WRATH'S STORM

TRINITY MASTERS: THE HAYDEN BROTHERS

BOOK THREE

MARI CARR

LILA DUBOIS

TRIGGER WARNINGS

The Trinity Masters series is a romantic suspense and all books contain explicit sex and depictions of violence (action scenes).

WRATH'S STORM

Hot sexy triplet #3 (The one who's both charming and a doctor.)

Dr. Walt Hayden is unflappable, but when a giant blond man walks into his rural medical clinic and starts teaching the youth to shoot bad guys...something has gone weirdly wrong. The last thing Walt expected was to deal with a wedding, a stalker, and a serial killer...in that order.

Attending his brother's wedding starts a journey that leads to the beautiful Annalise, whose life is threatened by a stalker, and her stoic, strong bodyguard, Jakob.

Walt may be the only man who can help put the pieces together to identify a killer who has already claimed one of the Masters' Admiralty's own. And if he falls in love with a member or two of that secret society along the way, well...

That love is doomed, because Walt is already promised to the Trinity Masters.

CHAPTER ONE

Walt stretched his arms overhead, working the muscles in his shoulders. He'd been hunched over for an hour reviewing slides of bloodwork, something most doctors didn't do again after college biology, or maybe a virology class in medical school.

In his type of medicine, he often had to do it all.

Normally, this was the kind of thing he'd assign to the shiny new doctors who rotated through. Working in a high-volume clinic where they'd see a diversity of issues—from acute traumas to routine care—was a great way for doctors to get tons of hands-on experience. But it was late, his current set of docs had all gone to their bunks, and, frankly, he was faster than they were. He didn't mind teaching, but between instructing and the natural nervousness of baby docs, everything took a hell of a lot longer than if he just did it himself.

He stripped off his PPE and washed his hands before grabbing his computer and taking it out onto the concrete patio. The patio area served as a waiting room, a triage center if things were really bad, and his living room, since every bit of space in the clinic besides his bedroom was devoted to medical care.

He sat back in one of the woven chairs and popped open his computer. He'd only been working for half an hour when he heard footsteps approach from the darkness.

He repressed an exhausted sigh and stood, turning back to the building, where various doors led out onto the large patio. Instead of his "lab" room, he headed for one of the exam rooms, leaving the door open behind him.

There were people who wouldn't come to him during the day. Oftentimes women with more personal concerns, but sometimes the occasional man who was experiencing anything from embarrassing ED, to injuries they'd ignored so that by the time they came to him, it was a salvage situation.

"Come on in," Walt called out in English, then again more hesitantly in French and Spanish, just in case. He was supposed to be studying Arabic in his free time. Free time. Ha. One of the nurses at the clinic was local and acted as a translator. She'd taught him a few helpful phrases in Nafusi, the Berber language many of the locals spoke, but not enough for him to confidently communicate with a patient. He'd call her to come in if needed.

He listened to the sound of footsteps on concrete as he put on a fresh mask and gloves. Whoever was coming was a large person, most likely male, and wearing shoes.

It was surprising how much information something so simple as a footstep could reveal.

"Hey, Doc."

Walt frowned in surprise and turned. A massive figure stood in the shadows just outside the door, where the overhang of the roof kept the bright light of the moon and stars from reaching.

The voice had a distinct Scandinavian accent. Danish, maybe. And it was familiar.

It took him several seconds to place it. "Oh, uh, Eric?"

Eric was the leader of the Masters' Admiralty, a European secret society founded around the time of the Black Plague. Honestly, it hadn't really surprised him to find out there was a secret, shadowy organization in Europe. What *had* surprised him was to find there was also a society in the United States—the Trinity Masters.

He and his siblings had been offered membership to both societies. Sylvia had fallen in love and moved to Europe to join the Masters' Admiralty. Langston had joined the American secret society and then fallen in love with the couple chosen to be his trinity. They were married now and living in Texas.

Oscar had joined the Trinity Masters as well and was about to be "called to the altar" to be placed with his trinity. Not that Oscar knew that yet. Langston and the Grand Master and a few others were in the process of planning a surprise New Year's Eve wedding.

Everyone expected Walt to follow suit—pick a society, join, and agree to an arranged ménage marriage, which was the foundation of both secret societies. Walt wasn't in a hurry to do that.

He hadn't had a lot of time for romance or relationships, given all his years spent in med school, with the military, and then with Doctors Without Borders, before taking over this small clinic. His career had kept him too busy to date. Regardless, he wasn't sure he wanted someone telling him who he had to marry. Personally, he preferred to fall in love the old-fashioned way, though he'd never admitted that to his brothers, who would most likely give him shit for the romantic sentiment.

Walt had only met Eric once, and he'd found him to be irreverent, though clearly commanding.

"Yep."

"What are you doing in Libya?"

"That's a long story. But not why I'm here."

"Sylvie?" It had taken Walt's brain a moment to get over the surprise and process what Eric's being there could actually mean.

"Your sister's fine, but I need your help."

"What's wrong?"

In response, Eric stepped through the open door and into the electric light of the exam room.

At well over six feet and heavily muscled, his nickname of "the Viking" fit him.

Especially now.

Because Eric was covered in blood.

Walt turned to the counter, snapped up a pair of safety scissors, and started for Eric. His questions, and he had a lot, no longer mattered. All that could wait until after he found out where all that blood was coming from. Eric's calm tone probably meant he was in shock.

He grabbed the hem of Eric's shirt and started cutting.

The Viking grabbed his wrist, stilling his hand. "Hey, Doc. This isn't my blood."

He'd heard that one before. "Take a deep breath for me." He tried to shove off Eric's hold. "I'm here to help. I won't hurt you." It was absolutely horrific how many times he had to repeat that phrase on a daily basis.

"Seriously. Not my blood." But Eric released his hand.

Walt finished cutting the shirt up the middle, then cut through the sleeves at the shoulders, quickly pulling the fabric away. The baby docs who came here to both help and learn were usually shocked by how brusque he was. He had to teach them that it was more important to get the patient into a position where they could be cared for than it was to gently remove clothes.

Given how much blood was on Eric's upper half, Walt expected long, shallow cuts. An arterial cut and Eric wouldn't have been upright and walking, which meant he needed to have a lot of bleeder wounds.

Instead, the man's chest only sported a few old scars and some fresh bruises around the ribs. Walt looked at Eric's scalp. It had to be a head wound. But there wasn't blood on his face.

"We done with the weird foreplay?" Eric was leering at him.

Walt pushed aside his doctor instincts—which were telling him to strip off the rest of Eric's clothes to do a complete check. "Whose blood is this?"

Eric's expression sobered. "That's why I need your help. Can you come with me?"

"Where?"

"I need you to patch up someone."

"Where?"

"About half an hour from here."

If they were bleeding this heavily, there was very little chance that the person would still be alive when they got there. Walt grimaced but grabbed his kit—a large duffel bag—and threw it over his shoulder. Eric followed him out of the exam room. Walt stopped only long enough to knock on the door of the small bunkhouse where the visiting baby docs slept, calling out that he was going out for an emergency.

Eric led him to a rusted jeep, and Walt hopped in, turning to see that one of the doctors—a young French woman—had opened the door. She raised her hand to wave at him as Eric started the vehicle. She was the most experienced of the lot and, though still slow in the way of new doctors, she was competent and confident.

There was no opportunity to talk on the drive, given the speed and open top. Walt was sorry he hadn't grabbed a jacket.

While the weather in December was fairly mild, it was chillier tonight than normal. They drove too quickly over rutted dirt roads here on the very furthest outskirts of the Bani Walid area. His clinic was in a densely populated, underserved area, but the direction they were headed...

Walt tensed because he was fairly sure they were now in an undeveloped area that was considered so dangerous, the local health authority had made it off-limits for him. For any foreigner. Even locals avoided it.

They came around a corner, the narrow road—which was more of a dirt path—opening up into a clearing with a few buildings.

Eric stepped on the brakes and dust spat up from under the tires as he stopped. When he turned the headlights off, Walt couldn't see anything for a moment—the only light here was a very faint orange glow coming through an open doorway in one of the three white buildings surrounding a small dirt courtyard.

Eric grabbed Walt's shoulder, guiding him toward the open door.

The long, low building seemed to be a storehouse and had probably started out as a barn. There were stall areas now full of army-green trunks. A table with four chairs near the door boasted a lantern.

He took all that in without actually acknowledging it because his focus was on the people in the room. Six men in mismatched camouflage were either kneeling or lying on the floor, their hands behind their backs.

Standing over them, holding very large guns, were a dozen girls, ranging in ages from what looked like ten to fourteen. The smallest girl turned to point her gun at them, teeth bared in a snarl that was no less terrifying coming from a little girl.

Eric gestured to the men. "I need you to patch them up."

"I won't work with someone holding a gun on me." Sadly, it was not the first time in his life Walt had used those words.

Eric looked at the girls. "Up to you."

"If I want to shoot them?" one of the older girls asked in soft, lovely accented English.

"Your call." Eric shrugged.

"What..." Walt wanted to channel his brother Oscar and say, "What the actual fuck is going on?" but he refrained because, despite the guns, the girls were still just children and his mama had raised him better than that.

"I need you to patch them up so we can finish questioning them."

Walt closed his eyes. "It's their blood. You're torturing them."

"Yep." Eric's hand came to rest on his shoulder. "They're the bad guys."

Walt glanced sideways at Eric. "If you're torturing them, you're a bad guy."

"But they deserve it."

"No one deserves—"

"They do." The same girl's voice cut through the room. "They deserve death."

Walt blew out a long breath. He'd been avoiding thinking about what the presence of the girls meant because even he had his limits to what his heart could handle. He'd seen far too much in his years as a doctor, on battlefields, traveling to ravaged, desperate places most people wouldn't dream of stepping foot in. But this... Walt fought hard to distance himself from what he was seeing. It was either that or walk back outside to throw up.

Walt set down his kit and dropped to a squat next to one of the girls. He was a big guy, though not as big as Eric, and could be intimidating for kids. "Are any of you hurt?"

What a stupid fucking thing to say. Of course they were hurt.

The reason he never came to this part of the region was because cells of extremist groups, with ideologies and fanaticism imported from other parts of the world, had started popping up here. The kind of extremists who thought they had the right to kidnap young girls.

She looked at him and spoke in Arabic. Walt shook his head, responding with one of the handful of phrases he knew in Arabic. "Sorry. *La atakallam arabi.*" *I don't speak Arabic.*

He should have been doing his Arabic language lessons instead of blood slides.

Many locals assumed he spoke their languages, that he was local. It was a common enough mistake since he was black, though lighter skinned than many of the people here.

Walt asked the question again, this time in Nafusi. It was one of the first phrases he'd learned.

The little girl brightened for a moment when he spoke what was probably her native language, then shook her head. Walt glanced around, from the other girls to the captive men. It was stupid of him to ask in front of all these people. He'd have to make sure the girls either saw doctors in their home villages or came to his clinic.

Walt stood and stepped back, not wanting to loom over the kids. The girls would need to be looked at in more private and comfortable settings, which left the men. "I won't treat them just so you can go back to torturing them." He glanced at Eric.

"Sure it won't change your mind if I said they deserve it?" Eric sounded only mildly interested.

"No."

"Stupid Hippocratic Oath."

"You don't need a doctor. You need the authorities. And... and these girls' parents."

The littlest huddled against the girl beside her and started speaking rapidly. The bigger girl nodded. "We want to go home, but not until Eric has the names of all their co-conspirators."

Co-conspirators? Walt looked at Eric, widening his eyes a little. No way the girl had known that word. Eric had taught it to them.

Eric grinned. "You don't cut the head off a hydra. You stab it in the fucking heart then rip out its guts."

The girls nodded.

"I will patch them up so they can be handed over to the authorities." Walt enunciated each word. He glanced at Eric and dropped his voice to a whisper. "Please tell me you didn't teach these children torture techniques."

"Of course not. I just made sure the fuckers couldn't move while the girls hit them. They went for the face. Most of the blood on my shirt was from broken noses."

"There are so many things wrong with this situation."

"And letting kidnapping victims beat the shit out of their abusers isn't one of them," Eric growled.

Walt wanted to argue with that—wanted to point out the psychological damage that could have been done—but honestly it was hard not to see his point.

The sound of a vehicle's engine charged the air in the room. One of the girls leapt for the table, dousing the light. The men on the floor started to make noise and were met with a flurry of kicks.

Eric pointed at two of the girls, who went to the door, dropping onto the floor, their guns at the ready. Walt flattened his back against the wall where he could keep an eye on the men and the girls.

Eric crouched near the door. "Don't shoot me," he stage-whispered. "Just shoot the bad guys."

The girls giggled. It was such an innocent, sweet sound that Walt had to swallow hard to dislodge the lump in his throat. The fact that they could giggle after the horrors they'd experienced, the nightmare they were all still swimming around in, actually gave him hope for their futures.

Eric slipped out the door and disappeared into the shadows. There was enough moonlight to just faintly see what was happening as a jeep matching the one he'd arrived in pulled into the courtyard. Four men jumped out, two of them pausing to light cigarettes. The flame from the lighters illuminated their faces—they were barely older than the oldest girls. Not quite children but not yet adults who could think and reason through the bullshit the extremists fed them.

They got within ten feet of the door—Walt saw the girls with guns tense, and he really, really hoped he wasn't about to see children committing cold-blooded murder—when Eric slid out of the darkness behind the men. He was easy to see, the pale skin of his bare chest silvery in the moonlight.

The Viking grabbed the guns slung over the rearmost guards' backs, using them as handles to hold them still as he stomped his heel into the sides of their knees. Walt was too far to hear the crack and pop, but the way the men dropped told him Eric knew what he was doing and had just broken and/or dislocated the knee joints.

The two who'd been in front whirled, fumbling to get their rifles off their shoulders. Eric grabbed one man's gun by the barrel, yanked it off him, then swung it like a baseball bat, hitting him in the ribs. This time Walt could hear the crack. Then Eric jabbed the butt of the other gun into the last man's stomach and kneed him in the face as he fell.

Eric stepped back, looking at the men on the ground, then called out, "You want to tie them up?"

One girl turned on the lantern again. Several others picked

up pieces of what looked like well-used rope before running out to bind the new captives. As they passed him, Walt saw the raw red skin around their wrists.

And for a moment, Walt wanted to pick up a gun and shoot the men himself.

Instead, he hauled his kit to the table and got ready to do his job. He was going to patch them up—all of them. The girls first, even if all he did was give them aspirin and Band-Aids. Then he'd stabilize the men, particularly splint the legs of the two with now destroyed knees. And when the authorities got here, he would throw whatever political weight he had behind the girls to make sure the men weren't simply released.

———

FOUR HOURS LATER, Walt sat on the floor with his back against the wall. He was in the small rural police station not far from the extremists' compound. The girls had been questioned —lightly, since he and Eric hovered—and most had been reunited with their parents. Some were orphans, some runaways. Most had been snatched while they walked to school.

The men were in jail, and Walt had pointedly and loudly talked about how great it was the authorities were going to make sure men like this didn't operate here. He was pretty sure at least one of the men had a politician parent, so he'd have to keep up pressure to make sure the men weren't released after a few months in prison.

Eric sat down beside him, groaning exaggeratedly. Walt had dug a spare scrub top out of the bottom of his kit for Eric. It barely fit, but Eric looked less like a deranged serial killer now that he was clothed, with only a few streaks of blood on his pants.

"Thanks for your help, Doc."

"I'm not sure how much help I was. None of them would have died." Suffered greatly but not died. Walt closed his eyes, weary beyond words.

Eric shrugged. "Never can tell with internal bleeding."

"And you know that because you regularly hunt down terrorists?"

"No. Happy accident. These guys beheaded some women. I was following that."

"You were looking for people who like to behead other people?" Walt didn't bother to open his eyes. This conversation wouldn't get any less surreal if he did.

"Right now I am. I'm...well, there's time for that later."

"Did you spend Christmas hunting down killers?" It was December twenty-seventh. He'd video chatted with his family on Christmas day, then talked separately with Langston about the surprise wedding for Oscar.

The Trinity Masters were insisting on keeping the wedding a surprise, including tricking Oscar into thinking he wasn't going to be one of the grooms until the last minute. Walt, like Langston, had a feeling it would go badly, but apparently no one was going to listen to them.

"Isn't that how everyone spends the holidays?" Eric said in a jolly tone.

"I'm flying home in a few days. For New Year's."

"You're leaving the clinic?"

"Don't worry, the baby docs can handle it, and anything serious will go to the doctor in the city." He hadn't had much notice about the need to be home for New Year's, but luckily there was enough coverage that he could attend the wedding. And then, he was going to take a few weeks off. Mental health breaks were necessary, and he was smart enough to know when he needed one. After tonight, he really needed one.

Eric merely grunted.

"Why were you looking for people who behead people?" That sentence was messy, but Walt was tired.

"Behead, dismember. It's the signature of...of a killer I'm hunting." Eric's voice had dropped to a growl.

"I'm guessing these guys weren't who you were looking for."

"No."

"But you decided to just stop and dismantle an extremist cell while you were here."

"Yep. I'm out of leads. I...I don't know where I'm going next." Eric seemed almost surprised by his own admission.

Walt turned his head, opened one eye. "Want to be my date to my brother's surprise New Year's Eve wedding?"

Eric blinked, then grinned.

CHAPTER TWO

W alt walked into the hotel conference room with Eric. They'd been summoned from Oscar's wedding reception by Juliette, the Grand Master of the Trinity Masters. They'd arrived at Oscar's wedding shortly after the ceremony had started. The fact he'd shown up in Boston with the head of the Masters' Admiralty had caused a stir.

As Walt took in the faces of Juliette, Franco, and Devon, he felt a bit like he used to when he'd been called to the principal's office back in school—something that occurred quite frequently, given Langston's love of blowing things up in chemistry class and Oscar's propensity for using four-letter words at all the wrong times. Walt's presence usually fell under the all-for-one-and-one-for-all rule of being a triplet. Though he couldn't deny he also was a big fan of jokes—he was often labeled the class clown—so he probably dragged his brothers down just as much as they did him.

Langston was already in the room, leaning against a side wall, offering Walt that same "we fucked up again" grin that was far too familiar to him. Eric was about to close the door, but before he managed, Oscar shuffled in.

"Seriously?" Oscar grumped, closing the door with more force than was probably necessary. "It's literally my fucking wedding night. This shit couldn't wait?"

Juliette narrowed her eyes at Oscar, and Walt suppressed a sigh. Oscar had a very bad habit of saying everything he thought as he thought it, with an extra fuck or two added to each sentence. "I'm aware it's your wedding night. By the way, you're welcome."

Oscar scowled, though Walt thought the expression was there to mask the tiniest bit of regret Oscar felt for his comment. After all, the Grand Master had just put Oscar in a trinity marriage with the two people his brother had fallen madly in love with. "Yeah. Uh. Thanks."

Juliette didn't reply but instead pointed at a chair.

Oscar—wisely—took it without comment.

"Great party. This is fun." Eric took a noisy sip from the signature cocktail he'd brought with him. "Congrats, Oscar. Though I would have given you two wives."

Langston raised his hand. "It was me who wanted that."

"Is this going to take long? I want another one of these." Eric jiggled his glass, the ice clinking noisily.

Walt gave him the side-eye, and then took a discreet half step away from the Viking.

Juliette Adams, whose identity as the Grand Master was a closely guarded secret, turned her cool blue gaze on Walt. He put his hands in the pockets of his pants and smiled. He was very aware of how tenuous his current situation was. He'd had plenty of time on the flights here to think about it.

He wasn't a member of the Trinity Masters, and yet he knew the Grand Master's identity, a secret most members did not.

He'd brought a plus-one when the invitation definitely hadn't included one.

And his plus-one was the leader of a rival secret society, though he wasn't totally sure if rival was the right word.

Some days he was as dumb as his brothers, and apparently this was one of those days. Hopefully the fact that Langston and Oscar were both in the room meant one of them would draw Juliette's ire away from him.

His money was on Oscar. The man had a gift for being an asshole.

"I'm surprised to find you here, Eric," Juliette said. "Apparently, you're a missing person."

"I am never missing. I am always precisely where I'm meant to be," Eric intoned.

Franco snort-laughed. Juliette glared at him.

"It's a *Lord of the Rings* reference. It was funny!" Franco grinned at his wife. Devon's eye seemed to be twitching.

"Why are you here?" Juliette asked Eric. "I thought we discussed this the last time we were together. You're not allowed in my territory without prior notice and my approval."

Eric pulled his phone from his pocket, passing his empty glass to Walt, who accepted it while trying to blend into the wall. Eric typed something, then stuck his phone in his pocket.

A second later, the small jeweled clutch Juliette carried pinged.

Juliette didn't even bother pulling her phone out. When Franco reached for her clutch, she smacked his hand away.

Oscar started to belly laugh. Langston slapped a hand over his brother's mouth. Walt shoved Eric's glass toward him.

Eric frowned at Walt. "You know, since you're my date, shouldn't you offer to get me a new drink?"

"If you get me killed, I'll haunt you," Walt muttered.

"Why. Are. You. Here. Eric?" Juliette repeated.

Eric bowed his head for a moment, and when he raised it, the teasing light was gone from his eyes. The air in the room shifted, and instead of just one powerful authority in the room, it became clear there were two. It was like Eric had put on a cloak made of duty and responsibility.

Devon took a step forward, standing at Juliette's side. Langston pushed away from the wall, stepping closer to Walt.

"I came because I'm out of leads." Eric's voice was low and dark.

Langston caught Walt's eye, and Walt vividly remembered the story Langston had told him about Eric literally ripping a man's head off.

"Explain." Juliette, unlike the men in the room, appeared perfectly calm, unafraid.

"I'm looking for a killer. A serial killer."

Juliette glanced at Devon briefly. "And you believe this person is on American soil?"

"No. I don't know where he is, and that's the fucking problem." The glass in Eric's hand cracked. Walt instinctively batted the glass away before it could completely shatter and cut Eric.

"He found me in Bani Walid," Walt said when the glass fell to the carpeted floor, rolling, ice spilling.

"Libya?" Devon asked, looking at Eric.

"The man I'm hunting dismembers, beheads, or both. There had been some beheadings in Bani Walid. I tracked it down. Wasn't him."

"Eric took out an extremist cell that was starting to take hold in the region. He freed the young girls they'd kidnapped." Everyone looked at Eric again, but this time there was approval in the attention. "He also wanted me to patch the bad guys up so he could keep torturing them."

"Did you?" Franco asked with interest.

Walt frowned. "No."

"Why not?" Franco pressed.

"Because I'm not a psychopath?" Walt couldn't believe he was having this conversation.

"Why are you, single-handedly, looking for a serial killer while also hiding from your own people?" Juliette raised a brow. "I've been working with Sophia."

"Oh. How's that going?" Eric asked. "Well? Because if so, I'll make her my ambassador to the Trinity Masters."

Juliette's lips twitched in a small smirk. "I have enjoyed it. She dresses better than you, and now that I have another woman to work with, we've made great strides in developing a useful relationship between our societies."

"Ouch." Eric rubbed his chest. "That hurt."

Oscar sighed loudly, rising and walking over to stand next to Langston—and closer to the door—making sure everyone knew he was still there and *not* on his honeymoon.

Juliette didn't acknowledge the sound. "Let's cut to the chase. Tell me what the hell is going on here."

Eric turned away from them all, staring at the wall. Everyone else exchanged glances, and Walt was aware of a horrible sense of fascinated anticipation, like listening to a true crime podcast or watching a train wreck.

"You know we had a traitor within the Masters' Admiralty. He killed my predecessor. Killed others. But he didn't do it all himself. He had people—puppets who danced to his tune. He dredged up old enemies and gave them new life. He's dead, as I'm sure Langston remembers."

"Vividly," Langston said.

Eric finally turned back around.

"He's dead, but killing him only freed the puppets from his strings. We have a religious cult who likes bombs..." Both Oscar and Langston nodded. "...and at least one serial killer."

"The serial killers were his puppets?" Franco asked.

"Yes. We caught one, who'd kidnapped our people on his orders, back before we knew how deep it ran. But when we were closing in, someone I was close to was murdered." He whispered her name. "Josephine." Eric's hands flexed, turning into tight fists and then relaxing. "He left her head in a fucking basket for us to find."

"My God," Langston breathed.

Juliette's eyes softened briefly. Walt's chest was tight, his throat closing as he considered what it must feel like to find someone you loved that way. Walt made the mistake of imagining it was Sylvia's head, or Oscar's or Langston's.

"Eric," Walt said softly, but the other man either didn't hear or he ignored him.

"The man I killed, Petro, the puppet master...the master-mind...whatever the fuck you want to call him, he didn't kill Josephine himself. He had one of his pets kill her."

"And so now you have to hunt him down," Oscar said quietly.

"When I cut off his head, it will be slow." Eric's voice was factual, as if it had already happened.

Devon cleared his throat. "That doesn't track, Fleet Admiral."

Walt looked at Devon and wondered if the man had brain damage that he would question Eric, who was clearly emotional about the death of Josephine, who, from the sounds of it, had been Eric's lover.

"Abort, abort," Franco whispered loudly.

Juliette looked at Devon, then motioned him to continue.

Devon stepped forward. "You have access to, and the ability to command through your membership, every law enforcement agency in Europe. They would be far better equipped to find a killer than you would be. Tracing specialists, forensic psychologists—"

Eric jerked, as if he was surprised or shocked by something Devon had just said.

"—and if what you wanted was to abandon any semblance of justice and murder the man yourself, I'm sure that could have been arranged."

"I'm being lectured on morals by someone who works for the CIA? Fuck that, you pompous ass." Eric took a threatening step forward.

Walt, for reasons he would never understand, grabbed Eric to hold him back. His brothers leapt to help.

Franco was his mirror image, though the arm he grabbed was Devon's. "Devon. Let the man speak. Eric, why didn't you seek help from the Masters' Admiralty? Why did you feel like you had to do this on your own?"

Devon opened his mouth, apparently ignoring his husband, but Juliette spoke first.

"Enough!" Everyone fell silent at her command. "Eric is going to explain."

Was that a command, or was she confident that Eric would open up?

Eric shook off Walt's hold, but then put a hand on his shoulder, as if to indicate he was calm. Then Eric very obviously tucked his hands into his pockets and relaxed his shoulders.

"I left," he said after a long moment, "to protect *them* from *me*."

"Protect 'them' who?" Walt asked.

"Everyone." The word was a dark rumble. "The members of my society, the people around me. Hell, all of fucking Europe. When I get angry..."

"Berserker rage," Langston muttered. It wasn't the first time

Walt had heard Langston use that term in reference to the fleet admiral, Eric's title within the Masters' Admiralty.

Eric nodded. "After my wives died, I left for a long time. I had to. Killing Petro wasn't enough. I was feeling that way again, but last time I felt like this I didn't have this much power." There was a bleak sadness to his voice. "You're right, Devon, I could have turned the full might of the Masters' Admiralty on finding the man who killed Josephine. And I would have destroyed us to get it done."

Walt, like the others, was probably thinking through all the grim possibilities, what exactly "destroyed us" might have looked like.

Juliette nodded slowly. "I understand. What do you need from us?"

The tension left the room and everyone's focus shifted. Now they had something to do: help Eric.

"Ten minutes ago, I would have said nothing." He pointed at Devon. "But you gave me an idea."

Devon grimaced.

"And that is?" Juliette patted her husband's arm.

"I need a forensic psychologist."

Juliette glanced at Franco, who was the most familiar with the backgrounds of every member of the Trinity Masters.

Franco pressed his fingers against his lips for just a moment, then said, "How would you feel about a criminal psychologist? We have one of those and they're basically the same thing."

Eric shook his head. "No, actually I have someone in the Masters' Admiralty who fits that bill. What I also want is a doctor."

"A forensic pathologist," Walt corrected slowly. "If you want someone to examine bodies, or look at existing autopsy records, that's who you need."

"No, I need a doctor." Eric clapped Walt on the shoulder. "Want to come help me hunt a serial killer?"

"Not even a little bit."

"I'll go!" Franco grinned.

"No," Juliette and Devon said in unison.

Juliette frowned. "I find it hard to believe there isn't a single doctor in your society. As a Trinity Masters' recruit, Walt isn't available to you."

Walt cleared his throat, and all eyes turned to him. He rarely pulled out the "I'm a doctor/authority figure" voice, but if there was ever a time to do it, it was now. "You don't get to say where I go."

Juliette's expression never changed, never revealed the slightest annoyance, though Walt would bet every last dollar he'd pissed her off every bit as much as Oscar did. "True, but you're an American citizen. Your work is funded by NIH and NSF grants, *and* your brothers are members."

Walt took a breath. "Is that a threat?"

"Yes," Eric said cheerily.

Juliette shrugged lightly. "No...not unless it needs to be."

"Let me take him, and I promise not to let him die," Eric said.

Juliette folded her arms. "No deal."

"You *also* don't get to say where I go," Walt told Eric. But the truth was he kind of wanted to go with the Viking. Which was surprising after the night he'd spent patching up the man's tortured victims in Bani Walid. Eric was a walking, talking time bomb, and an intelligent person would put at least a couple countries between himself and that.

Even so, Walt was tempted to say yes to Eric's offer. Or maybe it was more accurate to say he was intrigued and compelled. He didn't know who Josephine was, but if the woman had garnered such true loyalty and affection from a

man like Eric, it was safe to say she must have been an
extraordinary person.

"Shhh, Walt. Mommy and Daddy are talking." Eric patted
him again.

Of the triplets, Walt was the emotional middle. Oscar was
quick to anger, but it burned out fast. Langston rarely got angry,
but when he did, it was explosive.

When Walt got mad, it wasn't quite as bad as when
Langston did, but it was plenty destructive.

Eric had just pulled the trigger on his temper.

Walt pulled back his arm, ready to sucker punch Eric.

Langston grabbed that arm while Oscar hooked an arm
around Walt's neck.

"I'd prefer we all live," Langston said in a singsong.

Walt took a breath, slightly strangled because of Oscar's
arm. "Let go."

His brothers released him. Walt brushed at his suit jacket,
then turned to Juliette and Eric. "It's not up to you two to
decide where I go."

Juliette arched a brow. "Technically true."

"So I'll go with Eric to help him," Walt declared. "Not
because you said so, not because you wanted it this way, but
because Eric did something incredible for those young girls in
Bani Walid when he took out the extremists. And now he's
asking for our help. He saved those girls' lives. And while I
didn't know Josephine, I think she deserves justice too."

"Repaying a debt," Franco said with a nod.

Walt looked at Juliette, and her expression was cold,
remote. She had no hold on him, but the reality was that she
was a very powerful person. And he'd always figured that he
would join the Trinity Masters like his brothers, which meant
his fate, his *marriage* was at stake.

Juliette was silent, neither threatening him nor showing any level of acceptance.

Walt took a breath. "And after this, after I help Eric, I'll come back and I'll join—"

"A cult," Oscar snarked.

"You don't owe her that," Eric said. When Juliette arched a brow at him, Eric shrugged. "He doesn't."

"I know I don't," Walt assured the Viking. "But I was going to do it anyway. This way she won't torpedo my funding or something."

"Yes, of course I'd yank funding for a medical clinic." Juliette's voice was perfectly calm and cool. "I'd also evict orphans on Christmas."

"With their little frostbitten teddy bears!" Franco sang out.

Everyone looked at him for a long moment.

Oscar cleared his throat. "Yeah, I'm gonna go. Let me know if you need data mining. Because if so, I'm in."

"Eric, if I asked you to, would you rip Oscar's head off?" Juliette asked, gaze narrowed.

"Yeah, but are you sure? Then the score would be even."

"Score?" Juliette asked.

"The Hayden sibling game. You're winning two to one right now."

"Ah, yes, but now I have dibs on that one." She pointed at Walt. "A replacement Hayden."

"But he's so cute. I like him." Eric wrapped a possessive arm around Walt.

Juliette pursed her lips. "You'd make a cute couple. You know, Eric, I can think of several women who'd make a great third for you if you join the Trinity Masters."

"Tempting."

"Just think about it."

"I can't tell who's fucking flirting with who right now." Oscar crossed his arms.

"Should it be 'whom'?" Franco asked no one in particular.

"Oscar, go. You are never helpful in meetings," Devon said with a sigh.

Oscar grinned. "And that's why I do it. Peace, fuckers."

Walt looked back and forth between Juliette and Eric. He was pretty sure they were joking.

"Where in Europe are you going? We'll organize your travel," Devon said once Oscar closed the door behind himself.

"Frankfurt. That's where my forensic psychologist is."

Juliette looked at Walt and smiled, but her eyes were pinched with worry. "Please keep yourself safe, Walt. I'll give you the names of some people you can reach out to in Europe if you need."

"You have spies in my territory?" Eric's voice was no longer teasing.

Juliette gestured with one hand. "No, there's now a joint task force that Sophia and I created. Speaking of Sophia, I'm giving you a twenty-four-hour head start before I tell her I saw you."

"Where's the solidarity between secret society leaders?" Eric threw his hands in the air.

"And, I won't tell her where you've gone, but I will tell her you're doing an investigation."

"They may have figured out what I'm doing by now, but thank you, Juliette." Eric cleared his throat, then more formally said, "Thank you, Grand Master."

Juliette grinned. "Don't thank me, Fleet Admiral. You owe me another favor. I like having you in debt to me."

CHAPTER THREE

D r. Annalise Fischer shook her head as she walked into her office and spotted Jakob sitting at her desk. "You didn't have to come," she said, though she shouldn't have bothered wasting the breath. She had known the second she'd told him about her afternoon meeting with the American doctor that he'd show up.

"I did."

Jakob Bauer rose and stepped aside as she walked around her desk to claim the chair he'd just vacated. Jakob was a Ritter, a knight of the Masters' Admiralty in their home territory of Germany. The Ritter were the society's law enforcement—keeping the peace as well as enforcing the society's rules. They were also bodyguards when needed.

Jakob had been her personal shadow on and off for over four years.

When she'd joined the Masters' Admiralty fresh out of her doctoral program, a forensic psychologist about to embark on an exciting new career with the *Kriminalpolizei*, she hadn't realized she would come to rely on the secret society, less for the incredible connections within both the government and academia, and more for protection.

During her tenure with the *Kripo*, she'd attracted the attention of a highly disturbed individual. She wouldn't diagnose him without actually meeting him, though Jakob often referred to him as a psychopath.

Annalise had a stalker.

Even after years of work by the *Kripo*, herself, Jakob, and the Masters' Admiralty, she didn't know who he was or where they'd come into contact with one another. In a way, that was the worst aspect of the situation—with no idea how they'd met, she'd had nothing to give Jakob and the knights to aid in their investigation. No leads to help them track down the person who had destroyed her life.

Five years ago, she'd considered herself an independent, fearless woman. After all, she'd been recruited out of university, not only by the *Kripo*, but by the Masters' Admiralty because of her intelligence and drive. She'd wanted to revolutionize the way law enforcement dealt with mental health issues via advanced psychological screening techniques and by embedding mental health professionals within police and legal systems.

When the first note arrived—a vaguely threatening letter left on her doorstep—she'd shrugged it off.

By the fourth letter, she was angry with only a few hints of fear.

The fifth letter hadn't come alone.

When a box had arrived in the mail, bearing the logo of the cosmetics brand she preferred, she hadn't hesitated to bring it inside. When she opened it, hundreds of winged cockroaches flew out. She'd screamed and dropped the box. Only later did they find the folded note at the bottom. A note warning her not to ignore him.

That was the night she'd met Jakob. He'd been the one to coax her out of the bathroom, where she'd fled from the bugs.

That was the night she'd started to take the stalker seriously. He knew far more about her than just her address. He knew her favorite cosmetics brand, had known she'd take a box with their logo inside. And knew something very few others did—she had a near phobia of flying bugs.

The *Kripo* had created a task force, as had the Ritter. She'd been sure they would figure it out, would find this person who was stalking her and stop him.

They hadn't.

Her independence and bravery had been slowly chiseled away over the past four years, eroding with the passage of time, as her stalker continued to elude capture. Every lead—from some security camera footage that captured a hooded figure walking down her street after the fourth letter had been left, to tracking the bug package—had gone nowhere.

Her confidence in her abilities had taken a hit as well because she'd been unable to paint a picture of him. Jakob told her time and again—in his quiet, taciturn way—that she shouldn't lose faith in herself, insisting the problem was that she was too close to the case.

After the bug box, she'd been surrounded by guards, both the police and the Ritter, but they couldn't keep that up around the clock. There weren't enough resources to guard her, and a box full of bugs was hardly dangerous. Disturbing, yes, but not dangerous. Months passed, and when no more boxes arrived, only the odd letter, the task force was disbanded.

Except Jakob. Jakob stayed.

He was dark-skinned with close-cropped hair that was as no-nonsense as the man himself. He had thick eyelashes, an unexpectedly soft, almost feminine feature that she was slightly obsessed with.

Jakob had helped her move in secret into the vacant house adjacent to her own, installing a heavy door in the shared wall so she could walk in her front door, then immediately retreat to her hidden sanctuary, safe behind a steel door.

She'd lived that way for nearly a year, hiding within her own home. Once or twice a week, Jakob came and opened her mail. There were always new letters from her stalker—two to four per week. Jakob would check them, open them safely within a special box with built-in heavy gloves, then pass them to her once they were cleared. She read each one.

They'd grown steadily more explicit and hate-filled.

There were a lot of details in those letters that told her the man was still watching her, and he'd identified most of her security measures. The outdoor cameras on her home were routinely destroyed, each time capturing only glimpses of someone wielding a paintball gun. Even the hidden cameras failed to uncover anything because—beneath the hood—he always wore a balaclava, even in the summer. There had also been threats to drivers with the security service she started using for transportation, the restaurant down the street who sometimes delivered food, and her grocery store.

Little by little, he had whittled down her world until she never went anywhere, and only felt safe at work inside the police station or in her secret second home with its steel doors and barred windows. And the secret of where she actually slept was one thing he'd never figured out.

Then, two years ago, and after years of dealing with the stalker, the bottom had fallen out of her world when the man pursuing her had attacked her twin sister.

Annalise had always been the serious one, quiet and studious, while her sister, Adele, had been the easygoing one, happy, fun.

Adele lived and worked in Tokyo, living an interesting,

glamorous life there. She rarely came home to Germany, though they spoke at least every other week. Annalise hadn't wanted to worry Adele. Hadn't wanted to mar the happiness she saw in her sister's face. Once it was over, she'd planned to tell Adele, but not until the man was caught.

Adele also loved surprises, which was why Annalise hadn't known Adele had tacked a few days onto a business trip and decided to come visit. Though they lived continents apart, Adele had a key to Annalise's house.

Adele arrived late one night and let herself into Annalise's house, ready to surprise her twin.

She hadn't locked the door behind her.

And Annalise, safely asleep next door, hadn't heard her sister's alarm when the stalker followed her in. Hadn't heard her scream as she was raped.

Once the stalker realized he had the wrong sister, in a fit of fury, he cut off all of Adele's hair, telling her that it was so he could distinguish between them in the future. Adele had crawled to a phone and called the authorities when it was over.

Annalise hadn't known anything was wrong until Jakob, who'd been alerted when an ambulance was dispatched to her address, had called her.

Her sister's light had been extinguished after the brutal attack.

Since then, the sister Annalise had adored and wished she could be like was gone, replaced by a silent, angry stranger who stared at her with accusatory eyes. Before the rape, they'd been more than sisters, closer than the closest of best friends, but now Adele refused to speak to her, to see her. She had completely shut her out, claiming she couldn't look at Annalise without remembering the rape, without remembering what had happened to her.

And Adele, rightly, blamed Annalise for not telling her or

their parents what was going on. If Adele had known, she wouldn't have made a surprise visit. If she'd known, she would have been more careful.

If, if, if.

After the attack, the German admiral, Dolph Eburhardt, insisted Annalise once more have full-time protection. The reinvigorated task forces had been sure they would be able to catch him, using evidence from Adele's attack.

Jakob had been assigned as her bodyguard, a role he'd already been playing. A job he had taken very seriously since then.

Even after the trail ran cold.

Even after every lead had been followed, every possibility explored.

Even after she'd given up her job at the *Kripo*, no longer able to effectively perform her duties, her confidence and independence both ground to dust. She'd lost her objectivity and the ability to compartmentalize, which was necessary in her line of work.

Annalise was perfectly aware her one-sided longing for Jakob was most likely driven by the fact the two of them had been in close contact for an extended period of time and her interactions with other men had whittled down to practically nil. The only other men she conversed with were colleagues from the university and her male students.

Clinically, she knew the "why" behind her feelings, and it was more than just proximity and a lack of other people who could serve as suitable prospective romantic partners. It was quite natural for people to develop feelings for either their caregivers or rescuers, and he was both. He'd served as her Prince Charming and white knight and was the only person who really knew her anymore.

Jakob, a strong, silent presence, had stayed by her side as

her life changed. And now, because she was meeting with someone she didn't know, he was here.

"I know you have other duties to attend to, Jakob."

He put his arms behind his back in parade rest. His standard pose and one she was very familiar with. He didn't say anything, but the body language spoke for him.

I'm not going to let you meet a strange man on your own.

She sighed, wishing she had the courage to insist Jakob leave. In truth, she hadn't slept well last night, anxious about this afternoon's meeting. She'd been surprised when an American medical doctor, Walt Hayden, had contacted her. The email said he wanted to talk to her about the profile of a serial killer he was tracking.

Why was a doctor tracking a serial killer?

She'd forwarded the message to Jakob, and the Ritter had run background checks. Dr. Hayden ran a clinic in Africa, so maybe the local police force was overwhelmed and he'd stepped in.

Still, why would he come to her?

There were plenty of Americans he could have gone to. Maybe the suspect was a German national or someone she'd profiled before.

She'd tried to tell him she didn't do that sort of work anymore, even going so far as to give him the names of other profilers in the *Kripo* who could assist him, but Dr. Hayden had insisted that it be her.

After retiring from the *Kripo* shortly after her sister's attack, she'd accepted a position at Heidelberg University, about an hour south of Frankfurt. Her life had fallen into a comfortable, if boring, routine that consisted of her ping-ponging between her new Fort Knox-like home on the university grounds—and therefore monitored by university security and protected by the very fact that the university was never really quiet, with students constantly coming and going even late into the night—and her office. Her office was in the psychology building, which was next door to the lecture hall she used, both a seven-minute walk from her faculty housing.

Teaching abnormal psychology was far easier than her job with the *Kripo*. The people she discussed in class were already safely captured or dead, their names and faces known.

If Dr. Hayden had contacted her a few months earlier, she would have unequivocally rejected his request for a meeting. But lately it felt as if she was starting to come out of her skin. Hiding from the real world, drowning in the guilt she felt every time she thought of what her sister had suffered, hadn't done anything more than allow an evil man to remain free. While she couldn't profile her stalker, perhaps she could help bring whatever man the American was looking for to justice. Maybe the distance—helping hunt a man who was half a world away—would be easier than trying to profile someone she knew was loose in her city.

"You researched Dr. Hayden," Annalise said. "You said he is who he seems to be. Did something change?"

Jakob was a man of few words and even fewer expressions.

"Nothing is certain," he said after a long pause.

Annalise's lips twitched.

Right after Adele's attack, Jakob had stayed with her twenty-four seven, sleeping on the couch in her secret, secured house's living room. Eating every meal with her. And while she'd never admitted it aloud, she had been grateful for his presence and his diligence.

Because she'd been terrified.

As time dragged on and her stalker continued to elude arrest, Dolph had begun to pull Jakob away because he had other tasks that needed to be performed, and it appeared that the man pursuing her had lost interest. Then, when it seemed like it was over, another letter came. All it said was, "Don't try to trick me again. It wasn't right."

She'd spent hours trying to decide if the "it" in the second sentence was her "tricking" him or the rape itself. That it hadn't been right because it hadn't been *her* he'd attacked.

The day after she got that letter, she turned in her notice at the *Kripo*.

For the past year and a half, Jakob escorted her anytime she left the university grounds. Annalise suspected that, officially, Jakob was no longer on bodyguard duty and was now acting of his own accord. He would certainly never admit as much to her.

Just as she was fairly sure he, personally, was screening her mail. She'd made special arrangements for the university's mail-receiving office to set aside all her letters and packages for screening. Every package she received had been opened and resealed. And the letters she did receive were all safe, normal.

The letters hadn't stopped, though there were far fewer. Jakob had confirmed that much. He assured her that copies of all new letters were added to the still-open, but cold, case files that both the *Kripo* and the Ritter maintained.

In the dark quiet of night, the guilt would gnaw at her. Guilt over taking Jakob's free time. Guilt that so many people had to make adjustments and allowances for her because she hadn't been smart enough to identify the stalker or strong enough to deal with any more letters.

She'd been thinking about asking Jakob for a copy of the file. To read those letters and see if maybe with more materials, there might be something she could see that no one else did. Maybe she'd ask him today.

Annalise glanced at her watch. "Dr. Hayden should be here any moment."

Jakob nodded. "You intend to help him?"

"If I can," she said. "It's been some time since I've created a profile."

A long pause. "If you're uncomfortable, I will make him leave."

"I'm not," she interjected. "I'm..." Annalise took a deep breath, not sure what to say.

I'm ready. I'm tired of being scared. I'm done hiding.

All were true.

"Brilliant." Jakob's word was spoken so low, she almost didn't hear it.

Annalise gave him a slight shrug and glanced away. "It's been a long time, but I'd like to try to help."

Before Jakob could reply, though the taciturn man might not have, there was a knock at the door.

She sprang out of her chair, silently cursing herself for being so jumpy. Jakob, bless him, pretended not to notice her obvious nervousness.

Jakob glanced at her, and Annalise walked to the wall the door was in, leaning against it. She'd been with Jakob long enough to know there was no way in hell he'd ever let her answer the door. He'd taught her to position herself so that anyone coming in the door wouldn't be able to see her until they were fully in the room, but not so close to the door itself that she would be hit if the door were slammed open, or be in a position where it could be used to pin her in place.

In comparison, he planted himself squarely in front of the door, one hand resting on the short sword belted to his hip. He rarely wore the sword, which was a symbol of his office, but also very out of place in modern life. He must have come from another duty. Or perhaps he wanted to throw Dr. Hayden off.

Possibly both.

She braced her palms against the wall to steady herself as he opened the door.

Annalise heard a male voice with a distinct American accent say, "Uh, Hello. *Guten Tag.* I'm Dr. Walt Hayden. I'm looking for Dr. Annalise Fischer. *Frau Doktor Fischer.*"

She expected Jakob to step back and allow the American in, so she was surprised when he remained in the doorway.

That surprise morphed to alarm when Jakob stiffened, his fingers curling around the hilt of the sword. Something in the hall had alarmed or frightened Jakob.

Annalise barely suppressed a whimper of fear, and she shoved one hand into her slacks pocket, closing her fingers around her phone, ready to call for help.

"Surprise." This was a second voice, the accent Scandinavian. Danish, at a guess.

There shouldn't be a second man.

Was it her stalker?

Was he holding a gun on Jakob?

Before she could fully freak out, Jakob dropped his hand from his sword—and then said the last thing she'd ever expected.

"Hello, Fleet Admiral."

"Fleet Admiral?" Curiosity was one of the few emotions that could override fear. It was what made humans so dumb. Curiosity didn't just kill cats. It routinely killed people who liked to begin sentences with, "I'm sure it's safe..." and, "Let's just take a quick look..." Or the always dangerous, "I wonder what's in there?" or, "What's the worst that could happen?"

A blond giant shouldered his way into her small office. Jakob backed up to make space, backing toward her so that his body was between her and the giant.

Annalise had never met the new fleet admiral, but she'd heard him described, and most importantly, knew from Jakob that the fleet admiral was missing.

Except, apparently he wasn't.

Because he was in her office.

A second also-large-though-not-giant man squeezed in and shut the door. He leaned against it and smiled at her, raising a hand. "Hi, I'm Walt."

Annalise nodded her head in greeting. When in doubt, maintain social pleasantries. "Dr. Hayden. Welcome to Heidelberg. I trust you had a good flight to Frankfurt?"

Walt nodded. "We did. And I enjoyed the scenery as we drove here. Though this one should have his license revoked," Walt said, jerking his thumb at the fleet admiral.

"Annalise." The fleet admiral tossed a grin her way, ignoring Walt's jab. He was good-looking but intimidating, despite the friendly grin.

Jakob was looking back and forth between Walt and Eric. His shoulders were stiff but not tight as they had been. His body language said "the situation is dangerous but we are not in danger." Out loud, he said, "Dr. Hayden is a decoy."

"Yep," the fleet admiral agreed.

"You wanted to speak to Annalise. In secret."

"Well, that saves on explanations," Walt muttered.

"I wasn't expecting a Ritter," Eric said. "Someone tip you off I was coming?"

Jakob didn't say anything, and the smile melted off Eric's face. The tension in the air ratcheted up.

Annalise took a step forward and put a hand on Jakob's shoulder, but she addressed Eric.

"No, Fleet Admiral. Jakob is here to protect me. I have a stalker." If he wanted to know more, all he had to do was ask. Jakob and the Germany admiral would be obliged to tell him anything he wanted to know.

Eric frowned. "I'm sorry. I didn't know." He looked at Jakob. "You get the guy?"

Jakob's shoulder turned to steel under her hand, and

Annalise winced internally. She knew—though he'd never said anything—the fact that her stalker was still free ate away at his insides like a cancer. Jakob was a born protector, a man who'd dedicated his life to seeing justice done. Every single day her stalker roamed the earth as a free man was a personal affront to him.

"If I may ask, Fleet Admiral, why did you want to see me?" she asked.

Eric Ericsson had the smartest people in the world at his disposal. Why would he want to see her?

Because you're brilliant?

Jakob's earlier word echoed in her mind.

"Just what Walt here said. I want you to help me catch a serial killer."

Annalise's stomach knotted. "I'm no longer a practicing forensic psychologist. I teach now." She gestured around her small office, which included several stacks of papers waiting to be graded.

"Maybe we should sit down," Walt said. "Well, I'm going to sit down because Eric is squishing me against the door." Walt bumped past Eric, knocking him back against the bookcases before dropping into the chair on the other side of her desk, where normally panicked students sat.

She took a seat too, but Eric and Jakob remained standing.

"Facing off" might be a more accurate term.

"He really does want help with a serial killer. I'm just the smoke screen." Walt was glancing between them.

Annalise couldn't help the small smile Walt's comment provoked. Lately, she found it difficult to warm up to people—particularly men—as she was always suspicious and fearful. However, there was something about Dr. Walt Hayden that told her he was a good person. Since the appearance of her stalker, the only other man she'd warmed up to just as quickly had been Jakob.

"Don't sell yourself short, Walt. You're also here to consult on the fucked-up medical aspect of the killings."

Annalise hadn't expected the fleet admiral to be so flippant, so sarcastic. In her mind, she'd always envisioned Eric as stoic, stalwart, and intimidating. And while he had the intimidation thing in spades, he was lacking in the others. His sense of humor surprised her.

"You need a forensic pathologist." Walt had the air of someone saying something for the hundredth time.

Jakob, as always, didn't bother to mince words. "Serial killer?" he prompted.

"Straight to the point. No foreplay. Not exactly great on a first date." Eric's expression, in contrast to his words, was serious. He nodded at Walt, who reached into his pocket and pulled out a thumb drive.

Jakob took it, then glanced at Annalise. She opened the bottom drawer of her desk and pulled out the secured, untraceable computer that she used for anything personal. The laptop provided by the university was reserved for only class and research-related tasks. The slim black computer the Ritter had provided for her had no logo and, when opened, a single white cursor appeared on a black screen. She bent to the camera, which scanned her face, then pressed two fingers to the small touchpad in the corner. The computer unlocked, and she plugged in the thumb drive.

The content was hundreds of files divided into several folders: "Decapitation," "Full Dismemberment," "Cross Reference MA".

Annalise looked up from the computer, waiting silently for more information.

"Josephine O'Connor was one of ours. She was murdered

in Dublin, and her head left in a basket where I, we, would find it," Eric said in a dark, quiet voice.

Annalise shared a glance with Walt, since Jakob was wholly focused on the fleet admiral. Walt grimaced, and she found herself making a similar expression back to him, a moment of shared experience as they both processed Eric's words.

"Petro," Jakob said.

Petro meant Petro Sirko, the former admiral of Hungary. Annalise wasn't sure how many members knew the truth about what had happened. That Petro had turned against the society, that he had resurrected old enemies—the Domino and Bellator Dei. She knew about it because Jakob had told her.

One night, he'd arrived looking particularly grim. After pouring herself a glass of wine and him a cup of hot tea—she'd never seen him drink alcohol—she'd gotten him to talk to her. It was the first time Jakob had shared anything from his own life, even if what he shared was more about their society than him personally. Typically, he was a closed book, fully dedicated to the job he'd been assigned—in this case, protecting her.

That night, he'd been shaken, and she'd been touched when he had opened up to her. In some strange way, she'd felt less afraid that night, less alone. For too long, she'd been a target. Something like that had a way of causing a person to look inward. She had spent too much time lost in her own terrifying world. So much so, she'd failed to remember that there were other people suffering unspeakable tragedies as well.

Even now, Annalise's stomach clenched as she recalled Jakob telling her about the admiral who had turned against their society and the atrocities he'd committed against innocent people.

She glanced back to her computer, then did a quick search for "Josephine." The file popped up and she opened it.

Her gaze landed on a headshot photograph of Josephine, and her heart ached. The woman's wide smile, her bright, almost mischievous green eyes hidden behind glasses that were too large for her face, spoke of a kind, joyful woman. Annalise was briefly reminded of her sister, Adele, before the attack that had taken the light from her eyes.

"Petro targeted Josephine because he knew it would..." Eric looked away, his jaw muscle twitching.

Had the fleet admiral loved her?

Annalise studied his body language, and there was grief, but it wasn't the sort of shell-shocked grief she usually saw from people who'd lost someone. That usually looked like hunched shoulders, as if the weight of their grief was a physical presence. Eric's grief was fire. A burning grief-fueled anger that made him stand tall and take deep breaths.

"Petro organized it," Eric started again. "But he wasn't the one who actually killed her. We know he had at least one pet serial killer whom he helped fund and protect. Josephine wasn't murdered by him, so that means it was a different killer. A killer I'm going to find." The last words were a low, rumbling threat.

"You want me to create a profile of him, based on the case reports," Annalise said quietly. She didn't do this kind of work anymore. Couldn't. She'd lost whatever edge and insight she'd had. Except, looking at the files on her computer screen, she felt compelled. Anticipatory.

She glanced at Jakob, who was looking at her with interest. There was very little that got by her bodyguard.

No, her friend.

The passage of time had slowly changed their relationship from that of protector to someone with whom she felt a genuine connection.

He saw it. Knew before she'd even accepted the case that

she was going to do this. She'd failed Adele, but she would be damned if she'd fail Josephine.

"Yes. And Walt's going to look at the autopsy reports and tell us if this guy is, or was, a doctor."

"Damn it, Jim, I'm a doctor, not a *forensic pathologist.*" Everyone looked at Walt, who stared blandly back at them. "*Star Trek?* Seriously? God, I miss my brothers," he muttered.

"How many murders?" Annalise took a blank notebook out of her drawer and flipped it open.

"I don't know," Eric answered.

Annalise frowned and started opening the top-level files in the thumb drive. The decapitation file had dozens of names. She opened the dismemberment file. More names. She suppressed a groan when she realized what she was actually looking at.

"You're not sure which of these people were killed by the same suspect who murdered Ms. O'Connor." Annalise opened the folder with MA in the title. The list of names here was much shorter, but still long enough to make her wince.

"It could have been a professional," Jakob pointed out.

Eric shook his head. "No, I've had words with a lot of people in that business, and no one has heard of Josephine's kill."

"Wouldn't assassins lie about assassinating someone?" Walt asked.

"If they didn't talk about their kills, how would anyone know how good they are?" Eric raised one hand. "It's possible, but I've ruled that out, for the most part."

"This is why you disappeared," Annalise said. "So you could track down leads."

"The Spartan Guard would have a collective heart attack if they knew where I've been and what I've been doing. By the way, neither of you is going to tell anyone you've seen me, got it?" Eric's menacing tone made it very clear there would be hell to pay if they did.

Annalise nodded, but Jakob held his ground.

"No one," Eric reiterated. "That's an order from your fleet admiral."

Jakob gave one short, terse nod, making it clear he was following that particular directive under duress.

Walt looked almost cheerful as he said, "He took down an extremist group in Libya. Showed up at my clinic covered in blood. So I invited him to be my date to my brother's wedding."

Annalise blinked at Walt. That must be a joke. She'd never thought she had trouble understanding American humor...

Eric leaned forward, and once again Annalise got the sense that this wasn't the leader of the Masters' Admiralty working on behalf of his society.

This was a man on a mission. And it was personal. "I need a profile. If you can get me a profile and a list of other victims, great, but if you just want to do a profile from Josephine's file, I'll take it."

Annalise's brain was already folding and contorting the information she had, analyzing what she knew. "If the unsub killed Josephine at the direction of Petro, with whom he must have had some kind of trusting, possibly manipulative relationship, then a profile based only on her file won't be indicative of his personal pathology."

"I looked at the images on the flight," Walt said. "Of Josephine, I mean. I can tell you whoever removed the head knew what they were doing. I doubt it was their first time doing so."

Annalise made a note. "Then we assume the *modus operandi* of beheading is part of the pathology, part of the killer's need."

"That's why Petro sent him." Jakob was no longer staring

Eric down, but looking at her computer screen, then at her notes. "He knew how to cut off heads."

"Hey, this guy might be useful." Eric grinned at Jakob. "If I wasn't hiding from the admirals, I'd tell Dolph Eburhardt I needed you."

"Maybe you should stop hiding like a little bitch," Walt pointed out.

Annalise and Jakob both sucked in shocked breaths. One simply didn't speak to the fleet admiral that way.

"*You're* a little bitch," Eric countered.

"I have three siblings. You're going to need to up your insult game."

Eric and Walt's relationship would have been fascinating if she hadn't had a computer full of murder files to look through. Annalise jotted down a few more notes and flipped to a blank page. She looked around the room. "I will need time to go over these."

"How long?" Eric asked.

"A day. Maybe even a few days, if you want me to first identify murders potentially committed by the same unsub, then have Dr. Hayden verify the skills and incorporate all of that into a profile."

"Days." Eric folded his arms, looking like he wanted to argue with her, but then nodded. "Okay. I have a document in there with my notes. The things I've been using to try to trace possible victims."

Annalise found the file and opened it.

VICTIMS:

Humans, age 18 – 45.
Found in pieces 1 – 90 days after disappearance.
Last seen walking somewhere.

Other people also walking. Some with groceries and/or dogs.

THAT WAS IT. That was all it said. Annalise forced herself to smile. "Good, uh...job, Fleet Admiral. Will you be staying here or in Frankfurt, so I can consult with you and Dr. Hayden?"

"A little place between here and Frankfurt. When I leave Germany, it will be to go kill someone."

With that, the fleet admiral opened the door to her office and walked out. A second later he returned, grabbed Walt by the shirt, and hauled him out too.

When the door closed, Annalise looked up at Jakob. Her quiet, terse guardian sighed and said something that rather nicely summed up what had happened.

"Fuck."

CHAPTER FOUR

Annalise tucked her legs beneath her on the couch, her laptop resting on her knees as she read through one of the countless files on the thumb drive she'd received from the fleet admiral two days earlier. Outside her windows, a group of drunk students went by singing loudly enough for her to hear them. Classes would begin again in a week or so, and students were making the most of their Christmas break.

Jakob sat across from her, mindlessly clicking through the TV channels without stopping to watch anything. Given the fact he'd muted the sound, she suspected he wasn't interested in watching television at all. She'd felt his gaze slide to her several times over the past few minutes, but he hadn't spoken, even though she was certain there was something on his mind.

Jakob was a reserved man, a consummate professional, the type of person capable of compartmentalizing his emotions in order to focus on his job. It was an admirable quality in a Ritter. However, it was frustrating as hell for her, a woman who had once made a living from reading other people's words and emotions to analyze their actions and predict their reactions.

Of course, if Annalise was being honest with herself, it wasn't the psychologist in her who was frustrated by her inability to figure out what Jakob was thinking or feeling. It was the woman.

What had begun as a spark of attraction had grown, despite her best efforts, until now she was consumed by a longing she'd never experienced. She wanted her bodyguard, and the absurdity of that cliché was not lost on her.

She pretended not to notice Jakob's occasional glances, forcing herself to concentrate on the file she was reading. It was difficult. More and more she found herself thinking about Jakob. Not in a professional way but rather a naked, sweaty way.

She constantly reminded herself that her feelings for him were a byproduct of circumstance and situational intimacy. Perhaps a form of transference, since he was an authority figure with whom she had a close relationship, and who had "rescued" her from the bugs, then continued to protect her.

There wasn't a term for this particular situation, and she'd considered having one of her advanced classes do research on it. There was, perhaps, an interesting journal article that could be written about it. They could call it damsel-in-distress syndrome, though she disliked the gendered nature of it.

Unfortunately, knowing the psychology behind her feelings didn't dim them or make them easier to dismiss.

And to make matters worse, Jakob was locked up tighter than a drum, his own feelings toward her a complete mystery.

Annalise sighed and tried once more to push all thoughts of Jakob out of her head. She'd promised the fleet admiral she'd study the files and attempt to come up with a profile. Picking up a pen, she jotted down a note and for a few minutes, she was actually able to concentrate on the file she was reading.

That concentration was broken when Jakob turned off the television and shifted to face her.

She set down her pen and tipped down her laptop screen, not closing it all the way. "There's clearly something on your mind, Jakob. Say it."

"Are you certain you want to work on this case?"

"Do you think I should have said no?"

Jakob quickly shook his head. "No. I'm not saying that at all. I'm just concerned that..."

He didn't finish his statement, didn't have to. He'd been with her enough in the past few years to understand how hard her confidence had been shaken by her stalker, by Adele's attack, and her failure to find the man and bring him to justice. She'd morphed from an intelligent, assertive profiler to one who questioned everything she'd thought she knew about herself and her abilities.

Annalise gave him a sad smile. "I want to do this," she said, with a strength she didn't really feel.

Jakob frowned—of course her forthright response hadn't fooled him—but he didn't immediately speak. She was used to his long pauses, accustomed to his habit of thinking before he spoke. She appreciated that about him, preferring it to people who expressed inane or stupid sentiments without thought or care.

At last, he said, "I think it will be good for you. To profile again."

Sometimes she struggled to recall her time with the *Kripo*, her life as a profiler. It almost felt as if she'd been someone else back then, an entirely different person. Someone who, more and more, she wanted to be again.

"Perhaps it will."

Jakob nodded toward the pad of paper where she'd scrawled several of her thoughts. "What have you found?"

"The fleet admiral's search basis is too large, and as such, the victim pool is muddy. Plus the fact that Josephine O'Connor's body was not found—only her head—also complicates it. What I need to do is narrow the parameters without relying solely on Josephine's file. There simply isn't enough there."

"How?"

"I've done a cursory read-through of all the files, starting with victims who were dismembered." She held up two fingers. "There are two distinct classifications within the files."

"Classifications." Jakob looked at her with a calm, focused expectation.

"Most of the dismemberment files were attributed to organized crime or another potential source of societal violence, such as drug cartels or gangs, by the investigators. The victims often had either fingers, toes, ears, or noses removed before they died—as noted in their autopsies."

"Torture."

"And scare tactics, precisely. I'd say ninety-five percent of these files were correctly attributed, with the perimortem dismemberment a form of punishment or torture as you just pointed out. But, the cause of death is not the torture." She checked her notes. "Most often it was a gunshot wound, often to the head, or carotid artery severed with a knife."

"The *kill* was quick. Professional."

"Exactly, and for the files in this classification, my reading of it is that the postmortem dismemberment was a function of either necessity for disposal or extended punishment for those victims who come from cultures where funerary practices rely on an intact body."

"They were denied a proper burial."

"Yes."

"The other five percent?"

"Those, plus the dismembered, non-mob-attributed files,

are in the second category, which for simplicity we'll call non-organized-crime dismemberment. From there, I've split them into several subcategories. First..." She took a breath. "Women who suffered antemortem or perimortem torture and rape."

The word stuck a little in her throat, but she was focused on doing her job, and she blocked out everything else.

Jakob stared at her, his attention and focus complete and unwavering. "They could still be organized-crime kills."

She liked it when he talked. Liked it even more because he so rarely spoke that his relative chattiness when they were alone made her feel special.

"That's very true, but for one thing. I think that for these victims, the death was accidental. The focus for the unsub was the torture."

He was still for a moment, processing. "I hate it when I torture someone and they accidentally die."

Annalise blinked, then burst into laughter. Jakob rarely joked, but when he did, it was usually deadpan and delivered in such a way that people who didn't know him as intimately as she did wouldn't actually know if it was a joke.

When her giggles subsided, she looked up to see him smiling at her. Her heart skipped a beat. He had a gorgeous smile. His lower lip was full and luscious. More than once, she'd imagined biting his lip, maybe tugging on it to show him how much she wanted him. Then he'd growl and grab her butt, lift her up. She'd wrap her legs around him and then...

Annalise shoved the lid of her laptop up and stared at the autopsy photo of a severed hand.

Perfect libido killer.

"Of the two lists I've created, we've gone over antemortem rape and torture." She took a breath and straightened her shoulders. "Next are victims whose primary pre-death injuries were due to rape. Some also show signs of physical attack, but nothing that would be defined as torture."

"Annalise..."

She glanced up, holding herself tight. If he asked if she was okay, she might not be.

Jakob stared at her for a moment, and there was something in his eyes she couldn't decipher. But he didn't say anything, only nodded for her to go on.

"The commonality between the two subcategories is the rape and the postmortem dismemberment."

"Torture is odd man out in this group."

"Yes."

"How did they die?"

"This is where it becomes problematic—the causes of death are different." She flipped through her notes. "A fair number of those from blood loss. Though with those who died of internal bleeding, it was most likely not intentional, as it was with those who had arteries severed."

"Severed during amputation?" Jakob asked.

"Amputation means they survive the removal."

Jakob grunted. "Learned something new."

Annalise's lips twitched. "If we want to be very precise, I could have titled these categories defensive dismemberment— which is what we have with our organized-crime-related kills, in which the dismemberment was functional to aid in disposal and/or eliminating evidence. But the ones we're discussing, that this investigation should focus on, are offensive dismember-ment." Whatever amusement they briefly shared melted away as she refocused. "In offensive dismemberment, the focus of the dismemberer is the act of separating and sectioning the body."

That was going to be a major part of the profile, but for now she put it aside.

"Back to the causes of death. Given the state of many of the bodies, some CODs are listed as unknown or pending. Others have only a probable COD, not definitive."

"Offensive dismemberment, if done while still alive..." Jakob grimaced. It was a small twitch of an expression, but she saw it.

"Death most likely would be from blood loss, or from the trauma of the action causing cardiac arrest." She tapped her fingers on her notes. "Cardiac and respiratory arrest are the most common CODs in those files where one is listed."

Jakob stiffened, glancing at his hands before looking up at her. "If you break a man's neck correctly, sever the spinal column, the diaphragm is paralyzed."

Annalise held her breath, shocked by his words...but not surprised. She knew he was formidable, but he was also so chivalrous that she'd forgotten, or maybe never realized, that to become a Ritter, he was probably a dangerous man.

"Respiratory arrest is the technical cause of death," he finished.

Annalise gave herself a moment to see if fear would grip her. It didn't. This was Jakob.

Her Jakob.

No. Thinking like that was just as bad as imagining his hands on her.

Maybe worse.

Nothing about what the fleet admiral had asked her to do was easy or straightforward. If it had been, crime filters on ECRIS—European Criminal Records Information System— would have already flagged files with enough similarities to indicate a serial killer.

Annalise took a breath, flipping through her messy pages of notes. So many victims, so many ways to look at and assess the figurative reams of information.

"I'm sorry, I know this is a little confusing."

"Don't apologize." Jakob nodded for her to continue. "I understand."

She smiled softly. "Thank you, Jakob." She had so many things she needed to thank him for. "How about I skip to the actionable intelligence?"

Jakob stiffened, sitting forward, as if he were going to jump up and go get the bad guys as soon as she pointed him in the right direction.

"I narrowed it down further by gender—only women, though they were the majority of the victims anyway. Eliminated any who were dismembered but not decapitated, since we know Josephine's head was removed. I also filtered for some important similarities in relation to how the dismemberment was achieved. Then I made some judgment calls based on the other circumstances around the cases." It was those decisions made on interpretation of details that she was most worried about because she wasn't good at this anymore.

Except, right now...she felt sure of her choices. Confident in her analysis.

Brilliant.

"After all that, I have two names," she concluded.

"You took the list from hundreds to two."

Annalise looked down, self-doubt rearing its familiar head. Had she made the right calls? Focused on the right things? There were so many unknowns.

"Good job," Jakob said quietly.

"There are probably more, maybe I should check again, and without the rest of Josephine's body—"

"Trust yourself. I do."

Dammit. Annalise's emotions were already too close to the surface, and his words had just set her heart racing. She swallowed deeply. "Thank you," she said, her voice sounding thick even to her own ears.

"Where are the victims from?" Jakob asked, his question helping her switch her focus from how badly she wanted to kiss him to the case once more.

"Besides Josephine, one was killed in Brussels, the other in Krakow."

"Belgium, Poland, Ireland. But all large cities," Jakob said.

"Yes, and it means he is most likely a fluent English speaker."

Jakob folded his arms. "Convince me."

Annalise raised a brow. "Convince you?"

"Convince me this is actionable."

Annalise felt her brows climb higher up her forehead.

Jakob shrugged. "That's what we said at the BND."

"The BND?" *Bundesnachrichtendienst* was German foreign intelligence.

"I was a BND agent. Right after university. The Masters' Admiralty recruited me from there."

"I didn't know that about you," she said softly, though she didn't know why she should be surprised to learn he'd worked in intelligence. He'd proven himself highly intelligent, so much more than a bodyguard or hired gun, or even many of the police she'd worked with. And now his comment about neck breaking...

"It was years ago. Before I became a Ritter," Jakob replied.

"Very well then, I'll convince you." She set aside her notebook and laptop and adopted the tone she used when she was teaching. "The last known location of each of these people was walking down a city sidewalk. It's one of the things Eric noted. It might not seem that important, but it is. Why?"

Jakob's brows drew together, his arms still folded.

She waited a moment to see if he would say anything. When he didn't, she continued. "They lived in the cities where they were taken. These people were going through their daily routines."

"They were complacent."

"There might be an element of that, but for the most part, people are more secure when they are somewhere familiar. Habits and routine are a kind of protection...at least when it comes to this sort of situation. When you've seen something a thousand times, your brain will take note when there is change. People may be less consciously aware, but they are also more prone to pay attention to oddities. You notice things like when a business you've walked by many times changes their window display. Or they repaint the pedestrian crossing."

Window-shopping and walking around the city were things she'd had to abandon because of the stalker.

As if he'd realized what she was thinking, Jakob stood. She waited for a moment, holding her breath. Wondering if this time he'd come to her. If he'd hold her tight. He'd done it before, the night she'd opened the box of flying roaches, and then in the hospital hallway outside her sister's room after the rape.

Jakob went to the living room wall, standing sentry where he could see the front door and window.

It was the place he stood to keep watch, the place he stood when she had bad nights, nights she couldn't bear to even sleep. On those nights, she would sit up on the couch, essentially taking over his bed, and he would stand guard.

"They were on familiar ground," he said softly.

"Yes. Which means that their guard may have been down, as you said, but it also made them inherently less vulnerable. That, plus the public nature of where they were taken most likely means that the unsub approached them and used some sort of ruse or pretense to get them to deviate from that routine enough to be vulnerable."

Jakob nodded. "And English is widely spoken in all those countries?"

"Yes, I checked, and over half the population in both Belgium and Poland speak English fluently."

"And most of them are probably in the large cities."

"Precisely."

When she smiled, Jakob smiled back. It was for only a moment, but it was enough to take her breath away.

"Do you believe you have enough to start a profile?" he asked.

Annalise glanced at her notes and took a deep breath as something she hadn't felt in a very long time washed through her.

Excitement? Self-assurance? The thrill of the chase?

All of those things that had made her good at her job were suddenly there again, and she was tempted to rise from the couch, walk over to Jakob...and what? Hug him? Kiss him? Drag him to her bed?

She dismissed those notions and picked up her pen, flipping the pages of the notebook until she found a blank sheet of paper.

"Yes. Yes, I do."

CHAPTER FIVE

Walt added another teaspoon of sugar to his coffee after taking a sip as Eric smirked. The fleet admiral drank his coffee black and strong and obviously viewed Walt's desire for added sweetness as a personal flaw.

Walt rolled his eyes in response, unconcerned what Eric thought. He was a Southern boy through and through, so that meant he liked sugar. A lot. In his coffee, in his iced tea, and in his mama's so-sweet-you-get-a-cavity-looking-at-them Christmas cookies.

Maybe the flaw was Eric's. God knew the man could use a little sweetness in his life.

They'd arrived at the restaurant in Frankfurt a half hour before the meeting time they'd arranged with Dr. Annalise Fischer and her bodyguard, Jakob. Eric claimed he wanted to do some reconnaissance of the place.

The fleet admiral took paranoid behavior to the next level. But considering his position and the current case they were working—he, Walt Hayden, was on a case. Ha!—Walt didn't have a problem with the extra precautions.

He and Eric had spent the last few days cooling their heels in a Frankfurt hotel, while they waited for Annalise to create her profile of the serial killer. It was safe to say no one would ever accuse Eric of being a patient man. He'd prowled the room like a caged tiger, until Walt had hit his limit and gone out to play tourist in Frankfurt, a city he'd never had the opportunity to visit before.

"Hello."

Walt rose at the sound of Annalise's voice as she approached their table.

"Dr. Fischer. It's good to see you again." Walt reached out to shake her hand and watched as Jakob shifted closer. The man took his responsibility as Annalise's bodyguard very seriously.

"Please, call me Annalise."

Walt nodded, smiling.

Eric gestured at the other chairs at the table. "Join us."

Annalise took the seat next to Walt. Jakob hesitated for a moment, glancing around the restaurant.

"Sit, Bauer," Eric growled. "I've already checked the place out."

Walt thought it spoke to Jakob's level of professionalism that he didn't take a seat until he finished his quick survey of their surroundings.

"Fleet Admiral," Jakob said as he sat. "Dr. Hayden."

The waiter stopped by to see if Annalise and Jakob wanted to place an order. Well, that's what he assumed, since the server was speaking German.

Jakob's and Annalise's accents were crisp and sort of hip, the "s" sounds becoming "z's", yet also intimate in the way the words flowed and paused. Walt's knowledge of German accents was mostly from American-made movies. Neither Jakob nor Annalise had the harsh, guttural Indiana-Jones-Nazi accent he'd always associated with German. He was going to go ahead and never admit any of that out loud, since it was cultural racism. He'd just do better.

Eric was clearly pissed off by the interruption, impatient to discover what Annalise had found.

"We ordered coffee," Walt said, gesturing to their cups, hoping he was adding that comment at an appropriate point.

"That sounds good," Annalise said, then looked to the waiter and repeated her words in German.

The server replied in somewhat more heavily accented English. "Coffee, for you, very good."

Jakob raised two fingers. "And cream for her, please."

Annalise smiled at the Ritter, obviously pleased with Jakob's order. Walt wondered if there was something going on between the pretty psychologist and Jakob. The sexual tension between the two was unmistakable.

Once the server was gone, Eric sat forward, seeming both eager and grim as he looked at Annalise. "You have something."

She nodded. "Very preliminary. I only had time to go through the files you'd grouped under dismemberment."

Eric frowned. "But we don't know if Josephine was dismembered."

"Precisely. You don't know." Annalise pulled out file folders. "From the dismembered victim group, I've identified two potential victims." The top folder was labeled "Dr. Hayden." She passed it to Walt, then handed Eric and Jakob equally innocuous folders. She set her own stack of papers, which was a bit thicker, on the table in front of her.

Walt opened his, blinked, and muttered, "Jesus." The first page was a full-color autopsy photo.

"You're a doctor." Eric glanced at him.

"Yes, I like *alive, breathing* people."

"Dr. Hayden, I think the place we should start is with you."

"Me?" Walt raised his eyebrows comically high and was rewarded with a smile from Annalise.

"I'd like your assessment of the skill of the person who did the dismembering."

"Okay, give me a minute..." He glanced down at the papers and grimaced. "Actually, do you have higher-resolution versions of the photos?"

"Jakob had suggested you might ask for that." She reached into her bag, pulled out a tablet, and passed it over. "I loaded the images on this."

"Wow. It's exactly as bad as you think it would be in high def." Walt was inwardly horrified, but he was perfectly capable of viewing the images with a clinical eye. "I'll need a few minutes."

Eric craned his neck to look at the tablet, then turned his attention back to Annalise. "Start talking. I don't want to wait."

That was, undeniably, a command. Walt shook his head and sighed, but if Eric saw him, he ignored it.

"I always begin my first lecture on the first day of abnormal psychology with a single question." Annalise had a lovely speaking voice, calm, authoritative, and with that smart-sounding crisp accent. Walt could listen to her all day. "Do you know the definition of a serial killer?"

She paused, and Walt took a moment to appreciate the dramatic effect.

"My students' answers usually range from 'someone crazy' to 'someone who likes to kill people' or, for students who've already taken a psych class or two, the response is usually 'someone with a compulsive need.' Do you know the definition of a serial killer, Fleet Admiral?"

"Someone who needs killing," Eric replied instantly.

Annalise blinked, nonplussed, and beside her, Jakob stiffened a little.

"Fleet Admiral, if you'd ever like to talk to someone..." Annalise began hesitantly.

"Nope. I did plenty of therapy after my wives died, and I think I damn near broke the poor guy."

"I was sorry to hear about your wives," Walt said softly, recalling Eric mentioning to Juliette and Devon that his wives had died. "Was it an accident?"

Eric glanced in his direction, his jaw tight. "Assassinated."

Assassinated was an interesting word. Different from murdered. Obviously, Eric's wives, like him, held positions of power.

Walt wasn't sure how to respond to the fact that both of Eric's wives had been killed, but he didn't have an opportunity to when Eric looked at Annalise and said, "Just keep going."

"Right. Of course." Annalise took a breath.

Walt imagined she was putting the fleet admiral's mental health on a back burner, but only for now.

"A serial killer is someone for whom the murder of another person fills an abnormal psychological gratification." Annalise spoke quietly, though there was no one sitting near them. "Sometimes this is coupled with a mental disorder, other times rooted in trauma, but either way, the impetus for the killing is to satisfy a need, the same needs you or I might have, but which we satisfy in socially acceptable ways."

"He needs to kill people and cut their heads off," Eric said.

"Actually, the killing might be secondary. The fact that the people die may or may not be part of this person's motivation."

"You can't cut someone's head off and keep them alive," Walt pointed out.

"Precisely. But if what you need is to remove a head from a

body, the fact that they have to die for it to happen is a consequence, not the focus."

Beside Walt, Eric flipped open his folder, spreading out the papers. Walt turned his attention back to the images on the tablet. He told himself this was just like cadaver lab. He was looking at cadaver photos. Technically, they were pictures of cadavers, but...

"You think these two were killed by the same person who killed Josephine," Eric said. He'd laid three sheets of paper beside each other. They looked like the front page of a medical chart, except, that in addition to a smiling headshot, probably from an ID, on each page there was also a picture of the woman's head after death. The pale slackness of death made them bear only a passing resemblance to the people they'd been when alive.

There was also a large bold note with cause of death on each sheet.

The page bearing Josephine O'Connor's name said, "Unknown COD, Presumed Respiratory Arrest."

Yep, not having the brain connected to the heart was a pretty sure-fire way to cause respiratory arrest.

"Possibly," Annalise was saying, "but I'd like Dr. Hayden's opinion."

Walt refocused on the tablet, swiping to the next picture and then enlarging it to study the details while the rest of them continued to talk.

"Why?" Eric pulled a picture out of his folder. A woman's body in multiple pieces, laid out like a jigsaw puzzle on a steel autopsy table.

"Why do they do it? As I said, to satisfy their need—sexual, emotional, physical, intellectual."

"Intellectual?" Walt looked up at that.

Annalise nodded. "Britain and America have—and please take no offense, Dr. Hayden—"

"None taken, we're a dumpster fire a lot of the time."

"—a high number of, and therefore an extensive body of work on, serial killers." Annalise settled in her chair, leaning ever so slightly closer to Jakob. There was something about the two of them together that made him even more certain that they were in love. However, Walt couldn't tell if they'd acted on those feelings. They both seemed rather reserved with each other. Maybe they were just being professional in front of the fleet admiral.

"The Americans are nuts. Go on," Eric prompted.

Walt kicked Eric under the table, and the big man snorted in amusement. Everyone showed him so much deference, Walt felt like it was his job to take the Viking down a few notches whenever possible.

"Let's focus on the dismemberment and work under the theory that cutting up the victims is the act that satisfies the killer's need." Annalise pulled several papers out of her folder and spread them out, facing Eric and Walt. "The Cleveland Torso Murderer killed and dismembered at least a dozen people in Cleveland—that's a city in America."

Walt snickered. "My family traveled there once when I was a kid. My mama was determined to see the Great Lakes. Did you know the house from *A Christmas Story* is there?"

Eric scowled and pointed at the tablet. "Don't make me shoot your eye out."

"You get that reference but not the *Star Trek* one?"

"I got it. I just didn't think it was funny."

Annalise glanced over at Jakob, who shrugged.

"Sorry for the interruption, Annalise," Walt said. "Please continue before Eric has an aneurysm."

"Yes...well... The bodies in Cleveland were found in pieces, sometimes in boxes or a shallow pond or wrapped up in baskets."

Eric stiffened at the word *basket*. Walt had seen the picture of Josephine's head sitting in a basket, placed atop a cabinet in the famous Long Room of Trinity College Dublin's library, blood dripping down the glass of the display case. It had been horrific, and Walt hadn't even known her.

"This particular case offered potential insight into the need—the killer sent Agent Ness, the man in charge of the investigation a letter, stating," Annalise glanced down at her notes, "'I felt bad operating on those people, but science must advance. I shall soon astound'—spelled incorrectly a-s-t-o-n-d-e in the letter—'the medical profession.'"

"He was using them for medical experimentation," Eric said softly. "That could mean the rest of Josephine's body..."

The tense silence was broken only when Annalise flipped to another page.

"That is one possibility. Another is that the dismemberment was not the focus, not the source of the need, but secondary. Józef Cyppek dismembered his victim after killing her, claiming it was in order to transport the body. But viewed through a modern abnormal psychology lens, I'd say that dismembering the victims—only one confirmed, but reports indicate that Cyppek also killed dozens of children in addition to an adult female—had more to do with dehumanizing them. He needed to dismember them, not in a defensive sense but offensive." Annalise paused for a moment, seeming to consider how to phrase it. "If you butcher a human like an animal—remove the organs, setting aside those that are edible, removing the intestines for disposal, separating muscle from bone—you have stripped away the humanity of that person. Turned them into meat and offal."

Walt had seen plenty of gross shit in his time and yet her

words made him feel slightly sick to his stomach. "An indication of remorse?" he asked. "They feel bad they killed someone?"

Annalise pursed her lips. "Close. They are distancing themselves from the reality of the act, which may not be remorse but denial."

Walt looked back at the pictures. One of them was bugging him, but he flicked away, back to the image of the second body, which had been cut in half at the waist. "This body still had its internal organs."

"True, so again, it doesn't quite fit."

"The torso killer is closer," Eric said. "So you think the killer is a wannabe doctor?"

"Possible, but if the person you are hunting had that pathology, I'd suspect the volume of kills to be higher. Also, isolated in a central place." She shuffled papers and pulled out several sheets, placing them beside each other so she had a map showing Europe and North Africa. There were color-coded dots spread far and wide. "If they believe they are performing medical innovation or experimentation, they would be centralized around a private space, somewhere they think of as a lab or operating room."

"But this fucker killed whomever Petro told him to," Eric snarled.

"Every victim was selected by a partner?" Annalise asked it more as a leading question than an actual inquiry.

Eric's jaw clenched. "I'm not a student, Professor. And I'm not a complete asshole, so you can tell me if I'm wrong."

Annalise inclined her head. "Of course, Fleet Admiral. Let us put aside the issue of the partnership for the moment. Dismemberment could be, one, due to perceived medical experimentation, most likely to fill a need to be seen as intelligent and skilled. Two, a way to dehumanize the victim after death, or three..." Annalise hesitated. "A final act of control over the victims. It's close to the pathology of killers such as Giorgio Orsolano or Ted Bundy."

"Bundy." Walt looked up. He'd watched his share of true crime documentaries. "Bundy kidnapped, tortured, raped, and then kept the heads."

"Yes, and he often revisited the bodies. They belonged to him, and he was able to find sexual gratification with them, even after death. The heads were kept as trophies, or mementos, most likely allowing him to relive the act by looking at them."

Eric was so tense that the air around him was charged. "Orsolano cut up girls to dispose of the bodies after he raped and tortured them."

Annalise spoke very calmly, with the firm but compassionate tone Walt recognized well. It was the voice he used when telling a family their loved one was dead. It was the tone for delivering devastating news.

"Of the two potential victims we're focusing on, three if you include Josephine, we have the complete, pre-decomposition lower torso of only one." Annalise tapped the picture Eric had put on the table.

Most of the woman's body was there, laid out on a coroner's table. Unlike the other victim, the...pieces...of this one had been found before advanced decomp could set in.

The body had been laid out like a puzzle waiting to be put together. A puzzle missing two pieces—right hand, left foot—but otherwise intact. That picture was on his tablet, as were closeups of the places where the body had been cut—across the waist, arms severed at the shoulders, hands at the wrists. Her thighs were still attached to her pelvis, but the legs were severed below the knee and at the ankle.

"Alicja Lewandowski." Annalise placed a large picture of a

smiling woman who bore only surface resemblance to the corpse over the top of the autopsy photo. "A Polish woman who lived in, and was found in, Krakow. Vaginal and anal bruising and tearing indicates sexual assault, though no DNA was recovered."

Eric stood, turned, and hauled back his fist to punch the wall behind them.

The brick wall.

Walt and Jakob moved at the same time, both lunging for the fleet admiral. Walt hooked a hand around Eric's elbow, though since he was still sitting, stretched out across Eric's chair, it wouldn't have done much good.

Jakob, however, was both fast and effective. He grabbed the fleet admiral in a Full Nelson, arms hooked under Eric's armpits, his clenched hands braced against the back of Eric's neck, forcing his head down and hobbling the movement of his shoulders.

Eric snarled and started to turn. Jakob's shoes skidded across the floor as he was dragged. Walt and Jakob shared a glance, and there was a moment of understanding as well as a fair amount of *oh fuck.*

Even as Walt was scrambling out of his chair, bracing his body against Jakob's—which was rock hard with muscle—Annalise got up too.

"Fleet Admiral. Eric." She put a hand on his chest, her voice commanding. "This behavior is not productive. You are distracting us rather than helping us catch Josephine's killer."

That stopped Eric cold, and after a moment, Jakob eased his hold. Walt backed off so Jakob could let him go.

Annalise went to reassure the scared-looking waiter who was hesitantly approaching.

Annalise returned to the table, then cleared her throat when they remained standing. Walt sat down, and Annalise smiled at him. More slowly, Jakob resumed his seat. Finally Eric did too, but his jaw was clenched so tight that Walt was worried about his teeth.

"Dr. Hayden—" Annalise began.

"Walt."

"Walt, what can you tell us based on the photos?" Annalise gestured at the tablet.

"I hate to put a damper on your theory, Professor, but I don't think they were killed by the same person."

Annalise and Jakob shared a look.

"Maybe it is the same person, and they got better, but..." Walt shook his head. "I'm not a forensic pathologist, this is not my specialty at all. But on some of these, it's hard to see details."

"I have additional printed copies of the photos not in the folder."

"Well damn, you're organized. I like it." Walt shot her a smile, and when she glanced back and gave him a genuine, unguarded grin, he was surprised by his response to it. Annalise Fischer was—in a word—beautiful. Her chestnut-colored hair was currently pinned up, but enough tendrils had escaped that he could see it was long and wavy. Her light brown eyes captured his and, though it was a silly, romantic sentiment, Walt felt as if he could get lost in them. He forced himself to look away first, feeling the weight of Jakob's gaze on him.

Walt put down the tablet and quickly sorted through the paper copies. It took him a few minutes, during which everyone watched him make four piles.

"Why are there four?" Eric demanded. "I thought we were talking about two people and Josephine?"

Walt considered making a comment about Eric needing to be patient, then decided to choose life rather than having his face punched in.

"Okay, this pile is all Alicja." He stumbled a little over the pronunciation. "I matched up the closeups with the overall photo." He spread out the detailed shots. Up close, it was actually easier to deal with, because it didn't look like a person—just pinkish muscle, white bone, and cartilage. "If I was going to dismember a body, this is probably how I'd do it. Cut the legs off at the knees, and don't try and mess around with the hips. The joint there would be a pain in the ass to deal with, unless you used a bone saw, and the femur is a big bone.

"At the ankles, they cut off right between the bottom of the leg bones—tibia, fibula—and the top bone of the foot, the talus. That's hard to do because it's not straight across. They had to sort of go around the bottom of the tibia. And if you look at the legs, and the one foot, there's only one cut in the flesh. They knew exactly where to start. If they'd been an amateur, they might have started too high or too low and had to adjust, start over. The same thing at the shoulder. They knew just where to go to get in between the humerus and the clavicle and scapula."

He touched his arm and then collarbone and shoulder blade as he mentioned them. Probably unnecessary with this audience, but it was a practice he'd developed over the years he'd spent working abroad, using physical gestures in tandem with words to help explain for those with limited knowledge of their own anatomy or medicine.

He went on to the next stack.

"This body, though there's not much of it—"

"That's the victim from Belgium," Annalise said.

Walt nodded. "Again, the cuts are in just the right spot. Most people would try to cut straight across to sever a head, but they came in at a slight angle. See it?" Everyone leaned in to look at the line he drew across the profile shot of the head. "It's angled up from the back. The spinous process, the skinny fin part of your vertebrae that sticks out at the back, is angled slightly down in your neck. Whoever did this knew that and adjusted their angle so they'd go cleanly between the vertebrae."

Walt didn't look at Eric as he tapped the picture of Josephine's neck. "The same here."

"What's the fourth pile?" Eric asked.

Walt glanced at Annalise and Jakob, a little suspicious that they hadn't said anything or reacted.

"I guess this is the rest of the person from Belgium, but here, these incisions were made by someone who had no idea what they were doing." He spread out the photos of a knee, ankle, and right hand. "Compare these to these." He pointed to Alicja's photos. "See how there's a deep cut at the wrist, but they were too high? They hit bone, so then they started again, farther down, and managed to get it off. But see how the muscle looks sort of chewed? I'm guessing that's from either a dull knife or maybe hacking at it."

"Josephine and Alicja had the same killer, but the Belgium girl is only half this killer?" Eric sounded calm once again. Coldly analytical, even. "Maybe two killers."

"No," Annalise said. "They were all killed by the same unsub." Annalise picked up the fourth pile of pictures. "These are from another body. Not part of the victim from Belgium. One I ruled out, but I wanted to be sure."

"A test?" Walt tried not to be irritated.

"A test of my skill, not yours. The victim was a possible one, whom I ruled out based on the dismemberment, but I am far less an expert on human anatomy than you."

Walt relaxed and nodded. "A second opinion."

While he and Annalise had been talking, Jakob had twisted in his chair, scanning the restaurant. Eric, too, was looking around. Walt winced and checked to make sure no one was close enough to have heard them. The fact that they were speaking English wasn't a guarantee that no one would understand. Hopefully their poor server hadn't heard any of this.

"Now we come to the issue of the partnership," Annalise said. "Killer partnerships are not unheard of. I haven't had a chance to do an in-depth read of the reports from Rome about Ciril Novak, the man who killed a trinity, then kidnapped and tortured two other members. I want to do that before I make too many statements about how the partnership between Petro, who would most likely have been the dominant partner, and this unsub may be similar, or differentiate from the known—"

"Get the papers," Jakob said.

Annalise's brow furrowed at the same time Eric stood up, his chair teetering, almost ready to topple over.

Walt and Annalise shared a look, and then in tandem swept the papers off the table, shoving them into her bag.

"What's going on, Eric?" Walt asked in a low voice.

"Go out the back," was Eric's unhelpful reply.

"I will stay, Fleet Admiral." Jakob was on his feet, and he'd turned to the main dining room.

Now Walt could see them—a few people who had hats pulled low or newspapers open, but all of whom seemed to be looking their way.

They were being watched.

Why, and by whom, seemed unimportant as his body dumped adrenaline into his system. Walt pushed to his feet.

"Dr. Hayden..." Jakob didn't look at him, didn't take his attention away from those watching them, but Walt immediately knew what he was asking.

Walt looked at Annalise, who had her arms wrapped around her bag, holding it to her chest. Her eyes were wide, and she was trembling slightly. He remembered what they'd said in her office the other day. Something about Jakob guarding her due to a stalker. Something bad had happened to

Annalise, and now Jakob wanted Walt to look after her. He was pretty damn sure that request didn't come easily to the other man, which only ratcheted up the tension.

"Come on, Professor." Walt hooked a hand under her arm and pulled her to her feet. "Time to go."

"Jakob, follow us out." Eric grabbed Annalise's and Walt's shoulders and started dragging them to the door into the café kitchen. Walt hauled Annalise against his side so Eric wasn't dragging her.

Jakob's attention was focused on the room, on the potential danger, as he took calm, measured strides backward. Walt lost sight of him when they burst into the kitchen. Ignoring questions from the staff, he, Annalise, and Eric picked up speed, nearly running when they hit the back door. It opened onto an alley, and there were two large trash cans beside the door, reeking of old food.

Eric glanced left and right. The narrow alley was, luckily, not a dead end, with exits to the streets on both sides.

"You go left. Get someplace safe and stay there." Eric shot Walt a hard glance, and then turned away, toward the right.

"Where the hell are you going?" Walt called out.

Jakob emerged from the kitchen door. He glanced around, picked up a short broom, and held it like a bat, positioning himself so the first thing anyone who opened the door saw would be him.

"Knew three days here was too long." There was a wealth of feeling in Eric's words. "I'm the one they're after."

"Who?" Jakob asked, at the same time Walt said, "You're just telling me this now?"

"I pissed off a few people. If they find my body, start with the Albanian mafia or the guys running the port of Antwerp. They were smuggling cocaine. I kept running into assholes when all I wanted was a damn serial killer."

Walt thought about Eric casually taking down an extremist cell and teaching children how to fight and appropriately use words like "co-conspirator". Yeah, he could see that Eric might have made a few other enemies if he'd been rampaging all over Europe like that.

"Fleet Admiral," Jakob barked. "If you are in danger, the Spartan Guard—"

"I don't need a babysitter." Eric smiled grimly at Walt. "Sorry about this. We'll meet up later."

"When? How?" Walt was both baffled and terrified—the feeling reminded him a bit of being in med school.

"Jakob, get them out of here," Eric called back. He was almost to the street. "And keep them safe."

Then the fleet admiral disappeared around the corner.

Jakob dropped the broom and, without a word, went to the other side of Annalise, taking her hand while Walt still had an arm around her shoulder. She was pale and breathing too fast.

They heard a commotion in the kitchen.

Jakob looked at them. "Run."

CHAPTER SIX

I t was a testament to exactly how worried he was about Annalise that Jakob didn't object to how Walt's hand had rested on her shoulder during the car ride. He slid out of the armored, chauffeured car he'd called to pick them up after they'd taken basic evasive maneuvers, walking in a corkscrewing circle around Frankfurt. There'd been no sign of the people from the restaurant following them, but he'd opted to have a security service pick them up just in case and take them to his home, which he considered to be one of the most secure residences in Frankfurt.

A home he'd bought and remodeled for Annalise.

Because he was a stupid fucking fucker who was in love with a woman too good for him. Over his ears in love.

Years in intelligence work and then as a Masters' Admiralty Ritter hadn't beaten the stupid out of him.

His grandmother, if she were still alive, would have smacked him on the back of the head and called him an *Arsch mit Ohren*. Oma had never minced words, never hesitated to tell him when he was acting like a complete idiot. And God knew an *arsch mit ohren* was what he felt like. He *was* a butt with ears.

Walt guided Annalise up the steps to the front door. Jakob keyed in the code on the lock with one hand and subtly pressed his palm to the hidden scanner in the doorframe. It clicked open and he swept in, quickly checking and then disarming the security system before turning and motioning for Walt to guide Annalise inside.

She looked pale, even paler than her typical light complexion, with a gray undertone to her skin, set off by the darkness of her hair. It was pulled back today, the way she wore it when she was in her office at the university or teaching. But he'd seen her with her hair down, watched her scrub her fingers through it after releasing it from a tight bun. For a moment, she'd have glorious just-fucked hair, and then she'd smooth it down, tuck it behind her ears.

More than once, after she'd fallen asleep on the couch while he kept watch, he would crouch down and brush back any pieces that fell over her face.

Verdammt! He was no better than her stalker.

He was completely aware of exactly how ridiculously stupid he was, how creepy as fuck it was that he loved to watch her sleep, but that didn't stop him. He knew she felt safer when he was there.

And Annalise's feelings had become the single-most important thing in his life.

It was why his very precious free time was almost all spent with her or trying to ensure her safety in some way. Any moment he had where the vice admiral, who was in charge of the Ritter, didn't need him to be doing something else, Jakob was playing bodyguard for Annalise.

Sometimes, when he sat near her, either working on his own computer or watching TV while she graded papers, he could pretend they were a couple, relaxing together. And when they were done, they'd go to bed together. Their bed.

The bed in this house, in the bedroom he'd remodeled with her in mind.

He'd bought and redone an entire fucking house for a woman who would never live in it.

Verdammter Mist!

Arrrrgh.

"Okay, what do we do now?" Walt was looking around the foyer. Jakob had sanded down the exposed beams and varnished them himself, nearly breaking his fool neck when he leaned too far back and fell off the damn ladder.

"Come inside." Jakob motioned them through the door on the right.

The house was old but large, though by modern standards, the rooms were small. It sat in the middle of a large plot of land with trees that hid it from view on all sides.

Most of the trees had cameras, infrared sensors, and motion detection tech mounted to the trunks and disguised to look like bark. He'd toyed with the idea of adding automatic ground-level flamethrowers that would ignite when the motion or infrared sensors were tripped, but his beta test had resulted in several flaming bunnies that still haunted his nightmares.

The room he led them into was a small living space with two narrow windows on either side of a stone fireplace. There were three leather and wood armchairs, each with matching footstools, in a semicircle facing the fire.

In his deranged fantasy life, when he and Annalise were married and living here, there was always a shadowy third person—their third—so he'd made sure there were three chairs in this cozy little room. A cozy room with bulletproof glass windows and access to one of the seven safe rooms.

A second closed door led to the dining room, and beyond

that, the kitchen, which he'd enlarged considerably, since he knew she liked to sometimes work at the kitchen counter for a change of scenery. The inset marble block in one section of the counter was for baking, since she'd told him marble worked best for pastry making because it stayed cold.

The urge to say all these things, to give her—well, them, since Walt was here—a tour was so strong, he had to bite the inside of his cheek. He wanted to tell them that the chairs were custom made by a local furniture company. That he'd repaired the chimney for this fireplace himself and re-mortared the stone. Tell her, them, about the security system and his Oma's homemade quilt that covered the trinity-sized bed in the master suite.

Instead, he pointed at the chairs. "Sit."

Yeah, that was better.

Walt raised one eyebrow but guided Annalise over to the center chair. Then he crouched beside her. "Hi there, Annalise. Can you talk to me for a second?"

Oh, wait. Walt was a *doctor*.

And Annalise was either in shock or had done a mental retreat. Dissociated. He'd spent enough time with her that he had picked up his fair share of terms. He was pretty sure he'd attended more of her lectures than some of the actual students.

Either way, if it had been just him and Annalise, he would have been preparing to call someone to come out and check her physical health.

Her mental health?

Well, he had a pretty good idea of what was going on in that beautiful brain of hers, and he would have to find a way to break her out of her downward spiral.

"Annalise, is it okay if I touch you? I want to touch your wrist with two fingers." Walt held up two fingers on his left hand.

She didn't respond. No comment.

Walt turned to Jakob. "Can you repeat what I just said, in German?"

Jakob shifted so he could see Annalise's face and both doors, then quietly repeated exactly what Walt had said.

Annalise blinked and her eyes focused. She looked at Jakob and spoke in German. "You want to touch me?"

There was panicked, excited screaming in Jakob's head because he thought, hoped—*verdammter Mist*—there was longing in her voice. He held very still, replying in the same language. "I was repeating what Dr. Hayden said."

Annalise hugged her bag tighter against her chest, turning her face away from him.

The screaming in his head was now accompanied by a voice asking him why he hadn't just said yes. He could have confessed his undying love and devotion and...and...

Utterly betrayed her trust by crossing the line of professionalism, by taking advantage of her in a moment of vulnerability.

"Annalise, hey there." Walt shifted, an easy smile on his face, his eyes kind. "Can I touch your wrist? I'd like to check your pulse."

Mutely, she dropped her right arm to lay across her lap.

Walt tapped his smartwatch, starting a timer, then found her pulse. After half a minute, he looked up. "Your pulse is a little fast, so I'd like you to take a few slow, deep breaths for me. And maybe a glass of water?"

The last was addressed to him. Jakob stared at Walt, then pointed toward the door that led to the dining room and kitchen. He wasn't going to leave Annalise.

Walt looked back and forth between them and then said, "Okay, I'll go find some water."

When Walt was gone, Jakob let down his guard. Not all the way, of course. Without his walls up, his self-control dialed to nine, he talked too much. Said stupid, inane things no one wanted to hear.

And while his ability to remain quiet hadn't been a natural part of his personality, rather something that had been beaten into him—literally—right now, Annalise needed him to be calm, to comfort her.

He eased up on his control so that when he moved to stand in front of her and she met his gaze, he smiled, just enough that she smiled in turn. Seeing her smile made him feel like everything was right with the world. As if for all the good and bad he'd done in his life, he knew how to make this woman feel safe. How to make her smile. And that was a worthwhile achievement.

The door opened, and Jakob retreated a few steps.

Walt sat down on one of the footstools and passed Annalise the glass.

She took it, her hand shaking.

Jakob put his hands behind his back so she wouldn't see his fists clench.

Over the next five minutes, Annalise drank the whole glass of water, and Walt checked her pulse a second time, confirming that it had slowed.

Annalise finally relaxed enough to let go of her bag, which Walt took from her, placing it, and her empty glass, on the floor.

Jakob needed end tables in this room, one for each chair. What kind of end tables did she like? Maybe the guy who made the chairs would make end tables with hidden weapons drawers.

"I'm so sorry, Dr. Hayden," she said softly.

"Walt," he said. "And sorry for what?" Walt gave her an easygoing, friendly, reassuring grin that Jakob could never have managed. He wasn't sure his face could make that expression if he wanted it to.

"For putting you in danger."

"That was Eric, not you, and that was not nearly as alarming as Eric showing up covered in blood in the middle of the night."

Jakob made a mental note to check if the Spartan Guard, the poor, cursed bastards whose job was to protect the fleet admiral, had sent a cleanup crew to deal with whatever had left Eric bloody. He doubted they had, since no one in the Masters' Admiralty, except now himself and Annalise, knew where Eric was.

Of course, technically, he no longer knew.

And then he remembered that Eric had forbidden him from telling the Spartan Guard—actually anyone in the Masters' Admiralty—that he was here.

"I'm the reason we were in danger," Annalise insisted quietly. "I'm the one he was after."

Walt nodded as if he understood but shifted just enough to shoot Jakob a quick look. Odd that he understood exactly what Walt was asking—*Do you know what she's talking about?*—when they'd only met yesterday.

Jakob had so much he wanted to say to her, so many reassurances he wanted to offer.

You owe no one an apology. You are strong and brave and wonderful, and someday I'm going to kill the man who's tormenting you. I will kill him and make him real and mortal, not the dark, terrifying monster I know you see in your dreams.

Out loud, he said. "It wasn't him."

Annalise's lips trembled. "You don't have to lie to me so I don't feel guilty."

"I don't lie." That was a fat lie.

Annalise blinked and then her shoulders straightened, and she tipped her head ever so slightly. "Everyone lies, Jakob. I know you've sat in on that particular lecture at least once."

He could have cried with relief at seeing her looking so controlled and composed. Looking like, sounding like, herself.

He would never say it aloud, but he wished he'd known her before. Before the trauma of the stalking, and then her sister's attack, had robbed her of her self-assurance and confidence.

"Not him," Jakob said again.

Annalise studied his face, and then her expression relaxed ever so slightly, but she didn't just take his word for it. "How do you know?"

"There were three, maybe four people. Watching us."

Annalise's eyes widened. "That many? And you're sure they were after us?"

"When you went into the kitchen, they stood up," Jakob replied.

"If there were that many of them, shouldn't they have been able to catch us? I mean we weren't walking that fast."

"We took evasive measures." Jakob didn't think he needed to go into more detail than that, but she also had a point.

"Or they weren't interested in us and followed Eric," Walt suggested.

That was what he'd been thinking.

"We need to tell someone," Annalise said.

"Can't." The fleet admiral had expressly forbidden it at their first meeting in her office.

"Who do you think was following us...well, him?" Walt asked Annalise. "The people he mentioned? Someone else? Or is it top secret, secret society stuff?"

Annalise didn't tighten up or retreat the way Jakob expected her to. Instead, she turned her attention to Walt. "You are not a member of..."

"Of the Masters' Admiralty? No. But my sister is. She's married to a knight in England. Guy's name is Lancelot Knight and he sometimes carries a sword, if you can believe it."

Annalise's lips twitched.

Jakob grunted.

Walt made a face. "Crap. What's the German word for knight?"

"Ritter," Annalise said cheerfully.

"Aaaaand that's what Eric called you. Sorry, man. Oh shit, wait. You had a sword, didn't you?"

"He did." The longer they spoke, the more Annalise came back to life, shaking off her earlier shock.

Jakob stared at Annalise. She was clearly enjoying this, her humor, her genuine happiness something he'd only caught brief glimpses of. She grinned at him and his heart skipped a beat.

"I was jetlagged. That's my excuse for not taking note of that fascinating detail," Walt declared. He shook his head in apparent amusement at himself.

Jakob admired Walt's entertaining, while self-deprecating, manner of speaking. His calm assurance and confidence might have come from being a doctor, might just be who he was, but it meant he had no problem making fun of himself.

They were all quiet for a moment, but it wasn't awkward, especially when Walt slid from the ottoman to one of the other chairs, leaning back and sighing.

Jakob looked at them. The fact that Walt was sitting in the chair where he'd always pictured their shadowy, mysterious third was making him feel odd. Not bad, not good. It was a feeling he didn't fully understand, and so he couldn't name it.

It was winter, and though the heat in the house was on, Jakob turned to the fireplace, taking a few minutes to stack wood and then using a starter log to get it going quickly. Walt had his head back, his eyes closed. Jakob took a breath, and then went to the kitchen to make coffee. He didn't exactly *like* leaving Annalise alone with the other man now that they were out of the crisis situation, but after watching the American doctor take care of her and put her at ease, he found he could accept it.

Several minutes later, he returned with a tray including a French press waiting to be pressed, cups with saucers, delicate cut-glass sugar and creamer set, though the creamer had some non-dairy shelf-safe stuff in it, which was all he had in the house at the moment. He really needed to make time for a trip to the store.

"Cooffffeeee," Walt moaned, sounding rather like a zombie from a horror movie.

Jakob retreated to the wall, ignoring his desire to kneel and pour out the coffee, to take care of her, and of Walt, by providing for them. It was Walt who depressed the plunger on the French press and poured coffee into each of the cups.

Jakob drank his black, Annalise added a little of the cream, and when she was done, Walt dumped half the sugar into his own cup.

Annalise and Jakob both stared at Walt, her in amusement, him in horror. Annalise hid a smile behind her cup, shook her head gently, and finally sipped.

The fire was starting to warm the room, and the hot cup felt good in his hands. But Annalise's next words made him cold. She cleared her throat, faced Walt, and said, "I have a stalker, and someday he's going to kill me."

"Annalise," Jakob said, hating her words, but hating himself more for failing to catch the man, so that she didn't have to live her life with a guillotine blade dangling over her neck.

The sad smile she gave him told him she hadn't meant to hurt his feelings and she felt guilty for speaking her belief aloud. "I'm sorry," she said softly.

He didn't reply. He couldn't. His throat was clogged, his chest heavy with regret.

Walt, however, had no problem finding his voice. "Who is

this stalker?"

Annalise shook her head. "I have no idea." The breathy, self-deprecating scoff that followed those words made it perfectly clear how much she hated failing. "I'm a profiler, a psychologist. And yet I'm completely incapable of creating a profile of my own stalker."

"I don't find that surprising at all. You're too close to the case, too emotionally involved. There's a reason surgeons can't operate on someone they know. There has to be distance. And just because you understand the psychology behind an emotion doesn't mean you don't feel it," Walt said, his voice quiet and kind, soothing.

"I know that's true, but it doesn't make it easier to deal with. Someone...someone I was close to was badly hurt by this man."

Walt tilted his head. "Okay. Annalise, you don't have to tell me anything more if you'd rather not."

"You're...you're involved now. In a way. Maybe not, if you're sure it..." She glanced up at Jakob, her eyes wide and vulnerable.

"Wasn't him."

Walt leaned forward, elbows on knees, looking back and forth between them. "Who did this man hurt?"

The doctor was forthright, the type to ask questions he needed answers to. Jakob respected that. The question was, seemingly, directed at either of them, but Jakob sure as fuck wasn't going to answer.

"My twin sister."

Walt's brows rose. "You're a twin?"

Annalise nodded.

"I'm a triplet. Identical, so technically a quad since the number needs to be a multiple of two, but there's just three of us."

She and Walt shared a look that Jakob assumed only those who'd spent time in a womb with another would understand.

He was an only child.

Thank God. His father hadn't been cut out to rear children. A military man, he'd raised Jakob as if he was just another soldier under his command. And while he'd been terribly lonely as a child, he wouldn't have wished his upbringing on another simply to have someone to play with.

"My sister, Adele, lives in Tokyo. I didn't tell her that I'd acquired the attention of a dangerous man because I didn't want to worry her. And..." Annalise paused. "And because I had just enough pride that it bothered me to admit to her that I couldn't put together any sort of cohesive picture of the man tormenting me."

Walt reached over and placed his hand on top of Annalise's on the armrest of her chair when her voice started to wobble. Jakob stared at their touching hands, strangely compelled to rise and add his to theirs.

There was also an underlying desire to shove Walt away from her, because damn it, Annalise was *his*.

But he trusted Walt, or maybe she trusted Walt and that made him trust the doctor.

No, he decided, he trusted Walt.

Goddamn stupid feelings.

"She came to Frankfurt on business and decided to surprise me." Annalise swallowed heavily.

"If this is too hard..." Walt said, offering Annalise another out, a chance to end the conversation here.

She shook her head, refusing to take it. "I need to go back. To when Jakob started taking care of me."

Jakob's heart beat a little bit faster when she said he took care of her. That was what he wanted. To protect her, make her happy. Keep her safe.

"I have a near phobia of flying bugs. Clinically my reaction isn't quite extreme enough to be a true phobia, but I strongly dislike them, and I'm scared of them."

"You might not want to pay a visit to me at home in South Carolina then," Walt said. "I'm pretty sure you wouldn't like to run into a wheel bug."

Jakob made a mental note to look that bug up later. Actually, he felt compelled to research South Carolina as well, curious about where Walt came from.

"I'll consider myself warned."

"Why did you mention the bugs?" Walt asked.

"I'd begun getting threatening phone calls and letters. At the time, I worked for the *Kripo*, that's the German police."

Walt nodded, his calm, kind attention focused on her. His face showed empathy, compassion. Maybe Walt could teach him how to do that. His years of intelligence and knight work may not have beat the stupid out of him, but it had taught him to mask any and all emotions.

"It was disheartening that I couldn't identify this man. That I couldn't even give my colleagues a profile beyond the generic profile of a stalker. But I wasn't truly afraid until... well...one night when I went home, there was a package waiting. A package from a company I knew and used. Even more, I was expecting to receive that particular box. So I took it inside and opened it."

"Oh God, it was full of bugs, wasn't it?" Walt's complexion turned green. Not really—his skin was only a few shades lighter than Jakob's own and didn't pale the way he knew Annalise's did—but the horrified, slightly sick look was still readily apparent.

"Flying cockroaches. There were so many. The box was full, and they were angry." Annalise shook her head. "I know insects don't have emotions like that, but the instant I opened it, they were everywhere. I started screaming, and once I did, I couldn't stop. They got in my hair, touched my face. One crawled inside my shirt." Annalise looked as if she would vomit.

Walt made a horrified face, so comical that after a moment, she smiled, only for the expression to drop away once more.

"I screamed and cried and hid from the bugs," she murmured.

Jakob had a vivid memory of that night. Of the frantic call he'd been forwarded by the vice admiral Pia Klein. The call, a message Annalise had left on one of the numbers members called when they were in trouble, had been nearly incoherent, but she'd said her name clearly enough that they'd figured out who she was, and as the knight based in Frankfurt, he'd been the one sent out to help her.

If she'd never been in trouble, needed help and protection, he might never have met her.

"I didn't want my colleagues at the *Kripo* to see me like that, so I called the Masters' Admiralty. They sent Jakob. He cleared out the bugs, got me up off the floor, helped me stop crying. Later I explained about the stalker. Jakob and the other knights started working on the case too. Everyone wanted me to move, but I wouldn't move because I didn't want the stalker to know he had that kind of power over me. So Jakob came up with another solution. The house next door —in English, I believe the term is a row house, yes? Houses that share walls."

"I understand what you mean, though a lot of places in the States call them townhouses."

"It was for sale, so Jakob had the vice admiral buy it. He installed a hidden steel door between them. I went into what had always been my house but then passed through the door, into the safety of the place he'd made for me."

Annalise smiled at him, and Jakob could feel Walt's attention turn to him.

"As far as anyone other than Jakob and, I'm assuming, the vice admiral knew, I was still living in the same house."

"Vice Admiral..." Walt frowned, then grinned. "Y'all have fun titles."

Jakob narrowed his eyes ever so slightly at Annalise, who smiled sheepishly, the moment chasing some of the darkness away from her eyes.

"I forgot you weren't a member," Annalise said to Walt.

"If it makes you feel better, I'm going to be a member of the Trinity Masters, the American version of your secret society. My brothers are both members but fairly new to it, so I'm not familiar with many of their fancy titles."

Jakob filed that information away to pass on to his vice admiral and admiral. It was interesting—and by interesting, he meant fucking alarming—that the fleet admiral was running around hunting a serial killer with a man who already had ties to the Trinity Masters.

Then he remembered that he couldn't say anything about the fleet admiral.

Damned Viking.

"Years passed, and we never...I never could figure out who he was. Jakob kept guarding me, when he could, and I was safe in my secret house, but..."

"That must have been really hard. Living in fear," Walt murmured.

Annalise nodded before continuing. "My sister knew the code to my house, had a key, but she didn't know about the stalker. Didn't know I would be safe behind the secret steel door between my house and the place next door. She came by to surprise me, opened the door, and walked inside. She didn't pull it all the way closed. He, my stalker, must have been watching, seen that the door was still partially open, because he followed her in."

"Shit," Walt breathed.

"He attacked my sister. Raped her. And when he realized it wasn't me, he cut all her hair off so he wouldn't be 'tricked' again. All that happened while I slept safely on the other side of the wall."

"I know you know this, but hearing it again probably isn't a bad thing." Walt slid off his chair, kneeling in front of Annalise so his head was lower than hers, so he was less threatening than he'd been even when sitting. "What happened, both to you and to your sister, is not your fault."

"Agreed," Jakob said aloud. If he hadn't controlled himself, he might have told her how it broke his heart to see the pain in her eyes. Told her that no matter what she said, he knew her. Knew she felt responsible, aided in part by her sister, who had raged at her for not mentioning the stalker and who had now cut Annalise out of her life completely.

Jakob wanted to tell her that he was the one who should be blamed. He was the one who'd failed to catch the stalker in the nearly two years between when he'd been brought into the situation—the night of the bugs—and the night of her sister's attack.

Annalise didn't reply—it was clear she didn't agree—and the room fell silent for a few moments. Walt rose and walked over to the fireplace, staring at the flames in quiet contemplation. Jakob and Annalise shared a look before their gazes drifted over to the doctor, who had turned to face them once more.

"I have one more question," Walt began, "if you would indulge me."

"Of course," Annalise said.

Walt glanced from Annalise to Jakob, then gave them that dimpled grin that seemed to be an almost permanent fixture on his face. "How long have you two been in love?"

CHAPTER SEVEN

Walt tried to stifle a grin as Annalise and Jakob sputtered and stuttered their way through their rushed denials and assurances that they were nothing more than friends.

"I protect her," Jakob said—too fast and too hard.

Annalise said, "Oh no, no. That's not it at all. I'm the reason Jakob doesn't have any free time." She laughed, but it was forced. "I'm the reason he sleeps on a couch in Heidelberg instead of in this lovely home."

Walt nodded slowly. He'd thought maybe they just weren't talking about their relationship either because of professionalism, or because they'd been in front of Eric, or that whole trinity marriage thing. He'd heard from Sylvia about how the arranged ménage marriage could lead to dramatic, doomed love affair situations.

In literature, there was a device called the unreliable narrator. It was when the narrator of the story knew less about what was going on, or what their own feelings were, than the reader. His sister Sylvia might be a poet, but she enjoyed lecturing him and his STEM-oriented brothers on the literary arts.

As a doctor, he saw plenty of people who were their own unreliable narrators. Lying to themselves—about their symptoms, behavior, or both—but it was the first time he'd been confronted with two people who were so woefully unaware of, or in denial about, their feelings. "Riiiight," he drawled. "You're just protector and protectee."

"Honestly, Dr. Hay—Walt. You've misunderstood our relationship." Annalise looked like she wanted to say more but didn't seem to know what. Walt thought her assertion might be more convincing if she wasn't blushing and averting her gaze from Jakob.

Jakob had the role of a stoic bodyguard down solid. He did a pretty good impression of a pillar of ice. The man was locked up tighter than a drum. He was the kind of man who would walk into a clinic, say he needed to see a doctor, but then not actually explain why he needed a doctor and expect said doctor to guess he'd been shot.

Walt wondered if this was Jakob's natural behavior, or if it was due to his role within the Masters' Admiralty as a Ritter. He dismissed that idea out of hand. Sylvia was married to a knight in the secret society as well, and Lancelot was one of those guys with lots of funny things to say and personality to spare. It was Sylvia's second husband, the professor, Hugo, who was more reserved and quiet.

Walt's curiosity regarding Jakob was piqued. The man's short, to-the-point responses to basically everything offered no insight into what sort of man he was on the inside.

Walt had always considered himself a good judge of a person's character, but he was drawing a huge blank when it came to Jakob. The only reason he'd hypothesized for the man's silence was that Jakob was harboring feelings for Annalise.

Though in all honesty, she was giving off a stronger vibe as far as her unrequited feelings toward her bodyguard.

"Um..." Annalise rose from her seat. "How about a tour of your place, Jakob?" she asked, working overtime to change the subject.

The way Jakob quickly turned to the doorway told Walt she wasn't alone in trying to get off the hot seat.

Mmm-hmm. Feelings. He had them.

"That way first," he said, gesturing toward the kitchen Walt had found a few minutes ago as he went in search of a glass of water.

Walt hadn't done much more than glance around for a glass when he'd come to this room earlier. Now that he had a chance to study the room, he had to say that Jakob knew how to pick interior designers.

No. There wouldn't have been an interior designer. That would have been too invasive, meant giving up too much control. That meant Jakob had designed the space himself.

The kitchen was large—probably two rooms put together, since they didn't make kitchens this size in old homes, and from the outside, it was clear this home was at least a hundred years old and had probably been a mansion when it was built.

The cabinets were white shaker style, with plenty of glass-front cabinets displaying simple, elegant dishes and glassware. The stove was a six-burner Viking with a pot-filler above it. There were accents of soft blue and matte black—a pale blue veining in the granite and marble countertops. Three blue chairs were positioned around the end of the large island that was set up as an eat-in area. The backsplash above the stove was beautiful blue and white tile that looked almost antique—as if it had been either reclaimed from part of the original house or sourced from other old buildings. The hardware on the cabinets was black, a nice contrast to the white, as was a faucet that arched over the huge single-basin sink.

"Oh, Jakob," Annalise said, twirling slowly as she glanced around the room. "I swear this is my dream kitchen. I love this. And are those azulejo tiles?" She pointed to the backsplash, then hurried over, reaching to run her hand over them.

"Portuguese." Jakob's tone was calm, but the way his eyes tracked Annalise gave away how much he cared about her opinion.

Annalise made an appreciative noise. "I've always loved this style of ceramic. Well, ever since a visit to the Sintra National Palace in Portugal. I bought a few replica tiles, but they broke in my bag. I was so sad." Annalise stopped fondling the tiles. "I'm sorry, Jakob. I know I've told you that story before. Though it's not much of a story."

"You told him you loved that tile? Huh, interesting." Walt's gaze locked onto Jakob's face even though he was speaking to Annalise.

Jakob studiously returned Walt's look, managing to remain impassive.

Walt did an internal headshake. Jakob didn't know him well enough to understand that all he was doing was poking the bear. Walt had a lifetime of experience when it came to getting under his brothers' skins, teasing them about shit they didn't want anyone to know about.

"I swear if I ever remodeled my own place, I would design it like this. Clean, simple. Emphasis on a few beautiful details." She gestured to the tile. "Exactly like this," Annalise gushed. "Wait, is that a marble counter inset for dough?" There was both longing and envy in her voice.

"Just like this, huh?" Walt repeated, not bothering to hide his grin from Jakob. "Sounds like the two of you have similar tastes."

Annalise looked over at Jakob and smiled shyly. "Maybe we're rubbing off on each other. You *have* been forced to spend a lot of time with me."

Jakob scowled briefly before managing to school his features. It was apparent the Ritter didn't consider any time he spent in Annalise's presence as a hardship.

Rather than contradict her, however, Jakob gestured toward a second door in the kitchen. "This way."

Annalise walked ahead, her soft gasp of delight telling Walt and Jakob that she liked the next room as much as the kitchen.

"Jakob!" she exclaimed.

Walt followed her in, glancing around what he considered a fairly standard dining room. However, given the way Annalise's eyes widened as she looked at the table, she thought the room anything but ordinary.

"An antique clawfoot table! I can't believe you have one of these. My Oma had a table almost exactly like this in her dining room. My sister and I used to tease her, swearing that one night when she slept, we were going to paint the toenails on the claw feet."

Walt chuckled. "Sounds like you and your Oma were very close."

Annalise nodded. "We were, though I'm sure Jakob is tired of hearing all my stories about her and her house." Annalise ran her fingertips over the top of the table, the piece clearly evoking happy memories for her. "The hours Oma and I spent sitting at a table just like this, playing board games or doing puzzles."

"Wow. What are the chances you and Annalise's Oma would have the same table?" he asked Jakob, sinking a little too much faux surprise into his tone.

Annalise didn't notice.

Jakob did.

He stared hard at Walt, who blinked a few times, stopping just short of fluttering his lashes.

"The stairs are this way." Jakob pointed, but not before he narrowed his eyes at Walt, issuing an unspoken warning.

Ah. The game was afoot.

Walt loved this game, though it never lasted long when he played with his brother, Oscar. Oscar would have already stormed out of the room or house while using "fuck" as the subject, verb, and object of a sentence.

Walt ignored the sudden stab of homesickness and the sad feeling that followed when he remembered that "home" didn't mean what it once had. His siblings were all married now.

Once again, Annalise preceded them. She paused as they all reached the top, waiting for Jakob to direct them to the next room.

"The office," he said, opening the door directly at the top of the stairs.

Annalise's delight only magnified as they continued the tour. "Oh my God. I thought the kitchen was perfect. This room..." She spun around. "This is the best room in the house."

"You haven't even seen it all," Walt teased. "I'm betting the master bedroom is pretty special too."

Jakob growled, the reaction so out of character, Walt couldn't help but laugh. Perhaps that would have annoyed Jakob more if Annalise had a clue about the undercurrents of their conversation. Instead, she'd crossed to the center of the room, glancing upwards to take in the skylight.

"No windows," she said softly. "And yet there's so much natural light. It's perfect. You could work in here for hours and never be afraid."

Walt and Jakob exchanged a glance, but there was no humor this time. There was no question in Walt's mind that Jakob had remodeled this house with Annalise in mind, the

Ritter going to great lengths to create a home that Annalise would not only feel comfortable in but also safe.

"It is a great office," Walt conceded.

"There are two others." Jakob seemed almost reluctant to say that. "Connecting doors."

Annalise and Walt both looked around. "Where?" Annalise asked. Besides the door they'd come in, there were no other doors, just built-in floor-to-ceiling bookshelves that made it feel like a library.

Jakob walked toward a shelf, but Annalise gasped and ran past him. "Secret doors?!"

Jakob put his hands behind his back, a military parade-rest pose. Maybe it was to keep his hands off Annalise when she came close. Walt twisted to peer at the other man's face. And since Annalise wasn't looking at them, Walt grinned at Jakob, then made a heart shape with his fingers.

Jakob's lip pulled up in a snarl, but his eyes gave him away. The Ritter didn't like having his secret feelings exposed. He looked almost embarrassed.

Annalise was scanning the shelves. "A whole section on psychology. Austrian, of course, with Freud. Some more contemporary names. American, British, Canadian. Only one German?" She tsked but then paused, and though he had a three-quarters profile view of her face, he saw her cheek lift as she smiled. "Hermann Ebbinghaus. The man who first described the forgetting curve. Who better to hide a secret than the man who knows why we might remember or forget?"

She put her finger on the top of the spine and pulled. The book tipped, there was a click, and then the bookcase swung into the room on the other side.

Walt abandoned teasing Jakob and went to the other bookcase to start trying books. There were some things more important than poking the bear, and that included finding secret doors. It took him several minutes, but *Die Grundlagen der psychischen Entwicklung* by Kurt Koffka opened the bookcase on that side.

He stepped in, then looked over to where Annalise stood in the matching office on the other side. The second and third offices, flanking what was clearly Annalise's office, were almost spartan, with only desks and ergonomic chairs—facing large windows—and built-in sideboards that turned out to be combination storage and filing cabinets.

Walt walked back into Annalise's office.

"So whoever is in this room would be protected on both sides," Walt said with faux casualness. "Though the door is *right* at the top of the stairs..." Walt gestured to the entrance.

"Reinforced steel in the walls, with a remote-activated bolt lock, and it's also bulletproof," Jakob said.

"Of course it is." Walt smirked at Jakob, whose jaw muscle twitched.

Annalise was stroking the desk. "Very safe."

By the time they reached the master bedroom, it was painfully obvious what Jakob had done and whom he'd done it for.

Annalise glanced around the room, then turned to face Jakob. "Burgundy, my favorite color." The long wall behind the bed was painted a rich burgundy, while the other walls were a crisp, pristine white. The accent wall drew attention to the hand-stitched quilt covering the massive bed. It had to be Alaskan king or something like that. It was definitely made for at least three people.

Jakob hesitated for just a moment, then nodded once.

She pointed toward the bed. "Is that quilt homemade?"

Again, he paused briefly before nodding. "My Oma made it."

"Double-ring pattern?" she asked.

Jakob shrugged. "I don't know. It was always on her bed. I had fabric added so it would fit."

Walt's brows rose. That was the most he'd heard Jakob say.

Annalise smiled. "You were close to your Oma too."

"Yes."

Walt sighed softly, suddenly feeling bad. It had been fun to tease the man, joking around with him like he would have with Oscar or Langston, but now he wondered how long Jakob had been hiding his true feelings for Annalise. Given the fact he'd had time to learn Annalise's tastes and create this home with her in mind, Walt would say Jakob's affections had been engaged for quite some time.

And yet he kept them hidden.

"Your home, Jakob," Annalise said. "It's beautiful. Perfect."

This time, Annalise wasn't looking away from Jakob, her gaze instead intent, focused on his face.

"We should discuss the case," Jakob said, once again finding a way to avoid revealing his feelings for Annalise. The Ritter looked to Walt for support and he gave it, feeling bad for teasing the other man.

"I think that's a good idea," Walt said, noticing the way Jakob's shoulders relaxed slightly. "Should we return to the sitting room?"

This time it was Annalise's turn to hesitate. She wanted to question Jakob about his house, but it was clear Jakob wasn't ready for that conversation.

Walt gestured toward the door. Jakob and Annalise followed his direction, the three of them descending the stairs. He and Annalise claimed the same seats they'd vacated just a few minutes earlier, but Jakob remained standing.

Walt had to admit, Jakob had indeed built a wonderful, comfortable home. Everything in sets of three—three chairs here, in the kitchen, and a bed built for three.

After so many years, bouncing from war-torn countries to poverty-stricken towns, Walt was jealous of this oasis Jakob had created. This truly was the sort of place a person could come home to after a long day at work, prop his feet up, and just relax.

Even now he found himself sinking a bit deeper into the comfortable chair as his muscles loosened.

"Wine?" Jakob asked.

Annalise smiled and nodded. "That would be lovely, Jakob."

Walt nodded as well, certain that whatever bottle Jakob produced from the kitchen was definitely going to be Annalise's favorite.

When the Ritter returned, he had two—just two—glasses of red.

"You aren't drinking?" Walt asked.

Jakob shook his head.

Walt looked around the room, considering the tour they'd just taken. "Jakob, this house is safe, right?"

Jakob considered the question, then said, "As safe as I could make it."

"Have a glass of wine with us," Walt insisted.

Jakob nodded, disappeared briefly, then returned with his own glass of wine.

Walt's small house on his family's property back in Charleston was more utilitarian, a stopover more than a home. He was pretty sure his brothers used it as a spare bedroom from time to time. Every time he considered returning home, something stopped him, and the next thing he knew he was taking another field assignment with Doctors Without Borders. The longest he'd been in one place had been the clinic in Libya, which had been his home base for nearly a year.

His mama called him a nomad, but there were times when

Walt felt as if it wasn't a place he was searching for so much as a person. Langston and Oscar had found their "people" and Walt was suddenly anxious for the same. For him, it wasn't about the where, it was about the who.

His chest tightened a little as he watched the subtle interchange between Jakob and Annalise as he sat with his wine. She had slipped off her shoes upon sitting and her feet were resting on the ottoman closest to Jakob's chair. She shifted them over a bit so that there would be room for his feet as well. Jakob gave her a soft smile as he lifted his next to hers.

Annalise reached for her bag, which was resting beside her chair, and she pulled out the same files they'd been studying at the restaurant before someone—God knew who—had interrupted their meeting.

For a moment, Walt wondered where Eric was and if he'd gotten away. He dismissed that concern immediately. Satan himself would probably struggle to bring the fleet admiral down.

"I need more information," she said.

"Okay," Walt said. "How do we get it?"

Annalise separated out two case files from the pile on her lap. "We go and Walt speaks to the coroner."

"You want me to talk to a medical examiner?" Walt asked. "I'm not sure if I've said this before—oh wait, I have. I'm not a forensic pathologist."

"Travel?" Jakob said, his eyebrows furrowed. It was clear he didn't like the idea of Annalise being exposed any more than necessary.

"You said 'coroner' not 'coroners.'" Walt paused. "I thought there were two potential victims."

"Yes," Annalise said firmly. The professor was back in her voice. "We are going to Krakow. Alicja Lewandowski's case is the most complete, with the most potential for additional information. So, who's up for a trip to Poland?" she asked, holding the file up.

Walt looked at Jakob, then reached for the file. "I've always wanted to see Krakow in the winter. Anyone up for a walk around Old Town?"

CHAPTER EIGHT

H oly shit.

This was gross.

Jakob stood by the door of the morgue, glad that he had an excuse—keeping watch—to stay away from the autopsy table where Walt, Annalise, and Dr. Adamicz were bent over a body. Not the body of Alicja Lewandowski—she'd died nearly a year ago, before Josephine was killed. Given the state of Alicja's body, her relative—an elderly aunt—had opted for cremation, though that wasn't common in Poland. Scattering ashes was still illegal.

Jakob had listened while Annalise talked about Alicja's case. He would listen to her read the phone book. He loved the sound of her voice.

Loved her.

Which Walt clearly suspected, the *Rotzlöffel*.

"Would a hunter have that level of knowledge?" Annalise asked, dragging Jakob's attention back to death, away from his ridiculous, embarrassing, unrequited love.

She liked the house. She noticed everything you did for her, even if she'll never know the house was designed and remodeled with her in mind. Her safety, her happiness, her pleasure.

Maybe he could sell it to her and her trinity. Then at least she could appreciate it while she was happily married to two people worthy of her.

Dr. Adamicz was standing across the table from Walt and Annalise, who were both suited up in disposable white gowns, gloves, and plastic face shields. Dr. Adamicz reached across the table, grabbed the corpse's arm closest to Annalise and Walt, and tipped the body up.

"Feel here, along the back of the neck," Dr. Adamicz invited, pointing with his free hand. "Dr. Hayden was right to point out that the killer had to understand the human spine. If you are dismembering an animal to transport after a kill, you take the head off at the base of the skull." He pointed to the top of the corpse's neck, just under the hair. "On a human, it would be here. Now, would a hunter try for that point? Possibly, but hunters usually do not go between vertebrae like that one did." Dr. Adamicz let the body flop down.

The sheet slid off and Jakob was treated to a view of a flaccid, dead dick. He wondered who this poor fucker had been.

Annalise grabbed the medical drape, placing it back over the dead man's crotch. Shit like that was why he loved her. He could trust her to cover up his dick if he was dead.

Thinking about his dick and Annalise at the same time was a very bad idea. He stared hard at the Y incision on the corpse's chest.

"You ruled the cause of death as asphyxiation."

"Yes, due to the swelling of the right side of the heart and..." He paused, took a phone from his pocket, typed something in, and then held it out. "I had to look up the word in English."

"Cyanosis," Walt read aloud. "Lack of oxygen. Skin, mucus

membranes, will turn blue. That's a classic sign of strangulation."

Dr. Adamicz raised a finger. "Or suffocation. The decapitation trauma to the neck obscured any ligature or finger marks there might have been. But dilation of the heart, the blue skin, and a small amount of petechial hemorrhage could be from strangulation or suffocation." He raised one hand. "Asphyxiation."

"And you haven't had any other bodies here in Krakow that were dismembered?" Annalise asked.

"Not like that. Back when the mafia was more prevalent, we had some mob-style torture and killings. They cut off bits. If it's dropped in the woods in Wolski Forest, animals might eat the body. But they start with the soft bits. Face, guts."

This was *so* gross.

"Nowadays, we're dealing with gang kills. They're more straightforward. Shoot, bang, dead."

Jakob sucked in a breath, through his nose, and was overwhelmed by the smell of formaldehyde and...*verdammter Mist*...he didn't want to know what else.

"If you are here, you've found another body?" Dr. Adamicz rubbed gloved hands together and stared at Annalise, whose name he'd recognized based on a few papers she'd written. "A serial killer?"

"Possibly. But the geography is unusual."

"Where else were bodies found?"

Annalise smiled at the doctor, but it wasn't her real, good smile. It was polite, neutral. "We're keeping that information private."

"Yes, yes. In case I am the killer."

Dr. Adamicz seemed a little too excited about the idea he might be a suspected serial killer.

"Is there anything else you think we should know?" Walt asked. "Anything you didn't put in the report?"

Dr. Adamicz pursed his lips, then hustled over to his computer, which was on a rolling stand in the corner. How the fuck anyone could work with dead bodies just behind them was beyond Jakob's understanding. This...this was how zombies happened.

A few clicks later and the doctor had the now familiar images of Alicja's body up on the screen. He flicked through those, then pulled up the report itself. Annalise and Walt had wandered over to stand by him.

"I didn't have her all at once. Never did find the last few pieces. She came in bit by bit. The last few bits..." He raised and wiggled a hand. "They had to send cadaver dogs to the landfill. Actually, we ended up with an extra foot after that. But the head, which we found first, was wrapped in plastic, and then put in a wooden crate with a lid, before going in the garbage. The people who found it actually wanted the crate. It was a nice crate."

"Interesting. What makes you call it a nice crate?" Annalise asked.

"Good quality, finish still on it. Cedar, I believe. Like something your grandmother kept blankets in."

"A blanket chest," Walt said.

"Chest, not crate. Yes, that is the right word." They were speaking English, and though Dr. Adamicz was fluent, there were some words he'd stumbled over.

"I didn't see pictures of the crate in the file," Annalise said. "Do you have photos?"

"No, I saw it in the forensics lab when I went to flirt with Dr. Banik." Dr. Adamicz gave Walt the once-over, and then winked suggestively.

Walt didn't look put off or shocked.

He returned the wink with a playful grin.

Huh. Interesting.

Jakob rarely thought about other people's sexuality. It didn't matter to him for a number of reasons, first of which it was none of his damned business. Second, once he'd joined the Masters' Admiralty, he had started diligently watching gay porn so he was prepared if he got a husband and a wife. Jakob would do his duty toward his spouses, and if, at least at the beginning, he would be thinking of Annalise, that was something no one ever had to know.

And yet, the fact that Walt was interested in men intrigued him, and he wasn't entirely sure why.

He also wasn't worried about the fact that Walt was standing shoulder to shoulder with Annalise. He trusted the other man, based on nothing more than instinct. Well, that and his behavior toward her. He'd taken care of, and cared for her in a way Jakob could not. Annalise trusted him too, that much was clear, though if Jakob had asked her about it, she wouldn't say she trusted him. She no longer trusted her instincts or herself.

Though now that she was working this case...he wasn't sure if that was still as true as it would have been a year or even six months ago.

"None of the rest of her was as carefully packaged. Not by the time we found her. Maybe there were other chests, and people emptied out the body parts and took the chests."

That was a fun visual.

"I remember that the head smelled." Dr. Adamicz grinned. "Not the normal smell. I remember that it smelled floral. Something strong, almost enough to cover up the scent of desiccation."

Annalise arched a brow. "Why didn't you note that?"

"The smell didn't last long once it was unwrapped. Possibly her shampoo or perfume if she wore it here." He touched his neck just under the ear. "That kind of transfer should be noted at the scene. Here, there are too many other possibilities for contamination. That is the only thing I didn't put in the report because it couldn't be verified by my colleagues or the on-site investigator."

"Thank you," Annalise said. "This has been very helpful. Walt, do you have any other questions?"

"No, but thank you for letting me look at the aorta." Walt motioned to the man on the table. "I'd never seen a burst aortic aneurysm in person."

Dr. Adamicz grinned. "A good way to die. Ow, ow." He clutched his chest. "Then you're dead."

"Jakob, did you have any questions?" Annalise turned to him, smiling as she asked.

What he wanted to say was: *No, I want to get out of here and away from that lunatic coroner, and I might break his neck on the way out because honestly, he might be the killer, he's so damned weird and creepy.*

He shook his head once.

They said their goodbyes and rode the elevator up and out of the basement morgue. They checked out at the desk, quiet as they walked past somber, grim people in the waiting room, some of whom were probably there to identify bodies or find out how, exactly, loved ones had died.

Once they were out on the street, Annalise stepped to the side, motioning for them to join her, though Jakob never got more than half a meter away from her.

"Jakob, can you get a copy of the full report on Alicja, including the pictures of the chest her head was in? I assume they tried to trace it, but I want to know more."

He nodded, secretly thrilled she asked him to do anything. He angled his body so that she was fully protected—a wall at her back, Walt's big body serving as a shield from one direction and himself from the other. Jakob pulled out his phone and texted his vice admiral, who would be able to get the records, though Pia was none too pleased that Jakob was being closemouthed about why he and Annalise had gone to Krakow, and therefore into the Hungary territory. Luckily, everyone was so used to him not communicating, they accepted that he wasn't going to say anything until he was good and ready. Or in this case, until the fleet admiral lifted the gag order.

"If the head was carefully packaged, that means the killer... tried to take care of the body?" Walt asked as Jakob typed his text.

"Possibly." Annalise sounded slightly distant, as if she were more focused on her thoughts than what she was saying. "There are certainly parallels between this case and Josephine's, though the location of Josephine's head had, I still believe, more to do with shock value. But if that came from the partner, possibly the dominant partner..." Annalise was thinking out loud, words rapid, sentences unfinished. "Placing the head in a basket, then leaving it in a place of beauty such as the library...to satisfy the killer's compulsion...on the partner's order, if it was a dominant and submissive partnership."

"So Petro probably asked this guy to do the killing because he knew the killer had this need to cut off the head, and he could twist that so the head ended up where he wanted it." Walt folded his arms, shaking his head.

Jakob's phone binged with a reply. He tucked it into his pocket. "Pia Klein will send the files when she has them, though it may take some time."

Walt frowned. "Shit, did you just use up your whole allotment of words for the week?"

Annalise's lips twitched, but she playfully punched Walt. "Be nice."

"I was just teasing. Remember, triplet." He pointed at himself.

The mention of siblings wiped the smile from Annalise's face. Walt's eyes widened, and he glanced at Jakob, then put a gentle hand on Annalise's shoulder. "How about that walk around Old Town?"

"We should go back to the hotel." They'd arrived early yesterday afternoon, settling into their rooms and relaxing for a few hours before going downstairs for a quick dinner in the hotel restaurant. After dinner, they'd retired to their rooms for the night. Jakob had booked a secure suite for himself and Annalise—he'd slept on the couch—while Walt stayed in the room next door.

WALT LOOKED AT JAKOB. How could he not see that being stuck in the hotel room again today was the last thing she needed? Before he could say anything, Annalise spoke up for herself.

"No, Jakob," Annalise said. "Please. I need to do something normal. Something fun. I'm tired of hiding."

Jakob frowned, and Walt could tell how torn the man was. Given the fact he'd designed Annalise's dream house, it was obvious there was precious little the man wouldn't give her. But that truth was warring with the Ritter's unshakable determination to protect her no matter what.

"It's not safe," Jakob said as last.

Annalise shook her head. "I'm not going back to the hotel. We're in Krakow, not Frankfurt or Heidelberg."

"That doesn't mean—" Jakob started.

"He's not here," Annalise insisted.

Jakob wasn't going down without a fight. "You can't know that."

"Why would my stalker be in Krakow?" Annalise demanded.

"Jakob." Walt took a step closer to the other man and placed a comforting arm on his shoulder. "There are two of us now. We won't take unnecessary risks and we'll stay in well-populated, busy areas. We'll keep her safe. Together."

"Please," Annalise said softly. "It's been so many years since..."

Jakob sighed. Her quiet plea partnered with Walt's reassurances had won the argument.

"You will stay close to us," Jakob said. "At all times."

Walt was honored to have earned Jakob's trust. He suspected that when it came to Annalise's safety, the Ritter trusted no one.

Annalise's huge smile after his capitulation apparently overshadowed Jakob's concerns as he returned her happy grin with one of his own.

It changed Jakob's entire appearance...and Walt suddenly noticed exactly how attractive Annalise's bodyguard was. He was starting to understand the appeal.

Of course, because it was Jakob, the smile was short-lived and within seconds, he'd schooled his features once more, his intense, determined countenance firmly in place again.

"Where should we go first?" Annalise asked, as Jakob stepped to the curb and raised his hand, waving down a taxi.

Walt rubbed his hands together in glee. "I was hoping you would ask that. How would the two of you feel about a visit to the Pharmacy Museum?"

Annalise laughed and shook her head, even though Walt didn't doubt for a moment he was going to get his way. She was so happy about her brief respite from the terror of the past few years, she'd happily follow him anywhere. "You're joking, right?

I mean we're in Krakow and that's your first choice of tourist attraction?"

A taxi pulled up to the curb. Walt slid across the backseat first, Annalise next, and Jakob following last. It was a tight fit. Walt had a feeling he and Jakob would be flanking Annalise during every step of today's adventure.

"*Gdzie?*" the taxi driver asked.

While Walt didn't speak much Polish—okay, he spoke no Polish—it wasn't hard to figure out what the man was asking. "Old Town. Pharmacy Museum," he said, hoping the man spoke enough English to understand him.

The driver nodded to let them know he understood. "*Tak,*" he replied.

Walt grinned. Now he knew one word of Polish. Yes.

"*Dziękuję Ci,*" Annalise said.

Walt raised his eyebrows, impressed.

"Don't get excited," Annalise said in response. "I can speak enough to find us a restroom or order a cup of coffee. After that, we're in trouble."

Walt and Annalise both glanced over at Jakob, who grinned ruefully. "I only know curse words." There was a long pause, and Walt thought he was done, but then, Jakob added, "My friends from school and I taught ourselves how to say fuck, dick, and shit in twenty different languages."

Walt laughed. "Useful skill. Considering it appears we're up shit..." He paused, staring pointedly at Jakob.

"*Gówno,*" Jakob supplied without hesitation.

"Up *gówno* creek without a paddle," Walt finished.

The cab driver eyed them in the rearview mirror.

"You have such an interesting way of speaking," Annalise said, amused by Walt's joke.

"Oh, that right there is the Southern boy in me."

Neither Jakob nor Annalise seemed to have a clue what

that meant, but they both chuckled, shaking their heads as he accentuated his South Carolina drawl for their benefit.

It felt good to make her and Jakob smile. Until this afternoon, he didn't realize exactly how somber they'd been back in Frankfurt. His mama always liked to say that sometimes you didn't realize how unhappy a person was until you saw them truly happy. That was certainly true for Annalise and Jakob.

The trip to Old Town was relatively short distance-wise, though it was made longer by the traffic on the city streets.

When the driver pulled the taxi to the curb, Jakob paid the man and they left the car.

Old Town was crowded at this time of day. Walt had no trouble distinguishing the locals from the tourists, though he figured that was true of most large cities. He recalled his family's first trip to New York City when he was ten. He and his brothers had walked around with their heads thrown back, staring in amazement at the gigantic skyscrapers, while his mother snapped no fewer than a thousand pictures of basically everything.

Once they were on the sidewalk, Annalise glanced up at the museum and sighed. "It exists. I was hoping you were joking."

Walt winked at her as he placed his hand on her lower back, propelling her toward the entrance. Jakob followed, and Walt could feel the weight of the other man's eyes where Walt was touching her.

His grip on Annalise was intentional, a "piss or get off the pot" challenge to Jakob. What he hadn't expected was for Annalise to shift incrementally closer to him. Or for her to smell so good. Or for his body to react quite so strongly.

Walt did some mental math and realized he hadn't had sex in over seven years. Most people, with the exception of his brothers, would probably find his lack of sexual experience shocking. After all, he was in his thirties with a healthy sex drive. The problem was his work ethic was much stronger.

He'd graduated top of his class at medical school, then joined AMEDD—U.S. Army Medical Department—as a commissioned officer. The armed services had been desperate for doctors at the time, so he'd been able to join for just two years, while having some of the other requirements waived. He'd spent most of those two years stationed overseas, and that time had taught him more about what being a doctor really meant than all his years of medical school and residency.

After leaving the military, he'd joined Doctors Without Borders, traveling to some of the most dangerous places in the world, where he typically worked sixteen- to eighteen-hour days. Then he'd taken over the clinic in Libya, planning to be there for a few years before moving on to somewhere else.

Time for sex was something he simply didn't have. Not when there were wounds to bandage, burns to soothe, broken and beaten bodies to put back together, and most importantly, people who needed compassion and information in equal measure.

Annalise glanced up at Walt, their faces quite close. It wouldn't take much movement on his part to lower his head and kiss her. His eyes briefly slid to her lips. Annalise slowly licked her bottom lip before tugging on it with her teeth. He couldn't tell if her action was based on nerves or an invitation. He shifted even closer, his hand on her back, pulling her toward him.

Jesus.

Walt was being as subtle about his desires as a sledge-hammer to the head. He loosened his grip as they reached the door.

Jakob was standing even closer than before, his brows furrowed as he looked from Walt to Annalise, then back to

Walt. Their unsubtle interchange hadn't gone unnoticed. But Walt wasn't feeling jealousy from the other man, as expected. Instead, Jakob's eyes had taken their own lip inventory—but it was Walt's lips he was studying.

Interesting.

And...fuck him...also arousing.

Walt tried to push all thoughts of sex out of his head. Something he didn't usually have a problem with.

Today? The struggle was real.

Walt opened the door for Jakob and Annalise, then stepped in behind them, finally addressing Annalise's earlier comment about the existence of the Pharmacy Museum. "This place is very real. According to the article I read about it, it's a chemical odyssey. How could we miss it?" he joked.

Jakob glanced around, unimpressed. "Very easily."

Annalise laughed as Walt said, "Was that humor, Jakob?"

Jakob narrowed his eyes, but there was no heat behind the look.

For the next two hours, Walt and his traveling companions toured the museum, pleased when they both got into the spirit of the place, asking intelligent questions and approaching each exhibit with the same enthusiasm he felt. The museum was every bit as cool as the article he'd read about it, a true journey through the medicinal past of Poland. When he'd suggested they tour the museum, he'd planned to put them out of their misery quickly, stealing as much time as he dared before setting them free.

Neither Annalise nor Jakob gave the appearance of boredom. In fact, it was Walt who'd had to move Annalise along from the medical implements exhibit.

Once they were back on the street, they meandered around Old Town—this was clearly the part of the visit Annalise had been looking forward to—taking in the shops and sights until Annalise suggested they grab something to eat.

Apparently Walt hadn't been the only one to do a little Krakow research prior to their trip. Annalise suggested a restaurant she'd found online that she wanted to try, so they headed to *Bunkier Sztuki*. Thanks to the—relatively—warm January weather, they grabbed a table out on the large patio where sunlight and small heaters kept them comfortable. From here, they had an excellent view of Planty Park. They ordered a falafel and hummus plate to share as well as coffee. Annalise had looked around, delighted, admitting that before Eric and Walt had shown up in Frankfurt, it had been years since she'd actually eaten in a restaurant.

"Whoa," Walt said after tasting the falafel. "That is seriously good. You have to try this." Walt dipped a piece of falafel in the tahini sauce and held it out to Annalise, who leaned forward, accepting the bite from his fingers.

Her lips brushed his fingertips, and Walt stilled for a moment, his mind traveling over all the other places on his body he wanted to feel her lips. Annalise's gaze connected with his for just a moment, and he realized he wasn't alone in his attraction.

"That *is* good," she said, her voice suddenly husky and sexy as hell. "Jakob should try it too."

Walt nodded, then slowly reached for another piece of falafel. He turned to Jakob and held it out. He wasn't sure what he expected, but it certainly wasn't what happened.

Jakob, like Annalise, leaned forward, allowing Walt to feed it to him. Neither Walt nor Jakob looked away from each other, the moment so sexually charged, Walt forgot to breathe.

"I want to go back to the hotel," Annalise whispered, her voice so quiet, Walt wasn't certain he'd heard her correctly.

He and Jakob both turned to look at her, the Ritter's gaze

suddenly alarmed, as if he feared Annalise had been frightened by something.

Walt blew out a long, slow breath, muttering a softly spoken, "Damn."

Annalise wasn't afraid of a damn thing, and she wasn't retreating to the hotel to hide.

"Now," she added, her voice stronger, sexier...hungrier.

Walt rose from the table without hesitation. It took Jakob longer to react, but not much longer.

"I think that's a good idea," Walt said. "How do you say 'check, please' in Polish?"

Jakob turned his attention to their server, staring hard. The man stiffened and hurried over.

"Huh, that was a nice trick," Walt said. His stare didn't make people react like prey being hunted.

"It was this or yell 'dick'," Jakob murmured.

Annalise snorted in surprised amusement while Jakob paid the bill. "Let's go."

CHAPTER NINE

Annalise glanced at the couch where Jakob had slept the previous night. It had taken every bit of willpower she possessed not to suggest that they share the bed. Instead, she'd tossed and turned restlessly and spent most of the night fantasizing about what it would be like to have him there with her, while Jakob did what he always did—protected her.

Walt followed them in and the fact that he was there, in their room, made the attraction from the restaurant seem all too real. Flirting in public was one thing; being alone in a hotel room with two large, handsome men was something else. It had been so long since she'd flirted, always holding back her feelings —out of fear and guilt. She'd stopped denying her attraction to Jakob to herself a year ago, but given his role as her bodyguard, she hadn't allowed herself to act on it.

After all, what if he didn't feel the same?

For the foreseeable future, his life was tied to hers. He'd done so much for her, she simply couldn't bear the thought of making him uncomfortable. Wasn't it enough that he'd given up countless nights, remaining with her, keeping her safe?

Jakob had never once complained, so selfless, giving, wonderful.

The stalker had taken so much from her. Not only had he stolen her convictions, her instincts that had made her a good profiler, he'd also robbed her of her confidence as a woman.

Before her life had imploded, she'd taken more than a few lovers to her bed. She'd enjoyed the physical as well as the emotional aspects of attraction and desire.

Given her membership in the Masters' Admiralty, she'd kept her affairs short, not wanting to give any of her former lovers the wrong idea about a possible future between them. Her spouses weren't hers to choose, but while she was single, she'd very much enjoyed the flirtatious dance prior to inviting a man home with her for a night, maybe more.

It had been years since she'd let herself go, let herself truly feel anything real, hopeful, sensual. Today with Walt and Jakob, it was as if she'd found Annalise again. And she realized how much she'd missed her.

Walt put a hand on her shoulder, and she jumped, so lost in her thoughts *about* them, she wasn't paying attention *to* them.

His palm slid down her arm, fingertips stroking the sensitive skin of her palm before he took her hand in his.

Slowly, Walt raised their joined hands and kissed her fingers. It was a dry, closemouthed kiss that shouldn't have made her feel such intense desire. He parted his lips, placing a damp, openmouthed kiss first on the back of her hand, and then on the inside of her wrist.

When he did, she realized the desire she'd been feeling was only a pale shadow of what desire could be. It had been so long.

God...so long.

She looked up from Walt's bent head, her gaze colliding with Jakob's. His jaw was clenched, his eyes bright with a feeling that—despite how well she knew him—she could not name.

But then again, *did* she know him?

She'd never even been to his house before this week, and that experience had been eye-opening. Seeing his home was what had provoked her feelings of hope today. Because it had been the first indication—God, please let it be an indication— that her feelings were not one-sided. That house...it was too perfect to be a coincidence. But was it conceited of her to think that Jakob had redecorated with her in mind?

Walt straightened. "Annalise, I want to make sure I'm not reading this situation wrong."

"What is it you think the situation is?" she asked awkwardly, losing some of her fluency in English as desire muddled her brain.

The corner of Walt's mouth kicked up. "No. I don't think so. I want to hear *you* say it."

"Say that I want you?" Annalise shook her head at herself, acknowledging that she was avoiding giving a direct answer by framing it as a question, then she paused and gave in. The old Annalise had been drawn out of her hiding spot and the woman refused to hide, to cower again.

Walt remained quiet, waiting for the answer he wanted.

She gave it to him because she was tired of lying. Not to him—their acquaintance was too short. But to herself. "Yes," she admitted. "I do. I want you very badly."

Over Walt's shoulder, she saw Jakob turn his head away, his eyes closing briefly.

Stupid, imprecise language. English, unlike German, seemed to lack a clear plural form for the word *you*.

Before she could clarify, Walt grinned and slid an arm around her waist, pulling her against his body.

His chest was hard, his arms tight with muscle, and she was fairly certain his cock was at least semi-erect.

Walt lowered his head, and Annalise closed her eyes the moment before his lips touched hers. The kiss started out soft, just the press of dry lips. When she rose onto the balls of her feet and tipped her head to change the angle, that seemed to be the signal Walt was waiting for. His lips parted, his tongue stroking her bottom lip.

Annalise moaned and threw her arms around his neck. His tongue swept into her mouth, and she flicked it with her own. Felt him jerk in response. Her breasts felt heavy against his chest, her lower body already tight and tense.

Walt broke the kiss, breathing a little faster than before. "Wanna take this to the couch, sweetheart?"

"Or up against the wall," Annalise said. She'd always liked being fucked against the wall.

Walt blinked. "Damn, girl. I like it."

"You sound very American right now." Since it appeared Walt wasn't going to fuck her against the wall, she stepped back, grabbing his hand and tugging him toward the couch. Walt grinned and let her push him down, then stretched his long arms out along the back of the couch when she climbed on top.

Now that she had Walt where she wanted him...

Annalise glanced over at Jakob, ready to invite him over, but the look on his face stopped the words in her throat.

He looked heartbroken. Did he think she didn't want him?

"Jakob—"

"No." His voice was hard, and her heart froze. "No," he said again. "Do not make me watch."

Annalise's frozen heart broke. God, every frozen thing inside her burst into flames.

He wanted her.

"Jakob..." she said, no longer afraid of what she wanted, what she felt. She could sing an entire aria if someone asked, and she couldn't sing. "Come here."

"Hey, man, I thought we were all going to make out," Walt added.

Jakob stiffened but didn't look at them.

Annalise slid off Walt's lap. "Jakob."

The doubt and self-loathing that had been her near constant companions, though buried under her guilt and feelings of inadequacy, rose up once more. Maybe she was wrong. Maybe Jakob didn't want her. Maybe he was disgusted by her, and that was why he didn't want to see her with Walt.

Annalise retreated, the happiness she'd felt only seconds earlier evaporating as tears tightened her throat. She backed up, nearly stumbling over the low table.

Walt shot to his feet and grabbed her elbow, stopping her from falling. He looked back and forth between her and Jakob, then sighed.

He took Annalise's shoulders and turned her, pushing her to sit on the far end of the couch. Then he marched across the room and grabbed Jakob, who, to Annalise's shock, allowed himself to be dragged.

Walt shoved him down onto the other end of the couch, a cushion and too many unspoken words, separating them.

Walt moved a chair around so he could face both of them. "All right, you two, it's time for a come to Jesus meeting."

"A what?" Annalise asked, utterly confused.

"Time to put your cards on the table. Put up or shut up." Walt's lips twitched, and he winked. "I'm saying it's time to have a very frank and honest conversation about your relationship."

"We don't have a relationship," Annalise said softly. "I am the reason Jakob has no time for himself. I am just the...the coward who needs protecting. A burden." Every word she spoke felt like a dagger through the heart of the old Annalise, the one she thought she'd rediscovered. She wasn't certain she'd ever felt heartbreak until this very moment.

"No." Jakob's single word was hard and fierce. "You are not a burden. Not a coward."

"But I am. Objectively, I—"

"I protect you, take care of you, because I love you."

Annalise's breath caught.

Walt blinked. "Well, that escalated quickly."

"Jakob, you..." Annalise didn't know what to say.

"You remodeled, decorated that house for her, didn't you?" Walt asked.

Jakob nodded.

"I knew it!"

Jakob looked up and glared at Walt.

Annalise scooted over, reaching out to touch Jakob, but he shot to his feet, moving away from her. She pulled her hand back, utterly confused.

"I am no better than your stalker," Jakob said. "I can't stop thinking about you, Annalise. You consume my every waking moment. I stay close to you, protect you, because I can't imagine a world where you don't exist. I love the way your hair curls over your shoulders when you undo your bun at the end of the day and the way your forehead crinkles right here," he pointed to a spot between his brows, "whenever you're working on something difficult, something troubling. Walt's correct. I built that house for you because I wanted you to live in a place that didn't feel like a cage but rather a home. I didn't know who I was, what I wanted in life, until I met you. I would dedicate my life to making you happy, to making you smile, but I know... I can't help..." Jakob swallowed hard. "I'm like him."

"Wait. Stop." Annalise didn't know how to reply because

she hated his comparison. How could he believe that he was no better than her stalker? How could he truly think that?

Regardless, it was quite a speech from Jakob. It was more honest than even their late-night chats on her couch, the conversations that had made her fall in love with the real Jakob, the man whom no one else saw.

He loved her, but he didn't trust her.

"You are not like my stalker," she said.

"I am. I invaded your privacy—"

"To protect me."

"—I used what you told me to—"

"—build my dream house. That's not—"

"—it is, because—"

"Time out." Walt stood, holding a hand out toward each of them. "Take a knee."

Jakob looked at the ceiling, then crossed his arms. "Be less American."

"Be less literal and German. I'm saying you both need to go to your corners. Wait, damn, that's another sports analogy. Must be channeling my dad today because I don't even like sports that much." Walt shook his head. "You two aren't allowed to talk anymore because you're not listening to each other. You need a mediator."

What they needed was therapy. She should have been going to therapy this whole time but had thought she could handle it on her own.

"Annalise, how do you feel about Jakob?" Walt asked.

"I...I love him. I know I shouldn't, but I do. Even though it is not fair to him."

"Fair?" Jakob started.

"No. Not your turn." Walt pointed at him. "Okay, to sum up, you love each other, but neither of you has said anything because..." Walt looked first to her.

"Because it isn't fair to him. If I confessed my feelings, it might make him feel even more responsible for me, and I didn't want to put that kind of pressure on him."

Jakob was shaking his head, but Walt smiled at her. "Good. Okay, Jakob. Your turn. Why didn't you tell her you loved her?"

"Because she's being terrorized by a violent stalker. How could I take advantage of her when she's so vulnerable?"

"Both your feelings are valid, but, Jakob, do you think of Annalise as a burden?"

"No. Never."

"And, Annalise, do you think Jakob is taking advantage of you by spending time with you when you're stressed out?"

"No. Of course not," she murmured.

"Okay, great. Now kiss." Walt waved his hands at them.

Annalise turned to look at Walt, utterly stunned. "I'm sorry...what?"

"You love one another. Kiss."

Right.

Kiss Jakob.

Which she'd only been fantasizing about for months or maybe the better part of a year.

Annalise stood and faced Jakob. She could do this. Just walk over there and kiss him.

She didn't move. Couldn't. Jakob was right there, and a wild mix of embarrassment and uncertainty rooted her in place. She'd spent so long *not* kissing him that this felt awkward.

Jakob crossed his arms. Uncrossed them. Put his hands in his pockets. All the body language that said a person was unsure or uncomfortable.

They waited. The three of them. Standing there. Self-conscious and silent.

Walt sighed noisily, but he was smiling. "You two are lucky

I'm here." He reached out and took Annalise's wrist, then pulled her over to where Jakob was standing.

Walt didn't let go of her as he reached out with his free hand, cupped the back of Jakob's head, and kissed him.

A hot, sharp stab of desire lanced through her. She loved the way Jakob's eyes widened for just a moment, the shock and surprise so unlike his normal expressionless mask. Then he closed his eyes and wrapped one arm around Walt's waist, holding him close.

Walt pulled back, a bit breathless. "Damn, man, you can kiss." Then Walt glanced at Annalise. "Come here."

The husky command fired her libido even more.

Walt pulled her in, without really backing away from Jakob. Her shoulder brushed against Jakob's chest, but she kept her focus on Walt.

For the second time, he bent to kiss her. There was no chaste start to this kiss. His tongue slid between her lips, demanded entry to her mouth, and then swept inside. Walt was holding her wrist, but another arm, Jakob's, came around her waist. Jakob tugged her forward several tiny steps, sliding out of the way as he did.

For a moment, she panicked as Jakob pressed her against Walt's chest, allowing the other man to deepen the kiss even more. Was Jakob giving her to Walt? Saying he loved her but didn't want to kiss her?

Then Jakob slid behind her, his chest at her back, and his undeniably erect cock against the top of her ass. Hands curled around her hips, sliding up her sides until he cupped her ribs, fingertips on the sides of her breasts.

Annalise broke the kiss with Walt, twisting to try to look at Jakob.

"No," Jakob said, and she felt the word rumble through his chest and into her back. "Kiss him."

"I thought you didn't want to watch?" She sounded breathy, and the men reacted to that, both of them inhaling heavily.

"I'm not just going to watch," Jakob said. "Walt is going to keep you occupied while I play with your pretty tits. How do you want me to play with your nipples? Do you want me to stroke the tips? Or do you like a little pain? Shall I pinch them? Ah, I felt that, felt you jerk. You want me to twist and pinch and pluck and—"

Annalise was so aroused, she was light-headed, and though Jakob was only brushing the sides of her breasts with his fingers, her nipples were tight.

She looked up at Walt, who was staring past her at Jakob, with a baffled expression. That triggered her to think about exactly what Jakob had said. And exactly how *much* he'd said.

"So you'll talk as long as it's dirty talk?" Walt asked.

Annalise suppressed a giggle. This wasn't a giggling moment. This was a hurry-up-and-touch-me moment.

"Hold her for me," Jakob told Walt.

Walt reached down and grabbed her free wrist with his other hand. Experimentally, she tugged, but Walt held her firmly.

Jakob's hands slid under the hem of her shirt, his fingers slightly cooler than her skin. She shivered, but it wasn't really from the cold. Her shirt came up along with his hands and when he touched the band of her bra, he flipped the front hem of her shirt up, fully exposing her bra and breasts. The bra was utilitarian black with smooth cups, the only ornamentation a little bow between her breasts.

Walt stepped back, still holding her wrists, and took his time looking at what Jakob had revealed. It felt lewd in the best possible way to be standing between them, Jakob having exposed her breasts for Walt.

And he was about to really expose her. His hands were working the clasp of her bra, and a moment later, the band loosened. Without pausing, Jakob yanked the bra up, bunching it, along with her shirt, under her chin.

Then his bare hands touched her breasts, cupping them, lifting slightly. Despite what he'd said, his touch was gentle, almost reverent. She inhaled deeply, pressing her breasts into his palms, and he rewarded her by stroking her nipples with his thumbs.

Walt lifted her hands, guiding them to her neck. "Lace your fingers together. Good. Now don't move."

He released her wrists but waited a moment, eyeing her in a deliciously threatening way. If she moved after he'd ordered her not to, she'd be in trouble.

Maybe she wanted trouble. At least the kind of trouble that Walt was promising without saying a word.

She considered and dismissed it. Because more than anything, she wanted to know what he'd—what they'd—do next.

Jakob was tall enough that he probably had no trouble seeing over her arm, even when it was raised, bent, and out to the side. She felt his chin brush her hair as he leaned in, and then his thumbs made another lazy pass over her nipples.

"Are you ready for me to stop being gentle with you?"

Annalise blew out a long, slow breath. "I've been ready for you to stop being gentle for a very, *very* long time."

She felt Jakob's lips touch her hair, a soft caress—the first time he'd kissed her, though she wasn't going to count this one. No, she was waiting until he spun her around and kissed her the way Walt had.

Any other thoughts she might have had were driven from her mind when Jakob made good on his threat. No...his promise. He pinched her nipples with just enough pressure to make pleasure spark to life.

It was almost a relief because she'd been so ready for him, her breasts heavy, needy in his hands.

Then he rolled her nipples between his fingers and she let out a hissing breath, rising onto her toes for a moment.

In response, Jakob tugged her nipples. More pleasure, and then the first hints of pain as his fingers tightened, pinching hard on the sensitive buds.

"Damn, that's a pretty sight," Walt said.

Annalise looked at him through half-lowered lashes. His gaze was fixed on her breasts, on her nipples, as Jakob continued to roll and tug them.

Then Walt lowered to his knees in front of her. "All right, dirty talk us through this, Jakob. What do you think I should do to her from down here?"

Jakob pinched her nipples hard enough for her to cry out, his lips rubbing her hair in tender counterpoint to the sweet abuse of her breasts.

"Unfasten her pants," Jakob said, his voice rumbling. "Don't take them off, but reach in and shove her panties between her pussy lips. Then rub her clit, just a little bit. I want to see her trying to fuck your hand. I want to see her twitching and writhing while we play with her. By the time we put her on the bed, she's going to be so hot, so wet, that she's going to beg us to fuck her."

Annalise was ready to come just from listening to Jakob's description of what he wanted Walt to do to her, with her.

Actually having it happen...

Walt unbuttoned her slacks, then leaned in to lick the skin he'd just exposed, right above the band of her panties. These slacks looked good, cupped her ass enough to show a panty line, which was why she wore a black G-string with them. That was only going to make what Walt was about to do to her more interesting.

Jakob distracted her when he released her aching nipples and cupped her breasts, kneading them with his strong fingers. Then there were more fingers, between her legs, her pants pulled tight around her ass and hips, thanks to the insertion of Walt's big hand.

"Spread your legs for me, sweetheart," Walt murmured.

"Good," Jakob said when she did. "*Liebling,* you're going to keep those legs spread for me, for us, aren't you?"

Oh God. Was she his sweetheart? She wanted to be that. So badly.

"Yes. Yes, Jakob. Why didn't you touch me before th..." Her words trailed off into a moan as Walt ran his finger up and down the seam of her pussy lips, pressing the fabric in a little bit deeper with each pass. She wiggled her hips and managed to angle them so that his finger stroked her clit with his next pass.

Annalise nearly came from just that. She was so primed and ready that it wasn't going to take much more. Jakob's fingers pinched her nipples again, and the next time Walt's finger passed over her clit, she gritted her teeth. She needed her hands on them, so she reached down, sliding one hand over Walt's tightly clipped curls, which were long enough for her to grab, and with the other, she reached back to grab Jakob. It was an awkward angle, but she managed to lay her hand along his head, thumb on his ear. She ran her finger over the whorls there and felt him shudder against her.

"Naked," she demanded. "I want to be naked. I want you naked."

"Naked so we can fuck you," Jakob murmured, his words so low, she wasn't sure Walt could hear them. "*Liebling,* how do you want to be fucked? Do you want me to fuck your pussy while you have Walt's cock in your mouth? Or maybe you'll be on your hands and knees on the floor, Walt behind you, fucking you, while I slide my cock into your mouth. I want you to look at me when you suck my dick. I want to see your ass—"

A sound pierced the air, and for a moment Annalise thought she'd come—the combination of the slight touches on her clit, muted by her now sopping-wet G-string, the pinching of her nipples, and Jakob's words must have pushed her to orgasm. An orgasm so intense that her body registered it as a blaring alarm.

Then the light above the door flashed blinding white, and the alarm blared again.

That wasn't orgasm-induced.

"Fire alarm." Walt slid his hand from her open pants.

Annalise grabbed his wrist, tugging it back toward her. "Ignore it. Don't stop."

Walt chuckled and let her hold his wrist, but Jakob released her breasts.

Annalise groaned.

"I'll check." Jakob's voice was rougher than usual, and he walked a little funny, but the brevity was more like normal Jakob.

She liked dirty talking Jakob much better.

Walt rose to his feet as Jakob opened the door and stuck his head out.

Annalise felt slightly stupid standing there with her clothing all bunched up, but she didn't try to adjust it. She hoped they could continue.

With the door open, she could hear someone shouting and the sounds of hurried steps. Jakob closed the door and looked back at them. "We're leaving."

Annalise made an aggravated noise while Walt helpfully tugged her bra and shirt down.

She fastened her pants, irritation fueled by frustration, making her movements hard and fast. "This place had better be burning to the ground right now. Otherwise..."

"This is fun," Walt said. "I like turned-on Annalise and horny Jakob. They're demanding and talk dirty."

Jakob smiled, though it was brief, and then hustled them out into the hall. Just as he closed the door behind them, he leaned down, his lips against her ear so she could hear him over the fire alarm. "This isn't over yet, *Liebling*."

Annalise turned to look at him, so close, they were almost kissing.

And she froze. Experiencing that same feeling that had kept her from kissing him earlier.

Walt reached out and grabbed both their hands. "Can we go?" He had to yell to be heard. "I promise I'll make you kiss later."

That comment—which happened to coincide with the auditory lull between the alarm blares—earned a startled look from a passing woman who, apparently, understood English.

Jakob smiled, and this time, it lingered. Then he took the lead, guiding both her and Walt down the hall to the stairs. Leaving the room and the lovely bed she'd hoped to occupy with them, behind.

CHAPTER TEN

J akob tensed as they continued down the stairs, looking back at Walt and, with a jerk of his head, indicating...something.

Walt had been a doctor in the military but hadn't seen even a moment of combat, so he widened his eyes at the other man in his best "I don't know what you're trying to tell me" expression.

Jakob grunted and pushed Annalise so she was walking directly behind him. Jakob pointed, and the light went on as Walt figured it out, falling into step behind her so they were protecting her front and back.

It seemed a little ridiculous, especially when Walt almost stepped on Annalise's heels, but the second he tried to put a little space between them, Jakob glared back at him.

Maybe Jakob was channeling his sexual frustration into hyper-bodyguard mode.

Walt found it slightly amusing that Jakob could talk up a storm when it came to feelings and handing out sexual commands, but he was suddenly mute again when he shifted back into protector mode. Perhaps it would be more than slightly amusing if Walt wasn't still so turned on and pissed off by the interruption.

Blue balls fucking sucked.

Their rooms were on one of the upper floors, and that meant that with each step they took, more and more people filed in from the lower floors, until the stairwell was packed with people, some of whom looked a little panicked, others of whom looked either bewildered or—like him—annoyed.

At the bottom of the stairs, a hotel staff member was directing everyone out through the lobby and onto the side-walk. Jakob grabbed Annalise and tried to veer off down a side hall that led toward the back of the building. They were inter-cepted by another member of the hotel staff who didn't speak English, and neither Annalise's restaurant-focused nor Jakob's curse-word fluency in Polish were particularly helpful.

Walt and Annalise took pity on the staff member and turned around. Jakob's shoulders tensed as he took point again, his eyes sweeping left and right with the cold, commanding look of someone who could and would take out anyone he found to be a threat.

"Stop a second," Annalise murmured. She backed up, moving closer to one of the lobby walls.

Jakob scanned her as she stood with her back to the wall. "What's wrong?"

She had her hands behind her, elbows out.

Walt clapped Jakob on the shoulder. "She's fastening her bra, man. Take a breath."

"I don't like this."

"Fire alarms, or *coitus interruptus*?" Walt asked innocently.

Jakob stared at him.

Annalise sighed. "Jakob, we're in Krakow, my stalker isn't anywhere near here."

"We're hunting a killer," Jakob rumbled.

"No, I'm building a profile so other people can hunt him."

"A stalker and a serial killer? You know, if this was a romantic suspense, it would be two books," Walt joked. "And I'm pretty sure it's not 'people' so much as Eric himself who is going to hunt this guy down."

"Stand in front of me, please," Annalise said.

Walt shifted, facing her, while Jakob kept his back to them, scanning the now thinning crowd of hotel guests, whom they could see gathered on the sidewalk through the glass front doors.

Annalise reached into her shirt through the neck hole and adjusted her breasts, and Walt's blood headed south again.

Dammit, he'd just gotten his dick under control.

"Want some help with that?" he asked.

His tone must have alerted Jakob, who leaned a little toward Walt. "What's she doing now?" he asked without shifting his attention from the surrounding area.

"Playing with her tits," Walt murmured.

"Adjusting my bra," Annalise corrected, but then one brow twitched, and she reached out a hand, cupping Walt's crotch. "Do you need any help adjusting things?"

He grabbed her wrist, jerking her hand away, but it was too late. His cock, which hadn't entirely given up hope, hardened again.

"Excuse me. Please make your way outside." The accented customer service voice took Walt by surprise, but the pleased little smile Annalise shot him made it clear she'd seen the person coming and had timed it like this.

Walt shoved his hands in his pockets before turning around. Jakob glanced down at his crotch, then at Annalise, before leading them out of the hotel onto the sidewalk.

"That was mean," Walt murmured as they emerged into

the cool, crisp light. There was snow on the ground, but the sidewalk was clear. What little snow remained was mounds of dirty brown-gray sludge in the gutters and in shadowed corners where the sun couldn't hit it.

There were people all around them, milling about. Some seemed to be heading off down the sidewalk. Maybe looking for cafes where they could sit and kill time.

Shit, had any of them brought their wallets? He'd emptied his pockets of everything but his phone back up in the room and was pretty sure Jakob had too.

The crowd parted and Walt caught sight of a woman sitting in a lobby chair that had been pulled out onto the sidewalk. One of the members of the hotel staff hovered near her. She was grimacing and holding one leg out stiffly.

"I'm going to see if I can help," Walt said, his focus immediately shifting from sexy times to rendering aid. Before he could move, someone knocked into Jakob so hard that he stumbled into Annalise, who in turn fell into Walt. Walt staggered and managed to keep them all from going over like dominos. Jakob rubbed his shoulder, looking back, apparently for the person who'd hit him.

"Too many people," Jakob muttered. Then he grimaced, still rubbing the shoulder.

"You two want to go somewhere, meet me back here later?" Walt asked. He was antsy to get over to the woman and check her ankle, which looked a little swollen. It would have been easy to stumble on those stairs, packed as they'd been.

"We stay together," Jakob countered.

"Okay then, come with me."

Jakob growled and wrapped his arm around Annalise, clearly ready to double down on his bodyguard duties, as Walt pushed through the crowd, dropping to his knee. He looked from the staff member to the woman. "I'm a doctor. Do either of you speak English?"

"I do," the staff member answered. "We have called an ambulance."

"Can you translate for me, uh," Walt glanced at the woman's name tag, "Agnieszka. Sorry, I know I pronounced that wrong. I might be able to help until paramedics get here."

She smiled at Walt, clearly amused at his fumbling attempt at her name. "Yes."

"Tell her that I'm a doctor, and I'd like permission to touch her ankle."

Agnieszka repeated his words, and the woman's attention shifted to Walt. He carefully kept his focus on her as he asked what had happened, and then began a quick exam. Gentle as he was, she winced a few times but was able to flex her foot. Sadly, that could be a bad sign with ankles—cracked bones didn't affect the ability of muscles and tendons to shift and pull, and as long as it wasn't a major break, it might not even hurt. Then again, soft tissue injuries could be just as hard to heal, though patients enjoyed not having a cast, which meant showering was far easier.

Walt told the woman some of this, and then asked Agnieszka to get a stool so they could elevate the ankle. Just as he maneuvered the woman's leg onto the stool, there was a shout from farther down the sidewalk.

The crowd shifted, surging either to or away from the noise, depending on if curiosity or avoidance was their primary reaction. A voice called out, and Agnieszka, his translator, touched Walt's shoulder. "Someone has collapsed. Can you..."

"Of course."

With a nod to the injured woman, he and Agnieszka rose. They sidled through the crowd, emerging into the center of a ring of people who were looking at the figure of a prone man.

They were near the corner of the hotel, where a small lane, not large enough to be a proper street, separated the hotel from the building next door. The ring of gawkers was just far back enough that none of them felt any responsibility to do something. Of course, they were also close enough that they had a good view. People like this annoyed the hell out of Walt.

The figure they were staring at was lying awkwardly against the wall as if they'd slid down it before tipping to the side.

Jakob.

Walt leapt forward, dropping to Jakob's side and hitting his knees hard enough on the pavement that he was going to regret it later.

"Help me," Walt said, to no one and everyone. "We need to get him flat on his back."

Agnieszka crouched beside him, hesitantly moving Jakob's legs as Walt shifted his upper body and arm before rolling him onto his back. Walt wasn't gentle. He was fast. Most people associated medicine with being careful and precise. Gentle, attentive contact. In battlefields, and emergency medicine, that wasn't the case. The priority was to assess for critical injuries, and that meant grabbing and yanking when needed.

Jakob grimaced as he was being moved. He wasn't fully unconscious, though his eyes were closed.

Walt checked Jakob's pulse and breathing—fast and slow, respectively—and as he touched him, Jakob groaned, face contorted.

"Jakob." Walt pinched his trapezius muscle, right where his shoulder met his neck. It was a safe spot to pinch that hurt enough to either wake people up or shock them into focusing enough to answer questions.

"Hurts," Jakob said, barely moving his lips.

"You fell when you passed out. You might have hit something—"

"Didn't pass out. Pain. Shoulder. Chest."

Walt had seen men bigger and tougher than Jakob cry like babies while getting stitches, and tiny little women who could shrug off the pain of broken bones. Still, Walt didn't think Jakob would say something hurt unless it really hurt.

"Shot," Jakob said.

He'd been shot? Walt didn't panic. He simply processed that information and adjusted his next steps.

Walt glanced at the staff member, then at the circle of people. "Does anyone have scissors or a knife?"

A second later, a pocketknife hit his hand. He sliced up the center of Jakob's shirt. The fact that there was no blood on, and no visible hole in, the fabric didn't matter. Clothes could hide injuries, and one of the most important elements of triage was to assess for yourself. Even when patients were awake and talking, there could be injuries they didn't feel and therefore didn't mention, especially if they were in shock.

A moment later, Walt had Jakob's upper body exposed.

The only visible issue was a small area on his shoulder that was slightly swollen and flushed darker than the rest of his skin. There was no blood. No visible wound.

He hadn't been shot. A bad feeling curdled in Walt's stomach.

Walt bent closer, examining the swollen flesh. There was a small puncture mark. That plus the swelling...it looked like an insect sting.

Jakob's forehead was damp with sweat, and as Walt watched, the muscles of Jakob's arm and shoulder contracted. Jakob made a faint noise of pain so low, it was almost inaudible.

This kind of pain, the relatively small mark...

In medicine, when you heard hoofbeats you assumed

horse, not zebra. In Krakow, Poland, an insect sting meant a bee or maybe a wasp. Saying that Jakob had been stung by a bullet ant, an insect that injected poneratoxin into the body, was like predicting a zebra was coming when you heard hoofbeats.

And yet...

The paramedics who'd been called for the woman with the broken ankle rushed over, pushing him out of the way. Walt had just a moment to decide. To decide if he should trust what his instincts were telling him. Instincts that insisted this was a bullet ant sting, despite their location in Europe and not an equatorial jungle.

"Tell them he's been stung," he said to Agnieszka. "He needs to be treated for neurotoxin poisoning, and, given the location, they need to check his heart. His blood pressure. It might cause cardiac arrhythmia."

One of the paramedics glanced over. "What stung him?"

Walt was pathetically grateful to hear the man speaking English because that meant he'd understood what Walt had just said. "Bullet ant."

The paramedic frowned. Either he didn't know what that was, or he knew and now thought Walt was losing it, because how the hell would Jakob have gotten stung by a bullet ant?

Jakob let out a short scream when they got him to his feet. Sweat poured down his face. The sting of the bullet ant was the most painful sting of any insect. People who'd experienced it said it felt like being shot. Jakob started retching, and the paramedic whipped out a bag, holding it to his chin in case he vomited.

Right now, Jakob's nerves were all firing, unable to stop sending his brain the pain signals, while his skeletal muscles contracted and tensed beyond his control. Walt winced and followed as the paramedics guided him over to sit on the back bumper of the ambulance. While they strapped on a blood pressure cuff, Walt crouched in front of Jakob.

"I think you were stung by a bullet ant. I know it doesn't make sense, but I've seen a sting before, when I was in Nicaragua. It hurts, and it's going to keep hurting, but it isn't deadly."

"Ant?" Jakob wheezed.

"Yeah."

"Shot." Jakob looked at his shoulder, or at least tried but gave up with a grimace. The muscles of his shoulder and neck were visibly twitching.

"Nope. Ant sting."

"Hurts."

Walt could tell that admission cost Jakob something. Could tell it wasn't something he would have said if it wasn't someone he trusted.

Someone he trusted...

Walt sucked in air and shoved himself to his feet, frantically scanning the thinning crowd on the sidewalk. It looked like the hotel was letting people back in.

Jakob reached out, catching Walt's hand. Walt looked over, his stomach sinking even as his heart was in his throat. Jakob's eyes were wide, and a little glassy with pain, but he was functional enough to have figured out what—who—Walt was looking for.

"Annalise," Jakob wheezed.

Walt ran through the crowd, back into the hotel lobby, thinking maybe she'd gone inside.

But he knew. Deep down, he knew that there was no way she would have left Jakob, the man she just confessed to loving, all alone when he was vulnerable and in pain.

Walt checked the alleyway near the corner where Jakob

had collapsed and their rooms. He asked the staff if anyone had seen her and enlisted their help in searching.

An hour later, Walt, and a shivering, pain-wracked Jakob, who had refused to go to the hospital, sat side by side on a bench in the lobby. Walt had felt helpless before, though as a doctor, he could usually do something to make him feel like he was being useful.

Chest compressions even when he knew the likelihood of success was small.

Clamping arteries and ordering someone to hang blood even when the person had hit the point of fatal exsanguination.

This helplessness was different.

Because Annalise was gone, and he knew she hadn't gone willingly.

CHAPTER ELEVEN

J akob lay face up on the hotel bed, but only because Walt made him. He was twitching, his muscles spasming like crazy, and Walt was concerned he'd fall down. Every fucking part of his body hurt.

Walt had told him he could expect these waves of agony to continue anywhere from twelve- to twenty-four hours.

Jakob was certain that was information he could have lived without.

"Phone." Jakob tried to point toward the nightstand, but even that slight movement sent shock waves of pain through his body.

Walt crossed the room and picked up the cell.

"Need to call vice admiral." Jakob tried to lift his hand and take the phone, but Walt shook his head.

"Here." Walt grasped Jakob's fingers, pressing his thumb against the lock screen. "Is the number in your contacts?"

It spoke to exactly how much pain Jakob was in that he offered no resistance to Walt opening his phone and digging through the contacts list. "Yes. Klein."

Walt found the number, dialing it before putting it on speaker, shaking his head when Jakob attempted to reach for the phone.

"Klein," Pia, the vice admiral, said upon answering. "Jakob? Are you still in Krakow with Dr. Fischer?"

"Dr. Fischer missing. Abducted." With every word he spoke, Jakob felt crushed under the weight of his failure. "We can't find her."

"We?" Pia said.

Jakob's gaze locked with Walt's, but before he could summon the strength to shake his head in warning, Walt spoke.

"Dr. Walt Hayden here, uh, Vice Admiral. I've been working on the Alicja case with Annalise and Jakob."

There was a long pause on the other end of the line, and Jakob resigned himself to the tongue lashing he was going to receive when he returned to Germany.

"Dr. Hayden," Pia said at last. "You're American?"

"Yes, ma'am. Born and raised in Charleston, South Carolina."

"I see."

"And while I'm not a member of the Masters' Admiralty, my sister, Sylvia, belongs to the England territory."

"Your sister," Pia said slowly, though there was no question she was displeased with and confused by Walt's presence.

Jakob sighed. He was fucked. The Masters' Admiralty was a secret society—*secret* being the operative term. The fact that Walt was here, chatting to the vice admiral, was the equivalent of letting a Muggle into Hogwarts. If he could tell the vice admiral that Walt was with them on the fleet admiral's orders, it would clear everything up. But Eric had forbidden him from doing so.

"Dr. Fischer is missing," Jakob repeated. He'd take whatever punishment Pia saw fit to dole out to him after they found

Annalise. For now, finding her, saving her, was the only thing that mattered.

"Was she targeted? A political action against a German national? Someone moving against the Masters' Admiralty?" Pia asked.

Jakob and Walt exchanged a glance. They had no answer. Only more potential complications. Jakob tried to answer, but a fresh wave of pain swamped him. He rolled onto his side, pounding a fist into the mattress.

"Jakob was attacked too," Walt was saying. "Someone got him with bullet ant venom."

"With what?"

"I know it sounds crazy, but I've seen it before. He's in pretty incredible pain, and there's not a damn thing anyone can do about it."

"Are you in danger?" Pia asked sharply.

Jakob was able to push himself into a sitting position, though he was nauseous and sweating. "Unknown," he answered.

Walt looked at him, eyes wide, then glanced at the locked suite door, as if expecting someone to come barreling in.

There was a moment of silence, and when Pia spoke again it was with calm command. "I'm going to speak to the admiral. We will call in protection from Hungary."

Walt looked at the phone. "We're in Poland. Not Hungary."

The vice admiral wasn't talking about the country Hungary but the territory. Jakob didn't have the energy to explain that, not when agony was rippling through him.

"You will tell the harco everything," Pia commanded, clearly speaking to Jakob. "Do not involve the authorities."

"No," Jakob agreed.

"Uh, pretty sure we should call the police," Walt added.

"Keep me apprised." Then the phone line went dead as the vice admiral hung up.

"Why aren't we calling the police?" Walt asked.

Jakob swung his legs off the side of the bed. "Help me to the bathroom."

Walt slid an arm around his waist. They made it to the bathroom in time for Jakob to vomit into the toilet rather than on the bed. Walt sat on the edge of the tub next to him, silently passing him a wet washcloth when he stopped heaving.

Jakob sat back, leaning against the cool wall. He glanced down at his shoulder. A tiny pinprick incision point and a little bit of swelling. Given how much it hurt, it should have been a massive gaping wound, a broken bone, something.

"No police," Jakob said, addressing Walt's comment from several moments ago. "Because they will only get in our way."

"Okay. So we just wait?"

Walt's voice expressed exactly how horrified he was by that idea. Sitting here doing nothing while Annalise was...

Jakob couldn't think about it too hard. Couldn't let himself imagine what she was going through wherever she was.

"We'll get her back," Walt murmured. "We'll find her."

Walt was a good doctor. He knew what to say and how to say it. There was no denying his reassuring words and tone were on point.

Regardless, Jakob did *not* feel comforted.

"Call the desk. Get security footage," Jakob gasped. "I think I know..."

"You know who injected you?" Walt was already on his feet, pulling Jakob up too, to take him back to the bed.

When Jakob walked down the street, people usually cleared a path around him—he was big, intimidating. In the chaos on the sidewalk, someone had walked right into him, colliding with him hard enough for it to hurt, and to knock him sideways into Annalise. That had never happened to him before, but given the crowd, he attributed it to the throng of people and disorder.

There'd been a sharp pain when the man barreled into him. He'd assumed he'd caught him with hardware from a bag strap, a jacket buckle, or something like that. He'd looked back to see exactly who, or what, had hit him. He had a good mental picture of a medium-height blond-haired man striding away from him through the crowd.

Then Walt had gone to help the woman, and he and Annalise had followed...at least until he started to feel sick. Annalise helped him get away from the crowd, where he'd told her about the pain in his shoulder and arm. She'd been worried he was having a heart attack and then...and then there'd been a wave of pain so intense, it had dropped him, wiped out everything else. He'd slid to the ground, unable to think beyond the pain, his whole body tensed and cramped.

He told Walt this in fits and starts while the other man was on hold with the hotel manager.

The venom from the ant—an *ant*—had rendered him worse than useless. Annalise was gone, and he knew she wouldn't have left of her own accord. Walt had alerted the hotel, had been the one to search for her. Jakob hadn't been able to do more than stagger first into the lobby, then up here into their room.

Jakob's fear for her and guilt, along with all complete rational thought, was wiped away as a fresh wave of bone-breaking agony took him.

Twenty minutes after Walt had hung up the phone, there was a knock at the door, and Walt went to answer it as Jakob struggled to stand. According to Walt, the hotel general manager had said they needed to check with their legal counsel before releasing any security footage.

Walt opened the door, and Jakob cursed silently.

Because the man who walked in wasn't from the hotel.

Tall, heavily muscled, with short-cut hair, the man radiated danger. Jakob had expected Hungary to send one of the harco—a knight.

Instead, they'd sent a security officer.

If the knights served as the law-and-order enforcement of each territory, the security officers were the spies and assassins. Jakob had turned down a position as a security officer. He'd had enough of that life, and joining the Masters' Admiralty had given him the push to change the path of his own life. He'd been tired of being the bad guy. He'd wanted to be the good guy for once.

Vadisk Kushnir was born to be a security officer.

Jakob was a large man, but Vadisk made him feel small. And it wasn't merely the man's height that made him so intimidating. Vadisk was, without a doubt, the most muscular man Jakob had ever seen in his life. Vadisk had twisted slightly as he entered the room due to his broad shoulders and tree-trunk-sized biceps. If he was green, he'd be the Incredible Hulk.

"Hi, I'm Walt, the one you were speaking to on the phone, were you able to talk to—"

"No," Jakob said, interrupting Walt.

"No?" Walt looked at Vadisk, his shoulders tightening. "As in, *no he's not here with the hotel's security footage?*"

Vadisk eyed Walt.

Jakob eyed Vadisk.

Walt turned and mockingly thumped his head against the wall. "This is going to take forever if both of you are going to do the silent and dangerous thing."

Jakob didn't have time to respond because another wave of pain turned his world on end. He dropped back to the bed, blind and deaf to anything but pain for a few moments. The sound of his own agonized breaths were the first sounds he heard. A moment later, he was able to tune in to the conversation.

"This needs to be administered with imaging," Walt declared.

Vadisk scowled. "We don't have a CT scanner."

"Damn it. Langston and I were going to make a portable one of those next, but..." Walt sounded unsure, which was unlike him. "I can't blindly inject him with a nerve blocker."

"Then we will put him someplace safe. You come with me and we will find Dr. Fischer." Vadisk's English grammar was good, though his thick Ukrainian accent made him sound like a thug. German movies and TV liked to use Eastern European actors to portray villains.

Jakob opened his eyes, blinking back the tears.

Vadisk leaned over him, his face twisted in a grimace of sympathy. "I've heard bullet ant stings are some of the worst pain," he said to Jakob in passable German.

"It's true," Jakob croaked.

"English, guys. English. Please."

Vadisk, who was casually sitting on the bed beside Jakob, shrugged in apology. After the revelations about Petro and what had been going on in Hungary, the territories had all upped their inter-society surveillance. Jakob was glad now that they had because it meant he knew exactly how dangerous the man casually perched on the bed was.

Vadisk's military record had been sealed so tight, they'd only gotten mission reports for a few of his ops. He hadn't been a security officer for long—he'd been brought in by the new admiral of Hungary when she overhauled the entire power structure of her damaged territory.

"I brought you a nerve blocker." Vadisk held up two capped syringes. "The doctor won't give it to you."

Jakob's heart leapt at that. "Walt. Do it."

"No, and here is why." Walt took a breath, then paused, shook his head. "I was going to explain in detail, but I have this sinking feeling neither of you would listen. So I will use small words. This is a bad idea. This is dangerous."

Jakob looked at Vadisk. "You do it."

Vadisk uncapped a syringe. "Maybe in your neck?"

"Sweet baby Jesus, give that to me!" Walt lunged across Jakob and snatched the syringes.

Vadisk looked down at Jakob and winked.

There was a distinct possibility Jakob was hallucinating all of this.

"Okay, Jakob, I need you to take a deep breath. There's a nerve bundle in your shoulder, the brachial plexus, which, given the site of the string, is the most likely set of nerves to be affected." Walt's voice had gone into what Jakob now knew was doctor mode. Calm, controlled, explaining what he was doing as he did it.

Walt's finger probed his shoulder, and Jakob balled up the duvet in his fists.

"Want me to hold you down?" Vadisk asked.

Jakob's pride wanted to say no. But his pride didn't matter. What mattered was getting himself functional so he could find Annalise.

"Yes," Jakob hissed from between his clenched jaw.

Vadisk held him down at wrist and chest. Walt kept up a calm dialogue as he touched Jakob's shoulder. The pain of the needle didn't even register. The burn of the medicine was noticeable only because it was different from the deeper pain caused by the neurotoxin.

The pain ebbed, but it had done that before. It always came back.

"Can you make a fist for me?" Walt asked. "Okay, good. Now can you flex your wrist, like this?"

When Jakob was able to do both, Walt nodded, a little of the tension Jakob hadn't noticed fading.

"Better?" Vadisk asked.

"It comes and goes," Jakob said. "Not sure yet."

Walt checked his breathing, pulse, and had him move his arm, which didn't hurt as much as it had.

Experimentally, Jakob sat up. "I think it worked. Good job, Doc. Also, you have the best bedside manner. Has anyone ever told you that? Calm. Kind. Really good."

Walt's eyes widened. "Okay then. Nerve blocker turns you into talky Jakob."

"I love to talk," Jakob said. "But everyone told me I was annoying."

Vadisk nodded. "Seems accurate."

Jakob barked out a loud laugh. The Incredible Hulk was funny.

Vadisk stood. "You mentioned security footage. What do we need? I will get it."

"Footage from the hotel's front doors. Blond man knocked into me. He must have had a pin or something with the venom on him. You know, I should have just killed him for running into me. It's fucking inconsiderate."

"Sweet Jesus," Walt murmured.

"I will get the footage. You have a secure computer?"

"Of course." Jakob stood under his own power, even stretched. The lack of pain was nearly euphoric. "Then we find the woman I love and kill whoever took her."

"A good plan." Vadisk disappeared out the door. Jakob was starting to warm up to the guy. He was going to help him get Annalise back.

Walt tried to push Jakob back down on the bed. "I'd like to

take your vitals again. What I did was so fucking dangerous...so fucking stupid..."

"You just want an excuse to get your hands on me," Jakob said. "And I get it. I'm hot. You're hot. The sex will be amazing, but we have to wait for Annalise."

"Maybe I got it in your bloodstream and it's gone into your brain...no, you'd be dead." Walt was looking at his watch while he held two fingers on Jakob's wrist.

"Who do you think is after us?" Jakob mused. "I mean, it doesn't matter, I'm going to kill them, but do you think it's the serial killer?" Saying that sobered him up because if Annalise was in the hands of a serial killer, one who liked to cut off people's heads...

"Why would he?" Walt asked, but his eyes were pinched with worry. "I mean, we don't know anything about him yet, right?"

"Maybe her stalker. But no, he didn't follow her when she went to that academic conference." Jakob shook his head. "No, not him. If it was, he would have had to follow us from Frankfurt and..." Jakob let his words trail off. "But his letters have been getting more deranged. She gets at least three a week, but don't tell her that. And this is the first time in months, a year, Annalise has been anywhere besides her heavily secured house or office at the university."

"Maybe he's desperate and he followed her, hoping you would slip up—"

Jakob jerked away from Walt.

"Wait, wait. I didn't mean it like that." Walt put a hand on Jakob's shoulder. "I misspoke. I'm not blaming you."

"You should. She should. I'm not good enough for her. I should never have touched her." Jakob was haunted now by the feel of her body under his hands. Could hear the soft sound of her demanding moans.

"Don't say that."

"I never kissed her," Jakob said. "I was going to, but I didn't...didn't get to kiss her." And now he never would.

"Okay, there's a lot of emotion going on that we need to unpack, but we might have to set some of this aside." Walt was using his doctor voice again.

Jakob hadn't kissed her. Why the fuck hadn't he kissed her? He'd dreamed of kissing her for so long, there was a small part of him that believed he already had. It was as if his dreams of her had morphed into memories of things that had never happened.

He couldn't lose her. It would kill him.

Vadisk opened the door, holding up a thumb drive. He paused, looking back and forth between them, but before he could say anything, Jakob jerked away from Walt. He grabbed his computer, took the thumb drive from Vadisk, and plugged it in.

He scrolled through the footage. Watched people file out, the sidewalk filling. He saw himself emerge, followed by Annalise and Walt.

And then he saw the blond man. He wore a heavy leather jacket and had a thick winter scarf wrapped around his neck and chin—overkill given the relatively mild daytime weather.

He stood still and focused amid the milling crowd, one arm across his chest, cupping his shoulder. Covering, protecting whatever mechanism he was about to use to incapacitate Jakob.

Then he moved, walking quickly. Just before he reached Jakob, he dropped his hand, and there was a glint at his shoulder, like something metal or...? He angled toward Jakob, crashing into him. Any doubt as to the intentionality of what had happened was gone.

"Get his face," Vadisk said.

"We need to see if he takes Annalise first," Jakob countered.

"Get his face and I can start running facial recognition."

That was a good point. Jakob took a screenshot, quickly transferring it to Vadisk. It wasn't a full frontal shot. The camera angle meant they had a three-quarter profile shot that showed most of his face, with the bottom of his chin obscured by the scarf. Jakob stared at the screenshot.

Did he recognize the man? Was this the stalker? The serial killer? Someone else? Perhaps someone holding a grudge from Jakob's past as a BND agent?

Shoving those questions aside, he started the video again. They watched as Walt went to help the injured woman, and then as Annalise guided Jakob to the corner, her body language radiating concern.

She'd said she loved him.

But how could she? Annalise was everything that was good in the world, and he'd done things in his past that would forever leave a black stain on his soul.

"Is there another angle?" Walt asked.

"No," Vadisk replied. "This camera covers the entrance and is the only one on the front."

Damn it. He'd picked this place because it had good security, but he'd been looking for physical security in the room setup and access, not checking how many security cameras they had.

The corner was just barely in frame, but it was enough to see as the blond man, now wearing a sweater with no leather jacket or scarf, approached Annalise. She turned to talk to him, then quickly whipped back around to face Jakob when he started to slide down.

That was when the blond man grabbed her. The classic grab, one hand around her middle, the other clamped over her mouth. He was fast, efficient, yanking her backward into the lane. She was gone before Jakob finished collapsing.

She'd been right there, and he hadn't helped her. Hadn't even seen her be taken.

A moment later, a tiny Skoda Fabia drove out of the alley, going too fast. It went past the front of the hotel and then disappeared from camera range.

"Partial plate," Vadisk said. "I'll run that, and I've already started the facial recognition."

"You're a police officer?" Walt asked.

"No. But I have access." Vadisk tapped his phone.

"Check passport control," Jakob said. "Any German passport holders who entered Poland in the last thirty hours."

"Oh, you're a knight, then," Walt said.

"No."

Walt sighed. "Do I want to know who you are or what you do?"

"No," Jakob and Vadisk said in unison.

Ten long, tense minutes later, Vadisk's phone beeped. He looked at it and grinned. "Got him."

CHAPTER TWELVE

"I'm so sorry. I don't want it to be like this." Her kidnapper's brow was creased with worry as he put the car in park.

They'd only been driving for thirty minutes, and yet the wooded area where he'd stopped the car felt remote and isolated. They'd traveled on a highway before turning onto a smaller road, and finally this dirt track that took them deep into the woods, where he'd stopped in a large clearing. The sun beat down, warm and happy, but all around them the shadows in the forest were dark. Drifts of snow in those shaded spaces were a stark reminder that it was winter.

That she was alone in the forest with this man.

A caravan, on the other side of the clearing, was hooked to a black compact that looked as new as the shiny silver caravan.

When her kidnapper opened the driver's door, Annalise took a deep breath and threw her own door open. She'd been quietly plotting and planning during the drive, focusing on that to hold back her panic.

And yet, when he got out, all her careful, calm, rational

planning evaporated as her fight-or-flight response clicked firmly into "flight." It didn't matter how remote and secluded this place seemed. Didn't matter that there was still snow on the ground and she didn't have a coat. They weren't that far from the highway. All she had to do was make it there and flag down a car.

Her escape attempt was over before it started.

She barely had one foot out the hastily thrown-open door when he was there, looming over her, his brow furrowed. "I would have opened your door for you."

Annalise nodded slowly, her heart hammering so hard, she felt slightly light-headed. She needed to calm down and remain in control.

His hands were in his pockets. The knife was probably in one pocket, the lancing device in the other. He'd used the knife to get her into the car—there was a hole in her shirt and possibly a small cut to go with it.

Once in the car, he'd showed her the lancing device and told her exactly what was on it. No larger than a thumb, it looked like it had been taken from a diabetes testing kit. The tip of the small lancet retracted inside the plastic casing would shoot out with the press of a button. It was coated in the same venom he'd used on Jakob.

Jakob.

Thinking about him—about the lines of pain that creased his face and the way he'd collapsed—would cause her to panic, and she was not going to panic.

She'd bottled up her fear, stuffed it deep down, and remained calm and quiet the whole way here.

She couldn't, wouldn't, take any kind of decisive action, until she knew exactly who she was dealing with.

Was this man a serial killer...or her stalker?

She had her suspicions, based on his behavior so far, but if she was wrong...

He took one hand from his pocket and started to reach out toward her, his hand not grabbing, but palm up, offering.

Stalker.

She was about to bet her life on that.

Annalise put her hand in his, climbing out of the car. The man's eyes widened for a moment, and he squeezed her fingers painfully. Annalise kept her expression neutral, but the fear she'd just managed to suppress started to leak through her mental barriers.

The man looked down at their hands, at her fingers squashed in his, and his breathing sped up. Annalise's stomach knotted.

She didn't pull away, and after a moment, he turned and started walking, pulling her along with him, the bones of her fingers still grinding against one another in his too-tight grip.

He hauled her across the clearing to the caravan, releasing her hand so he could pull out a key and unlock the door. While he wasn't looking, she flexed her aching fingers.

He put the caravan keys back into his pocket, then pulled out a small black cell phone. It was an older style, with actual buttons for the numbers rather than a touchscreen. He frowned down at it, then tapped the keys. He didn't dial enough numbers to be a phone number, but after hitting a few buttons, he stuffed it back in the same pocket as the keys. Finally, he opened the caravan door and gestured, gallantly, for her to precede him into the dark interior.

Her courage, the shell of calm she'd pulled around herself, cracked. Silence and compliance were no longer her best bet.

Annalise shook her head slowly. "I don't like caravans."

The man frowned, the first hints of anger touching his face.

"You used to go camping in caravans all the time when you were younger."

Before now, he'd mostly been silent, uttering only a few terse warnings and commands, then the apology as they arrived. This sounded more like his normal speaking voice.

If she hadn't already figured this was her stalker, that comment would have sealed it. It also meant that if she got into the caravan, she was likely facing a long imprisonment punctuated by rape. Which, admittedly, was far better than her fate of being raped, then murdered and decapitated if he were the serial killer.

"You remember that," she said neutrally.

He preened, as if her words had been a compliment. "Of course I do."

"But," she said softly. "I didn't actually enjoy it. Too small. Too enclosed."

His frown deepened. "I bought this *for you*."

"I understand that," she murmured, internally wincing. So his desire to please her was, and would be, rooted in his expectations of her needs, not in what she actually said.

He shook his head. "You'll love it, Anna. You will."

A pet name. An intimacy that no doubt made sense to him because it was appropriate in his version of reality.

Annalise slowly and deliberately shook her head, making sure the movement didn't seem panicked.

His expression darkened, and her stalker's hand shot out, closing tightly around her upper arm. He jerked her forward, her shins cracking against the metal step just below the door opening. Annalise cursed in pain, and he yanked on her arm so hard that her shoulder joint started to throb.

"Inside. You will love it," he declared.

One of her side duties at the *Kripo* was to work with the *Polizei* on outreach. Mostly she'd written scripts and pamphlets the officers could use when talking about crime prevention to community groups. One of the things she'd written had been a script officers used when speaking at schools, where one of the main points the officers had hoped to drive home was *never get into a stranger's car*. No matter what they said, never get in the car.

The script for the children hadn't included the statistics. Hadn't told them they were far more likely to be kidnapped by a family member than a stranger. Hadn't told them that if they got into a vehicle, the chances of being found decreased dramatically.

Never get in a stranger's car. Too late on that one. But the sentiment still applied.

Never get into a stranger's caravan.

Especially if you know that the stranger is very dangerous.

"I would prefer to stay out here, in the sunshine and fresh air, and talk." Annalise knew it was probably futile. Her words were slightly breathless, thanks to a combination of panic and pain.

"No, I got this for you. It's nice. We are going inside." His voice was rough with anger.

The stalker hauled up on her arm, and Annalise reluctantly stepped into the trailer. It was either that or run. It was safer, and smarter, to do her best to keep him calm.

Once inside the caravan, which smelled new, he directed her toward a small built-in bench. There was enough light coming from outside that she could see the L-shaped bench, with its artfully arranged pillows, with a small dining table in front of it.

The daylight also glinted off the chain and single handcuff coiled on the table.

Annalise panicked, backpedaling. She knocked into her stalker and he teetered in the open doorway. If she was lucky, he'd fall hard enough to be knocked senseless and give her a chance to escape.

But she wasn't lucky, or maybe he was too focused, too prepared. He caught himself on the doorframe and then shoved her forward. Annalise stumbled into the table, winding herself when her lower abdomen hit the edge.

He shoved her sideways, sending her sprawling on the bench. Then one of her arms was jerked up and back. A click and the cold metal of a handcuff encircled her wrist.

The caravan door closed, sealing them together in utter darkness.

Annalise had never felt so small, so scared.

There was no steel door, no Jakob.

No hope.

All she had was herself...and a doctorate in abnormal psychology.

Annalise forced herself to sit up, then cleared her throat. When she spoke, her voice was calm. "Could you turn on a light, please?"

A moment later, lights clicked on. The small camper was elegant inside, with polished wood compartments and recessed lighting. There was a double bed at the back, which she ignored, even as dread and fear formed a tight ball in her gut.

Annalise tugged her shirt down so the front was smooth, brushed back her hair, and dropped the wrist bearing the cuff onto her lap, out of sight. As she moved, the chain slid from the table top, falling onto her lap and to the floor, pooling around the base of the metal table leg to which it was attached.

With no outward signs of either fear or her captive status, Annalise looked at her stalker.

The rage and aggression he'd displayed outside retreated, leaving him looking a little nervous.

"This is quite lovely." She gestured around with her free hand. "How did you select this particular model of caravan?"

"Oh, um, I thought you would like the wood details." He smiled, seemingly pleased to be discussing his choices. "And I wanted to make sure we had some place to cook and to eat." He turned toward the bed, and her stomach lurched. "Those fold up into a couch and a desk. I knew you'd want to be able to work."

"Can you show me the desk?" Annalise asked, forcing mild curiosity into her voice.

"Of course, Anna. Of course."

While her stalker went to fold up and stow the bed—which proved to be two single beds, allowing it to essentially split in half for storage—Annalise forced herself to take calming breaths and then to assess the behaviors he'd just displayed.

She was about to use her knowledge and skills to manipulate, and possibly mentally harm, this man. It went against both professional ethical principles and her own personal ethics. She would do this man harm, and since, unlike Jakob, she couldn't harm him physically, she'd do it mentally.

And she just had to hope that whatever she did would be enough to give Jakob and Walt time to find her.

VADISK WAS DRIVING, and they were all going to die. Walt braced his back against one rear door, his foot on the other, and held on for dear life. Jakob—still in talky mode—was in the front passenger seat and had only stopped talking so they could hear the directions being called out by a man named Dimitri, who had a slight Ukrainian accent, his voice coming through the car's speakers.

Dimitri was, apparently, someone of considerable power

and authority—Vadisk called him "sir"—who also had access to every security camera in and around Krakow.

"No, he did take that exit. Go back," Dimitri said.

Vadisk screeched to a halt. "Check," he barked at Jakob.

Jakob swiveled, put a hand on Walt's head, pushed him down, and looked out the back window. "Go," Jakob commanded.

Vadisk threw the car into reverse and hit the gas. Walt thought it might be a good time to switch from agnostic back to the God-fearing Methodist his mama had raised him to be. He needed Jesus to take the wheel from Vadisk.

There were some honks and the car lurched to a stop, then shot forward again, taking a curve so fast, the G-forces pushed Walt even harder against the door.

"What else do we know about him?" Jakob asked, his voice calm, and maybe even a little chipper.

"Axel Richen. Age twenty-nine. German national with no living relatives. Software developer," Dimitri said.

They knew that much already—Vadisk had read out stats as they raced from the hotel room to his car.

"No known connection to Dr. Fischer," Dimitri continued.

"There wouldn't be. Annalise didn't have any exes who fit the profile of a rejected stalker subtype, and we looked at other associates."

Walt raised his head enough to look at Jakob.

"I tried to find him," Jakob said. "We looked at everyone she knew."

"She worked for the police," Vadisk said. "Revenge?"

"That would be the resentful subtype, and we looked into that too. I went through every case she worked on."

Vadisk looked over at Jakob. "You went through every single casefile and checked out each man who might want revenge on her?"

"Yes."

"That's dedication." Vadisk sounded shocked.

"I love her," Jakob declared softly. "I would have killed each possible suspect on the off chance it would keep her safe. If my imprisonment wouldn't have also meant leaving her unprotected, of course."

"No killing. Killing bad," Walt said.

Vadisk, Jakob, and Dimitri all laughed.

Well, that was really fucking scary...

"He's headed out of the city. Toward an undeveloped area," Dimitri said. "We have the car on a highway camera about ten kilometers in front of you. There isn't going to be much after this."

"Keep looking," Jakob demanded.

"I'm not going to take offense at that," Dimitri said mildly.

"Faster," Jakob demanded of Vadisk. "The longer he has her..."

Walt's stomach sank. She'd already been gone nearly two hours. He couldn't think about what Annalise might be going through right now. If he did, he'd start sobbing or raging, and neither reaction was helpful.

Vadisk put his foot down, and the car picked up speed.

CHAPTER THIRTEEN

Annalise set down the cup of coffee, smiling at the man. "Just the way I like it."

He grinned, looking relieved. "I've been practicing."

The man vacillated between angry and sweetly uncertain. Those seemingly disparate reactions, paired with the relatively stable fantasy reality he'd built for himself, were making her attempts at on-the-fly diagnoses difficult.

There were five types of stalkers. Rejected were people who stalked their exes; resentful, those who usually sought revenge for a perceived wrong. Neither was applicable to this situation. Though it was entirely possible she'd done or said something that he perceived as worthy of revenge, his behavior didn't fit with the psychopathy of someone who felt humiliated.

Predatory stalking usually involved sexual fantasies. Given what he'd done to her sister, that would make sense, but predatory stalkers rarely fantasized about relationships with their victims, and it was very clear that he either wanted, or already believed they were in, a relationship. Of course, the sexual component couldn't be discounted.

That left the incompetent stalker and the intimacy seeker. Of those two, he fit most of the markers for intimacy seeker—belief in a relationship with a complete stranger, a delusion that the feelings were reciprocated.

Intimacy seeker with predatory elements would have to do for her quick-and-dirty diagnosis. A clinical way of saying he'd created a delusion-based fantasy relationship with a complete stranger, but also showed paraphilia centered around abnormal control and authority over that person.

An incredibly dangerous combination.

She'd decided to try and figure him out so she could manipulate him. Use her knowledge and skills as a weapon. The only weapon she had, considering she was chained to the table. However, there was a great deal to be said for ignorance being bliss. She might have been happier not having a preliminary diagnosis that made it clear exactly how dangerous he was.

Given her analysis, there was no denying this man was capable of doing horrific things. Her sister's face as she lay in the hospital bed the morning after her rape flashed in Annalise's mind. In the past, those memories haunted her so badly, she'd failed, lost her dream job, let it shake her confidence right off the foundations until there was nothing left but a pile of dust.

But not today.

Today, she would seek to find justice.

For Adele.

For herself.

Annalise took another sip of coffee, considering what she should say next. Indulging his delusion was dangerous, and not something she would ever normally do, but it might buy her the time she needed. Then again, if she didn't behave exactly the way he expected, thereby breaking or ruining his fantasy, he might lash out.

And the one thing she wanted to do, and absolutely could not, was ask him his name.

After all, if they were in a relationship as he believed, she would know his name. Asking would break his fantasy.

Given all those factors, her best option was to...

Annalise sucked in a deep breath, steadied herself, and grabbed hold of every last ounce of courage she had. She was going to challenge his delusion that he was "caring" and "cared for" her, without outright confronting him with reality.

Annalise dipped her head, letting her hair fall forward to hide her face, hide that she was looking at him. "Why did you send me the flying bugs?" she asked softly. "It was very scary. I was really afraid."

He jerked, as if she'd poked him. His mouth opened and closed, two lines appearing between his brows. For the first time, he turned away, no longer staring at her with an intensity that made her hindbrain nervous.

He turned his back to her, opening the small refrigerator. "I have your favorite cheese. Crackers. Dried fruit."

Annalise often made a meal out of a simple charcuterie platter. Her stomach knotted that he knew that even though it wasn't a surprise.

She watched him fumble for a few minutes, getting things out of the refrigerator, and then setting everything on a small cutting board. He brought it over, placing it in front of her expectantly. Annalise was nervous about eating any of it. Though the cheese was still wrapped up in what looked like its original wrapping, it was a soft cheese, and maybe he could have injected something into it, through the packaging. Same with the dried fruit. She took a cracker, carefully taking a small bite. He smiled, relaxing.

"Why did you choose a caravan?" she asked, keeping her focus on the tray, as if she were just making conversation. He hadn't been able to engage with a direct question, so she'd have to try to work her way around to it.

"You had one, growing up."

"Yes, but I also had a house. You chose something portable."

"To keep you safe."

Annalise folded her hands, looking up. "Am I in danger?"

"Yes."

"From whom?"

He pushed to his feet. "I have wine too." He took her coffee cup, tipping it into the sink.

"No, thank you."

"I got it *for you*."

"I understand that, but right now I'm nervous. Will you tell me why I'm in danger?"

He didn't answer. Instead, he pulled a bottle of white wine from the refrigerator, setting it on the small counter. But he didn't move to open it.

"This must have been very expensive," she said. "The caravan. The cars."

He relaxed, opened a cupboard for a corkscrew. "I'm rich. Very successful. I could have anyone I want."

"But you want me."

"Yes."

"Why?" she asked mildly.

"Why?"

She wanted, oh God, she wanted to say, *"Why me? Why are you doing this? Did we meet? Do I know you? Please say something that will make everything make sense."* Instead, she said, "Women like to know what men appreciate about them."

He frowned down at the corkscrew in his hand. "I know what women want."

She was on dangerous ground. Rather than risk saying anything else, she picked up another cracker. Her mouth was dry from the last one, so instead of eating it, she broke it in half.

"I could have any woman I want. But I want you. Not just because of how you look." He rushed to add, then smiled as if he were proud of himself for not being shallow. "You're cerebral, like me."

She was many things but "cerebral" wasn't one of them, though the term was amusing, given what she did. What Annalise was, was determined, hardworking, and, in many ways, insightful. But something about her made him identify her as "cerebral"—an odd and specific choice of words.

Or maybe after he'd focused on her, selected her as his victim, he'd decided that the object of his affections had to be extraordinary, according to his own definition and terminology. "You're cerebral too, of course. Tell me about work." She hoped she'd phrased that generically enough.

He set down the corkscrew, running his fingers up and down the bottle of wine. "I don't want to talk about me."

"Well, I think we should. I'd like to talk about you." Her tone was a little too clinical, too much like a therapist, and she knew it the moment the words were out of her mouth. She saw his shoulders tense, and his hand tightened around the bottle. "Where did you buy the camper?" she rushed to ask. "Here, or in Frankfurt?"

For a minute, she thought she'd managed to distract him, but the tension was still in the lines of his body. "I knew you might do this," he murmured. "But I'm not like them."

"Of course not," she soothed. *Them* could be anyone from the people she'd helped the police hunt to other men in general. Who exactly they were didn't matter as much as assuring him she agreed with his distinction between himself and those who were "other".

"You're in danger, and I'm protecting you." He said the words steadily and calmly. They had the tone and cadence of words often repeated, almost a mantra.

Had there been a slight stress on the word "I'm"?

"And I need protecting," she said, neither question nor statement but an ambiguous place in between.

"You do. You might not see it, but I do. The people you try to find, they're too dangerous. One of them will want to find *you*. Hurt you."

One like him?

Anger welled in her, and though she knew better, though her control should be better, Annalise raised her chin, her soothing tone becoming accusatory. "Yes, I am in danger. Some coward broke into my house one night and attacked my sister."

"Coward?" He whirled, wine bottle in hand, eyes narrowing. "She was in your house, pretending to be you."

"She was welcome in my home," Annalise snapped, ignoring the way his body language had changed from tentative and unsure to aggressive. "She was invited. She has a place in my life."

She saw the words hurt him, knew she had wounded him by highlighting a reality—in which he was unknown and unwelcome—that was so different from his delusion.

And now she would pay for attacking his fantasy.

He raised the bottle.

Annalise threw up an arm and leaned to the side. She saved herself from a concussion, the bottle striking her upper arm instead of her head. Pain lanced through her humerus and shoulder, stopping the breath in her lungs for a moment. Then she screamed, a high, thin sound that wasn't deliberate, but reactionary.

He raised the bottle again.

Annalise scrambled off the bench, running for the door. She'd forgotten about the cuff, the chain. She managed to put a hand on the door latch before she was pulled up short, the chain suddenly taut, the cuff digging into her wrist.

Then his body slammed into her, forcing her against the closed door, the cuffed arm stretched back painfully. She didn't turn her head in time, and her nose impacted the door, hard enough that her eyes instantly watered. Her stalker shoved his hips hard against her ass, and his lips brushed her cheek. With a small cry of horror, she twisted her face to the other side, only to have him grip her hair, pulling so tight she felt little pops as the hairs were ripped from her scalp. He brushed his lips against her other cheek, his breath washing over her face. He smelled like mint.

"Don't worry, Anna," he murmured, his lips roving over her cheek. "I've got you. You're with me now. I'll protect you."

Annalise hated the whimpers that escaped her. Hated that she couldn't think, could barely breathe through the thick fear. This man had terrorized her, brutalized her sister. He was the unseen towering monster that had destroyed her life...

But he wasn't unseen, unknown. Not anymore.

He was just a man. Delusional, yes. Mentally ill, without a doubt. Able to physically hurt her, yes, as her throbbing shins, arm, wrist, and nose could all attest.

But he was just a man, and Jakob and Walt were coming for her.

VADISK WHIPPED the car off the motorway. The last video they had of the kidnapper's was from a camera about five kilometers behind them. Another traffic camera seven miles ahead showed no image of the vehicle, which meant it had exited somewhere in this twelve-mile stretch. They were well outside of Krakow now, surrounded by forested areas, the only sign of human habitation the four lanes of road snaking through the trees.

There were four possible exits between the two points. Two exits connected to slightly smaller, but well-traveled roads. Dimitri, the security minister of Hungary, was getting access to cameras along those roads now, since they weren't looped in to the same traffic monitoring system as the major motorway. The third exit was the private driveway to a small luxury hotel nestled in among the trees. They'd stopped there first, though Jakob's instincts were screaming at him that Axel wouldn't have dared take Annalise someplace so public. Still, they'd stopped, flashed both Annalise's and Axel's pictures—Vadisk spoke conversational Polish and was able to ask questions—and when no one recognized Annalise or Axel, they'd jumped back into the car.

With Dimitri working on footage from the two larger roads, Vadisk had driven them to the fourth exit. A road just wide enough for two cars, but with flat shoulders where the trees had been cut back. This road was clearly less traveled, especially in winter.

According to Dimitri, it led to a popular campground deep in the forest. On a summer day, the road would have been clogged with cars pulling caravans or massive motorhomes on their way to the wide, mowed lawns of the campground that included amenities like showers and bathrooms, and even a small shop.

In January, the campgrounds were closed, the buildings locked, but the road wasn't blocked off.

Jakob's already tight shoulders tensed as Vadisk shot up the road.

Walt leaned forward, placing his hand on Jakob's shoulder.

"We'll find her," he murmured.

Jakob nodded woodenly, his gaze focused out the front window though he wasn't really seeing anything. He'd gone to the hospital when Annalise's sister had been there after her attack. He remembered her glassy, shocked eyes. Remembered the way Annalise had looked—heartsick, guilty, utterly destroyed.

"We'll get our girl back." Walt squeezed his shoulder.

Our girl.

That sounded right. Felt right. He and Annalise...there was too much between them. But Walt made them work.

Walt Hayden had shown up with the fleet admiral and flashed him and Annalise that easygoing smile of his, while attempting to speak German with his charming American drawl. Jakob had never met anyone so comfortable in their own skin. Somehow the kind doctor had become the bridge between Jakob and Annalise, tearing down what had previously been a wall. One he and Annalise had built out of unspoken longing, attempted professionalism, and far too much self-doubt.

He reached up and squeezed Walt's hand, blinking to clear his vision, which was abruptly blurry. Damn it, between the venom and the drugs, he was unable to control his words, to shield his feelings. He was wearing his heart on his sleeve and fighting like the devil not to cry.

He was a mess.

Jakob blinked again, his gaze focusing. He let go of Walt's hand and reached across to the driver's side, jerking the wheel.

Vadisk cursed and stood on the brake. The car screeched in protest as they were all flung sideways. They spun around before wobbling to a stop on the wide dirt shoulder, facing back the way they'd just come.

"Church every day," Walt wheezed from the backseat. He was wedged in the footwell behind the driver's seat.

Jakob didn't wait for the car to stop. He threw open the

door, leapt out, and ran back toward the break in the trees he'd been looking at, but hadn't really *seen* until it was almost too late.

It was unseasonably warm in Poland, and in the city, the snow had melted away from the streets and sidewalks. But up here, in the mountains, it was colder, winter more evident. The ground was frozen hard, the undergrowth dead and dry. Snow was still present in some of the deep pockets of shadow.

Including a wide drift that spanned a barely discernible break between the trees.

Tire tracks cut through the hard-crusted snow.

CHAPTER FOURTEEN

"Could I have that glass of wine now?" Annalise asked. She was still pressed against the door, the stalker's lips on her cheeks. "I like to have a glass of wine when I'm stressed."

He paused. "A glass of wine to help you relax."

"Yes," she agreed.

He backed off, and Annalise turned her face to the door, squeezing her eyes tight.

Don't challenge his delusion. Use the clues he's giving you and pretend to be the person he wants you to be.

Indulging a delusion like this was highly unethical and incredibly unhealthy for the patient. It was why hostage negotiators were rarely psychologists. They would do or say whatever was needed to form a relationship with the subject, even if that meant going along with the delusion, or worse, adding to the narrative.

Add to it.

She could try that. It was not without heavy risks. Especially given that she hadn't been able to keep her rage and fear totally under control.

She heard him pick up the wine bottle, heard the squeak of a corkscrew going into a cork. Annalise gathered herself and returned to the bench, sitting gingerly, and then tucking the chain out of sight under the table. She couldn't afford to panic and run again, so she wrapped the chain several times around her hand and gripped hard enough that the chain dug into her skin, a constant reminder of her captivity.

A reminder not to try to run.

He poured her a glass of wine, setting it on the table. Annalise lifted it and took a small sip. Not because she trusted that the wine wasn't tampered with—much like the cheese, if he'd wanted to, he probably could have tampered with it—but because she needed to be the fantasy version of herself he'd created.

She smiled at him after she took that first sip. "Lovely. Are you going to join me for a glass?"

He blinked and his shoulders were once again hunched in what would have seemed like cute embarrassment on someone who wasn't delusional and dangerous. He poured himself a glass and then slid onto the edge of the other bench, so they were seated at right angles to one another.

They sipped in silence, a silence that lasted far too long to be anything but horrible and awkward, though he didn't seem to realize. She was going to assume he had a low interpersonal IQ and difficulty with social norms. If he had the financial resources to follow her to Poland, to plan for her kidnapping to the extent that he'd bought an expensive caravan, then he most likely either had independent financial resources or a way to make money that didn't involve him having to interact with people.

Annalise needed to get him talking, to keep him engaged,

so he wouldn't focus on the next thing, the next part of his fantasy, which could involve him doing something to her that she didn't want to happen.

It was time to take a risk, to gamble, if not with her life, then certainly her physical safety.

After taking another sip, she smiled and gestured toward the small desk that had been revealed when he folded up the beds. "Have you had a chance to read my latest paper?"

He perked up, smiling back at her. He seemed so normal. Medium height, blond, with a nice jawline. His hair was longish, but not as if it was a style he'd chosen. Rather, it was long in a way that screamed lack of self-care. His oily skin and ill-fitting shirt also added to the overall impression of a man who didn't know how to dress or take care of himself.

A man who'd never had a friend or lover to guide him on how to present himself to the world.

"I always read your papers," he said. "I support you, Anna."

That's what she'd expected from a man who labeled both himself, and her, as cerebral. "What did you think about the commentary on the dichotomy of positive and negative representations of therapy and psychiatry in pop culture?" she asked with as much genuine curiosity as she could feign.

He frowned down at his wine glass, and she gripped the chain tighter, trying not to visibly tense in anticipation of the blow if she'd miscalculated and he reacted badly. An academic discussion should appeal to the "cerebral" aspect of his fantasy construct, but if he felt she were challenging or quizzing him...

"I don't think we need to make people feel like therapy is acceptable," he said after a moment. "The people who need it just need to do it."

That was the dumbest thing she'd ever heard. Annalise nodded, even leaned into him. "Interesting. And what of people who might feel ashamed of needing help."

"Do they even matter? I mean, if they need that kind of help, they're probably useless."

She swallowed down a slightly hysterical giggle. The utter lack of self-awareness was comical.

"I want people who need help to get it," she countered ever so gently. "If they don't come to see people like me...well, then we'll never know how to explain the ways a human mind works."

That statement was also nonsense because she wasn't a therapist. If he'd actually *understood* the papers she wrote, and what she did, surely he would realize that what she'd just said was off.

But he didn't react except to reach out for the wine bottle, plucking it from the tiny counter and setting it on the table. "You can just talk to them after they catch them."

Annalise nodded again, now confident that hubris was a driving factor in his actions. This man thought he was far smarter than he actually was. Which also meant, if she was careful, and controlled her own reactions, he could be manipulated. Manipulated into sitting there and talking to her. Into drinking wine that might lower his inhibitions and reaction time.

Annalise reached for the inelegantly presented plate of charcuterie. "Do you want me to make you a plate? I love to have some wine with fruit and cheese."

He shifted awkwardly, then squared his shoulders. "Yes. You should make me a plate."

Annalise unwrapped the cheese, and when she put a lost and helpless expression on her face, he rose and grabbed her a table knife, then a plate. She cut cheese, arranged a plate, then passed it to him before lifting the bottle of wine. "Do you want some more wine? Anything else I can get you?"

He preened, clearly enjoying her in the role of subservient

female. He'd said he wanted to take care of her. What he wanted was to control her, to have power over her. Rather than allow him to choose the shape and manner of it, she would do it. Give him perceived power over her by making herself subservient.

Buy time until Jakob and Walt arrived.

Only how long would it be? How far behind her were they?

God. Please let them be on the way.

She asked for his opinions of her other papers and journal articles, careful never to ask or say anything that might remind him that she knew nothing about him.

The minutes dragged on into an hour, maybe more, and Annalise's fist was so tight on the chain that the links felt like they were fusing with her skin.

Jakob and Walt were coming for her...unless they weren't. Unless Jakob was in the hospital fighting for his life, Walt beside him. Because if Jakob was hurt, that was where Walt would be.

Or worse, what if Jakob was dead?

She'd been so careful to keep herself from even obliquely considering that possibility, but now that she'd let that horrific thought in, she couldn't get rid of it. Couldn't shake the memory of Jakob's face drawn tight in pain, of him falling back against the wall of the hotel, and then sliding to the ground.

"Anna."

His hand clamped tight around her wrist and Annalise jerked, brought back to the moment, fear for Jakob fluttering high in her chest.

"You weren't listening to me." He sounded disappointed and angry.

Annalise twisted her wrist in his grip, so her hand was palm up, fingers softly curled, a deliberately vulnerable position.

"I'm so sorry. Something you said gave me an idea for another paper." Was she talking too fast? It felt like she was.

He was still frowning at her.

"I'm so sorry," she said again, lowering her gaze. "It was very rude of me."

He grunted, an arrogant noise of satisfaction that made her body burn with rage. She hated this, hated sitting here playing pretend while the man she loved, and who loved her, might be sick or dead.

No. Jakob was okay. Walt was there with him.

Just the thought of the sweet American doctor had the tightness in her chest loosening. How Walt had managed to sneak under her defenses—and Jakob's—so quickly was a mystery to her. She thought she'd lost the ability to trust others, to let people in. For so long, it had been her and Jakob against the world.

Walt changed that. He challenged them to open themselves up to possibilities they'd only dreamed of.

As well as possibilities she'd never considered.

What would she give to be back in that hotel just before the fire alarm sounded? Jakob standing behind her, kissing her neck, his hands on her breasts, Walt teasing her with his big hand, thick fingers. She had never felt so safe, so adored, so...

Damn it.

She should get the conversation back on track, keep him talking about her work, about anything that would play into his fantasy. And yet...

She needed to know what he'd done to Jakob.

Annalise swallowed hard and accepted that she might be about to fuck everything up. That in the next few minutes, she might be suffering the consequences of breaking his delusion. Annalise glanced up, smiling softly. He released her wrist but then placed his hand atop hers, lacing their fingers together. She felt physically ill at the intimacy.

"Oh," she said, as casually as she was able. "I keep forgetting to ask, is that a new poison you have?"

He glanced sharply at her, and Annalise nearly whimpered in fear. She tried to hold on to rage, to her anger, while maintaining a calm, slightly curious expression. In his delusion where they were in a relationship, she should know things about him. Things like his interest in poison, or his profession if that's where he'd gotten whatever poison he'd managed to slip to Jakob.

After a moment, his brow cleared. "Venom, not poison."

"Oh, of course. Wrong word."

"Bullet ant venom." He said the words with relish. "It's the most painful insect sting. They call it a bullet ant because it feels like being shot. Days of agony."

Days.

Jakob wasn't coming.

"Oh dear," she murmured, her tone noncommittal as she desperately tried to hide her panic.

She must have failed, because his face darkened. "I'm protecting you. From him."

Annalise nodded, but this time it didn't seem to appease him. Her stalker squeezed her hand so hard she once more felt her bones creak. Though she tried to keep her composure, a small sound of pain escaped as he continued to crush her hand.

"It was going to be fine, until him. That's why I had to get you away from him. I knew when you came to Krakow that you wanted me to rescue you, and I had to act fast. That it was our chance to be together."

"So you pulled the fire alarm," she gasped. "Very clever."

"Clever? Are you making fun of me?" He jerked her toward him.

Annalise tipped sideways on the bench, catching herself with the chain-wrapped hand. "No, of course not."

He looked down at the chain and smirked.

Damn it, damn it.

The chain would serve as a visual signal that he could have other, more direct power over her.

He released her, then stood, coming around to her other side. This time when he grabbed her, Annalise clung to the table. It wasn't fear, but rage that clamped her fingers around the wood. Rage that wanted to lash out. To fight him, hurt him. Punish him for what he'd done to her, to her sister, to Jakob.

Rage that wouldn't be enough. Unless she could incapacitate him. Lashing out would only serve to escalate the situation and put herself in danger.

And Jakob wasn't coming. Walt would tell someone, someone would be looking for her, but Walt wasn't a member of the Masters' Admiralty. He'd go to the police. It would take time.

Which meant rescue was hours, maybe days away.

If this were a movie she would have grabbed something, managed to knock him unconscious, and then get away. But this was reality, in which she had considerably less physical mass than him, was hobbled by the chain, and there were no conveniently heavy objects besides the nearly empty wine bottle, which may have been enough to knock him out if she managed to hit him in just the right spot, and with enough force.

Too many mights and maybes, especially when she knew that any aggression on her part would only escalate his own behavior.

And so, when he grabbed her by the hair and yanked, she let go of the table, scrambling off the bench in a desperate effort to alleviate some of the pressure on her scalp.

When he pushed her up against the wall, his hips against hers, his hand tight on her jaw, forcing her face up, Annalise closed her eyes.

And when he kissed her, she stayed passive, holding her need to thrash and bite in check, even when he forced her mouth open. Even when his hand trailed down from her jaw as tears slipped from under her lashes.

JAKOB LOOKED from the tracks back at Vadisk, who'd jumped out of the car and come running up beside him.

Vadisk looked at Jakob, and together they turned and raced back to the car. Walt had just managed to get the back passenger door open and his shoulder and head were hanging out the open door, his hands scrabbling on the seat to try to gain purchase to pull himself upright, or maybe out.

Jakob stopped, grabbed Walt's shoulders, heaved him up, then shoved him back into the car, slamming the door. He raced around, jumping in his still-open door even as Vadisk put the car in drive.

"What's going on?" Walt demanded.

"Tire tracks." Vadisk said.

"Fresh tire tracks," Jakob added.

"You think it's Annalise?"

Jakob wished he had a more tangible reason than some tire tracks for the instincts screaming inside his head. For his absolute, unshakable belief that Annalise was down that nearly hidden tract through the forest. He didn't. Just a feeling that she was close. Very close. And he would give up his own life if it meant saving hers.

"Yes, she's there," Jakob said.

Vadisk steered them off the road and into the dark, cold woods.

. . .

ANNALISE HUDDLED in on herself when her stalker stepped away. Something, somewhere, in the caravan was beeping, but all she cared about was the reprieve. With the chain at its limit, she couldn't cross her arms, but did her best to cover and protect herself.

He'd cut her shirt off, but left on the bra.

The part of her brain that was detached from reality, that wasn't trembling in revulsion at the way he'd "kissed" her and mauled her breasts, was able to look at it clinically. She doubted he had sexual experience, meaning his frames of reference were porn, where the women often started out naked. But he wouldn't have any respect for those women, so some part of him was rejecting the idea of stripping her naked and making her like those women he didn't respect. Women he would never have called cerebral.

On the other hand, lingerie companies regularly posted billboards in public spaces of women in bras. Branding and advertising where women wore bras were common and familiar.

Right now he was probably uncomfortable with the idea of her naked, and so he'd left her in her underwear because it was a more familiar visual.

But whatever he might be feeling, it ultimately wouldn't stop him, only delay him.

And once he did strip her naked, he might begin to feel the contempt toward her that he most likely felt for women in pornography.

The beeping got louder, and she looked up to see that he'd opened a cupboard. Inside there was an open laptop, which continued to sound an alarm.

He tapped the keyboard, then hissed in anger.

Annalise froze, scared to hope, but sure that anything he didn't like was good for *her*. She craned her neck so she could see the screen—a grainy security camera feed of the clearing. The camera must have been somewhere on the caravan and showed everything, including the car he'd brought her in parked on the far side, near the slight break in the trees.

He peered at the screen, intent. There was nothing there.

Maybe the alarm was some kind of motion sensor or early alert system that someone was approaching. Maybe that was very wishful thinking on her part.

A car shot out from between the trees, going far too fast. The driver swerved to avoid hitting the parked car and then rocked to a stop.

The doors opened. The driver was someone she didn't know, but the two men who climbed out on the passenger side...

"Jakob," she breathed. "Walt."

Her stalker spun to her, his eyes wide and enraged. He took two quick steps and slapped her. Annalise saw it coming and ducked, his hand just clipping the top of her head.

Then she balled up her fist and punched him in the dick.

At least that was her intention, but she was using her non-dominant arm, which still throbbed from the wine-bottle blow —a huge bruise was already forming.

She hit him hard enough to make him yelp and step back, but not hard enough to drop him.

Her stalker snarled and grabbed her by the hair, hauling her over to the cabinet, forcing her to look at the laptop. "I want you to watch this."

"Watch what?" she gasped, one arm outstretched to accommodate the chain, the other desperately gripping his wrist as if that would lessen his hold on her hair.

"After this, we'll be leaving. Don't worry, there's another way out, so we won't have to deal with the debris."

"Debris?" Annalise stared at the grainy footage. Her men were so close. Less than fifty meters from the camper. Jakob had gone to check the stalker's car, while the man she didn't recognize kept his attention on the camper, standing in the space between the car he'd been driving and the one she'd been kidnapped in.

Debris.

The phone. The old, simple phone he'd used when they first arrived.

A bomb. There was a bomb in the car.

Annalise screamed as loud as she could. Hoping to warn them.

"It's soundproof." Her stalker laughed, then propped the phone up by the laptop. He tapped the green send button.

A fifteen-second countdown window appeared on the screen. Fourteen, no, thirteen seconds and then Walt and Jakob were going to be blown to bits. She screamed again.

Her stalker turned her, forcing her against the wall once more, but this meant she had a perfect view of the laptop.

He drew the knife from his pocket and placed the tip at the waistband of her pants.

Annalise had no more room for fear. Her horror at what was about to happen filled her until there wasn't space for anything else.

THERE WAS nothing in the car. No sign of Annalise, but the plates matched the partial plate they'd seen on the video.

"If she's not in the car, is she in there?" Walt asked.

Vadisk, looking at the caravan on the other side of the clearing, didn't immediately respond.

Every muscle in Jakob's body was tense with the surety that she was in the caravan. That she was trapped in there with a man who would hurt her.

Not might hurt her. Would.

He probably already had.

"Maybe," Vadisk said. "But it is too obvious."

"No." Jakob looked from the car to the caravan and back again. "It's too easy."

"Trap?" Vadisk asked.

"He's smart enough to evade me for years. He left no clues. He's organized enough to plan this kidnapping on the fly in a city he isn't familiar with." Jakob's words were several seconds behind his thoughts. By the time the last word left his lips, he was already moving away from the cars.

"Run," Jakob snarled. "Into the trees."

Neither Vadisk nor Walt questioned him. They turned and sprinted toward the trees.

A second later, the world flashed bright white, then a wrecking ball slammed into his back an eighth of a second before a deafening noise wiped out all other sound.

THE EXPLOSION ROCKED the camper slightly. The camera feed whirled drunkenly, then stilled, now pointed at the sky, only the tops of the trees visible—it must have been knocked to the side by the blast.

Annalise forced herself to exhale when her lungs started to hurt. She'd been right. There had been a bomb in the car.

A bomb that would have killed Jakob, Walt, and the stranger if they hadn't moved.

She'd seen them start to run, just before the timer hit zero.

Had they gotten far enough away?

Annalise stared mutely at the screen, until her stalker

dragged her down to the floor, forcing her onto her back. Her pants were gone, and when he forced her legs apart, the G-string didn't feel like much protection.

She should be horrified or scared. Should be angry enough that she'd started fighting.

Instead, she craned her head, trying to see the laptop screen. Hoping that the camera would have shifted again. Would show her what had become of the men she loved.

God, she loved them. Both of them.

Her stalker slapped her, hard enough to make her ears ring.

"Pay attention to me!" he snarled. "You can't hide. You're mine. Mine!"

"No, I'm not, and I never will be, you delusional, pathetic waste of humanity." There was no heat in her words, only disgust.

He screamed in her face, his spittle hitting her cheek. Annalise turned her face away, breathing hard through her nose.

"I won't cut your hair. I only cut hers so I wouldn't be tricked again." He was on his knees, scrambling for the knife. "But there are other places I can cut. So you'll know you're mine."

"But you protect me," Annalise said firmly, though she was trembling. "Is that protecting? Or are *you* the one I need protecting from?"

He raised his hands, including the one now holding the knife, and clamped his hands over his ears. "Shut up!"

"No, you have to decide. Do you want to love me or hurt me? It cannot be both."

"I said shut up." The hand holding the knife rose.

Annalise tensed to roll out of the way.

The caravan door exploded inward, bouncing against the

wall and ricocheting back only to be arrested by Jakob as he barreled into the opening.

He was dirty, his shirt torn, blood on his face and lips, but he was here.

And alive.

"No!" Her stalker screamed the denial, turning toward Jakob. She could see fear in his expression.

He still held the knife, and he was far closer to her than Jakob, though given the size of the camper, the distance wasn't great. But she knew she was still in danger.

Or would have been if Jakob hadn't taken one big step, half turned, and lashed out with one foot, kicking her stalker so hard in the face that his head snapped back.

Blood spurted and her stalker slumped to the floor, knife clattering from his hand. Jakob took two more steps, grabbed the man's head, shoved it down, compressing his neck, and then twisted with a short, sharp jerking motion.

Annalise scrambled to her hands and knees, crawling as far as the chain would allow. Then Jakob was there, crouching in front of her, his dark eyes haunted. He started to reach for her, but stopped, his hand hovering in the air between them.

Walt bounded in, dropping to his knees beside them. Without hesitation, he gathered Annalise into his arms, then pulled Jakob in too.

It was then—safe and in their arms—that Annalise started to sob.

CHAPTER FIFTEEN

Walt stood by the hotel window, looking down on the busy street below them, replaying yesterday's events over and over. Annalise had fallen apart in their arms after they'd found her. It was as if she'd stored up too many years' worth of tears and they all came out at once, the dam breaking.

It had ripped his heart out, hearing the unadulterated terror and anguish in her cries.

He glanced back at the bed, feeling the need to check on her again. He'd felt that same need every few minutes since he'd woken up.

She was still in the center of the mattress, her arm curled over Jakob's waist. Jakob lay on his back, one arm around her shoulders, tucking her close to him, the other thrown above his head.

Both of them were dead to the world.

Not that Walt was surprised. It felt as if they'd lived ten lifetimes in just a few days.

Given the pain-free, peaceful way Jakob slept, it was

apparent the effects from the bullet ant sting had subsided. Walt grinned as he recalled Jakob's reaction to the nerve blocker. The medication hadn't just loosened the tension and burning agony in his muscles. It had loosened his tongue as well, allowing Jakob to speak every thought, every feeling aloud. During the course of the day, he'd revealed quite a bit about his love for Annalise.

Walt hoped Jakob wouldn't retreat back to his silence. He enjoyed hearing his thoughts and for such a seemingly serious, stoic man, Jakob had a great sense of humor and a very dirty mind. Walt shook his head when his thoughts traveled to the sexy activities that had been interrupted by the fire alarm.

He wasn't sure how to return them to that moment.

No, he wasn't sure if he should.

Walt didn't have a clue how long he and Jakob had held Annalise on the floor of that caravan before Vadisk had cleared his throat and told them he was going to make sure the car they'd arrived in hadn't been damaged by the blast. Really, Vadisk had been giving them a few minutes to pull themselves together, as well as telling them it was time to leave.

It spoke to Walt's intense fear for Annalise's well-being that he'd forgotten about the man lying just a few feet away from them.

Walt had released Jakob and Annalise, crawling over to Axel's body. He'd witnessed the kick, seen Jakob's boot connect with Axel's face, and he'd known immediately that the man was dead. And if that hadn't done it, the terrifyingly professional and efficient way Jakob had broken the man's neck would have.

Walt had taken a pulse, but hadn't searched for a breath. Axel had died instantly, his spinal cord snapped. Most likely if they looked on an X-ray, he would have died from atlanto-occipital dislocation—commonly referred to as an internal decapitation.

After that, things had moved in slow motion, as every action felt like they were performing it neck-deep in thick mud. A fog had settled in all their brains, their motions performed by rote. They'd found a clean T-shirt and sweatpants in the caravan—Annalise's clothing had been sliced to ribbons—and helped her dress, then Jakob had carried her to the car.

Vadisk had promised to call and make arrangements for someone to take care of the clean-up at the site, then he'd driven them—in a car that now sported some serious dents and a missing back passenger window—to the hotel just as the sun was setting.

None of them had spoken a single word during the ride. Annalise looked shell-shocked, battered and bruised—inside and out. Meanwhile, he, Vadisk, and Jakob appeared as if they'd just walked out of a war film, filthy and bloody after coming far too close to being blown to Kingdom Come by the car bomb.

Exhaustion—mental and physical—had taken them all down quickly last night. Walt had wanted to take Annalise to the hospital. There was a severe contusion on her arm, as well as several on her shins, and the start of two black eyes. But he'd held his tongue. Not forcing her to go to the hospital was only the second-worst medical decision he'd made yesterday, after the blind injection he'd given Jakob.

They'd returned to the room they'd vacated earlier in the day, climbed into the bed together, and fallen fast asleep. They hadn't even undressed or washed up, hadn't done more than slip off their shoes.

Walt glanced at the clock on the nightstand. It was nearly noon, but he didn't have the heart to wake them. He'd only spent a few days aware of Annalise's stalker, of the horrors the man had subjected her to. Meanwhile, she and Jakob had spent years wallowing around in that nightmare. With the threat removed, they were obviously catching up on years of lost slumber.

If they weren't still knee-deep in the hunt for a serial killer, the doctor in him would have suggested at least a few days of serious bed rest for both of them, and he probably would have prescribed a sedative to ensure that happened.

Glancing at his phone, he realized he'd missed an early-morning text from his new friend Vadisk. The man said they were getting a one-day reprieve, but that the admiral of Hungary intended to pay them a visit.

Apparently, the admiral was looking for answers. Answers Walt knew they couldn't provide. Not without betraying the fleet admiral.

Walt sighed as he looked at the bed once more, surprised to find Annalise had turned toward him, her gaze on his face.

"How do you feel?" he asked softly, not wanting to disturb Jakob.

Annalise's brow furrowed, and he got a sense she was genuinely searching for a response to his question. He could almost imagine her doing a mental check-in, trying to analyze her condition. Finally, she said, "Numb."

After the avalanche of emotions she'd released yesterday, he wasn't surprised. "Maybe that's a good thing for now."

She gave him a ghost of a smile. "Maybe it is." Then she twisted her head to look at Jakob. "How is he?"

"The effects of the venom, and the nerve blocker, should have subsided by now." Walt walked over to the bed and sank down next to her. "I would like to examine you."

He'd wanted to do at least a field exam last night since they weren't going to the hospital, but Annalise had refused, allowing him to do little more than a cursory exam, insisting she was fine.

"I'm fine," she persisted.

"You aren't getting another bye, Annalise."

Before she could continue the fight—or ask him what that meant—Jakob rolled toward them, propping himself up on his elbow. "Let Walt look at you."

Annalise sat up gingerly. Walt kicked himself for not demanding to examine her last night, but she'd been emotionally fragile and he hadn't wanted to push.

She tried to take off the T-shirt, but stopped, unable to hide her wince of pain. Walt gently took her hand in his, holding it steady, as he stretched the material until he was able to pull her arm out.

"Shit," he murmured, a similar curse coming from Jakob as well, when their gazes landed on the large black bruise covering one entire shoulder.

"Wine bottle," she said quietly.

At Walt's questioning glance, she elaborated. "He hit me with a wine bottle."

Jakob growled. "He died too quickly."

Walt sighed and shook his head. "Jakob," he started, perfectly aware that he and the Ritter would never see eye to eye when it came to the value of a human life. Jakob saw the world in terms of good and evil, an eye for an eye. Walt, however, had sworn to preserve life—all lives—and the lightness or darkness of the souls within those bodies was immaterial.

Jakob didn't give him a chance to contradict him. "He deserved to suffer more."

The tone in Jakob's voice told Walt he would never be convinced otherwise, so he returned his attention to Annalise.

That was when he saw the bite mark on her neck—and for

the flash of a second, Walt found his own humanity wavering, his anger toward Axel and the pain he'd caused Annalise sparking a desire for payback.

Walt swallowed the foreign feeling down, digging deep for the clinical detachment that allowed him to do his job competently, without emotion getting in the way of the work.

He ran his fingers over the bruise on her shoulder, gently probing. Given the range of motion she'd already displayed, he was fairly certain she hadn't suffered a break, but even so... "I want to get an X-ray of this arm. I don't think it's broken, but there could be a hairline fracture."

She sighed. "Does that have to be today? I really don't want to get out of bed. I just feel..."

"Numb," he said, repeating her earlier assessment.

"And tired. Though I don't know how after last night. I can't remember the last time I slept so soundly. I didn't dream and I didn't roll over."

Walt cupped her face, stroking her cheek with his thumb. "The X-ray can wait until tomorrow. I agree that bed rest is the best thing for you today."

Reaching behind her back, he unfastened her bra, his eyes locked with hers, awaiting a signal from her that this was okay.

She gave him a slight nod and he gently pulled the bra off. There were several fingerprint-sized bruises on her breasts and her nipples looked tender. Axel had been rough with her, brutal even.

"Annalise," he whispered.

"They're only bruises. They'll fade with time."

Walt hoped that was true. While her body would recover within a few days, he worried the mental anguish she suffered would take longer to heal, and he didn't even fool himself into pretending it wouldn't leave a scar.

He continued his exam, lowering his gaze to her side.

There was a small cut, but it was not too deep. He doubted it had even bled much.

When she realized what he was looking at, she explained, "He took me away from the hotel at knifepoint."

"I should have protected you," Jakob said, his expression filled with guilt.

Annalise shook her head quickly. "Don't do that, Jakob. You were hurt. Badly. There was nothing you could do." As she spoke, she rubbed a spot on her head.

Walt followed the movement, running his own hands through her hair, once again probing for bruises, lumps.

"He pulled my hair a few times. My scalp is a little sore. Nothing more."

"What else?" Walt asked. "Where else does it hurt?"

"Just some more bruises on my shins. That's the worst of it," Annalise said. "You arrived before he..." She visibly swallowed, unable to speak the word.

Walt was grateful for that. He'd spent too much time this morning as Jakob and Annalise continued to sleep considering what would have happened if they hadn't arrived when they did. She would have been raped, possibly disfigured. The bastard had been holding a knife, one he wouldn't have hesitated to use if Jakob hadn't reacted without hesitation.

Even so, it had been a close call. Too fucking close.

Jakob had remained silent through most of the exam, but now that Walt was finished, he stirred, sitting up next to her.

Jakob reached for her hand, lifting it gently to kiss the bruises around her wrist, left there from the cuff and the chain.

"Annalise—" he started.

"Please, Jakob. No more guilt. No more blaming yourself for things you had no control over."

Walt reached out, placing his hand over Jakob's, the two of them holding her hand. He'd never felt such an instant or powerful connection to two people, but there was no denying this pull, this desire. And it had less to do with sex—okay, the sexual attraction was definitely there—and more to do with who they were and how they made him feel.

While he'd grown up a triplet, Walt had always been the brother standing just a step or two away from the others, too focused on his career to join in on the more normal aspects of life, like friendship, dating...love.

"He's gone," Annalise whispered, the first sign that the magnitude of what had happened—ended—yesterday was beginning to sink in.

"He's gone," Walt repeated. "He can't hurt you ever again."

"I'm not sure I know how...how to live a normal life," she confessed.

"Me either," Jakob admitted.

"So what I think I'm hearing is that the two of you genuinely believe you were normal at some point?" Walt joked.

Jakob snorted, the uncharacteristic sound capturing Annalise's attention.

"Wait. Was that a laugh?" she teased.

Walt was sorry she'd missed meeting drugged-up Jakob. That guy was a hoot.

Jakob smiled widely, but sadly, he didn't speak, didn't rattle off every thought in his head.

Walt missed the running diatribe and wondered how he could get Jakob to start sharing his thoughts again without having to inject him with another nerve blocker.

Annalise shifted slightly and Walt caught the glimpse of pain. Her shoulder was going to be very tender for a few days. He rose from the bed and rummaged around in his duffel bag until he found the bottle of ibuprofen. Tapping three out into his hand, he went to the bathroom and got a cup of water before returning to the bed.

"Here. Take these. They'll help with the pain." Walt handed her the tablets.

Annalise took them, then her stomach growled loudly.

"You need food," Walt said, reaching for the room service menu he'd spotted earlier on the small desk in the corner of the room. He'd run down for a bag of ice later.

The three of them passed the menu around, called in their order, then settled on the bed, sitting with their backs against the headboard to wait for it to be delivered.

"I still don't even know his name," Annalise said.

"Axel Richen. Age twenty-nine. A software developer," Jakob informed her.

"Did he mention anything about how he knew you?" Walt asked, curious. Apart from the few details she'd given them in regards to her injuries, Annalise hadn't told them anything about the hours she'd spent as the man's captive.

She shook her head. "No. And I couldn't ask him without triggering his anger. His delusion allowed him to genuinely believe we were in a relationship. I didn't do or say anything—well, I tried not to—that would contradict his belief. Asking his name or how we met would have disputed his worldview."

"Now that we have his name, I bet Jakob can figure out where he met you or saw you," Walt said, hoping, for her sake, there would be some kind of closure.

"In the end, it doesn't really matter. He could have seen me on TV, or at a conference, being interviewed..." Her voice trailed off, and her expression turned almost rueful.

Jakob nodded, then looked to Annalise. "Intimacy seeker."

She grinned. "Very impressive, Mr. Bauer." Annalise leaned to bump her good shoulder against Jakob's. "You continue to be my best student."

"Well, that has some kinky potential," Walt said.

"What?" Annalise asked, laughing.

Walt soaked up the sound. Annalise had a great laugh.

He kept smiling as he said, "Jakob nearly drowned in regret yesterday after some pretty powerful drugs."

Walt had certainly captured Annalise's attention.

"What kind of regrets?" she asked.

"Jakob..." Walt said, lifting his hand as if yielding the other man the floor.

"Walt." It was incredible how much warning Jakob could put into his tone with a single word.

Of course, the funny thing was Jakob still didn't understand the power of the triplet. "I believe it had something to do with a kiss. Isn't that right, Jakob? Jakob is definitely hot for teacher."

"Just a kiss?" Annalise asked, turning toward Jakob, catching on quickly.

Damn...Dr. Fischer would have zero trouble when it came to dealing with his siblings and their off-color sense of humor and constant teasing.

And Walt was beginning to think the same of Jakob. If he ever managed to get the stick out of his ass.

Walt bailed out of the conversation, merely answering her question with an eyebrow he cocked in Jakob's direction.

"Yesterday," Jakob began slowly, "when we realized you were gone..."

Walt tried hard to hide his grin. Jakob was talking. His word count rising.

"I...Annalise...I...all I could think about was that I'd never..." He paused just before the best part.

Walt was two seconds away from saying, "Carry on," when Annalise spoke first.

"You never what?" she asked.

"Kissed you," Jakob said, the words more breath than sound. "I want to kiss you."

Annalise smiled. "Then kiss m—"

She didn't have the chance to finish her invitation before Jakob leaned closer and stole the words with his lips on hers.

Annalise's hands found their way to Jakob's chest, her fingers tightening in the material of his shirt.

Walt sat there, spellbound, watching as their lips parted, their tongues touched. Jakob had reached up to hold her face in his large hands, but the grip was soft, tender, cognizant of her bruised face.

Before he could think about his actions, Walt shifted closer, placing a kiss on Annalise's bruised shoulder before adding one to the bite mark on her neck.

Jakob stopped kissing her at her breathy laugh.

"Kissing it all better, Dr. Hayden?" she asked.

Jakob lifted his chin just once, an unspoken directive for Walt to continue. He didn't need to be told twice.

He twisted Annalise toward him and lowered his head to her breasts, placing "healing" kisses to the bruises there as well before stroking his tongue over the firm tip of her nipple.

"Ah," Annalise sighed, her head drifting back, her eyes closing.

"No."

Her eyes flew open, finding Jakob, who said, "Don't close your eyes. Watch us."

Annalise sucked in a shaky breath, then nodded.

Walt hadn't meant to take them from zero to sixty. Hell, he hadn't even meant to step in, part of him still feeling like the outsider here, the interloper.

Annalise and Jakob had been together for years, quietly longing for each other. Now that they'd come clean, now that they were free to explore that longing without fear of danger lurking in the shadows, shouldn't he step away and give them that chance?

Lost in self-doubt, Walt didn't realize he'd stopped until

Jakob's hand landed on his shoulder. "Keep going. *Our* girl, remember?"

Walt had used those words yesterday in the car as they raced to save Annalise. They'd slipped out unbidden, but there was no denying they'd felt right.

And they still felt right, hearing them repeated back to him by Jakob.

"Our girl," Walt whispered, just before he stroked his tongue over her nipple again.

"Oh God," Annalise cried out, one of her hands latching onto the back of his head as he continued to kiss and lick her breasts.

Jakob tugged off his shirt, then shifted, spreading his legs to pull Annalise between them, her back now resting against his bare chest. Jakob cupped her breasts, holding them up to Walt's continued ministrations.

Walt kept his kisses soft, not wanting to hurt her. He startled for just a moment when Jakob released one of her breasts, so that he could run his thumb over Walt's lower lip. Walt captured his thumb and sucked it into his mouth.

"So hot," Annalise breathed.

Jakob pulled his thumb free, then rubbed the wet digit over Annalise's nipple.

"Are you going to watch me fuck Walt, Annalise?" Jakob asked. "Watch me bend him over this bed and take him hard and fast?"

"Yes," Annalise said. "Please."

Jakob sure as shit made up for his silence outside of the bedroom. The man was the master of dirty talk.

"I want you to be sure to concentrate, to pay attention while I take his ass."

"I'll pay attention," she promised.

"It won't be easy, because Walt's going to be between those

sexy legs of yours, sucking on your pretty clit, driving you wild with his fingers and tongue."

"Jesus," Walt murmured, so turned on he couldn't see straight.

Jakob ran one finger over her bruised shoulder, placing a kiss on it as well. "I'm afraid your body isn't ready for more just yet. You need time to heal."

"No. I am ready. I want you. Both of you," Annalise insisted.

Jakob shook his head. "And you'll have us, but not today."

"Jakob—" she started.

"Don't worry. Walt's going to make you come. Going to make sure you're well taken care of, aren't you, Walt?"

Walt didn't bother to reply. Instead, he straightened, pulling his shirt off, ready to put every single one of Jakob's promises into action. He was just reaching for the waistband of Annalise's sweatpants when there was a knock at the door.

"Shit," Walt cursed. "Room service didn't take long."

"Fucking interruptions," Jakob muttered.

Annalise released a shaky laugh. "Guess I should get it. Don't want to traumatize the hotel staff."

Walt looked down and realized he and Jakob were sporting very pronounced hard-ons, their pants tented.

Jakob pulled Annalise's T-shirt back over her head, but didn't bother with her bra. "*Liebling,* stay here. I'll grab the food. We'll eat it in bed."

Annalise curled one leg under her, smoothing out the sheets for their bed picnic, as Walt attempted to adjust his jeans, the denim uncomfortable as hell.

Jakob, ever vigilant, looked through the peephole, then cursed.

"What's wrong?" Annalise asked.

Jakob sighed as he opened the door. He nodded his head

once as a show of respect before stepping back to allow their company in.

Walt frowned as Vadisk entered, followed by a slim woman with long dark hair and piercing eyes. Walt looked at Vadisk, then pointedly at the bed. "I thought your text said we wouldn't see you until tomorrow."

Vadisk gave him a rueful grin. "The admiral wasn't inclined to wait."

Walt glanced back at the woman as Vadisk did the introductions, gesturing to her as he spoke. "This is Nikolett Varda, the admiral of Hungary."

CHAPTER SIXTEEN

Nikolett's brow quirked as she glanced at all of them. Annalise wished she had a bra on. The men, her men, looked a little bit less than respectable at the moment too.

Vadisk, whom she hadn't really paid attention to yesterday, had retreated to stand by the door, taking up a position as guard. A position she was used to Jakob occupying.

She didn't need protection anymore. Jakob could go back to his normal life.

Is that what would happen when Walt left? Jakob would leave too, the emotions between them unsustainable without Walt?

The idea pierced, causing her chest to ache, but there wasn't time to think about that now. Annalise gingerly scooted to the edge of the bed and then stood. Walt put an arm around her waist, supporting her. His lips dropped to her ear.

"Is an admiral...the admiral?...showing up a good thing or a bad thing?"

That made Annalise smile, as she thought he'd intended.

"Admiral Varda." Jakob inclined his head, his normal quiet reticence drawn around him once more. Looking at him now, there was no hint of the man who'd been planning a sex scene that included him fucking Walt's ass while Walt licked her clit.

Annalise cleared her throat, forcing her attention back to the moment and away from what might have been. "Admiral," she murmured, inclining her head.

Admiral Varda wore an air of command along with her long wool coat, belted at the waist. Though her hair was down, it was neatly combed, each strand in place.

"Ritter Bauer, Dr. Fischer." She nodded to each of them in turn. "Dr. Hayden," she said with a slight emphasis on his name.

"Uh, hello, Admiral," Walt said uncertainly.

Nikolett's gaze slid back to Annalise, then softened. "Please, sit down."

Annalise hesitated, then nodded. Instead of sitting on the bed, she and Walt made their way to the suite's small sitting area. She and Walt took the couch, while Jakob stood beside them, his hands in parade rest at his back.

Nikolett sat in one of the armchairs, unbelted her jacket, and then leaned forward, elbows on knees, hands clasped. "I won't ask if you're all right, since that would be a stupid question. Instead, I'll ask what you need. A private medical facility? Crisis counseling?"

Annalise's throat tightened and tears threatened. Her men had been planning to help her by having wild, kinky sex with and near her. It wasn't a bad plan, but there was something about another woman offering to get her to counseling that made her feel safe and cared for in an entirely different way.

"No, but thank you," she murmured.

"You'll see someone? Talk to someone?" Nikolett asked, still intent and focused.

Annalise nodded. "I will." She'd resisted doing so before now. First, because she thought she could handle it, then because the guilt she'd felt over what happened to her sister made her feel like she hadn't deserved the help or understanding a counselor would provide. As a psychologist, she knew exactly how stupid that was, but she hadn't been able to stop herself from feeling that way.

This time, she would get therapy.

"Actually," Walt said. "Do you have access to an X-ray?"

Nikolett's brow rose. "I do."

"She either needs her upper arm X-rayed here, if you have a portable one, or we're going to a hospital."

"She might have a broken bone and you were having sex with her?" Nikolett's brows rose higher, and her gaze turned accusatory as she looked from Walt to Jakob to the bed and back.

"They were comforting me, Admiral." Annalise was suppressing a slightly insane urge to start giggling.

"Uh-huh..." Nikolett twisted to look back at Vadisk, who stared down at her, then shrugged one shoulder. "Call Nyx about the X-ray," she said.

Vadisk retreated a few steps and then took out his phone.

"Thank you," Walt said.

"You're welcome, Dr. Hayden." Nikolett scooted forward a little on her chair. She was intense, her focus, when it landed, absolute. "Now, please tell me why you're here, and why we're covering up a murder."

Annalise opened her mouth, closed it, and looked at Jakob. He twisted so Nikolett couldn't see his face, then grimaced ever so slightly. There was a key piece of "why" information they couldn't answer—because Eric had forbidden them to.

"No lies, please." There was a warning in Nikolett's voice.

Annalise took a breath and looked at the other woman.

Someone knocked on the door.

Nikolett raised her gaze to the ceiling in exasperation as Jakob and Vadisk, who had finished his call, went to first check, and then welcome, room service. Food was placed on the coffee table, a coffee station set up on the sideboard, and everyone took a few minutes to get what they needed. Nikolett and Vadisk both got cups of coffee.

At Walt's urging, Annalise took more pain pills along with a bite of her quintessentially Polish breakfast—a slice of bread topped with kielbasa and scrambled eggs.

Nikolett didn't pressure any of them to start talking, but she also didn't make the silence easy. Her focused regard was a sort of pressure that made her seem far bigger than her small frame. She was a presence, her authority and power quietly radiating from her.

Annalise ate until she knew what she was going to say, then set down the rest of her breakfast and wiped her fingers.

"We came to Krakow to talk to the medical examiner. I believe an unsolved murder here may be linked to other unsolved crimes from around Europe."

Nikolett's back straightened. "A serial killer?" She twisted to look at Vadisk. "I thought you said this was about a stalker." She swiveled back to Annalise. "You were kidnapped by a serial killer?"

"No, I was kidnapped by a stalker. My stalker. In Frankfurt, and then Heidelberg, I had taken extreme measures to protect myself. Jakob came to Krakow because he is with me anytime I go anywhere or see anyone new."

Nikolett eyed Jakob. "Extreme measures, indeed."

"My coming here, breaking routine...my stalker—" Annalise stopped, forced herself to use his name. He was no longer an unnamed, shadowy threat. He was just a very sick person. Well...had been. "Axel followed me here, and took advantage of the opportunity."

"The stalker is not linked to the serial killer?" Nikolett asked doubtfully.

"No," Annalise said firmly.

"We had some time on our hands, so we just thought we'd take on all of Europe's bad guys," Walt said cheerfully.

Nikolett snorted out a surprised laugh, covering her mouth with her hand. "You lead a dangerous life, Dr. Fischer."

"I assure you I don't mean to," Annalise said.

"Let us approach this logically." Nikolett set down her coffee cup with a click. "Walk me through what happened yesterday."

Annalise opened her mouth, but stopped, suddenly overwhelmed.

Walt, still seated beside her, put his hand on her thigh and squeezed gently. Then he began the story, starting with the fire alarm, and ending with Jakob's agony and Vadisk's arrival. By the time he was done, she was ready, backing up to describe what had happened to her once she'd been pulled from the crowd. She hadn't really spoken about what had happened to her in that caravan. She hadn't needed to, or wanted to, because the bruises and marks told the story. Yet, once she started talking, and as long as she kept her attention on Nikolett, she was able to disclose everything.

Her calculated and unethical manipulation.

The raw fear and rage she'd had to keep at bay.

The first fruitless escape attempt.

How she'd played along with, and into, his delusions.

How she'd been willingly and intentionally submissive in a bid to buy time.

What it had felt like when she hadn't been able to pretend, those moments when he'd hurt her.

The fear and horror of the bomb going off, not knowing if they'd survived.

Eventually she ran out of words, and when she did, she felt both empty and lighter, as if by talking she had expunged some of the negative emotions. Really great sex could probably have done that too, if they hadn't been interrupted.

"Thank you for telling me," Nikolett murmured. "And I'm so sorry for what you suffered."

Annalise nodded, her throat a little tight.

"I wish I could leave it at that..." Nikolett's face twisted with regret, but only for a moment. "However, since I now understand the dead body and bomb scene, I need to know more about this serial killer. And," she looked at Jakob, "why I wasn't informed of the possibility of there being a killer in *my* territory."

Annalise winced. She'd never been in a position to play inter-territory politics, but she knew that what they'd done was a major breach of etiquette, if not officially against any rules.

Wishing she had case files to hand out the way she'd had at the restaurant with the fleet admiral, Annalise started to explain. She carefully omitted where she'd gotten the original list of potential victims, and why *she* was working on this case when active profiling was no longer what she did.

Given the way Nikolett exchanged the occasional glance with Vadisk, the vagueness and omissions didn't go unnoticed.

When she was done walking them through the profile, Nikolett stood. "Very well. I have further questions, but rather than ask them now, I'll save it until the meeting."

"What meeting?" Walt asked.

"The meeting you're going to attend in Budapest." Nikolett looked at each of them in turn. "You're coming with me, back to Hungary headquarters."

. . .

JAKOB KEPT his arm on the small of Annalise's back as they entered the modest three-story building. Admiral Varda's headquarters were tucked away on a side street in the heart of Budapest, in a quaint neighborhood that boasted cafes, bakeries, flower shops, and boutiques.

There was no sign on the building and nothing of interest to draw the attention of passersby.

Nikolett pointed at Vadisk. "Please take them up. I will find Dimitri and have him join us in Nyx's office."

Vadisk led the way, gesturing to a set of stairs. "The admiral and vice admiral have offices on the second floor."

Vadisk had flown the three of them and Nikolett to Budapest in his helicopter. Mercifully, prior to the trip, Nikolett had given them enough time to shower, change into clean clothing, and pack.

Walt carried Annalise's bag containing her printouts of the case files. Their luggage was apparently on its way to a nearby hotel, where they would be staying while they were guests of the Hungary admiral.

Jakob figured they might be "guests" until the admiral was satisfied. That could take a while if they couldn't find a way to answer Nikolett's questions without betraying Eric.

None of them spoke as Vadisk led them up the stairs, then down a wide corridor. They passed several open doors, revealing a couple of conference rooms and what looked like a break room, complete with a refrigerator, microwave, coffeepot, table, and chairs. Vadisk paused outside that room.

"Would you like some coffee or perhaps a bottle of water?" he asked.

"No, thank you," Annalise said as Jakob and Walt shook their heads.

Vadisk continued down the hall, stopping in front of a closed door. He knocked.

"*Belép*," a female voice called out.

They all stepped inside and Jakob took in the slight blonde woman sitting behind the desk. The office was large, with three big windows that let in lots of natural light. In addition to the desk, there was a rectangular table with six leather chairs off to one side and a huge, fully loaded bookshelf against one wall.

The woman rose and regarded them coolly. "Hello, I'm Nyx Kata." Jakob noticed the long white scar that bisected her cheek from eye to jaw. He'd heard the story about how she'd nearly lost her life at the hands of a brutal killer, Petro's *other* pet serial killer, Ciril.

Vadisk introduced each of them in turn. "Vice Admiral, allow me to present Dr. Annalise Fischer, Ritter Jakob Bauer, and Dr. Walt Hayden from America."

"I've had the pleasure of meeting your sister, Sylvia," Nyx said to Walt. "Her husband Hugo and I are close friends. I'm quite a fan of her poetry."

Walt grinned. "Sylvia is the best of us and incredibly talented," he said sincerely, though Jakob found it hard to believe anyone could be better than Walt.

Before they could say more, the door opened and Nikolett entered with two men, the first of whom held his hand out to Annalise.

"I'm happy to make your acquaintance, Dr. Fischer. It is good to see you safe and sound after your ordeal yesterday."

Jakob recognized the man's voice from the car phone. "Dimitri. I want to thank you for your help."

"Dimitri," Walt said, shaking the man's hand. "Nice to have a face to go with the voice."

Annalise looked at Jakob curiously, so he explained. "Dimitri was instrumental in helping us find you."

She smiled at Dimitri. "Thank you, truly, and please, call me Annalise."

Dimitri nodded his head.

"And this," Nyx said, pointing to the other man, "is my husband, Grigoris Violaris."

Grigoris shook Jakob's and Walt's hands.

Jakob cleared his throat and forced himself to say something rather than make do with the silent nod. "It is good to meet you, *chorbajis*."

Grigoris smiled. "I'm neither janissary nor *chorbajis* any longer, but thank you."

The upheaval in Hungary had affected not only that territory, but others. When Nikolett pulled Nyx in to be vice admiral, Grigoris had come with her, relinquishing his position as leader of the janissaries—the Ottoman territory knights. Security minister Dimitri and his trinity, which included the former leader of the Spartan Guard, Mateo, had moved here from England. Petro had left Hungary in shambles, and Nikolett had pulled in the best to help her revive the territory.

"You need medical attention," Nyx said, turning to Annalise and Walt. "I've had a portable X-ray machine set up in one of the conference rooms down the hall."

"Thank you," Walt said. "I'm fairly sure she's okay, but based on the bruise, there could be a stable closed fracture to the humerus." He gestured to her arm, which was in a simple sling they'd bought at a pharmacy on the way to the helicopter.

Nyx studied Annalise's face. "Are you in pain?"

"Oh no," Annalise interjected. "I'm fine. Walt has given me medicine for the pain and I'm certain nothing is broken."

Nikolett gestured toward the long table. "Good, because I'd like to begin. However, if you find yourself in pain, we can get you enough drugs to allow you to function."

Grigoris shook his head and walked up to his wife, placing a hand on her back. Being in the same room as Nyx and Nikolett was giving Jakob the twitchy feeling he got when in the presence of powerful, dangerous people. Vadisk and Dimitri weren't exactly non-threatening, but they were more of a physical threat.

Now, as in the hotel, Vadisk took his place beside the closed door to Nyx's office, while the rest of them claimed chairs at the table. Jakob didn't like having Vadisk doing a job he would prefer to be doing himself, but he had no authority here. Another thing that was making him twitchy.

Nikolett took a spot at the head of the table, the other end occupied by Nyx. Dimitri and Jakob sat together on one side, facing Annalise and Walt. Grigoris had rolled Nyx's office chair over to sit next to and slightly behind his wife.

"Walt, can you set up my laptop?" Annalise asked.

"Do we need a whiteboard?" Nyx asked, sounding almost hopeful.

Annalise blinked. "No, but do you have a projector?"

For the first time, Nyx grinned. "I like visual aids."

Grigoris helped Nyx set up a small projector on the table-top, then lifted a painting down off the wall to give them a wide white surface.

Annalise was working one-handed—Walt grumbled at her each time she tried to slide her arm out of the sling—so Jakob got up and acted as her assistant. He knew how she worked, what she would need. In a way, he could imagine he was helping her prepare for a lecture.

Finally, Annalise tapped the trackpad and projected on the wall was a window showing two files. One titled "Decapitation," the other "Dismemberment."

Grigoris murmured something in Greek, Dimitri stiffened, and Nikolett sat forward, all their attention on the screen.

Nyx had gone perfectly still.

Annalise began. "I was asked to consult on the profile of a possible serial killer."

"By whom?" Nyx turned dark eyes to Annalise.

Jakob tensed, the feeling that he was amongst dangerous people increasing. Annalise ignored the question.

"As you can see, the potential uniting factor is that the bodies are not left intact. From that broad categorization, there are two subcategories, each with possible different pathologies."

Annalise clicked open the decapitation file, and a list of subfolders appeared, each bearing the name of a victim. Annalise clicked on the folder labeled Josephine O'Connor.

Nyx jumped to her feet, her chair toppling backwards. Her face was stark. Pale. "Josephine."

Annalise looked over. "Oh, I'm sorry, I should have warned you that you might know of some of the victims."

"Know of?" Nyx snarled.

Grigoris reached over and closed the laptop.

The projection cut off.

"We don't...didn't...just know her," Grigoris said softly. "She was our wife."

CHAPTER SEVENTEEN

Annalise stared at Grigoris and Nyx, utterly horrified by what she'd just done. A wave of nausea passed through her.

Josephine had been their third? Nothing in the file the fleet admiral had given her mentioned that Josephine was married. She'd thought, given his unyielding determination to bring the killer to justice, that perhaps she and the fleet admiral had been lovers.

Nyx closed her eyes for a moment, then put a hand on her husband's arm. When she opened her eyes, she stared straight ahead and sank down into her chair, which Grigoris had righted.

"She would have been our third," Nyx said softly. "If she hadn't been murdered. But most importantly, she was my friend. I felt her death keenly."

Nikolett was looking at Nyx with such compassion that it softened the admiral, who struck Annalise as the sort to take no prisoners. Of course, at the same time, Nikolett was the kind of woman who wouldn't have broken, wouldn't have gone into hiding from a stalker. She would have stood her ground in the middle of the street and dared the villain to come for her, especially if, by doing so, she was protecting someone else.

Annalise glanced at Walt, then Jakob. They each smiled back at her, and she tried to let their kindness ease her guilt over upsetting Nyx.

"I'm so sorry," Annalise said quietly. "I didn't know."

"Please continue," Nyx said.

Annalise glanced at Grigoris, unwilling to traumatize Nyx any further. He was looking at his wife, but after only a moment, he nodded.

Annalise opened the lid of her laptop, her mental notes already reshuffled to approach this from a different direction.

"I am attempting to identify murders that may have been committed by the same person who killed Josephine."

"Petro murdered her," Nyx said softly. "Even if he didn't actually cut off her head, he was the killer."

Annalise nodded, but she was going to approach this as if she were giving a profile to a roomful of officers, all of whom usually had their own theories or assumptions. She had learned during briefings such as this that she had to ignore their comments, keep calm, and speak with authority.

"Our primary victim's head is the only part of the body recovered to date." She tapped her computer, bringing up Josephine's autopsy report. "I'd like to warn you all there will be graphic photos of bodies in this briefing. If you'd like me to warn you before showing one of those photos so you can look away, please let me know now."

She waited, but no one said anything.

Annalise nodded and pulled up the screen showing the original files Eric had given her. "We started with these lists. As you can see, the victims were divided broadly into those who were just decapitated, and those who were dismembered, either with or without decapitation."

"What about that list?" Nikolett pointed. "Cross-referenced with Masters' Admiralty. Who is in that file?"

"That isn't important," Annalise said.

"How could that not be important? Petro is, was, the mastermind." Nyx sounded cold, angry.

"And we know he mentored other killers," Dimitri added.

"Thank you for bringing that up. Let us start with the possible partnership between our unsub and Petro.

"I believe their relationship was not a full partnership. Not in the way of the González sisters, the Hillside Stranglers, or Wolfgang Abel and Marco Furlan. Nor, I think, is the unsub we're looking for the submissive partner, but I will explain my reasoning for that further in a moment.

"What we have here is a partnership where, I believe, *both* parties considered themselves the dominant partner." Everyone, including Jakob and Walt, looked at her. This was news to them too, because it was part of the profile she hadn't been able to give at the coffee shop meeting with Eric before they were interrupted.

"Petro provided resources, and in at least one instance that we know of, identified a victim, using our unknown subject as a weapon." She very carefully didn't mention Josephine's name again.

"Why would he think he's in charge if Petro was telling him who to kill?" Walt asked.

"Have you ever worked in a hospital, a large one?" Annalise asked, deciding it might be easier to explain this by way of analogy.

"Well, during my residency, yes. And I was in the military, so if you want to talk about large organizations..."

"And did you have people above you in rank, or with more

authority than you, but who were not doctors? They knew less about how to treat a patient, about medicine and taking care of another person, yet had some authority over how you did your job."

Jakob's brows rose and he sat back, a sort of faraway expression in his eyes. He'd figured out not only where this conversation was going, but the implications.

Her best student.

Walt nodded. "Okay, Dr. Fischer, I see what you mean."

"Thank you, Dr. Hayden." She didn't wink. It wouldn't have been appropriate, but she wanted to. "In the examples Dr. Hayden provided, he is the medical authority, and yet there are people of authority to whom he reports. Both parties have authority, but their authority is inherently different."

Nikolett nodded. "So the killer saw Petro as an unskilled supervisor."

"That is what I believe. A submissive partner would not have been able to carry out the murders of Josephine and Alicja on their own. Oftentimes in killing partnerships, it is the submissive partner who is forced to commit the worst aspects of the crime, but they are in the direct sphere of influence of the dominant partner—either living with them or maintaining regular contact."

"Petro could have done that by phone."

Annalise shook her head. "Possible, but highly unlikely. I believe the unsub saw Petro as a patron. Someone who appreciated their work and therefore was willing to provide resources and support."

"Ciril, one of the other serial killers, referred to Petro as his 'friend'," Nyx said.

"That supports my theory that Petro's relationships with the killers were not the same as say that of U.S. killers McClintic and Rafferty."

Several people frowned, and Nikolett reached for her phone.

Annalise cleared her throat. "For your own sakes, I would suggest not doing a search. They murdered a child."

Everyone looked grim.

"So Petro was a patron to this killer. We know Petro appreciated what this person, man, did." Grigoris sounded harsh, and he made the word "appreciated" into something disgusting with his tone.

"Patron is, based on what information we have, an informed hypothesis, the most appropriate term," Annalise agreed.

"How did you figure out which of the names on that list were killed by the same man who murdered Josephine?" Nikolett gestured at the wall where Alicja's autopsy report and the list of files were projected.

Annalise talked them through the difference between defensive and offensive dismemberment—killing and then dismembering, or death as an unintended consequence of the dismemberment, which was the focus of the pathology. She went on, now with Walt's help, to explain the skill with which the cuts on Alicja had been made. She didn't talk about Josephine directly, only saying that the decapitation of the Polish woman was nearly identical to the decapitation of the primary victim.

She went over Alicja's antemortem injuries, her voice compassionate but firm as she talked about the rape, the lack of DNA, and how the case had gone cold. The way Alicja's body had been disposed of, the head carefully packed in a small blanket chest, other parts loose in dumpsters.

She explained the psychology behind a possible medical-invention-based killer, like the Cleveland Torso Murderer, and why they had dismissed it given the geographic diversity. She showed them the file of the victim in Belgium, explained that was the second place they'd considered going, but had decided to go to Krakow since almost all of Alicja Lewandowski's body had been found.

Finally she told them what the medical examiner had revealed—the blanket chest, his agreement with Walt's assessment of the skill, the floral scent that may have been the victim's perfume.

Everyone but Nikolett was nodding.

Grigoris and Dimitri had both been taking notes. Dimitri spoke first. "What do you know about how they were taken?"

Annalise flipped over to the very last known image of Alicja. A still from a store's security camera footage. "She was taken while walking down a city street. A route that was part of her normal routine."

Grigoris grunted. "He'd watched her."

"Yes, I believe the unsub was stalking her for quite some time. Enough to not only know her routine, but to have identified physical locations along her regular walking commute where there were no cameras."

"Drove up in a van and grabbed her," Dimitri said.

Annalise shook her head. "No van is visible on any of the tapes."

"Then how is he getting his victims?" Dimitri asked. "How did he physically move them somewhere where he could kill them?"

Annalise had been thinking about the case, the profile, on and off for days, even with all the other things that happened. She'd come to some possible conclusions that were both alarming and interesting. "I believe the victims are going willingly with the unsub."

Grigoris frowned. "You mean he's using a gun, knife?"

Annalise briefly froze, remembering the feel of the knife grazing her skin. Nyx, too, looked stiff.

"No," Annalise said slowly. "I think the unsub has more skill, and more subtlety, than that."

Nyx shook her head. "I would not follow a strange man no matter what he said. And Josephine, she was kind, generous, but not stupid."

Annalise raised one eyebrow, took her time looking around the table. "Who said the unsub was a man?"

There was a collective shocked inhale.

Nyx was the first to recover. "You said Alicja was raped."

"Which doesn't actually require a biological penis," Annalise pointed out. When no one spoke, she went on. "Using a blanket chest, plus the care that was put into wrapping her head...these are both more typically female behaviors, as, anthropologically speaking, it is traditionally women who care for bodies, wash them, tend them."

Nyx nodded in agreement.

"The killer is a woman." Dimitri sat back, clearly thinking. "Nyx, Admiral, if a woman approached you on the street and asked you for help, would you go with her?"

"Yes," they answered in unison.

"Don't," Grigoris said.

While Dimitri grunted and added, "Not anymore you don't."

Annalise took a moment, considered her next comment before turning toward Nyx. "Even Josephine's head...it was deliberately placed in order to shock and horrify, correct?"

Nyx's face was smooth and calm, but frozen, a marble bust, the only flaw the line down her cheek. Grigoris just looked grim.

"But if shock and horror were the end goal, why the basket?" Annalise asked.

"Putting someone's head in a basket is horrifying," Grigoris pointed out. "Or maybe it was about forcing someone to look in the basket."

Annalise raised a brow. "Wouldn't a decapitated head sitting on the table, or placed on some sort of spike, be more horrifying?"

Nyx closed her eyes. "Yes. *Displaying* the head would make it more like the aftermath of an execution."

"Let us say that Petro asked the unsub to place Josephine's head in the library where it would be seen. The killer...she compromised by putting it in a basket." It was getting harder and harder for Annalise to maintain her objectivity. She could sense Nyx's grief, but the vice admiral was made of sterner stuff. Though the conversation was no doubt painful, she remained in the room, clearly determined to listen and understand.

"Where we would find it, but no one would see Josephine unless they looked inside," Nyx murmured.

Annalise nodded, then gave everyone—Nyx and Grigoris most of all—a few moments to process before clearing her throat. "Another point we haven't discussed in detail yet—"

"There is more? *Ebat'*," Dimitri spat.

"—is that our three victims, Josephine, Alicja, and the woman from Belgium, are all from places that are either English speaking, or where the majority of the population is bilingual, with English as the second language."

"So we start there," Grigoris said.

"There is more work to be done analyzing the last video we have of Alicja," Jakob said. Then, to Annalise's delight, he continued talking. "It is possible the killer is on that tape, though their meeting isn't, as nowhere on the footage does Alicja stop to talk to anyone."

"Were you checking for women?" Nikolett asked.

Jakob nodded, but slowly. "I need to check again."

"We," Nikolett said firmly. "Not just you, Ritter."

"And Josephine?" Nyx asked.

Annalise took over once more. "According to the case file, she was with her brother and left to get dinner. She was going to a restaurant she frequented, so though that was not something she did every day at that time, it was a somewhat predictable activity."

Dimitri shook his head. "There is too much information in play. Simplify it, please."

Jakob glanced at Annalise, his lips tipping up in a small smile. "Make it actionable."

Annalise squared her shoulders, taking a moment to glance around the room.

It was time to give the profile.

"The unsub is most likely a woman between the ages of twenty-five and forty-five. She is a native English speaker, though is bilingual and well-traveled enough that she doesn't stand out by the fact that she only speaks English. She appears non-threatening. This means, most likely, she does not have any visible tattoos or piercings beyond her ears. She also would not be taller than average, and may even be on the shorter end of the female height spectrum.

"She has either studied or worked in a medical setting, but does not have a full-time, steady job in that field. She may currently have a job that involves either butchering animals, or something to do with hunting, but that is not where she learned how to dismember. Her knowledge of human anatomy shows a skill that indicates training and practice. We should look not just at doctors and nurses, but medical examiners, possibly morticians or those who might have had access to human cadavers to practice on.

"The unsub will rely on the compassion and trust of her

victims. She approaches them by asking for some sort of help that requires the victims to either walk with her or direct her. This action diverts them from their previous course or path and brings them into a place where she is able to incapacitate them, most likely using something with an instantaneous effect, such as a stun gun.

"It is unlikely that the investigators of our victims' disappearances had contact with her, and in contrast to many killers, she may move on to another place, another victim, relatively quickly. She is organized, with logical, careful pre- and post-behaviors. The crime scenes, if they were found, would most likely be not just cleaned as a countermeasure, but tidy."

Annalise stopped there, looking around the table.

Almost as one, Dimitri, Grigoris, and Jakob all leaned in, Dimitri and Grigoris peppering her with questions. Annalise took what paper copies she had of photos and reports and passed them out. They divided up the task of reviewing footage, focusing on other female pedestrians. Notes and plans were made, digital files copied, and...

And the admiral of Hungary was frowning, and had been for quite some time.

"Question, Admiral?" Annalise asked.

"You no longer work for the German police, correct?" Nikolett asked.

Uh-oh.

"That's correct. I'm a professor at Heidelberg University. I left my position due to the issue with my stalker." She hoped that would divert attention, but given that no one seemed surprised, she guessed Dimitri or Nikolett had briefed the others about what had happened yesterday.

Nikolett raised one brow. "Then why are you looking into these killings? If our killer is crossing borders, Interpol should be handling the investigation."

Shit.

Annalise smiled to hide her pounding heart. "You're right, and though I'm no longer working directly for the police, I have consulted with Interpol in the past. I've also engaged in research on various abnormal psychology topics." Maybe they would assume she'd figured all this out as research. She didn't want to outright lie.

Nikolett's brow rose higher. "You weren't hired by the admiral of England to consult on this."

"No, you're correct." Annalise looked at Jakob, wondering if things were about to go very bad. If the admiral thought she, Jakob, and Walt were lying in order to hide something, there would be consequences.

"Then why are you looking into this?" Nikolett demanded.

"Josephine deserves justice," Annalise said, hoping that would end the conversation.

"You care enough about Josephine to try to find her killer, but you didn't know her well enough to have been told that she was placed in a trinity, posthumously, with Nyx and Grigoris?"

Nikolett wasn't going to let this go. Annalise settled for smiling vaguely.

"And those lists of names, the files...you didn't get those yourself. Not without help from someone at Interpol, someone who had access. And I just checked," she held up her phone, "there's no record of you requesting these files from Interpol."

"I have other resources," Annalise murmured, hoping Nikolett couldn't hear how loudly her heart was pounding.

"I'm sure you do. But not enough to have compiled all this without having to tell someone what you were doing. And so far, no one I've messaged had any idea a psychologist from Germany was looking into a potential serial killer. Not Rome, England, certainly not here in Hungary."

Dimitri stiffened. "Annalise is the killer."

The room exploded, nearly everyone coming up out of their chairs. Walt yanked Annalise back across the room away from the others, while Jakob stepped around the table, coming between her and Dimitri, who was now holding a gun that hadn't been there the moment before.

Demands were flying—Dimitri demanding Jakob step aside. Jakob demanding Dimitri drop the gun. Grigoris demanding that Nikolett and Nyx—who were still seated—get out of the way, and when his wife didn't move in time, Grigoris dragged Nyx, chair and all, away from the table. Vadisk had moved to the admiral, putting his hands on the back of her chair, as if planning to copy Grigoris and haul both her and the chair out if needed.

Annalise wanted to laugh. The situation would be funny if it wasn't so ridiculous. If she hadn't just been beaten and terrorized by her stalker yesterday, she might have even been scared. But that emotion appeared to be dormant at the moment.

"Enough." Nikolett stood, her voice ringing with authority. "Dimitri, I don't think she's the killer."

He hesitated. "Admiral, if she's not the killer—"

"Where did she get all the files and who told her to investigate?" Nikolett stepped closer, so close that Jakob wasn't between them anymore. Annalise felt the weight of the other woman's attention, her utter focus and resolve. She was a force of nature, the kind of woman who would have ridden at the front of her army in custom-made chain mail rather than stay safe in the castle.

And Annalise couldn't answer her question. Eric had forbidden it.

"I took it on as a project because I am thinking about leaving academia and returning to law enforcement." That statement was half-lie and half-truth. Because on the helicopter ride here, to keep herself from dwelling on what had happened to her, she *had* been thinking about going back to the *Kripo*.

"Please do not lie to me. Who gave you this information, the files? Why are you investigating?" Nikolett was relentless.

Annalise opened her mouth, but nothing came out. She grabbed the back of Jakob's shirt, scrunching the fabric in her fist. She'd run out of half-truths and deflections.

"Ritter," Nikolett snapped. "Tell me the truth."

Jakob did silence much more calmly than Annalise. He was composed and resolute as he quietly stared down the admiral.

"I want to believe your intentions are good, but there are too many secrets within our society, and those secrets have left people dead." Nikolett looked grim.

Enough was enough. "If I could tell you, I would, Admiral," Annalise said with a resigned sigh. This answer was the truth, but the sort of statement that only led to more questions, which was why she'd avoided saying it before now.

"And if I could ignore what you're doing, if I could afford not to question it, I would." Nikolett stepped back. "Dimitri, take them into custody."

"Sweet baby Jesus, y'all are too dramatic." Walt, who'd had his hands on her hips, moved, pulling Annalise back another step and then putting himself between her, Jakob, and the rest of the room.

"Dramatic?" Nyx murmured.

"Maybe he's the killer," Dimitri muttered with the paranoid suspicion that probably made him an excellent security minister.

"No," Walt said. "I'm not the killer, and neither is she. They can't tell you because they were literally forbidden by someone higher ranking than you." He looked at Nikolett.

The admiral exhaled slowly. "I knew it."

"Wait...you mean...?" Grigoris looked at Walt.

Walt nodded. "The fleet admiral gave Annalise the case. He gave her the files, brought me along to be her medical expert, and forbade her and Jakob from telling anyone anything."

"The fleet admiral," Nikolett murmured. Her sudden smile was both predatory and grim. "Eric is back."

CHAPTER EIGHTEEN

J akob, Walt, and Annalise stepped into the hotel suite without speaking. Annalise kicked off her shoes before dropping heavily onto a chaise lounge, while Walt walked over to the bar. Jakob remained by the door, out of habit more than necessity.

After all, Nikolett had sent two knights to accompany them to the hotel, and he knew they would stand sentry outside the door of this suite until the one thing they'd failed to resolve in today's meeting was...well...resolved. Though God only knew how they'd accomplish that. Because what Nikolett wanted was Eric.

Looking around, Jakob had to admit to himself there were worse places to be. At least Nikolett had gotten them a suite to share, rather than forcing them to stay in their own rooms. And she had spared no expense in setting them up in what was basically their prison cell for the foreseeable future.

Nikolett hadn't been pleased with their answers to her questions about Eric's whereabouts. Probably because they'd had no answers. So she'd all but insisted they remain in

Budapest. Jakob imagined she was on the phone with his and Annalise's admiral, Dolph Eburhardt, at this very moment—the two admirals trying to figure out how to extract information he and Annalise didn't possess, and even if they did, the fleet admiral's gag order took precedence.

No one had seemed to believe that Walt had told them everything he knew, despite the fact that Walt *had* told them everything, from Eric showing up in Libya to the unknown people who'd been in the restaurant in Frankfurt.

"Nice digs," Walt said, too cheerfully for the situation, as he lifted a bottle of red wine from the bar. "Wine?" he offered.

Annalise nodded, exhaustion rife in her tone as she said, "God, yes."

Walt chuckled. "Should I bother with a glass or do you want to just chug it straight from the bottle?"

Annalise laughed softly. "You decide."

Jakob wasn't sure how the American always managed to lighten the heaviest of loads. He admired the other man's sense of humor, wishing it was as easy for him to laugh things off, make a joke to break the tension.

When he was much younger, he'd been quite the clown—in his family and in school. But his silliness wasn't appreciated in either place. While his Oma was amused, his father—a staunch military man and strict disciplinarian—had viewed Jakob's humor as something that needed to be silenced...and as such, he hadn't spared the rod.

That same "be seen, not heard" viewpoint had also been shared by the instructors at the boarding school he'd been sent to when he was ten years old. Jakob figured there were just so many times a child could be told to "be quiet" before the lesson stuck.

And considering the number of times his father had punctuated that request with a belt, and his teachers with a ruler, Jakob learned it very well.

Walt handed Annalise her glass of wine and Jakob noted the way she reached for it with her uninjured arm. After their meeting, Walt had X-rayed Annalise's shoulder. Fortunately, as she'd suspected, she had suffered no broken or fractured bones, and while the bruise was deep, Walt assured her it would heal completely within a week or so.

"How about you, Jakob? Wine?" Walt asked again.

"I..." Jakob glanced toward the closed door, his action not lost on Walt.

"At ease, Ritter Bauer. You're not on guard duty anymore," Walt said, pouring two more glasses of wine before handing one to Jakob. "Our prison guards will keep the bad guys out, and us good guys in."

"Old habits," he murmured.

Annalise gave him a sad smile. "I think it's going to take both of us some time to become accustomed to the new—old?—normal. He's not out there watching or waiting anymore."

Annalise had made a similar comment after they'd woken up this morning.

Axel was gone, the danger gone.

Their reason to be together...gone?

"I keep wanting to call Adele, to tell her he's dead, but...I don't think..." Annalise swallowed heavily.

Jakob gave her a sad smile. Adele had completely cut her twin sister out of her life and every attempt that Annalise had made to mend the rift between them since the attack had been met with outright derision and anger. Eventually, Annalise had stopped trying because she believed she was only hurting her sister more. Adele couldn't look at Annalise without remembering, so Annalise removed herself from her life in hopes it would help her sister move on.

"Drink your wine," Walt said, joining Annalise, lifting her feet to his lap as he claimed the end of the chaise. "Both of you. Actually, finish those first glasses now, so we can go ahead and get our buzzes going."

And just like that, Annalise laughed, Jakob grinned, and once again, Walt had managed to break the tension, to pull them out of their heads and into the moment.

"Are you trying to get us drunk, Dr. Hayden?" Annalise asked, though Jakob didn't miss the big gulp of wine she'd taken before her question.

Walt quirked an eyebrow, his face pure mischief. "Absolutely. And then I fully intend to take advantage of both of you. With any luck, the wine will loosen Jakob's tongue and we can get him to serenade us in bed with some more of that dirty talk of his. God, I love a kinky bastard."

Jakob liked the way Walt said his name, with a slight American accent. He'd been named after his paternal grandfather. He'd never met his Opa—he'd died before Jakob was born—but from his Oma's stories of him, he knew his Opa had been a prominent man in their city, a judge and a politician. The name had always felt too big for him.

However, hearing it from Walt didn't feel ridiculous at all. It felt right.

Suddenly, this Jakob—Walt's Jakob—felt like the sort of man who went to a football match with his friends, who drank a pint of Krombacher in the pub, who laughed and joked and fell in love easily. He wasn't the kind of man who stood by the door all night, silently pining for a woman he knew was too good for him, but still wanted.

"I like the way you say my name." Jakob inwardly cringed when he realized how weird that probably sounded, but he found it harder and harder to conceal his thoughts from them.

No. It wasn't hard. He could do it if he wanted to.

Walt tilted his head. "Am I saying it wrong?"

Jakob shook his head. "No. Just sort of American. Makes me feel less like my Opa's namesake and more like my own man."

"You've got a cool name," Walt said. "Guess you could figure out I'm Walter, but no one except my mama called me that. And only when I'd pissed her off but good."

"But good?" Annalise asked with a giggle. Jakob laughed as well, enjoying the playful way Walt liked to deepen his American—Southern, he called it—accent to amuse them.

Walt gave him a cocky grin. "I have to admit I was hoping you'd pick up on the two more important words in my comment earlier. Kinky and dirty."

Annalise made use of the feet in Walt's lap, flexing them against the crotch of his pants. It didn't take more than a few strokes before Walt's erection became evident. "Dirty *and* kinky, you say?" she teased.

Jakob threw back his glass of wine, swallowing it all in one long drink, before placing the glass on an end table. "I'm not sure your body is ready for that, Annalise." She'd taken quite a beating yesterday and the effects were written too clearly on much of her body, from her bruised and swollen shoulder and shins to the black eyes she'd attempted to conceal with makeup. "And I don't think..."

"What do you want?" she asked Jakob.

He glanced from her to Walt, then back again, trying to decide if he should speak what was truly on his mind...no, in his heart.

Walt lifted her feet from his lap and stood, reaching down to help her rise as well. Holding her hand, the two of them walked over to Jakob, the three of them standing so closely, Jakob could feel the warmth of their breath on his face.

"Say it, Jakob."

Walt was using his name, saying it with that American accent on purpose, offering Jakob the opportunity to be his own man tonight, with them.

"I want to make love to you, Annalise. I want to make love to both of you."

Jakob only caught a glimpse of her smile before she moved even closer, their lips touching in a kiss that was more powerful than he could have imagined.

Her lips parted and he tasted the wine on her tongue, savored it. Her hands rested on his hips, pulling him closer. Had her shoulder not been so damaged, he suspected she would have lifted her hands higher, wrapped them around his neck.

Jakob broke the kiss when he felt Walt's hand on his back, his hand fisting his shirt. Opening his eyes, he saw that Walt had a similar grip on Annalise. He was embracing both of them, as much a part of the kiss as they were.

Annalise turned toward Walt, who gave her his own gentle kiss. Both of them were cognizant of her injuries, of the need to take care with her.

Jakob watched as they kissed until he couldn't wait a moment longer. "My turn," he all but growled.

Annalise smiled when Walt turned toward him. The kiss he shared with Walt was completely different from the one he'd just given Annalise. There was no need for softness, gentleness. With Walt, he could unleash all his darkest, roughest passions without fear.

Walt gave as good as he got, biting Jakob's lower lip as they pulled apart.

"I want both of you to go to the bedroom," Jakob commanded. "And take off your clothes. Nothing is stopping us tonight. I don't care if the building burns down around our heads."

Walt grinned. "I suspect we're going to be the ones setting this place on fire."

Annalise led the way to the bedroom, glancing over her shoulder with eyes that reflected pure seduction.

As they entered the bedroom, Jakob took in the large king-size bed. Obviously, they hadn't done a very good job hiding their attraction from Nikolett. Despite the fact she was angry at them for not telling her about Eric's return, she'd still gone out of her way to offer them comfort and time to be alone together.

Annalise twisted to face them as she slipped each button on her blouse free.

Neither he nor Walt looked away as she slowly parted the material and slipped it over her shoulders. Jakob's gaze slid to her shoulder once more, and he had to force back the guilt he felt every time he saw her injuries.

"I should have—"

Before he could finish, Walt's hand landed on his shoulder. "No. There's no place for guilt or regret here tonight."

Annalise nodded. "Tonight is for us. The three of us."

Walt gave them a crooked grin. "If I was a good guy, I'd ask if you all were sure you really wanted me here. But I'm not taking any chances you'll say no."

Jakob lifted his chin as he pierced Walt with his gaze. "I thought I told you to take your clothes off."

Walt reached over his head and pulled his T-shirt off in one smooth tug. Jakob let his gaze slide over the man's bare chest. It was apparent the doctor took very good care of himself, with the trim physique of a man who was no stranger to running.

Annalise stepped between them, turning her back to Jakob. "Can you help me with my bra?" she asked him as she reached out to run her fingers along Walt's pecs.

Jakob unfastened her bra, tugging it away from her body

before dropping it to the floor. He wrapped his arms around her, cupping her breasts in his hands.

"I believe this is where we left off," Jakob murmured before placing his lips against the side of her neck, which she'd tilted to allow him easy access.

"At least one of the times," Walt joked as he stepped closer, the two of them caging Annalise between them. "Not sure I'll survive another case of blue balls."

Walt kissed her. As he did so, he reached around her body, tugging the hem of Jakob's shirt from his jeans, drawing it upwards.

Jakob took the hint, stepping back for just a moment to remove his shirt completely.

"If this affair between the three of us continues for much longer," Walt said, his eyes meeting Jakob's over Annalise's shoulder. "I'm going to have to start lifting weights. Buff up a little so I can compete with our man."

Annalise turned so that she was facing Jakob, placing her hand on his bare chest, her fingers exploring his muscles. Her palm stilled just over his right pec, so Jakob reached around her, for one of Walt's hands, pressing it next to hers, letting them both feel the heavy thudding of his heart.

"Take off your pants and get on the bed," Jakob said, his cock throbbing, in need of release. "We're going to finish what we started this morning."

"And yesterday," Annalise whispered. "It feels like it's been a million years..."

Annalise and Walt wasted no time divesting themselves of the rest of their clothing. Jakob watched as Walt pulled back the duvet and gestured gallantly for Annalise to climb in before he joined her.

Annalise laughed softly and Jakob shook his head, amazed

that he was here, and shocked by how naturally, how easily the three of them fit together.

He'd spent too much of his life as the square peg trying to squeeze his way into the round hole. None of those feelings of inadequacy were present here. More than that, he felt a freedom he hadn't experienced in a very long time.

The freedom to ask for what he wanted, to laugh with reckless abandon, to say everything that was on his mind, and to love without fear of loss or rejection.

Walt kissed Annalise, his hand skimming along her side, causing her to shiver with desire. "It's been so long," she admitted.

As Jakob opened his jeans, pulled his cock out over his boxer briefs, precum dripping from the head, he felt the truth of her words intensely. "Too long," he added.

Walt lay on his side, his weight supported by his elbow. "I'm going to go out on a limb and say neither of you has taken a lover since you met."

Annalise nodded. "Been sort of busy. Stalker and all that."

Jakob barked out a laugh, shocked by her words.

"Joking about it? Already?" Walt asked.

"I'm tired of crying," she admitted.

"I get that," Walt said, placing a soft kiss on her cheek. "No more crying then."

"How long has it been for you?" Jakob asked, curious about this funny doctor who crash-landed into their lives just a few days earlier.

Walt shrugged. "Jesus. I don't know. Maybe seven, eight years?"

"What?" Jakob and Annalise said in unison.

"If you want the truth, I've only ever had sex with two people."

"Long-term relationships?" Annalise asked.

Walt shook his head. "No. Casual flings and neither lasted too long. I had a brief affair with another one of the doctors I did my residency with. He popped my guy cherry. Then—if you'll excuse the cliché—I had an off-and-on, friends-with-benefits deal with a nurse who was stationed with me in Guatemala, during my first tour with Doctors Without Borders. She popped my girl cherry."

"And that was it?" Jakob asked, stunned.

Walt winked at Annalise. "Been sort of busy. Saving lives, hunting serial killers, and all that."

Annalise pushed on Walt's shoulder, straddling his waist. "So we're going to pop your threesome cherry?"

She slowly slid up and down, Walt's erection nestled between the slit in her legs, his dick suddenly slick from the juices of her body.

Walt blew out a long, unsteady breath. "Too much more of that, sweetheart, and this will be over before it even starts."

Jakob walked next to the bed and ran his fingertips along Annalise's spine, not stopping until he reached between her legs to touch her opening and Walt's now-wet cock.

She leaned forward, taking her weight only on her good arm, lifting her ass in obvious invitation, wanting Jakob's fingers to delve a little deeper. Rather than yield to her unspoken desires, he lifted his hand and lightly slapped her ass.

"Patience, Annalise," he warned. When her body healed, he had every intention of exploring the pleasure to be found in sweet discipline, the vision of Annalise draped over his thighs as he and Walt spanked her causing him to go light-headed.

"Jakob," she breathed.

"For now, we're going to play this out exactly as I said this morning. Roll over onto your back and spread those pretty thighs."

Walt didn't wait for Annalise to follow his directions.

Instead, he shifted, moving until Annalise was caged beneath him.

Jakob watched as Walt kissed Annalise, their tongues touching. They remained that way for a few minutes, neither of them in a hurry to move to the next part. And Jakob, for his part, loved watching them.

Eventually, Walt slowly started maneuvering his way down her body, kissing her neck, licking a trail between her breasts, then sucking her nipples into his mouth.

Jakob continued watching them, even as he walked away from the bed backwards.

His actions caused Walt to lift his head.

"Jakob?"

Jakob smiled. "Getting lube and condoms from my bag. I picked them up earlier when we went to get Annalise's sling."

"Oh yeah? Carry on then. And while you're at it, undress."

Damn. Walt had been happy to let Jakob take the lead in the bedroom thus far, but the doctor's husky voice issuing that demand of his own sent so much blood to regions south that Jakob actually felt dizzy.

Walt held his gaze for just a moment and Jakob could almost hear the words "look sharp" in his expression. Jakob unfastened his jeans and pushed them off.

Satisfied he was being obeyed, Walt lowered his head once more to play with Annalise's breasts.

Once he was naked, Jakob retrieved what he'd purchased at the pharmacy and returned to their side. He tossed the condoms onto the nightstand, then uncapped the tube of lubrication.

He paused and took a deep breath. This moment, these wonderful, amazing people, what was about to happen...it felt almost surreal. If he was prone to fits of fancy, he'd pinch himself.

Then he grinned, reached over, and pinched Walt's ass.

Walt didn't even bother to look back at him, though he did release Annalise's nipple with a pop. "Don't make promises your dick's not willing to cash."

Jakob laughed. Loudly. Joyfully.

For the first time in his life, he dialed his control all the way back to zero and set himself free.

Tonight, he was their Jakob. And he was exactly who and where he wanted to be.

CHAPTER NINETEEN

Walt groaned when he felt the mattress dip next to his knee, a sign that Jakob was ready to join the party.

Annalise shifted slightly, trying to look over Walt's shoulder.

"You've got a bit of voyeur in you," Walt teased.

Annalise nodded, not bothering to deny it. "I like to watch."

"Then watch," Jakob said. "Sit up with your back against the headboard, but keep those legs spread open wide."

Walt helped Annalise shift into position, aware it was still too painful for her to put much weight on her injured shoulder. She ran her hand over his head as he bent it to place a closed-mouth kiss against each of her inner thighs.

"Tease," she whispered, her breathing suddenly more rapid.

Walt glanced up at her and winked. He'd intended to lower his head and give her a much more intimate kiss, but he stilled when he felt Jakob's hand on his ass.

"You've done this before?" Jakob asked. "This way?"

Walt nodded, understanding Jakob's question. In his affair with the other doctor, he'd been the bottom as well. "Yeah. This way."

Jakob moved until he was kneeling behind Walt, who pushed upwards to give Annalise a quick kiss.

"You're gorgeous," Walt murmured.

"I have two black eyes," Annalise said, laughing softly.

"Walt's right," Jakob added. "You're the most beautiful woman I've ever known."

Annalise didn't respond, but her slight blush and pleased smile said it all. "I thought I was getting a show."

Walt returned to his previous position, on his hands and knees, his face just above her pussy. "Not just a show." He bent down and ran his tongue along her slit as Annalise opened her legs farther, a soft "oh" escaping her lips.

Walt continued to stroke her with his tongue, teasing her clit with the tip of it, before circling the opening to her body. Her soft sighs and whispered "yes" drove him on. She was wet and hot and it would take very little to draw out her first orgasm.

Walt had just determined to make that a reality when he stilled, something cold on his ass taking him by surprise.

He groaned loudly when Jakob worked that cold lube into his ass with one thick finger. After several thrusts, he added a second.

"Sweet Jesus, Jakob," he breathed. "You heard the 'seven, eight years' part, right?"

Jakob paused briefly. "You want it soft and sweet, Walt? Or are you gonna let me fuck you the way I want to?" His voice deepened further. "The way you need?"

Walt rested his head briefly on Annalise's stomach. He'd always wanted to experience rough sex—something he hadn't done with his previous two lovers—and somehow Jakob, a man he'd only known for a few days, had figured that out.

"Take me hard," Walt said at last, lifting his head and glancing over his shoulder at Jakob.

He expected Jakob to smile. After all, the man had become more free with those sexy grins over the course of the day. But Jakob didn't smile. Instead, his expression was one of lust, of determination, of hunger.

Annalise cupped Walt's face, pulling it around until he looked at her. She leaned forward to kiss him before leaning back once more and waving her hand, the gesture so regal, so like a queen on her throne that he couldn't help but laugh when she said, "Continue."

And like the perfect, obedient subject, he opened her mons with the thumb and forefinger of one hand and sucked her clit into his mouth. Like Jakob, he didn't go the soft and sweet route. Instead, he took her exactly as he wanted. As he sucked on her clit, he drove two fingers inside her and, just as he'd thought, Annalise came quickly, after no more than half a dozen rough thrusts.

"Oh my God," she cried out, her back arching, pushing her breasts forward. Jakob reached over with the hand not buried in Walt's ass to grasp one, stroking the nipple, the action—along with Walt's continued ministrations below her waist—drawing out her orgasm.

Walt slowly withdrew his fingers, her inner muscles clenching and spasming in such a way he thought she might come again. Jakob gripped Walt's wrist and pulled it up until Jakob could suck his wet fingers into his mouth.

Annalise watched them for a few moments before she whispered. "Take Walt, Jakob. Make him feel as good as I do right now."

Jakob tugged Walt's wrist away, though he increased the

suction on his fingers, his tongue tickling his fingertips. The powerful pull made Walt wish it was his cock in his lover's mouth instead. Jakob would give one hell of a blow job.

Releasing Walt's fingers, Jakob ran his hand along his spine and back to his ass.

More of the cold lube hit Walt's ass and he hissed slightly until Jakob drew his fingers through it, pressing those same two fingers deep on the first pass. "You're so tight, Walt. I can't wait to drive my dick inside you. All the way to the hilt. This ass is mine. All mine."

"Fuck," Walt said through gritted teeth as Jakob thrust over and over into his ass, stretching him in a way he hadn't experienced in years. The pinching pain of it was overridden by how fucking good it felt.

When Jakob added a third finger, Walt's own clenched the sheets by Annalise's hips in a white-knuckled grip. Annalise ran her hand over the side of his face to his jaw, using fingers under his chin to tilt his head up, forcing him to meet her gaze.

"Beautiful," she murmured as she studied what he could only imagine must look like pain in his expression, though God knew nothing had ever hurt so fucking good before.

Or so he thought.

Until Jakob reached around his waist with his free hand to grip Walt's dick.

Walt jerked and cursed, swearing he wasn't going to make it much longer. Jakob ignored him, firmly stroking his cock as he continued to ream Walt's ass with three thick fingers.

"Jesus, Jakob. Fuck, man." Walt's forehead was once more pressed against Annalise's lower belly, her hand cupping the back of his head, his mouth near her sex, each inhale smelling her arousal, his mouth watering for a taste.

"While you're down there," she teased, prompting Jakob to laugh.

Jakob pulled his fingers out slowly. "Give our girl her second orgasm while I put a condom on."

Walt's head was swimming and it was taking every ounce of strength he had not to come, even with no one touching him anymore. "Goddammit. You're both trying to kill me."

Regardless of his impending death, he stroked Annalise's clit with his thumb, increasing the pressure and the speed until she was in the same state he was. She slid lower on the bed, no longer sitting, but instead reclined, propped up against the pillows, with her feet flat on the mattress. Her hips lifted and tilted, an unspoken plea for more.

He knew what she wanted, but after spending the last few minutes on the receiving end of Jakob's sensual torture, he wanted to make sure she really understood what he was going through.

He kept the pressure on her clit, and then used the other hand to tease the rest of her. He drew circles around her opening, loving the fact that she was still so wet and ready for them. Using some of her body's natural juices, he wet his fingertips, then slid them lower, teasing her anus.

"Walt," she said, his name air, not sound. There was no mistaking the naked desire behind it.

Walt had been following Jakob's progress, not through sight, but through sound. He'd heard the crinkle of the condom wrapper as well as the snap of the cap on the lubrication opening and closing. He knew their lover was sheathed and ready to move to the next part.

Jakob left his place behind Walt, shifting to the side. "What did you do?"

"I think someone else is going to enjoy your cock in their ass as well."

"Fuck," Jakob breathed. "Touch her there again. Let me see."

Walt lifted up enough that Jakob had the perfect view as he gathered up more of her juices, then returned to her ass. This time, he didn't just tease the opening. Instead, he pushed inside until he was one knuckle deep.

Annalise's hips rose, inviting more.

Jakob watched for a few seconds before rising. Rather than kneel, he stood at the end of the bed, gripping Walt's hips to draw him down to the edge of the mattress. Walt followed suit, dragging Annalise downward as well.

"Fuck her ass with that finger while I fuck you. I want all of us to come together. Better grab that lube, Walt. Get her nice and slick. None of us is getting soft and sweet tonight."

"*Halleluja. Beeile dich,*" Annalise murmured in German.

Walt wasn't exactly sure what the last part meant, but he could sure as hell infer from the urgency in her tone. Annalise's patience had reached its end.

He reached for the tube, lathered up his finger, and then slid inside her ass again, just as he felt the head of Jakob's cock pressing against his anus.

"Sweet Jesus." Walt forced himself to focus on Annalise, on bringing her to the same precipice he was already dangling from. This was not going to take fucking long. He'd let too many years pass between lovers.

Unlike Jakob, Walt attempted to go slow, pressing inside her ass with one slippery finger, trying to read her body's clues about what was good and what might hurt.

Jakob wasn't reading a fucking thing. He gripped Walt's hips, pulled him back, and entered him in one full, deep thrust that would have hurt if he hadn't taken the time to prepare Walt's body for it.

"*Verdammter Hurensohn,*" Jakob bit out, just before withdrawing and slamming back in.

After that, the race was on. Walt lowered his upper body,

the position allowing Jakob to take him deeper, while allowing him to suck Annalise's clit into his mouth as he finger-fucked her ass.

None of them spoke a single discernable word after that—not in German or English—conversing instead in a litany of guttural groans and breathless cries.

Annalise went over first, crying out his name and Jakob's as her body trembled with the force of her orgasm. Walt was mere seconds behind her. There was no stopping him. He reached down, gripping his own dick, stroking his fist over it once, twice, before he erupted, his come splashing out on the comforter, some hitting Annalise's thighs and stomach.

Jakob thrust inside him only a handful of times more before his fingers turned to vises on Walt's hips, gripping hard enough to bruise as he exploded.

They all remained there, a frozen tableau as they each attempted to land. Jakob moved first, holding on to the end of the condom as he slowly slid out.

"Now you're gentle," Walt said with a grin. He pushed himself backwards trying to find the strength to stand. His back was stiff and his knees slightly weak. It had been quite a workout.

"Are you okay?" Jakob asked him, placing a steadying hand on his back.

Walt twisted and gave Jakob a hard kiss that let him know exactly how okay he was.

Together, they turned to Annalise.

"How about you, sweetheart?" Walt asked, belatedly concerned that perhaps they'd gotten too carried away with lust.

Annalise grinned like the cat who'd eaten the canary. "Never been better," she all but purred.

He and Jakob chuckled as they padded to the bathroom to

wash up. Jakob tossed the condom and washed his hands. Walt did the same, then tapped a few ibuprofen into his palm and got a cup of water. Regardless of how happy Annalise looked now, Walt was certain once the post-orgasmic pleasure had waned, she'd be sore again.

They returned to the room together. Annalise sat up to swallow the pills as they climbed into the bed, he and Jakob flanking her. Walt sighed as he sank into the warm soft bed, chuckling as he murmured softly, "I live here now."

CHAPTER TWENTY

Nikolett rubbed her eyes wearily. She, Nyx, Grigoris, Dimitri and Dimitri's spouses had been up all night, poring over the video footage from each of the case files off Annalise's thumb drive. She'd called in the knights and security officers stationed in and around Budapest when she accepted this couldn't be done with a handful of people in a matter of mere hours. It was going to take more— more work, more people, more focus.

Once briefed on the situation, the new additions were given assignments.

The larger conference room on the second floor, just down the hall from both her and Nyx's offices, had become the headquarters of the investigation. Eventually they'd spilled into the other conference room as more and more people arrived to help.

She had a moment where she wondered if she was doing the right thing. This killer had operated in her territory, but Alicja Lewandowski wasn't one of her members. Josephine had been a member, but from Dublin, which—though it was essentially neutral thanks to the presence of the archive—was in England's territory. England belonged Arthur, Sophia, and James.

And she knew from past conversations with Arthur that the investigation into Josephine's death was a cold case with both the English knights and the Irish *Garda Síochána*.

Still, she could have turned this over to England rather than put the resources of her territory toward the investigation—a territory still suffering from the manipulations and abuse perpetuated by their former admiral.

There was no reason for this to be Hungary's responsibility.

No reason, except that she'd known Petro was duplicitous and manipulative. She'd known there was something wrong and thought she could handle it. That overconfidence, coupled with obedience, had kept her from reaching out and telling someone what was going on.

Though very few people would think of her as "obedient," she took her oaths very seriously. The oath she took upon joining the Masters' Admiralty included obedience to her admiral. But leveraging power and allies wasn't disobedient, so she'd decided to take on Petro the way she'd been trying to change the Hungarian government as a member of Parliament.

Given enough time she'd thought she could build allies within the territory leadership and bring pressure to bear on the admiral that would force him to change. And while she'd been playing a long game and holding her oath of obedience, people died. Petro hurt and killed, and even after his death, his reach was long and bloody.

Now she had a new way of looking at the world. Oaths of obedience held only so long as the person you were to obey was sane, and no authority was beyond being questioned. Including her own. It was one of the reasons she'd chosen Nyx as her vice admiral, and why those in her inner circle routinely questioned and challenged her decisions.

If she could have fit a nice round table in her's or Nyx's office, she would have gotten one so they could all sit around it, equals in private, though they would maintain formalities when in the presence of others.

Speaking of Nyx, the former academic had found a whiteboard and hauled it into the conference room. On it were listed the main points from Dr. Fischer's profile, as well as pictures of Josephine and Alicja.

The picture of Alicja was of her face, but from the autopsy, not her ID photo, and cropped so the severed end of her neck wasn't visible. Josephine's was a smiling candid shot of her, alive and happy.

Nikolett didn't need to see the picture of Josephine's severed head ever again. It was burned into her memory.

"Admiral," Dimitri murmured. "Let us do our work. You should sleep."

She'd sent Vadisk to do precisely that—sleep and eat—hours ago. But Nikolett didn't believe in asking people to do things she wasn't willing to do herself.

"When we have something, I will," she murmured, turning back to her computer.

"You might be missing things," Nyx said coolly. She hadn't even looked up from her computer. "If you're tired, you'll make mistakes."

Nikolett arched a brow at her, but then nodded. It was one of the reasons she liked Nyx—the other woman didn't bother with niceties when she felt they weren't needed.

"I will take a few hours," Nikolett said. "I was working on this block in Dublin." She pointed at the map beside her computer, her assigned section traced out in highlighter.

"One of us will take care of it," Grigoris murmured, standing and stretching.

Nikolett rose, her back muscles protesting. Her shoulders, which had been knotted for what felt like hours, physically ached.

For one quick, weak moment, she wished she had someone waiting for her. Someone she could go to. Someone who would take care of her, rub her shoulders, the way Grigoris was now rubbing Nyx's. When Nyx leaned her cheek against her husband's wrist, Nikolett jerked her attention away.

She glanced around the room and cleared her throat. "I'd like to thank each of you for coming in to work on this."

People replied in murmurs and nods.

"If you're tired, take a break. Sleep. Eat." She smiled. "That's what I'm going to do."

Instead of looking at her with derision, or maybe contempt, her people smiled back at her, some nodding. Having the respect of not only her peers, but the people under her command and care, was still novel.

Prior to her position as an admiral for the Masters' Admiralty, she'd been a politician. She'd been thought of as a ball buster, making waves in the National Assembly by taking a strong stance in the opposition party. Nikolett had spent too many years being called a bitch—either behind her back or to her face—during her time in politics, for doing the same things her male peers did that got them labeled intrepid or innovative.

She stopped in the second conference room to deliver the same message—thanking everyone and reminding them to stop and rest, eat when necessary. In here, a printer had been set up, and stills from the various surveillance videos the team was scanning were posted on the walls—one wall for Krakow, one for Dublin. A third was covered in Post-it notes all related to victi-

MARI CARR & LILA DUBOIS

mology. Because the killer most likely hadn't picked Josephine so much as had her name suggested by Petro, Annalise had told them that any study of victimology might be futile at best, and misleading at worst. Still, one of the harcos who'd come in to help had insisted on starting a victimology study.

All these images were also being run through facial recognition, where possible. As it was explained to her earlier, even the most advanced facial recognition needed a decent photograph of the person in order to analyze as many of the nodal points on the face as possible to create the facial signature. Then the facial signature was converted into a mathematical formula that was compared to others.

They were sourcing security camera feeds from both public and private sources—traffic cameras, security feeds from banks and restaurants. None of those were mounted at eye level, many had low pixel numbers, and those factors combined with the angles meant there were relatively few faces they'd actually be able to run. The only reason Dimitri had been able to use facial recognition to help find Dr. Fischer's stalker was because the Ritter had told them to check with passport control for any German nationals. That had meant a small pool of potentials, and allowed the less-than-ideal still image to render a match that it wouldn't otherwise have selected.

So far there were no matches between the two sets of pedestrians—aka, potential serial killers.

They'd find something. They would.

Nikolett went to her office, closing the door behind her. Her office was the same size as Nyx's, but instead of a conference table, she had a couch and two armchairs, perfect for less formal meetings.

That had been deliberate. Nikolett knew she could come across as too aggressive, too outspoken and demanding. Again, if she'd been a man, and older, those words would have been "commanding" and "decisive."

So when she had a meeting in her office, they sat in the deliberately informal space.

It had the added benefit of giving her someplace to sleep if she worked too long.

Her vice admiral and security minister might work long hours, but Nyx and Dimitri had people to go home to. People who made sure they ate and slept. People who brought balance to their lives.

Nikolett took off her earrings, grabbed a makeup wipe out of her drawer, and removed her long-wear lipstick. Her mascara was waterproof and she didn't want to deal with it, so she would just have to hope it survived.

Then she went to one of the wide wooden filing cabinets and pulled out a fluffy blanket. It was pink and soft and matched nothing else in her office or her life. She loved it.

Nikolett wrapped the blanket around herself and collapsed on the couch, head pillowed on her arm. She closed her eyes, relaxed her shoulders, and...

Was no longer tired.

With an aggravated sigh, she rolled onto her back and fished under the blanket, digging her phone out of her pocket. She'd been ignoring it, but as she looked at the dozens of waiting messages, she grinned.

Each of the other eight admirals had texted, with messages ranging from, "Thank you for the information" to "What new information do you have? What's going on?"

Nikolett cackled quietly.

She could have kept the information Dr. Fischer had brought her quiet, but she'd had a much better idea. After checking in with Sophia, who was the acting Fleet Admiral, and Arthur, to make sure he agreed with her reasoning for her keeping the case, Nikolett had reached out to the other seven admirals and let them know that she and her territory were actively investigating who had murdered Josephine O'Connor and that they could confirm it was a serial killer.

That hadn't just been about sharing information—something she was pushing for the territories to do more openly, rather than each acting in isolation and in perceived competition with each other.

No, letting the admirals know, and then asking them to pass on any information they might have that could help—including names of any women who'd been murdered or gone missing in their territories—had served a second purpose.

She wanted word to spread. She wanted the fleet admiral to resurface and come to her.

The fleet admiral had decided to shirk his duties and disappear. Yes, it had been in a quest for justice for Josephine, whom popular gossip suggested had been his lover. As noble and romantic as that was, it was also stupid.

He'd left Sophia in charge, but his instructions had been so brief that her authority was undefined and amorphous. Their society was on unstable ground. The revelation that one of the admirals had been their greatest enemy, and that his death hadn't eliminated threats such as the Bellator Dei, had only served to deepen that unease.

Though she knew the Spartan Guard had been looking for the fleet admiral, he'd evaded them, and possibly would continue to evade them. The fleet admiral needed to come back and either resign his position or actually do his job.

She intended to be the one to tell him because, though he outranked her, she had no qualms about questioning his decisions and actions. Her oath of obedience no longer came with a side of silence and caution.

The time to act was now.

Before more people died.

No one else seemed to be willing to call the Viking on his bullshit.

She responded to each of the messages with a brief update, plus a slightly longer one for both Arthur and Hande, whom she considered her closest allies. The Spartan Guard would hear through a less formal, but just as effective mode of communication—Dimitri's husband, Mateo would call his former compatriots and fill them in.

When she was done, she stuck her phone back into her pocket and settled in to try to get some sleep. The fleet admiral had been hiding for long enough. Whether it took days or weeks, he'd hear about what she was doing, and he was going to come to her.

"I CAN SEE I'm going to have to learn German or forever be in the dark in the bedroom with you two," Walt joked as he rolled to his side to look at his lovers. A small voice in the back of his head reminded him that there wasn't a forever with them. There wouldn't even be a next week.

He pushed the dark thoughts aside.

Annalise had curled up facing him, Jakob spooning her from behind. The only word to describe their faces was exhausted bliss. And yet, despite the whirlwind of the past few days, none of them seemed anxious to go to sleep.

Perhaps because they knew their time together was fleeting.

Annalise gave a breathy laugh. "Let's see. I told you to hurry up and Jakob was calling someone a son of a bitch." She sighed contentedly. "I can't believe I'm still awake. I should be exhausted after that amazing sex combined with the past few days," Annalise admitted, her thoughts mirroring his own.

"I was thinking the same thing," Walt concurred. "It's just…

I don't want to waste a second of this, you know?"

Jakob pushed up so that he could give Annalise, then Walt, quick kisses. "Maybe there's a way..."

When his words drifted off, Walt knew there wasn't an answer to this. There was no happy ending here. Not for the three of them.

Jakob and Annalise were members of the Masters' Admiralty. That meant their spouses weren't theirs to choose. And even if, by some stroke of amazing luck, the admiral of Germany put them together in a trinity, Walt wouldn't be there with them.

"Why did Eric come to you in Libya?" Jakob asked Walt.

"As I said, our paths crossed when he was following a lead about Josephine's killer. He walked into my clinic, covered in someone else's blood. But that wasn't the first time we'd met. We'd met once before. In America. He pissed off the Grand Master of the Trinity Masters by offering me and my siblings membership to the Masters' Admiralty."

Annalise shifted to her back, then sat up.

"The Grand Master?" Annalise asked. "That's the leader of the American society, right?"

Walt winced. "Damn. Yeah. I'm sort of shit when it comes to keeping all this secret society stuff secret. That's not something y'all knew?"

"Our knowledge of the American society is fairly limited. I suspect the admirals know a great deal more," Annalise explained. "The Trinity Masters sort of falls in the same category as your American IRS. We know they exist, but because they don't impact our lives, we don't bother to learn much about them."

"My brothers, Langston and Oscar, both recently joined the Trinity Masters, and I've made a promise to the leader— they call her the Grand Master, which is not as cool as fleet admiral if you ask me—that once Eric and I catch Josephine's killer, I will return to join as well." Walt hadn't really considered that promise a hardship at the time. His brothers had joined and he'd intended to follow suit. Now, however... Now there was nothing he wanted to do less.

"You mentioned that before...so you're really promised to join the Trinity Masters?" Annalise asked.

Walt sighed, swallowing heavily. He'd always made it his goal to live a good life, one where he could crawl into bed each night, close his eyes, and not have any regrets. And for the most part, he'd managed to do just that.

Until now.

He should never have made that promise to Juliette because returning to America and pledging his life to the Trinity Masters was something he would truly regret.

"I am," he said at last.

"All of us knew, going into this," Annalise said, her voice quiet and sad, "that it couldn't last." She looked at Jakob. "You and I..."

"The stalker is gone," Jakob said.

"Which means your reason for being with me is gone."

Jakob frowned and shook his head. "Annalise, I haven't been assigned to protect you for a very long time. I wasn't with you just because of Axel. I was with you because that was where I wanted to be. I love you."

She smiled. "I love you too, but we can't steer our destinies any more than Walt can. The admiral will put us in trinities that he chooses."

Jakob didn't respond to that, not at first. Walt didn't believe it was the silent stoic returning as much as Jakob was weighing what he said next.

"Perhaps. But what if we talk to the admiral together? Plead our case."

Annalise glanced at Walt. "We could, but..."

"But Walt wouldn't be with us." Jakob scrubbed his hand over his close-cropped hair in frustration. "He's a part of us now. *Mist!* I can't stand this. Can't stand the thought of losing both of you. I've spent years dreaming of this moment with you, Annalise, never imagining we'd be together. And now that we've found Walt...I never knew love could feel like this. So intense. So right. So perfect."

Though the sheer agony in Jakob's tone cut deep, Walt was thrilled that Jakob no longer held back with them. "I feel the same way," Walt admitted. "I've spent the last six months watching my brothers fall head over ass in love, wondering if something was missing inside me, some vital piece, because I'd never experienced anything even close to what they described feeling for their partners. Now? Well, now, I get it."

Annalise turned to her back, taking their hands in hers. "Let's not talk about the end tonight, please. I've spent the last four years fearing what may happen in the future. For right now, I want to live in the present. I'm happy here. It's been so long, so damn long..."

"You're right," Walt said, squeezing her hand. "Now isn't the time to worry about what's to come. Let's steal as much joy as we can during the time we have left together. Let's make it all count."

Jakob placed a soft kiss on the side of Annalise's head. "Let's make it count," he repeated.

With that decision made, sleep came much easier and quickly.

Walt pushed away every other concern, focusing only on his happiness, a happiness so big, he was surprised he could hold it all.

When he closed his eyes, he drifted away with a smile on his face, his dreams the sweetest he'd ever had.

. . .

Nikolett rolled off the couch, unable to untangle herself from the blanket in time to make it graceful. She landed in a heap, struggled inelegantly, and finally unwrapped herself. Bouncing to her feet, she threw off the blanket. Panting, she looked around to make sure her office was empty and no one had seen her looking ridiculous. No one. Good.

Nikolett cleared her throat, tugged down her shirt, and smoothed back her hair.

She wobbled for a moment—damn it, naps always made her feel odd—then folded and stowed the blanket before going to her desk.

Needing a minute, Nikolett jiggled her desktop computer awake and opened major news sites in Romania, Hungary, Bulgaria, Serbia, and the Ukraine. She was fluent in Hungarian —her native language—English, and Romanian. She had basic conversational language skills in Ukrainian and Bulgarian and was working toward both verbal and written fluency.

Pulling a small toiletries bag out of her desk, she scanned the headlines as she applied some moisturizer and brushed the sleep tangles out of her hair. She'd take a few more minutes to herself, and then she'd go back into the conference room and—

Nikolett's eyes narrowed, then widened as she clicked on "more" to keep reading an article. It wasn't one of the top news articles—the story had been toward the bottom of the home-page on the *Ekspres*, a major Ukrainian newspaper, which she'd had the computer translate since she wasn't up for trying to muddle through it.

Twenty-seven-year-old Zasha Romanov, an international trade lawyer and native of Odessa, had been missing for four days, last seen leaving her office in a city-center building.

Nikolett clicked over to read the original article from the

local Odessan newspaper, but it was in Russian. Sadly, her Russian was terrible, and though predominantly ethnically Ukrainian, Russian was the main language in Odessa, as it was along much of the coast of the Black Sea.

Nikolett shook her head, telling herself to calm down. Odessa was a large city, but not on the scale of Krakow or Dublin, and it didn't have a large English-speaking population. She glanced at the picture of Zasha—brown hair, light gray or blue eyes. Brown hair was the only similarity between her and the other victims. In fact, brown hair and a white-collar job were some of the only commonalities they'd been able to put together for victimology.

And Zasha fit both of those.

Nikolett couldn't ignore this tense, tight feeling. Maybe it was a product of lack of sleep. Maybe she was hoping for there to be similarities because she wanted to find and stop this killer. Hesitating for only a moment, she quickly tapped the keys to translate the article, then searched for other articles, in languages she did know, on the Zasha Romanov disappearance.

Her printer whirred to life and Nikolett snatched up the papers as she stood.

Zasha had seemingly vanished, and it appeared the authorities were ready to say she'd fled the country for unspecified reasons. One article included a quote from her brother, a former Ukrainian Navy officer, now CEO of a major stevedoring company based out of the port of Odessa, vehemently denying that his sister was connected with any criminal activities and insisting that she had no reason to flee.

Nikolett marched into the conference room, sweeping her gaze around. Grigoris and Nyx were gone, Dimitri was slumped in a chair in the corner, apparently asleep, but Vadisk was there, his massive body looking ridiculous hunched over a tiny laptop. Nikolett thrust the papers at him.

Vadisk had apparently been concentrating so hard he hadn't heard her approach. Startled, he reached out and grabbed her wrist, starting to jerk her forward before he realized what he was doing. Nikolett didn't show any outward reaction, though internally she yelped in surprise and a little fear.

"Admiral. Sorry." Vadisk grimaced and released her.

She waited, still holding out the papers. After a moment, he took them and started to read. His brows drew together, and after what felt like far too long he looked up. "It could be, but they don't speak English in Odessa."

Nikolett let out a long breath. "My exact thoughts, but the similarities were enough that for a second—"

"They do." Maxim Kovalenko, seated at the other end of the table, was looking at them. Nikolett turned her full attention to the harco, who'd just recently accepted a position as a knight. The Ukrainian man was tall and lean, at least in comparison to Vadisk. A former Spetsnaz operative for the SSU's Alpha Group, Maxim was quietly dangerous, fiercely loyal, and deaf and blind on his right side, though no one would know it based on his behavior. The disability had forced him out of the Alpha Group, and he'd been consulting for corporate security firms before she'd asked him to step up as a harco.

"They do?" she asked.

"Many, maybe most, people in Odessa speak some English, because of the tourism, and TV, internet."

"Who would know that?" Vadisk asked.

Maxim was quiet for a moment, seeming to consider his answer. "Anyone who has been to Odessa. I believe the guidebooks, websites, they say you can get by speaking only English there."

Nikolett took a deep breath, then let it out slowly. "Vadisk, put together a team. I want to go to Odessa."

CHAPTER TWENTY-ONE

Annalise managed not to groan as Walt kneaded her good shoulder. Letting him know exactly how good that felt would hardly be appropriate with Admiral Varda, Vadisk, and a knight from Hungary, Maxim Kovalenko, seated around the table with her, Jakob, and Walt.

They were at yet another hotel, this time in Odessa. Last night had been both physically and emotionally exhausting. As she'd said to Jakob and Walt, she was determined to focus on the here and now, rather than worry about the future, but that was easier said than done. Her heart was already beginning to crack and she was still with them. What would happen when the three of them had to say goodbye for good?

They'd been woken up after too little sleep when Admiral Varda had called to inform her that she was taking a small team to Odessa, and Annalise was coming with her. Jakob had demanded to accompany her, as had Walt.

She didn't need Jakob's protection anymore, but that fact didn't make it any easier for her to accept that she could walk down a street without him. That freedom was still too new and she feared she would continue to see shadows everywhere. Maybe those shadows would never go away.

It would take time for her to feel comfortable being alone. Old habits died hard, but the truth was she didn't want to break the Jakob habit. Even though she didn't need him as her body-guard, she still wanted him—and Walt—with her, desperately.

Vadisk flew them to Odessa in his six-seater helicopter, and they'd arrived by mid-morning. The flight hadn't been the sort where she could sip wine while reviewing files, so it wasn't until they'd reached the hotel, and the two-bedroom penthouse suite complete with the large dining room, that she'd gotten to look at the information about Zasha Romanov.

Annalise had specifically told Admiral Varda that victi-mology was not a good basis for continued investigation because of the patronage partnership between the unsub and Petro. The unsub hadn't chosen Josephine, and because they hadn't had a chance to gather more information about the potential victim in Belgium, the only victim they could work for a victimology study was Alicja.

Reminding Admiral Varda of these issues would be point-less, since they were here now. And since they were, maybe she, they, could do something to help find Zasha, assuming her disappearance wasn't tied to the bratva, or voluntary, as the reports implied.

Maxim rose from the table, phone in hand. He spoke briefly with the admiral in what she assumed was either Romanian or Ukrainian—though for the most part they'd been speaking English for Walt's benefit. A moment later, Maxim walked out the door.

"They've finished going through the footage from Krakow," Vadisk announced, looking up from his computer. The poor man looked uncomfortable, hunched over the computer, his massive arms pulled in tight so he could type.

"Facial recognition?" Nikolett asked.

"Still running. With every database..." Vadisk shook his head.

Walt took his hand from her good shoulder, raising it like he was in class. "Question."

Nikolett's lips twitched. "Yes?"

"You have to check every female resident in all of Europe?"

"And parts of North Africa," Vadisk said.

Annalise cleared her throat. "Even if this has nothing to do with Josephine's and Alicja's murders, we may be able to help this investigation, and we can continue to work on the serial killer case." Annalise gestured to Vadisk, who, unlike Maxim, had been focused on what was happening back at the Hungary headquarters rather than what was going on in Odessa.

"Like I said, we're here to take on all the bad guys," Walt said cheerfully.

Nikolett folded her arms, turning to stare out the window. From their luxury hotel near the seaside, they had a view of Odessa's famous Duke de Richelieu Monument. The admiral of the Ottoman territory—they'd crossed the border into the other territory once they came within fifty kilometers of the Black Sea—had helped arrange for the hotel, and had janissaries on their way to meet them and assist, but it would take several hours as none were currently stationed in the part of Ukraine that belonged to Ottoman.

"Budapest is sending over pictures." Vadisk's voice rumbled through the room. "But the Dublin team is still working."

Annalise put aside the police report she was reading on Zasha's disappearance—she had to use a translation software, and that meant the information probably wasn't perfect anyway.

A moment later, a file appeared on her borrowed laptop. She opened it to find nearly a hundred still images and video clips, sorted and organized by the dozens of women they'd identified. There were different angles and variations in video and still image quality, and in far too many of them the women were wearing hoods and scarves. It had been cold the day Alicja disappeared.

Annalise clicked on the first video, watching the forty-second clip that appeared to be from the exterior of a cafe, the main focus the small, deserted sidewalk seating area. Pedestrians were visible on the right-hand side of the frame.

The door opened, and Jakob, seated beside her, rose, angling his body just slightly to put himself between her and the door. Annalise sucked in a breath, remembered terror clawing at her. But she wasn't in danger. Axel was dead. Still, Jakob's mannerism was setting off alarm bells.

A second later, she saw why. Maxim had returned, bringing with him two strangers. The first was a tall man, though not quite as tall as Maxim, wearing an expensive silver suit, sans tie, shirt open at the neck. His face was hard, cold, but the way the skin was pinched at the corners of his eyes spoke of pain. Behind him was a man who might as well have had "bodyguard" tattooed on his forehead—black pants, T-shirt, and leather jacket, with a small clear earpiece easily visible thanks to his shaved head.

Maxim led the newcomers to Nikolett, and the guy in the suit and she exchanged greetings, briefly shaking hands. Nikolett's voice was softer than Annalise had ever heard it. Compassionate.

She glanced at the newcomer, assessing for a moment, before whispering, just loud enough for Jakob and Walt to hear her. "Leonid Romanov, Zasha's brother."

"How do you know?" Walt asked.

"Nikolett is consoling him. He's angry and afraid, for his sister. See it in his body language?"

Walt nodded. "Damn. Now that you say it, yeah."

Vadisk must have overheard some of their conversation because he glanced at her, brows raised and clearly impressed.

After Nikolett and Leonid exchanged a few more words, Maxim standing off to the side, the trio turned to the table.

"Mr. Romanov, are you comfortable if we continue in English? Two of my team are German, the other American. It is the common language among us."

Leonid nodded. "I'm comfortable with English."

Nikolett caught Annalise's eye, and there was a warning in her gaze. "Maxim and I have spoken with Mr. Romanov about our task force. And that, though we aren't sure of a connection, we came to Odessa to look into his sister's disappearance."

Ah, so that was the cover story.

Annalise looked at Leonid, at the pain, fear, and rage he was barely hiding. They couldn't give this man false hope, it would be too cruel.

"Mr. Romanov, I want to caution you that our investigation may not link to your sister's, and therefore, we won't have any additional insight. There is no guarantee we can provide any assistance with finding your sister."

"I understand," Leonid's voice rumbled, low and pleasant despite the tension underlying the tone. "But any help you can give, I will take. The *politsiya* have given up on her because of me."

"Because of you?" Annalise asked, when no one else spoke.

"I have enemies. I have done hard things in my life."

"That is why they think the bratva took her?" Vadisk asked.

Leonid's hands clenched into fists. Annalise watched with interest as he forced himself to relax, uncurling his fingers one by one. "Yes."

"You said you had copies of the police files," Nikolett interjected.

He nodded. "And my company did its own investigation. But missing persons is far different than the security we maintain at the port."

Vadisk, Maxim, Jakob, and the unnamed bodyguard all nodded as if they understood exactly what that meant.

Leonid reached into his jacket pocket and pulled out a thumb drive, passing it to Nikolett.

To Annalise's surprise, Nikolett gave it to her. "He gathered surveillance footage from places along Krasnova Street, which is how his sister walks home from her office."

Annalise resisted the urge to once again remind Admiral Varda that this may have nothing to do with their case, and plugged in the thumb drive, copying the files before passing it over to Jakob, who did the same.

Conversation turned to Zasha's disappearance—the details of what they knew, what they didn't know, and what the authorities had and hadn't done. Annalise listened, ready to give her perspective, but it seemed that Maxim had some investigative experience, because he knew how an investigation should have been handled and was able to point out weak spots and mistakes.

Seeing she wasn't needed, Annalise yielded her seat at the table, going to sit on the designer couch with her laptop. Everything in the suite was elegant, designed in the classic French style.

Out of curiosity more than anything, she watched the surveillance footage of Zasha, following her path home from camera to camera, until suddenly, she wasn't there.

Annalise's eyes narrowed. Disappearing between one block and another, in a spot that just happened to be blind of any security cameras...well, that was a far more compelling similarity between the cases than pointing out that they were all white-collar missing brunettes.

Annalise watched the videos a second time, this time studying the pedestrians. Leonid had clipped the footage to show the street at the exact time his sister had appeared on camera, but they needed to look at the footage for at least several hours beforehand. That was part of what was taking so long with the footage from Krakow and Dublin.

The unsub was highly organized and patient, which meant she may have been waiting in the blind-spot area for hours, just waiting for her target to pass by.

She checked the files Leonid had provided, finding the larger video files with the entire day's footage. Raising her head, she looked at Jakob. After a moment, as if he could feel her watching him, he—and Walt—came over to her.

"I need you to pull out clips from the videos for two hours before Zasha walks by," she murmured.

Jakob nodded and without a word went back to the table and his laptop.

"You think they might be related after all?" Walt asked.

"No one here is unbiased," Annalise said. "I am trying not to let my desire for these to be connected, for us to have recent and actionable information on the unsub, cloud my objectivity."

"But maybe?" Walt raised his brows.

"Maybe," she agreed after a moment.

Walt swallowed. "But if our killer has Zasha, she's already dead."

Josephine had been taken and killed within twenty-four hours. There'd been no way to determine the date of death for Alicja due to the state of her remains, so there was no way of knowing how long she'd been held.

Annalise started to say yes, that no matter what had actually happened to Zasha, she was most likely dead, but instead, she closed her mouth, thinking.

"Admiral Varda's instincts told her these cases were related. Now...now I think there's a possibility she's right."

"And you didn't before?"

"No." Annalise paused as her computer dinged, the first edited video file starting to download as Jakob sent it over. "But now, it's possible by a slim margin." She opened the video file, setting it to play at triple speed. "And my instinct is telling me that Zasha might still be alive."

It was like being in an action movie. Actually, ever since Eric showed up covered in blood, Walt's life had gone from boring if exhausting to action-packed and terrifying. But also romantic and sexy, so that part was cool...if temporary.

Argh.

Sadly, there wasn't much he could do to distract himself from thoughts about the future—Annalise said she needed to review the video herself—so instead, he got her some aspirin, checked on Jakob, and ordered room service coffee. At least he was pretty sure he'd ordered coffee. The menu was, unsurprisingly, in Ukrainian or maybe Russian. Either way, it was in a Slavic language, with an alphabet Walt didn't know, but the nice woman who answered the phone had seemed to understand his plea for coffee, sugar, and food. He was hopeful for a basket of rolls or something to snack on.

When there was a knock at the door, the paranoid security-type people—so, basically everyone in the room but himself, Annalise, and the admiral—whipped their heads around.

"I ordered room service," Walt said.

The bald guy who'd come in with Leonid was the one who actually opened the door, conversing with whomever was outside in terse tones. He stepped back to let two servers roll in carts bearing heavy trays, but stopped them just inside the door, checking under the tablecloths and domed lids of the plate covers. He even opened the coffee urn.

Walt looked at Leonid, wondering exactly what this guy did that he needed a bodyguard who was even more paranoid and security conscious than Jakob. During their discussion, someone had mentioned he owned a company that handled unloading and loading cargo at the port of Odessa, which was one of the largest and busiest ports on the Black Sea.

An Eastern European longshoreman boss. Right.

The hotel staff set up an elegant silver coffee service as well as some light refreshments, including Black Sea mussels, goat cheese, seasonal grapes, and some thinly sliced, fresh baked bread.

Walt made Annalise and Jakob each a cup of coffee and delivered them before going back to make them plates of snacks. He clasped Vadisk on the shoulder and asked him if he wanted anything, and then, since he sure as shit wasn't being helpful with the investigation, he took everyone else's orders.

That done, Walt took his own cup of coffee and went to look out the window. He wondered if, somewhere out there right now, Zasha was suffering. Hurting.

People became doctors because they wanted to ease suffering. He'd learned, long before his fellow doctors whose careers kept them in the relative safety of hospitals and medical offices, that no matter how hard he worked, no matter how dedicated he was, people would suffer and die. He could, would, help some of them, but he wouldn't be able to help everyone he wanted to.

If they found Zasha alive, he would be there. He wasn't useful for much right now, in fact he was only there because he hadn't wanted to be separated from Jakob and Annalise. Not when their time together was nearly over.

A sharp inhale from Annalise brought his attention away

from the view. Walt went over to the couch, sinking down beside her.

The screen of her laptop was a mess of video windows, three or four of which were currently playing.

"Whoa, what am I looking at?" Walt asked.

"Wait, I don't want to influence you." Annalise clicked, then enlarged one of the videos.

Walt watched the video feed of a random city street. Three people walked by—two men and a woman. He focused on the woman, leaning forward.

She walked more slowly than the men, her hands in her pockets. Tall, with short blonde hair and a fluffy wool scarf wrapped around her neck and tucked into her jacket.

"Now watch this one."

Annalise started another video. This clip was longer, with half a dozen people, two of which were women.

And neither of whom was the tall blonde.

Walt glanced at Annalise out of the corner of his eye. Maybe lack of sleep was getting to her. "What am I looking at?" he asked again.

"The woman."

"Uh, which woman? There were three different women."

"Were there?" Annalise arched a brow, the professor back in the saddle again.

Walt leaned forward. Damn it, he was a good student. He'd pass this test. "Play them again."

The blonde from the first video looked wealthy—something about the way her coat fit, the perfect golden tan, and her haircut. She walked with her shoulders back, a slow sort of saunter. Walt motioned for Annalise to bring up the other video.

The first woman in this one was a short brunette with her hair in a bun, wispy pieces framing her face. She wore a winter jacket and boots.

The second was another brunette, her hair loose under a beanie-style winter hat. She wore a scarf wrapped around her neck, nearly covering the entire bottom half of her face.

"The scarf," Walt said. "The blonde woman was wearing a scarf, and so is this one. But they're not the same height. I mean the hair could be a wig, but the height."

"You're right that hair color can be changed with a wig. And height with the right kind of shoes. Don't focus on what they look like. Watch how she moves. How she walks." There was a tight excitement in Annalise's voice. Jakob, who'd been leaning on the table to look at something Vadisk was doing, pushed up, coming to stand behind the couch and watch as Annalise played the videos again.

This time Walt saw it. The first woman in the longer video wasn't walking as fast as everyone else. There was an almost arrogant slowness to the way she moved that was at odds with her rather drab appearance. It was the tall blonde's walk, and it had fit her appearance—wealthy, powerful, self-assured—when she was a blonde far more than when she was dressed as the brunette.

"She also has one hand in her pocket," Annalise said. "She's wearing a glove on the other hand, so she clearly has gloves. My guess is she has something in that pocket she needs to hold onto. Either because she's worried about losing or dropping it or because she needs it for reassurance."

"Are there any shots of her face?" Walt asked, suddenly anxious and antsy.

"Here." She clicked, opening a still of the woman. "This video is from Krakow. I checked and though they've been running facial recognition for hours, the team in Budapest hasn't identified her yet. This one, where she's blonde, this is from here in Odessa."

Jakob straightened. "Admiral Varda."

Nikolett had been watching them, and the instant Jakob said her name she came over, dropping down beside Annalise.

Annalise had the still images of the woman's face up on screen—neither of them a front-facing image, but there was enough to see that they weren't the same person.

"Okay, the walk is something, but... They look nothing alike," Walt said.

"Yes, they do," Annalise assured him. At the same time Nikolett said, "Makeup."

Walt looked again. The shape of the eyes was different, wasn't it? He peered closer. The blonde version had almond-shaped eyes, while the brunette had rounder eyes. The blonde's nose was skinnier, her lips full.

But the closer he looked, the more he saw. Comparing the actual size of visible sclera of the eye, as well as the curvature of the lower lid...those were the same. Her nostrils were the same too, they just seemed skinnier on the blonde.

"Vadisk," Nikolett barked. "Run this woman's face against passport control for the past—" Nikolett looked at Annalise.

"Six, to be safe."

"Six months," Nikolett finished.

Leonid was on his feet. "What have you found?"

It was Annalise who answered. "The footage you provided shows a woman who is very, very similar to, if not the same person, as one of the persons of interest we have in relation to the case in Krakow."

Leonid's cheek twitched. "A serial killer took my sister."

"Facial recognition running," Vadisk said. "Six months' worth of passport photos isn't a small number, but it's a hell of a lot better than trying to check against all of Europe."

"Show me," Leonid demanded.

Walt followed after Annalise as she took her computer to the table, stepping back so other people could crowd around her as she played the videos, pointing out the similarity in the way the woman held herself, her gait, if not the stride length of her steps thanks to the difference in footwear.

Annalise was still talking when Vadisk shoved to his feet. "Got her."

The air went perfectly still, as if everyone in the room held their breath for one frozen, tense moment.

"Ava Chapman. British citizen," Vadisk said.

"Where is she now?" Leonid snarled.

Vadisk clicked. "She rented a private residence in Teplodar. Four-month lease that ends in two weeks." Vadisk grabbed his phone off the table. "She has a flight booked to Paraguay five days from now."

Before Vadisk was even finished talking he, Jakob, Maxim, Leonid, and the bodyguard were all in motion, headed for the door. The conversation had switched from English to Ukrainian, and Nikolett was quick-fire translating for Jakob.

Less than five minutes later, the suite was empty.

Walt stared at the door, shocked at how quickly things had happened.

Nikolett was at a computer. "We will watch. Vadisk is wearing an advanced comm system." A second later, a video feed popped up. All they could see was the front window of a car that seemed to be racing through the city traffic.

Nikolett straightened, looked at Annalise. "What is the likelihood she's still alive?"

Annalise shook her head. "I don't know, but it's not good. The killer has a flight booked. She's ready to leave the country."

Nikolett looked grim. "Then we'll hope they are there in time to recover her body."

CHAPTER TWENTY-TWO

T he ride to Teplodar was quiet, tense. Jakob's memory flashed back to times he'd sat in tanks and vans, trying to calm and focus himself before an op. He was riding in an elegant, expensive SUV, Vadisk in the front passenger seat, Leonid—the car's owner—beside him, Maxim on the third row bench seat.

Leonid's bodyguard, whose name Jakob still didn't know, was driving, though that term was far too sedate for the way the vehicle had whipped through traffic, finally leaving the elegant city of Odessa behind.

As they barreled by the Baraboi River, Jakob understood why their killer had chosen this location. It was close to the city of Odessa, but it felt like a ghost town.

In the front, Vadisk said something to the bodyguard, who nodded. After checking his phone, Vadisk turned around to look back at Jakob and the others. He spoke first in Ukrainian, and then repeated it in English for Jakob.

"We are less than five kilometers away. No one, not our people or his," Vadisk nodded at Leonid, "have been able to get detailed schematics of the house. Our Turkish friend," code for the Ottoman admiral, "sent help," the janissaries, "but they are hours out."

"Blind and weaponless," Jakob murmured.

"There are rifles in the trunk," Leonid replied in English. "Hunting rifles."

"Better than nothing," Maxim said.

"Once we go in, we use Ukrainian. We know she speaks English."

Jakob nodded once. He would be left out of the communications because he didn't speak the language, but he could handle it.

"Did you serve?" Maxim asked him.

Jakob twisted in his seat to answer. "Not directly. Intelligence."

There was a beat of silence as everyone processed that. Leonid repeated Jakob's words for the driver, who grunted.

Vadisk, Maxim, and Leonid all nodded.

The car turned off the road into a seemingly abandoned residential area. The houses were far apart, the trees and vegetation between them overgrown. The car slowed, and the pre-action silence descended once more.

"My sister is the priority. We get her out safe...alive." Leonid's voice was fierce and...scared. Jakob remembered how he'd felt when he knew Annalise was gone. Knew she was in danger.

The driver pulled the car to the side, wheels half on the greenery that made a narrow strip between the edge of the road and the half wall that marked the front boundary of a two-story house that was barely visible through the untrimmed trees that crowded the front lawn.

Vadisk checked his phone and opened his door.

"Wait."

Everyone looked to Leonid.

He was frowning, looking through the front window. "When we find my sister, I will help her. I have...enemies. And I taught my sister how to fight. Survive. She would not have expected betrayal from a woman, but she will think you are enemies." He looked from Vadisk to Jakob to Maxim. The driver was frowning back at his boss, who said something quickly to him. The bald man's eyes widened, and he nodded empathetically.

"Who will she think we are?" Vadisk asked with what might have been resignation in his tone.

"*Solntsevskaya* Bratva."

"*Layno*," Maxim cursed.

That sounded enough like the Polish word for "shit" that Jakob was fairly certain of the translation. And he heartily agreed with the sentiment.

"When we find her, I will approach Zasha." With that, Leonid opened his door.

Ten minutes later, rifles had been dispersed to Leonid, Maxim, and the bodyguard. Jakob and Vadisk were unarmed, but he didn't mind. He was better in hand-to-hand combat.

The fact that Leonid had a weapon would be concerning if they didn't find his sister alive. In his grief, mistakes might be made.

The house Ava had rented was fifty meters from where they parked. The whole road seemed deserted, no doubt because the city of Teplodar was originally created to provide housing for workers at an atomic thermal power station. However, development of the station was postponed after Chernobyl and completely halted in the nineties.

Using hand signals, Maxim, who had taken point, split them up. Vadisk, Leonid, and the guard were going around the side to find alternate entrances, while Jakob and Maxim were taking the front door.

The two-story white house was blocky in the way of Soviet buildings, and like the houses around it, there were signs of neglect. The overgrown foliage, the rutted gravel driveway that was more weeds than rock. But there was a car parked just in front of the small stoop. Ava was here.

Jakob snuck forward, using the untamed bushes and tall grass in what may have been a well-landscaped yard. Crouching down next to the car, he quietly unscrewed the valve stem and depressed the valve, air whooshing around his fingertip. He could have knifed the tires—he had a long matte black knife in a holder on his back—but if they were wrong and Ava wasn't here, it would be better to do something that wouldn't raise the alarm. One flat tire would be enough to slow down her getaway.

Maxim seemed to understand because he watched Jakob, and then nodded.

It felt as if hours had passed, but in reality he knew it was less than two minutes before he and Maxim rose and ran at a crouch around the car and up the front steps. Jakob flattened himself beside the door and gingerly tested the handle. Locked.

Maxim passed Jakob the gun, reached into his pocket, and pulled out a set of lock picks. Forty seconds later, they were in, the door swinging open with a loud, rusty squeal.

But that sound was drowned out by the screams that echoed up from somewhere deep in the house.

Jakob checked the urge to run in, waiting instead for Maxim, who could see into the house, to raise two fingers and do a quick double point. Jakob slid past him, pressing the rifle into his hand even as he drew his knife, holding it in a reverse grip, the blade along his forearm.

The house was far nicer than the outside would have

suggested, with pleasant furnishings and clean, if well worn, floors. Jakob didn't bother to stop and check the rooms. He wasn't law enforcement, not really, and his training had focused on getting the job done, no matter what it took, and with little to no regard for his own safety.

The scream had been muffled, which meant interior room or the second floor. Vadisk and Leonid passed by an open doorway ahead and on the left. They were being more methodical in their search, but everyone was headed to the stairs.

In a quirk of construction, the foot of the stairs were toward the back of the house, closer to where Vadisk and Leonid were. Maxim was behind him, and when Jakob looked back, he saw Maxim half turned to cover their rear, gun in place with the butt against his shoulder, but the barrel pointed down.

Jakob headed for the stairs, planning to follow Vadisk and Leonid—the bodyguard had taken position in an opening where he could see the stairs and the back of the house.

He passed the opening to a dining room and a small door to an under-stair closet as another scream echoed through the house.

He paused, head swiveling. The sound had come through the small door.

Not upstairs...but down. In a basement.

Jakob raised a hand, forming a fist. Everyone stopped, and he leaned in to the door.

He could just faintly hear voices. One rose in volume, though not enough for him to make out the words, and then there was another scream.

It didn't sound like a scream of fear, but more like one of rage.

Jakob started to ease the door open. Leonid tried to knock him out of the way, but Vadisk grabbed him, slapping a hand over his mouth. For a moment, Leonid's eyes were wild, and

Jakob's heart went out to him. Vadisk held the other man easily —a testament to exactly how strong he was—and whispered something in his ear.

Jakob shot a glance at Maxim, who nodded.

Resettling his grip on the hilt of the knife, Jakob went through the door, as a vision of Annalise and Walt, the way they'd looked last night as the three of them had come together, flashed through his mind. He'd been in dangerous situations before, even faced down death, but it had been easier back then. Because he'd never felt like he had so much to lose.

There was a tiny landing, really more of a wide step, just inside the door, then stairs so steep they were almost a ladder. Lights were on in the basement, illuminating a section of the gray concrete block floor and walls.

Jakob went down two more steps, until his feet were nearly in the light, then stopped. Bracing the hand not holding the knife, he leaned as far as he could, taking a quick glance at the room and silently jerking back up before processing everything he'd seen.

Two women, one medium height with hair a color somewhere between brown and blonde, the other dark haired...and locked in a cage. Ava held what looked like a spear, but it might have been a knife taped to the end of a broom handle. Zasha, the woman in the cage, was bloody, her clothes ragged and each slice in the fabric rimmed in blood, some of it old enough to have dried black.

Was Zasha...holding a knife of her own?

Ava was standing to the side of the stairs, which meant she would most likely see any movement. The best option would be to have Maxim shoot her.

Both women were panting, Zasha occasionally letting out a little sound of pain.

Jakob looked back and held up two fingers, hoping the

others, who were crowded above him, Vadisk still in the hallway since there was so little space, could see.

Jakob held up one finger, and then changed it into a gun.

Target one, neutralize by gunshot.

Maxim nodded, but Leonid vehemently shook his head, pointed at the rifle he held, pantomimed using a sight, then shook his head again.

Jakob nodded once, fairly certain that Leonid was saying they weren't precision rifles. He didn't want to risk his sister.

There was enough space between them, and they were close enough, that it would take only a mildly adept marksman to hit Ava without getting Zasha...unless the rifles were loaded with buckshot. Leonid called them hunting rifles. They might have scatter-shot cartridges.

Jakob gritted his teeth in frustration, and then tucked his knife back into his scabbard. This was going to have to be a surprise attack.

Repositioning himself so his hands were on the walls of the stairwell, his feet braced on the narrow step, Jakob looked over his shoulder, hoping they could read his expression, then jumped.

His palms skidded down the walls, controlling his descent to some degree. When he hit the ground, he rolled, not away from, but toward Ava.

An enraged scream was all the warning he got before the makeshift spear stabbed the floor where he would have been had he rolled the other way. Bracing his elbows, Jakob swept out one leg, taking Ava down at the ankles.

She fell, but held on to her weapon. Jakob saw the blade flashing in the too-bright light, and brought his arms up in time to protect his head. In his peripheral vision, he saw Maxim and Leonid hitting the ground. Maxim raised the weapon and snarled, "Stop."

But Ava was in midfall, and the business end of her spear was headed right for Jakob. He saw it coming, and though it felt like it was happening in slow motion it was only a fraction of a second before the blade came down. He felt the knife bite into his arm, felt the thump as it hit bone.

Grabbing the shaft of the weapon, Jakob gritted his teeth and held perfectly still, half-sprawled on the floor, stuck that way since, until he was in the presence of a medical team, the knife needed to stay in place.

The woman in the cage snarled something, and then to Jakob's alarm, she raised her own weapon, an exact copy of the knife currently embedded in his arm. She seemed to be planning to stab through the bars into Jakob's foot, which rested against the cage.

Jakob made a noise that might have been a yelp of alarm—though he would deny it—but Leonid dropped down, straddling Jakob's legs, his hands raised, a steady stream of words falling from his lips.

Jakob could no longer see the woman, but he heard her gasp, heard the soft sob as she said her brother's name.

Maxim had Ava on her stomach, arms behind her back.

"Stop!" she demanded, sounding panicked rather than angry. "I have to finish. You don't understand."

The bodyguard produced a pair of handcuffs, passing them to Maxim, who locked them around the English woman's wrists.

"Keys," Leonid snarled. "Where are the keys to the cage?"

"No, no, no." Ava shook her head as Maxim hauled her to her feet.

Vadisk was standing off to the side, speaking quietly into a phone and staring at the far corner of the concrete room.

"The cage isn't part of my mission. She was being difficult.

She stole my instrument and hurt me. I had to control her so she wouldn't hurt me!"

"Fuck you, you fucking bitch," Zasha snarled. Her voice was a cracking rasp, and now Jakob could see her lips were cracked. She needed water.

Leonid snapped something to his bodyguard, and then walked over to where Ava stood.

The room seemed to get twenty degrees colder. Or maybe that was shock as blood started to soak the sleeve of Jakob's shirt.

"Where is the key?" Leonid asked quietly.

Ava shook her head, eyes filling with tears. "Please leave. You're not allowing me to do this properly."

"I have never hit a woman before." Leonid's words hung heavy, punctuated by the rasping breath of his still-caged sister. Then he drew back his arm and backhanded Ava across the face. "But you are not a woman. You are a monster."

Maxim released Ava, who crumpled to the ground, utterly silent and with a faraway look in her eyes. Leonid's man returned, holding a bottle of water and a crowbar.

Vadisk hung up the phone, and then came over to Jakob. Without a word, he hooked his arms under Jakob's. Jakob tightened his hold on the spear to make sure it didn't shift, then nodded that he was ready.

Vadisk hauled him to his feet.

Jakob ground his teeth together, swore a blue streak in the silence of his head. Out loud, he said, "Ouch."

"Your doctor is on his way. Actually, both of them. Maybe Dr. Fischer can figure out...her." Vadisk took the knife from the holster at Jakob's back and cut away the heavy-duty tape that bound Ava's weapon to the end of the pole. Jakob blew out air in relief as the weight and pressure of the pole torqueing the knife was eliminated.

Jakob glanced at Ava, who was statue-still. In person she didn't look like either of the women they'd seen on video. She was pale-skinned with large blue eyes and thin lips, pretty, but not so much that anyone would ever look twice at her.

Leonid had managed to use the crowbar to pop open the door of the cage. He dropped to his knees and hauled his sister out, wrapping her in his arms. She hugged him back, still holding the knife she'd somehow gotten ahold of. Even when her brother gave her the bottle of water, she didn't let go of the weapon, instead taking the water with her free hand and desperately chugging it down, only to start retching a moment later.

Looking away to give her some privacy, however illusory it might be, Jakob caught sight of what Vadisk had been looking at in the corner.

Ten square feet of the room had been carefully tarped in plastic. Scalpels, butcher's blades, and a small saw were laid out on a stainless steel tray. Heavy, black webbed straps and cuffs hung down from the ceiling.

Jakob looked back to where Zasha now clung to her brother, shaking, and he was grateful they'd made it in time. Saved Zasha from the same gruesome fate that had taken Josephine and Alicja.

If only they could have been there to save those women as well.

CHAPTER TWENTY-THREE

Annalise smiled and leaned forward, lowering her voice and using a you-can-tell-me-a-secret tone. "What's your favorite food?"

Ava blinked, but returned the smile. It was the first time Annalise had managed to get her to react with anything other than frustrated tears or icy silence.

"Scones," Ava said softly. "A fresh, warm scone with nice jam, maybe a bit of cream."

"You're making me hungry," Annalise laughed softly. "A fresh scone sounds delicious. Mine is a really nice spinach salad. I know it's boring, but I love a salad with walnuts and cranberries, maybe some cheese, onions. Well, a nice salad and *Kartoffelpuffer*—German potato pancakes." Annalise leaned back in her chair, sighing a little. "My grandmother made the best *kartoffelpuffer*."

Everything Annalise said was true. It was dangerous to lie to someone with a complex psychosis because often they were far better at spotting lies than a normal person would be. It was also dangerous to share personal information with them, but that was a risk she was willing to take.

"One of my family's *empregadas* would make *xima*."

The word sounded like "chi-mah". Annalise nodded as if she understood, trusting the small concealed mic she wore would pick up the word.

"Comfort food," Ava said softly. Then she raised her chin, and her whole demeanor changed. She went from soft and sad to bold and ruthless with nothing more than the way she held her shoulders and the angle of her chin.

The hairs on the back of Annalise's neck rose, a primitive and instinctive response to being in the presence of an unpredictable predator. Outwardly, she made sure her expression didn't change. Inwardly, she reminded herself that Jakob and Walt were in a room not far away, watching everything that was happening on a video feed and listening through the hidden mic she wore.

"I wasn't raised to think things like chips and fried fish were comfort food. My parents were better than that."

Now they were getting somewhere.

Annalise faked a grimace. "In Germany, there is too much fried food also. It is good that your parents protected you." The choice of the word *protect* was a calculated risk. One that paid off.

Ava jerked and seemed to fold in on herself once more. "My parents *did* protect me." She'd lowered her voice, ostensibly so that no one else would hear her.

Annalise had been very deliberate in how she'd set up the small room. A camcorder sat on the long built-in counter desk along one side of the as-yet-unfinished safe room. A small folding table and two chairs had been brought in, the tools and materials the construction crew was using hauled out.

They'd started out handcuffing Ava to the table, but

Annalise had stopped them, demanding that she instead be cuffed to the chair with a chain that was long enough for plenty of slack. It wouldn't do much to slow Ava down if she decided to attack, but seeing Ava shackled to the table had made Annalise have a flashback to the caravan, to being at Axel's mercy.

Everyone had objected to that—what if Ava picked up the chair and started beating her with it—but there was a guard stationed just outside the door, and having someone in the room would destroy the trust she needed to build.

It was midafternoon now, nearly twenty-four hours after she'd spotted the similarities on the videos. They were back in Budapest. Getting everyone here, including Ava and a wounded Jakob, had taken some logistical planning, and a large, expensive helicopter.

Annalise suspected that Nikolett had also had to do some fast-talking or serious negotiations in order to get Leonid to agree to let them take custody of Ava. From what she'd seen of him, Leonid wasn't the kind of man who let his enemies go. And based on what Walt had said about Zasha's substantial injuries, it was even more surprising that Leonid had let them take Ava and helped arrange it so they could leave Odessa via the helipad at his company's facility on the port.

Between Leonid and assistance from the Ottoman territory janissaries, who had arrived a few hours after everyone was hauled back to the hotel, they'd managed to leave Odessa in the early hours of the morning, before the sun rose.

Rather than going to downtown Budapest, Vadisk had flown them to Nikolett's private residence in the Zugliget neighborhood to the east of Budapest.

The modern-style villa was lovely, but much of the inside was still under construction—though the exterior was done and the security systems were all up and running.

The safe room, which wasn't yet fully functional, was now both prison cell and interrogation room. Jakob, Walt, Nikolett, and a few others who'd been working the case at the Hungary territory headquarters were in Nikolett's large home office, which had secure phone and internet connections, and a live feed of everything going on in this room.

"That's a parent's job. To protect their children."

"It's not a parent's fault if something bad happened," Ava shot back, the predator back in her voice and posture.

The way she was vacillating between victim and predator was dazzling in how completely abnormal it was.

"Sometimes," Annalise agreed. "Bad things happen that no one can stop. Accidents. Sickness. Other times the parents could have done more to protect—"

"My father wasn't wrong! They needed him. Too many of them called themselves Christians, but they were bound for hell. My father was saving them."

"How did he save them?"

"He taught them. Showed them the right way to be good. There were Zionists, Catholics." She spit the words as if they were foul.

Her earpiece beeped quietly before beginning transmission.

"*Empregada is the Portuguese word for servant,*" Nikolett's voice was tiny but clear. "*We think the other word she said earlier is xima. It's a porridge they serve in Mozambique, where upper classes speak Portuguese. No progress on her records.*"

At least one of the forms Petro's presumed patronage must have taken was to wipe away any trace of Ava's past. They'd found her birth record in England, but then there was nearly no trace of her—only the odd record of her entering and exiting countries in South America and the Far East. Her immigration records within the EU had all been deleted.

Annalise stayed quiet, waited until some of the rage had seeped from Ava's posture.

It was time to take another calculated risk, based on the information she had. "There aren't many Anglican missionaries in Mozambique."

Ava jerked as if struck. She turned away, shoulders hunched. The posture of someone who knew to protect their chest and stomach from incoming blows.

It was all but certain that Ava had suffered some kind of steady, sustained abuse in her childhood. It was rare for people with severe abnormal behavior, the kind that resulted in the psychopathy of a serial killer, to have a trauma-free past.

"How old were you when your father took you to Mozambique?" Annalise asked softly.

"He was called when I was four. We went with him. To support him. That was our duty."

"Duty? But you were just a child."

"I was more. God had a purpose for me." Little by little, Ava started to unfold, morphing once again.

"Is your purpose something you can talk about?"

Ava looked down her nose at Annalise. "You wouldn't understand."

"Oh? Why not? I'm a pretty smart person."

"This isn't about intelligence. It's about moral fortitude."

Annalise took a breath and reminded herself that this was police interrogation, not a diagnostic interview. No matter how fascinating Ava would be to diagnose. That job would be left to others, mostly like a psychology team with whatever government or prison system Ava ended up in.

But before they could turn her over to those authorities, there was information the Masters' Admiralty wanted.

Annalise had rarely been the one to conduct interrogations when she worked at the *Kripo*. Usually she was where Jakob and Walt were now, on the outside of the interrogation room, watching, listening, and assisting with ongoing interview strategies.

Of the people currently in Nikolett's house, she was the most qualified.

"How do you know if someone has moral fortitude?" Annalise asked.

A genuine, peaceful smile graced Ava's lips. "I can see it."

"What does it look like?"

"It's a halo around them. I first saw it on my mother."

"Your mother has a halo."

"Not has. Had. My mother *had* a halo."

"My condolences on the loss of your mother."

"No need. She sits at the feet of my father, who sits at the right hand of God."

"Did she die when you were young?" It was time to start pushing Ava, and asking more specific questions would give the other woman fewer opportunities to spout rote religious statements.

"I was ten."

"And how did she die?"

"They killed her."

"How did they kill her?"

Ava jerked, as if she hadn't expected that question. She'd probably expected "who killed her?" which was why Annalise hadn't asked that.

Ava's eyes seemed to glitter with an emotion Annalise wasn't ready to name.

"They tortured my mother. Raped her. Cut off one hand, then the other. Then they cut off her head."

Annalise nodded, keeping her expression sympathetic. It wasn't hard.

"I watched. With my father. They made us watch, and I

begged him to do what they wanted so they'd stop hurting my mother. He wouldn't. He was a righteous man."

"Your mother's halo, was that because of how she died?"

"No, the halo appeared before. When they started to hurt her. When she died, it was so bright it blinded me."

"Did the woman in Odessa, Zasha, have a halo?"

Ava nodded. "Yes. Faintly, but it was there."

"Is that why you chose her?"

"Why ask when you know the answer?" Ava snapped.

"Because I don't know. I'm listening to you and trying to understand. Can you explain, help me understand?" Annalise reached out, put her hand on Ava's forearm, squeezing gently.

"The halo is faint and will fade if I don't help them."

"What you're doing is helping people to be like your mother. To have moral fortitude, like she did."

"Yes. If I didn't, their halo might vanish. They have the right to ascend with the grace of angels."

"Everyone you helped...they all had halos?"

"Yes."

"Even Josephine O'Connor?" Annalise reached into her pocket, pulled out a small photo of Josephine and held it up. "She lived in Dublin."

Ava glanced at the photo, and then reached for it. Annalise put it back in her pocket.

"She did," Ava assured her.

"But you didn't pick her, did you?" Annalise asked. "Someone else gave you her name."

Ava's shoulders straightened and she raised a brow. "Oh?"

"There's no need to protect him. He's dead."

"No," Ava said slowly. But before Annalise could reply, she said, "I knew that. I knew he'd ascended."

Annalise reached into her other pocket, taking out the picture of Petro. "Who was he to you? A friend?"

"Melech understood me." She reached for the picture, and this time Annalise let her have it.

"Melech," Annalise repeated.

Ava studied the picture of Petro. There was no longing in the way she looked at it. Whatever had been between them hadn't been romantic.

"He could see the halos too." Ava passed the picture back. "He saw it on Josephine. It took me time, but I also saw."

"But he told you what to do with her body, didn't he? So he did more than just see the halos. He told you how to...help them."

"If he saw them first, then I had to listen." Ava stared at the wall, seemingly lost in thought.

"Melech is a Hebrew name, but also translates to 'king'," Nikolett said in her ear. *"Subtle."*

"You had to do what he said, because he identified Josephine first. But you would have done it differently, wouldn't you? If you'd seen her first."

Ava looked back to Annalise, frowning. "It wasn't proper, what happened to her." Ava touched her cheek.

"It wasn't dignified," Annalise agreed, noting that when it came to Josephine, Ava was speaking about it as if someone else had done the action.

"Dignity is not... A body isn't important." It sounded like Ava was trying to convince herself. "My mother's body had to be left so it could return to the earth." Ava swallowed. "Even so, I treat them with care."

"Yes, I saw how you cared for Alicja. The box you used was lovely," Annalise murmured. "But with Josephine, he didn't think there should be anything, did he? You chose to do more than he'd told you to. To care for her."

"Melech didn't fully understand. He wasn't there to see my mother."

"Of course not. It makes sense he wouldn't know as much as you. What did he suggest you do with the other pieces of Josephine?"

"I didn't have time to do what I needed with her." Ava shook her head. "So I gave her body to the fire, so it could baptize her."

Annalise's heart hurt for Eric, and Josephine's brother, that there would never be any additional remains they could bury. None of what she was feeling showed on her face as she kept her expression calm and slightly sympathetic. "That must have been hard, to build a fire big enough to burn a body without anyone seeing."

Ava's attention snapped to Annalise. "Please don't be obtuse. I didn't build a...a pyre." Another sneer. "Like a pagan. I put her pieces in the hospital's incinerator."

"Hospital?" Annalise's heart was pounding, and through the earpiece she thought she heard muttering, quickly shushed.

"St. James's Hospital. In Dublin. That's where I was stationed."

"Stationed?"

Ava looked down her nose at Annalise. "You're pretending to know things, but really you don't know anything important."

"Then why don't you tell me? Tell me what you were doing at St. James's Hospital."

"Locum work." Ava smiled. "I'm an orthopedic surgeon."

CHAPTER TWENTY-FOUR

It was late when Walt returned to the hotel suite in Budapest with Jakob and Annalise. They'd cut the interrogation of Ava short after she'd dropped the bomb about being an orthopedic surgeon. They needed time to gather more intel from Leonid and Zasha before they continued with the questioning.

It had been a hell of a week. He, Jakob, and Annalise had spent the previous night in Odessa together, but they'd done nothing more than climb into bed, sleeping restlessly. Jakob had been in a great deal of pain from the laceration to his arm—the subcutaneous cut had only required external stitches—and Annalise had never had time to properly heal—physically and mentally—from her time with Axel.

Walt was beginning to think it was a good thing he was around. The two of them seemed to need a full-time physician on hand.

He'd spent more than a few anxious moments in the car on the way to the house outside Odessa after learning Jakob had been wounded. While the knife had been lodged deeply in

Jakob's upper arm, after careful bandaging, Walt had been able to remove it safely.

When he'd seen the knife wound through the grainy feed of Vadisk's body cam, he'd been concerned about vascular damage, so he had been relieved to discover the knife hadn't struck an artery. An injury like that could have effectively ended Jakob's career as a Ritter of the territory.

Leonid's bodyguard had been frighteningly prepared when they arrived at the house where Zasha had been held. He'd helped Walt set up a makeshift field hospital in one of the upstairs bedrooms, supplying everything he needed from a first-aid perspective—gauze, nylon sutures, needle, antibiotics.

They'd been awakened this morning in Odessa an hour or so before dawn by Vadisk, banging on their hotel room door, telling them they were all flying back to Hungary to question the serial killer.

It wasn't until they'd returned to Budapest that Walt had been able to take an X-ray of Jakob's arm. Dimitri had delivered the portable machine from the conference room in headquarters to Nikolett's home at Walt's request. It had been the second time in as many days that Walt had made use of the portable X-ray machine. As he'd hoped, the bone in Jakob's arm —like Annalise's—was fine, no fractures or breaks.

Walt felt like he was running on fumes, waiting for the next catastrophe to strike. And given the way Annalise walked over to the couch like a zombie, dropping down heavily, he'd say she felt the same way.

"Fuck me," Annalise muttered.

Jakob followed her, his arm, like hers, in a matching sling. He joined her on the couch, the two of them mirror images in damaged bodies and weary expressions.

If Walt weren't so damn tired, he might have had enough energy to make a joke about the slings, but like them, he'd been ridden hard and put away wet. So he merely claimed the chair across from them, rubbing the palms of his hands into his scratchy, dry eyes.

Annalise broke the silence first. "It's been a challenging few days."

"So much crazy," Jakob murmured. The three of them were still shaken after hearing about Ava's mother's death, and Walt was particularly disturbed by the fact Ava, the serial killer, was a trained orthopedic surgeon. He was struggling to understand how she'd been able to hide her psychosis all through medical school.

"Nikolett wants us back at her place tomorrow early. She's asked me to continue leading the questioning," Annalise said after a few quiet minutes.

Jakob sighed. "Are you okay going back in there? Talking to Ava? No one would blame you for stepping aside after everything that happened with Axel."

She gave Jakob a soft smile. "I'm fine. Truly. It's a bit like playing chess. I'm not used to being the primary investigator, so it's a different way of approaching the suspect. A different style of questioning. It's challenging."

It wasn't until that moment that Walt realized how much Annalise had changed over the course of the past week. When they'd first met in her office at the university, she'd seemed a bit like a caged puppy, one who'd been kicked a few times too many, and was torn between cowering or biting back.

None of that was apparent now as he was seeing the reemerging of Annalise and the forensic psychologist she'd been before Axel had come into her life and slowly, insidiously, ripped it to shreds.

No. Walt changed his mind. He'd bet his entire life savings this was a totally new Annalise. A woman who was much wiser and stronger after unspeakable mental abuse. She was just now coming out on the other side of hell, and he was blown away by the confident, intelligent woman sitting across from him. She rocked his world.

As did the man sitting next to her. Jakob hadn't hesitated to race off to rescue a woman he'd never met yesterday. He'd risked his life to save Zasha. But that shouldn't surprise Walt. Even after a short acquaintance, he'd come to know Jakob as the type of man who'd throw himself in front of the speeding bullet. Jakob faced down danger with nothing more than his courage and his strength and his need to protect.

They were incredible people, and Walt felt grateful to be sitting here with them. He'd had no idea when Eric had stumbled into his field hospital in Libya, covered in blood, that his life would be so irrevocably changed in such a short time.

He stared at them in silence for a few minutes, trying to push away the dark thoughts starting to close in on him. When that failed, Walt leaned his head against the back of the chair and closed his eyes, debating whether or not to ask the question that was on everyone's mind, the big-ass elephant in the room.

The serial killer had been found and Annalise's stalker was dead. Their reasons for being together were at an end, but the idea of returning to Libya to continue his work with Doctors Without Borders held very little appeal to Walt right now, something he'd never experienced before. With him, work had always come first.

Before he could speak his concerns, Jakob beat him to the punch. "What now?" There was no denying from his tone Jakob was afraid to hear the answer.

Just as there was no denying the thought of leaving these two, knowing they could never be together, killed Walt. He had never expected to feel a tighter bond between three people than the one he shared with his brothers. And while this bond was different, it was definitely just as powerful, as strong.

The clinical, practical part of him tried to explain away the closeness he felt. After all, they'd shared a life-or-death experience that—coupled with their obvious attraction—could have Walt seeing and feeling things that weren't there.

But he discounted that instantly. He might be relatively inexperienced when it came to romantic love, but he knew enough to understand that this was it. The real deal.

Walt's eyelids lifted as he captured Jakob's gaze and decided he couldn't leave them. Not yet. "I still have some time before I'm due back at my clinic. I could come back to Frankfurt with the two of you for a little while."

Jakob considered that, and then turned to look at Annalise.

"I have some time before the semester starts. And perhaps I could also take additional time off," she said. "In truth, I think it is time to do more than teach. I'd like to return to the *Kripo*."

Jakob gave her a sad smile, sighing. "Damn. I was afraid you were going to say that."

Annalise reached out and grasped his good hand with hers. "Your job is just as dangerous, you know. I lost ten years off my life yesterday when I saw that knife in your arm. We'll have to worry about each other equally."

Jakob lifted her hand and kissed her knuckles. "Agreed. But Walt has the most dangerous job. Wasn't he talking about taking down extremist cells in Libya with the fleet admiral?" he asked with a chuckle.

"Then we would be smart to keep him here with us for as long as we can." Annalise glanced in Walt's direction.

Walt rose, closing the few feet that separated them, kneeling before them on the floor. "The future is coming. It's not something we can outrun or escape. But let's steal a few days more. Keep living in this incredible present just like Annalise suggested."

"I'd like that," Annalise said.

"So would I," Jakob added.

Walt smiled, rising up to kiss Annalise and then Jakob. They were quick, sealed-with-a-kiss busses, a promise that he would give them everything he could in the time they had remaining.

After that, words were no longer necessary. Annalise rose, Jakob's hand still clasped in hers. She gave Walt a pointed look that said "follow," and the three of them walked to the bedroom.

Once they arrived, Jakob kissed Annalise gently, his two lovers standing by the side of the bed. Walt had stopped at the bedroom door to watch them.

When they turned in unison, he couldn't hold back the brief bark of laughter at the sight of their matching slings. "This keeps getting trickier."

"Good thing there's a doctor in the house," Jakob said.

"Stay still," Walt said as he approached them. With slow, careful movements, he removed Annalise's sling, then Jakob's. Annalise lowered her arm, flexing it a bit to work out the kinks. Jakob winced, keeping his upper arm close to his side. The sling wasn't really necessary, but Walt used it as a way to immobilize Jakob's arm so the muscles could start to heal. The knife wound had gone about as deep as it could without striking an artery, and without the sling and the painkillers Walt had given him earlier, Jakob would be in a great deal more pain. Even now, Walt suspected his arm was hurting him more than Jakob was willing to admit.

Together, he and Annalise worked to remove Jakob's clothing, taking care not to jar his arm too much. Once he was naked, Walt placed a steadying hand on his good arm and guided him to the bed.

"Sit up with your back against the headboard," Walt directed.

"You think you're going to be the one giving the orders tonight just because I've got a little cut on my arm and a few stitches?" Jakob asked in that deep, rich, commanding voice that had Walt's cock rising from half-mast to rock hard in an instant.

Walt merely chuckled, then waved his hand, gesturing for Jakob to take control. He sure as shit wasn't going to argue with him or suggest they arm wrestle for it. There was nothing on earth hotter than Jakob's dirty demands in the bedroom. Unless, of course, it was Annalise's pleas for more.

"Undress our woman," Jakob said, looking for all the world like a king on his throne as he sat propped up against a pile of pillows.

Regardless of what Jakob might ask for, Walt wouldn't let him go too far tonight. His lover really did need to keep his arm as still as possible. There was no way Walt was going to risk him tearing out the stitches.

Walt twisted toward Annalise, who gave him the sexiest come hither smile he'd ever seen. He could tell he surprised her when he shifted until he was standing behind her, her back to his chest. He looked at Jakob over her shoulder, sliding his hands along her arms and sides until he reached the hem of her shirt. His light touch made her shiver.

Gripping the bottom of her shirt, he pulled it upwards, taking his time in order to tease Jakob as he bared her to their lover inch by inch.

He pulled the material tauter on her injured shoulder side, trying to limit her movement, but Annalise was clearly feeling better. She lifted both arms over her head to help him remove her shirt completely. Walt kissed her bruised shoulder, then the other, as he unfastened her bra.

Jakob was uncharacteristically—well, for the bedroom— quiet as he watched, but he was by no means an uninterested observer. He gripped his erection in his hand, slowly stroking the hard flesh, his gaze glued to Annalise's breasts as Walt tugged the bra off and dropped it to the floor.

"Cup them," Jakob said, his voice husky with need. "Pinch her nipples."

Walt narrowed his eyes at the second command, but Jakob shook his head and continued speaking before he could voice his concerns. "The bruises are faded. And she likes the way we make her nipples ache. Do it."

The doctor in Walt tried to glance over Annalise's shoulder, tried to make certain she'd healed enough. He couldn't see her nipples well enough to tell, but it didn't matter. Not when Annalise repeated Jakob's demand. "Do it," she whispered.

He cupped her heavy breasts, lifting them up before closing his palms over them, squeezing them, gently at first, before kneading them more firmly. The way Annalise's breathing increased and the slight arching of her back drove him on. Taking her nipples between his thumbs and forefingers, he pinched, the action provoking the sweetest moans and whimpers.

Jakob's grip on his own dick tightened, his strokes harder. "Turn her around, Walt. Take those pretty nipples in your mouth and suck them. Hard."

Walt had Annalise facing him before Jakob had finished issuing his demand. He bent his head lower, drawing one of her nipples in with rough suction. Annalise's hands flew to his head and she nearly suffocated him in her soft breasts as she drew him closer.

"Harder," she gasped.

Walt gave her what she asked for, teasing the taut tip with his teeth.

"Fuck, that's hot," Jakob murmured. "Take off the rest of her damn clothes and yours and the two of you get over here."

Annalise and Walt wasted no time getting naked, racing to undress each other, and once they were done, they both turned to face Jakob, awaiting his next command. Walt had never been a passive lover in his previous sexual encounters, limited though they were. He had never realized how much he liked being told what to do in bed.

Maybe he'd get Annalise to explain the psychology behind it for him later. Nothing like a little light pillow talk. He grinned at the thought, his sudden amusement catching Jakob's attention.

"Something funny?" Jakob asked.

Walt shook his head. "Tell you later."

It was obvious Jakob had other things on his mind because he dropped the subject. "I thought I told the two of you to get over here."

Annalise stepped closer to the bed, but Walt stopped her from climbing on the mattress and straddling Jakob's thighs by gripping her wrist.

She looked over her shoulder in question.

"Regardless of what Jakob might ask for," Walt warned, "we need to go slow tonight, take care."

Jakob growled, but didn't argue—which told Walt the man was indeed still in pain. "One of these days, the three of us are going to be completely healed and I'm showing you exactly how hard I want to fuck you. Both of you."

"But until then..." Walt said, releasing Annalise's wrist and kissing her on the cheek. "We're just going to have to be creative."

Annalise grinned. "I think I can handle that."

Walt sucked in a deep breath as Annalise proved just how creative she could be. She climbed onto the bed, but rather than straddling his waist, she settled between Jakob's outstretched thighs. Bending low and supporting her weight on her good arm, she ran her tongue along Jakob's dick from balls to tip before sliding it back down again and sucking one of Jakob's balls into her mouth.

Jakob's eyes closed briefly and Walt wondered if their lover was praying for the strength to hold on. God knew Annalise could tempt a priest to sin.

While she teased Jakob with her mouth, she took Walt down in a different way, wiggling her ass suggestively.

Walt reached out and ran his hand along the soft, smooth globes of her ass, then drew one fingertip along the slit between her legs. He teased the rim of her anus, then moved lower, circling the opening to her body. She was wet and hot and ready.

Annalise lifted her ass higher, spreading her legs apart even farther. He grinned and accepted the offer, pushing two fingers inside to the hilt.

She released Jakob's balls with a pop, a breathy moan escaping her lips.

Jakob was watching him, his gaze locked on where Walt was fucking her with his fingers.

"Use three," Jakob demanded. "Get her nice and ready for that big cock of yours."

Walt added a third to the first two, circling her waist with his other hand so that he could play with her clit. Annalise was a clit girl. The second he touched hers, she jerked and cried out, "Yes!"

Jakob placed his hand on the back of her head. "Pay attention to your work, Dr. Fischer," he growled.

Annalise shuddered, but lost no time wrapping her hand around the base of Jakob's cock and taking the head into her mouth.

"Get on the bed, Walt. You're going to fuck our woman while she sucks me."

Walt shifted, claiming his spot at the bottom of the bed between her legs. "Shit. I forgot the condom," he muttered, starting to rise.

Annalise released Jakob, shaking her head. "Birth control. Nothing between us. Please."

Walt glanced at Jakob and saw his own emotions reflected in the other man's eyes. They were both head over heels in love with this woman, and Walt was certain that would be true until the day they both took their last breaths.

Jakob and Annalise had fallen in love slowly over the course of the past few years. Their feelings had been born from protection, and then turned to friendship, before settling into this comfortable yet passionate love.

Walt was jealous of the years they'd had together without him. It was a weird sentiment, considering he'd only met them a week ago. His brothers would no doubt give him shit. Walt had always seemed the least likely of the Haydens to fall in love at first sight, too practical, too driven, too distracted by his career.

Oscar, though a grumpy fuck, had fallen fast for his first love, Faith, while Langston, a bit of a playboy, had always been open-minded, ready to find his soul mate—or in his case, mates —and fall in love. Walt, on the other hand, had brushed aside the concept of a close relationship, content to settle for casual, infrequent hookups that didn't interfere with his work.

Now...well, now, he wanted them with a passion that bordered on reckless. He felt completely out of control and he wasn't about to try to change that fact. Walt lowered his head and bit Annalise's ass. Not exactly hard, just enough to tease.

She jerked in surprise, his actions catching her off-guard. "Walt?"

"I've never felt like this," he admitted. "Never wanted anyone as badly as I want the two of you. And it's not a normal desire. It's overwhelming, consuming. It's like I'm willingly walking into the fire." He ran his tongue over the red mark left behind by his teeth. Then he lifted his hand and spanked her. Just one hard smack that cracked in the quiet room. "I want your pain, your pleasure, your body, your heart. I want to own you, and I want you to own me. I want to lose myself in your arms every single night and never wake up if it means leaving you."

Annalise studied his face as she looked at him over her shoulder. "Walt," she whispered.

He held her gaze but didn't respond. Couldn't respond. His throat constricted, tight. Had he gone too far?

"Everything. You can have everything you just asked for."

Walt swallowed heavily, placed his hand on her hip, guided his cock to her pussy, and he thrust in hard. Buried deep, he froze and chanced a look at Jakob.

"Take it," Jakob said. "Take everything. It's yours."

Annalise took Jakob into her mouth once more and this time, she followed Walt's lead, drawing their lover in deep, half his cock disappearing until he heard the quiet gag that told him Jakob's dick was touching the back of her throat.

After that, everything went out of focus, so he closed his eyes. Walt thrust in and out of Annalise's tight, beautiful body. He couldn't get deep enough, so he took her harder. He stroked her clit with firm fingers, drove the tip of his thumb into her ass, and still it wasn't enough.

He heard Jakob's grunts, his demands that Annalise take him deeper, open her throat, swallow him down.

He opened his eyes, watching as Jakob fucked Annalise's mouth. Or maybe she was fucking him.

Jakob's fist was clenched around her hair, lifting her up, drawing her back down. His face was etched with pain chiseled from pure ecstasy.

Jakob must have felt Walt's eyes on him because he glanced up. Walt hadn't stopped fucking her—he couldn't.

A muscle in Jakob's jaw twitched. "She's ours," he said through gritted teeth. "Prove it to her."

It was all Walt needed to hear. He increased his pace, spanking her ass over and over until her orgasm crashed over her, She lifted her head briefly from Jakob's cock, releasing a loud, beautiful cry, as her inner muscles clenched Walt's dick so tightly, he saw stars.

Walt came on the next rough thrust, groaning because it felt so fucking good it hurt. He filled her with jet after jet of come.

Annalise lowered her head as her climax began to wane. It only took a few seconds more before Jakob came as well, holding Annalise's head as she swallowed every drop.

The room was quiet except for the harsh inhale and exhale of breath, all three of them struggling for air.

Walt felt a drop of sweat slide along the side of his face, and for the first time, he was aware of just how hot the room had gotten.

Annalise released Jakob's dick, placing her cheek on Jakob's stomach, even as her ass was still raised, still holding Walt's softening dick. He pulled out slowly, the action prompting her to open sex-dazed eyes and look at him.

"I love you," she whispered as she stared at him, then she turned to look at Jakob as well.

Just three words. Spoken for all of them.

Neither he nor Jakob said them back. They didn't need to. There was no question they felt the exact same way.

And it was then it occurred to Walt that while he could mend broken bodies, he didn't have a clue how to fix a broken heart.

And his was about to be shattered.

CHAPTER TWENTY-FIVE

J akob stood with his back to the wall, outwardly silent, while inwardly snarling.

There were way too many damned people in the room.

When Nikolett's house was finished, this room would be a combination home office and off-site backup for the Hungary territory headquarters. Large as both the house and this room were, right now, it was crowded.

When he, Walt, and Annalise had arrived half an hour ago, the Hungary territory leadership had just been finishing up an early morning meeting. Attendees included Admiral Varda, Vice Admiral Kata, the security minister Dimitri, plus the three finance ministers, four knights—including Maxim, and three security officers. Vadisk hadn't been at the meeting because he'd been the one to pick them up at the hotel and escort them back here.

Nikolett had acknowledged them with a nod when they walked in. A few others had looked their way, but no one seemed surprised by their presence or confused as to who they were. That meant at least part of the meeting had included briefing the people he, Walt, and Annalise hadn't met before as to who they were and how they were involved.

Nikolett finished speaking to the assembled members of her territory in Hungarian for several minutes before dismissing people. About a third of the room cleared out, and before they were even out the front door—which was steel set in steel-reinforced surrounds like the door of a bank vault—the remaining knights and security officers had taken positions near the doors and just behind the admiral.

All this security to keep danger out, when danger was already inside.

Nikolett motioned Annalise forward. His love spoke with Nikolett and Nyx for several minutes.

His love.

After all these years, Annalise was his love. But not for much longer.

Because life fucking sucked. Maybe they could have an intense, carnal affair when they got back to Frankfurt. He would fuck her on the bed he'd bought for her, in the room he'd decorated for her.

Nope. Wouldn't work. Because Walt couldn't stay there for long, couldn't live there with them. Hell, the two of them couldn't even remain there together forever.

Irritated, Jakob crossed his arms, keeping his attention on Annalise. His arm immediately protested, and that just increased his irritation. Dropping his bad arm with a grunt, he considered telling everyone in the room to fuck off. All these people wanted Annalise to go lock herself in a room with a bat-shit crazy woman who hacked people up both professionally and for fun.

Walt's hand landed on Jakob's shoulder. "I would feel better if you'd use the sling."

He wasn't going to use a damn sling. A little stab never hurt...actually it hurt quite a fucking bit. But still, if he needed to fight to protect Walt and Annalise, the sling would be in the way. The odds weren't good if they had to fight their way out of here, even if he hadn't had one arm that had recently been used as a knife block.

Out loud he said, "No."

Walt laughed silently, a little huff of sound.

Annalise nodded in response to what Nyx was saying, then turned to face the room. Nikolett and Nyx both stepped back to give her the floor.

"Everyone here speaks English?" Annalise asked in her professor voice, a file folder in hand.

All but one of the people in the room nodded, and Vadisk moved to stand by him, promising to translate.

"Your admiral has asked me to brief everyone as to what we know so far."

Annalise looked at Jakob, and his stupid, stupid heart fluttered in his chest.

"This includes some new information pieced together thanks to the work of several of the people in this room."

A few of the security officers and knights Jakob didn't know nodded. Oh. That was why she'd looked at him. She was about to say something new. He was an idiot. An idiot in love with a woman he couldn't handle when it was just the two of them, and a man whose life and future was an ocean away.

Annalise glanced down at the paper in her hand and began to summarize the information on the page.

"Ava Chapman was born in Devon, England. When she was a child, her father joined and eventually became a priest in a strict, devout Anglican church. Shortly after, he moved his family, including a four-year-old Ava, to Mozambique where he set up a small mission, focused strictly on conversion. In particular, they were focused on members of the Catholic and amaZioni churches, which were the two primary houses of worship in the township where her father opened his mission.

"Relatively little is known about what exactly happened over the course of the six years that the Chapman family lived there. This may be due to the records having been deleted, as were most of Ava's records beyond her birth certificate, or it could be due to the fact that the mission wasn't affiliated with any international faith-based aid groups. Either way, based on the outcome, I think it would be safe to say there was a divisive relationship between the English family and the community."

Everyone was listening intently, and Jakob realized he was seeing the pre-stalker Annalise. He'd never loved her more.

She continued speaking. "Thanks to Maxim, who found recently digitized copies of a local paper, we know that when Ava was ten, the mission was attacked. Five people were killed —three locals, as well as Ava's father and mother. The article mentions that they were beheaded and then dismembered."

"She saw it happen," Vadisk said after translating for the man beside him.

"Based on her statements, yes. Her mother was raped, and had limbs removed, prior to her death. Again, Ava saw this. I am not going to offer a diagnosis, as I haven't done a diagnostic interview with her, but given what we know, I believe she has been recreating her mother's death, in what is not an act of rage, but one of mercy."

"She's mercy killing and torturing people?" Walt asked incredulously.

"Not mercy killing in the sense of euthanasia, but as a release." Annalise paused to think. "Perhaps a better way to phrase it would be exactly that. She believed she was releasing or freeing women who, like her mother, have what she calls 'moral fortitude'. Her victims are selected based on what she describes as a visible halo."

Jakob felt the first stirrings of pity for Ava. It didn't excuse what she'd done. The woman was undeniably nuts and needed to be—at the very least—locked up for life. Jakob had seen plenty of death in his time before becoming a knight. Death that came without trials, judgment rendered and execution carried out in darkness. When he became a knight, he walked away from that mindset, though clearly not the skillset, as evidenced by Axel's death.

As a Ritter, enforcing their laws and carrying out any punishments was his duty, but he acted in response to laws and at the direction of his admiral and vice admiral.

Despite all that, there was a part of him, a remnant of who he had been, who wanted to walk into that safe room and snap Ava's neck.

"She was torturing Zasha," Maxim said softly.

"Yes, and there is no doubt that her other victims also suffered prior to death, but her actions were not rooted in a desire to cause them pain. I don't believe there is a sexual sadism fulfillment element to her action, despite the fact that she is raping the women using, based on what was found in Odessa, homemade wooden phalluses."

Everyone took a minute to process that horrific detail. Annalise cleared her throat and continued.

"Though her records and information are missing from most major databases, by searching lower-level—provincial, parish, individual academic institution—records, some of her life has been pieced together. Several years after the death of her parents, she was brought back to England where she became a ward of the court until the age of eighteen. I suspect she suffered some abuse, most likely in those years between when her parents died and before she returned to England."

A ten-year-old suddenly orphaned in a small town where her parents had been hated and she was an outsider in every possible way. Yeah, some really bad shit could have happened.

"Though," Annalise went on, "it is possible the abuse came from one or both parents. She attended medical school in Brazil—we can and should assume she speaks fluent Portuguese."

"How did she get from being an orphan with nothing to medical school?" someone asked.

Annalise nodded slowly. "That is an important question to which we don't have the answer. It is one of the things I may ask her in today's interrogation."

"Do you think the traitor Petro was helping her back then?"

Jakob noticed Nyx stiffened a little, only to relax when Grigoris wrapped an arm around her, leaning in to whisper in her ear. Nikolett glanced at the couple, and then quickly looked away.

"It is possible, given what we know of the timeline," Annalise replied. "But it would mean that Ava was one of Petro's first—"

"Pets." The word echoed with menace, the speaker's tone quiet but full of rage.

Around the room, men and women jumped to their feet, weapons appearing in their hands—everything from swords to small guns. Maxim and Grigoris had stepped in front of Nyx, Annalise, and Nikolett, protecting them from the speaker who filled the open doorway into the large office.

Walt propped one elbow on Jakob's good shoulder and raised the other hand in a little wave. "Heya, Eric."

Halt deinen Mund, Jakob thought, wishing Walt knew when to shut his mouth.

Out loud, Jakob muttered. "*Mist.*"

"Fleet Admiral." Grigoris was the first to speak. From the

way some people jerked in reaction, not everyone had recognized the massive blond man on sight.

Eric was wearing snow camo, the jacket unzipped to reveal a white T-shirt that was ripped in several places, but not bloody. In the doorway behind him, one of the security officers was grimacing and cradling his ribs.

Nikolett stepped out from behind Maxim and Grigoris, her eyes narrowed. "How did you get in here?"

"Where's the psycho?" Eric countered.

"My security—"

"Is pretty good. I'm better." Eric flashed a toothy smile at the Hungary admiral and Nikolett seemed to visibly swell with outrage.

"I will need a detailed accounting as to how you got in here. Wait, did you harm any of my people?" Nikolett's words were sharp, forceful.

Eric's smile melted away, and he took a step into the room, toward Nikolett. "He'll be fine, and I wouldn't harm any of *my* people."

"Make no mistake, Fleet Admiral, these are also *my* people." Nikolett paused, seemed to collect herself, and then smiled coolly. "We will come back to the issue of your breaking and entering—"

"No. You're going to tell me where—"

"But first—"

"—so I can—"

"—thank you for accepting my gracious invitation."

Though they'd been talking over one another, Nikolett's last statement made Eric's teeth click together. He took a second, glaring down at her.

"Your invitation?" he snorted, shaking his head dismissively.

She arched a brow. "Of course. You think it was a coincidence that you heard I was coordinating the investigation you went walkabout for? I made sure word would reach you."

Eric's face went blank with either surprise or shock. Then his eyes narrowed. All the hair on the back of Jakob's neck stood on end. Around the room, those who had lowered their weapons when they realized who Eric was adjusted their grips.

If the fleet admiral attacked a territory admiral, where would loyalties lie? Jakob was very glad it wasn't Dolph antagonizing the fleet admiral.

"While I understand grief can make people do illogical things, the Masters' Admiralty needs you, so hopefully bringing Josephine's killer to justice will ensure that you start performing your duties once more," Nikolett continued.

"Talk about poking the bear," Walt murmured low enough that only Jakob could hear.

Eric took another step, looming over Nikolett, who had to tilt her head back to stare up at him. When he took another half step, fully invading her personal space, Nikolett raised her hand, planted one finger in the center of Eric's chest, and pushed.

"Back. Up."

Eric scooted back maybe ten centimeters, no farther. "You and I need to have a private conversation, Admiral." His voice rumbled, his tone so low Jakob almost couldn't hear it.

Annalise was watching them with what appeared to be clinical fascination. Nyx had one eyebrow raised. Vadisk's face was drawn in a grimace. He'd inched closer to Eric and Nikolett, so he and Maxim were about equidistant from them. If it came to a fight, either Maxim or Vadisk looked like they were ready to step into Eric's path. Maybe together they'd be able to take the fleet admiral...

"I look forward to our private conversation, Fleet Admiral. There are some things I'd like to say to you also."

"Watch your tone," Eric rumbled in warning.

"There is nothing wrong with my tone." Nikolett smiled, and it was a sharp, dangerous expression. "I'd suggest you watch yours. You're a guest in my house." Before Eric could respond, Nikolett turned her back to him, focusing on Annalise. "Dr. Fischer, please finish the briefing."

Everyone was looking at Eric, who was staring at the back of Nikolett's head with an expression somewhere between shock, irritation, and maybe admiration.

Walt leaned in. "Wanna bet on whether they fuck or kill each other?"

Jakob snorted—quietly—before saying, "Both."

Walt's laughter broke the tension in the room, even if it meant they got some uncomfortably intense looks.

Annalise stepped out from behind Grigoris, shooting a quick smile their way before clearing her throat and facing the room at large.

"Today's interrogation is going to be focused on getting names and locations of any of her other victims. Given that she watches them for quite some time in order to plan the abduction, the maximum number of victims is most likely three per year. If possible, I'll try to fill in some of those gaps, including asking her how she met Petro," Annalise very carefully didn't look at Eric, "whom she knew as Melech." Annalise turned and looked at Grigoris. "If you could bring up the video?"

They waited while a large built-in cabinet was opened, revealing a bank of monitors with a massive screen in the center. A second later, the video feed from the safe room was brought up. Ava was curled on an air mattress under a blanket. She looked small and soft in her sleep.

"There are some other details I'm going to question her on, specifically, how she approaches the victims, and how she is able to transport them from one location to another. From the information we have from Zasha, we know some of this, so it will be a test to see if she's answering me honestly. Are there any questions or suggestions before I start?"

Jakob stopped listening as people peppered Annalise with comments. He was looking at Eric.

The fleet admiral was staring at the screen, his face blank. Little by little, his expression started to shift. First, his jaw clenched so hard the muscle in his cheek was visible. His hands curled into fists, his shoulder and arm muscles seeming to swell.

When Annalise left the room, accompanied by Vadisk, the fleet admiral was still staring at the screen.

Jakob wasn't the only one eyeing the fleet admiral. He wondered if anyone else had the feeling that Eric was like a kettle coming up to boil, the heat—his anger—increasing with each second that passed. He almost said something to Walt, but held his tongue. It was one thing to start talking more in front of other people, another to say something ridiculous and fanciful about emotions being like kettles in front of strangers.

On the monitor, they saw Vadisk and Annalise walk into the room. Annalise helped her get up, then the three of them left—taking Ava to the bathroom—returning ten minutes later. While they were off screen, Eric seemed to calm a bit.

Once back in the room, Annalise handed the other woman a breakfast bar and some water, chatting quietly all the while, her voice calm and steady through the small concealed mic and earpiece she wore.

"*I'd like to know more about what you do,*" Annalise said. "*Orthopedic surgeon. You fix broken bones?*"

Everyone settled into place either in chairs or leaning against the walls. The man who'd been in the hall was holding an ice pack to his ribs. The room had the air of people prepared to wait and watch.

The Fleet Admiral's next words changed that.

"She killed Josephine." Eric's low snarl brought everyone to their feet. "She raped her, murdered her, and then left her head in a fucking basket."

He turned to the door and managed four purposeful strides before someone jumped into his path.

The only one insane enough to do something that stupid was Nikolett.

"Fleet Admiral," Nikolett snapped, planting herself in front of him, her eyes wide. "I understand that this is personal for you, but we need her alive to question her. We, I, need to know more about what Petro did. Who else he hurt, who else may still be out there waiting to hurt us." She put her hands out, settling them on Eric's chest. He paused, looking down at her, and for a moment, the rage that had transformed his face faded.

"Eric," Nikolett murmured. "Please listen. Don't do this."

Eric reached out, hesitating for a moment, and then letting his hands settle on her upper arms. For a second he almost seemed to be caressing her, and Nikolett said something, whispering so low that no one could hear. Eric stared down at her, thumbs rubbing her shoulders...

And then Eric's grip tightened, he lifted Nikolett off her feet and set her to the side, then stalked out the door.

Nikolett spun the minute he put her down and managed to get her hands on Eric, grabbing his forearm. Eric shook her off without breaking stride.

"Grab him," Nikolett ordered, for the first time a hint of fear in her words. "Later, he'll thank us for making sure he doesn't kill her."

The knights and security officers obeyed their admiral, streaking out after Eric. Jakob had started moving the instant he saw Eric's hands tighten on Nikolett's arms. As a result, he was only half a step behind the knights near the door, and two steps behind Eric. As they sprinted down the hall, Jakob nearly pulled even with Eric.

The safe room was off a short connecting hall, and since Eric didn't know that, he shot past it, catching sight of Vadisk standing guard outside the door too late to change course. Jakob slapped a hand against the corner so he could take it at speed, whipping around, shoes slipping on the unfinished concrete subfloor.

Vadisk was already at attention, clearly having heard the sounds of running feet.

Jakob didn't bother to say anything, figuring Vadisk was smart enough to figure it out. Instead, Jakob shot past him slapping his hands on the door. Because it was meant to be a safe room, there was no lock on the outside, and since they didn't want Ava locking them out, the internal lock had been disabled. That hadn't been an issue because Nikolett had pairs of people stationed outside all night as guards.

But now it meant there was no way to keep Eric out of the room, and Annalise was inside. Annalise, who was still brave, even if she didn't think about herself that way. If Annalise saw an enraged Eric burst into the room, she might put herself between Eric and Ava.

Jakob was going to get into the room before the fleet admiral. And he was going to protect Annalise. Ava...well, there were plenty of other people who could stop the fleet admiral from murdering her. This wasn't Jakob's territory. He had no obligation to make sure the prisoner was treated fairly.

Or kept alive.

Vadisk stepped forward to meet Eric, his shoulder turned and lowered like a rugby player.

Meanwhile, Jakob burst through the saferoom door.

Annalise, who'd pulled her chair around so she was close enough to Ava to have her hand on the other woman's shoulder, jumped to her feet. As Jakob had feared, she stepped between the door and the insane serial killer. Jakob had too much momentum to stop, so he reached out, grabbed Annalise's arm, and yanked her to the side. He heard her gasp, knew he'd grabbed the arm with the bruised shoulder. The chair clattered as she caught her hip on it, knocking it to the floor.

He turned so when they hit the long wall with the built-in counter, he took the brunt of the blow. He was going to have a long line bruise on his butt. Maybe Walt would kiss it better. Annalise thumped into his chest a second later. Jakob wrapped his arms around her and then spun, his back to the door, his body between hers and danger.

There was the sound of fists thudding from outside the door.

"What's happening?" Ava sounded scared, and chain clanked as she moved around.

Right. Better not turn his back to the insane serial killer. He had no desire to have her wearing his face after she peeled the skin off his skull. Jakob turned, sandwiching Annalise between his back and the counter.

"Jakob, what's going on?" Annalise asked in breathless German.

"*Der Flottenadmiral ist hier.*"

Annalise sucked in a breath, realizing in an instant how the situation had changed.

Jakob pinned Ava with his stare, hoping his expression conveyed his utter ambivalence as to whether she lived or died, and his willingness to do whatever it took to protect Annalise.

"Annalise?" Ava's eyes were wide, her lower lip trembling.

For a moment, Jakob's resolve wavered. She looked so frightened and helpless. The cuff dangling from one wrist, securing her to the chair, seemed suddenly obscene.

"The woman you killed in Dublin, her friend is here," Annalise said.

Ava's shoulders pulled back. "I gave her a gift because if I—"

The door slammed open, hitting the wall so hard, concrete cracked. Eric's face was a mask of rage. He'd lost the camo jacket, and now his already ripped T-shirt was stippled with blood. More blood trailed from the corner of his mouth. Out in the hall, Vadisk and several others were struggling to rise from the floor.

Eric's lips pulled back from his teeth, a savage, feral expression.

Ava stepped back, eyes wide. Her mouth opened and closed several times, but no words came out.

Annalise stepped out from behind Jakob. He grabbed her arm, halting her when it seemed she would put herself between the fleet admiral and Ava. Maybe she didn't know the stories about Eric Ericsson. About how, after the death of his wives, the loss of his trinity, he'd become a mercenary. How he'd taken on jobs where death was all but certain, only to come out alive because he, like the Vikings he was nicknamed for, suffered from berserker rages. The kind of rages that allowed him to quite literally rip a man's head off with his bare hands.

"Fleet Admiral." Annalise's voice cracked with authority. It was a tone Jakob had never heard her use before.

It caught Eric's attention, and though he didn't look away from Ava, he cocked his head.

"This woman is responsible not just for Josephine's death, but the deaths of others. Potentially many others. We need her alive so she can tell us about them. Help us find and locate their bodies, their loved ones."

Eric shuddered, an actual physical shudder working its way down his body from his shoulders to his feet. He rolled his head on his shoulders and finally released a slow breath. He was calming himself down, hopefully either coming out of, or preventing himself from fully entering, a berserker rage.

They were so close to getting out of this without any dead bodies.

But then Ava decided to seal her own fate.

She turned with a predatory grace, sneering at Annalise. "Is that what you thought you were doing? That you were going to manipulate me and make me do things? Tell you things?" Ava shook her head, almost sadly. "You would never understand, and quite frankly, you don't deserve to know who those I deemed worthy were."

There was a beat of silence, and then Eric took two long strides, grabbed Ava by the neck, and shoved her body back against the wall.

"You deserve to suffer." He yanked her forward, lifted her by the neck with one hand, and slammed her back against the wall once more, this time with her toes a few centimeters off the ground.

People rushed into the room, but Eric snarled, "Out."

Reluctantly, a battered Vadisk and Maxim obeyed and backed out. Jakob started edging Annalise toward the door.

"No," Annalise whispered furiously. "We have to stop him because I can get her to talk. Eventually she will, it will just take time..."

There was no time. Jakob very much doubted the British woman would leave this room alive.

Ava's nails scratched Eric's hand and wrist as she gasped and struggled to breathe. But she *was* still breathing. Jakob could hear the air wheezing in and out of her lungs. Eric wasn't killing her...not yet.

"Josephine died in pain and alone because of you." Eric's

accent had thickened, his tone guttural and dark. "She died thinking I would come for her, find her."

Eric's fingers tightened, and Ava's struggles became frantic, her heels scraping the wall as she tried and failed to find any purchase that would allow her to leverage out of his hold.

"I promised them I would protect them. Josephine is dead and Colum is drinking himself to death. He's locked himself away, given up his job, disappeared from the world."

Eric's rage and grief were almost palpable. Even Jakob could tell that it was deep, pain-filled grief that threaded through the fleet admiral's voice. He'd mistakenly believed perhaps Josephine had been a lover, but hearing him talk about her and a man he didn't know, it sounded more like a father speaking about his children. But the fleet admiral had no children.

No one spoke. No one moved to stop him, not daring to get too close lest they be consumed by the inferno that raged so hot inside the fleet admiral, it could turn them all to ash.

Ava's choked, desperate sounds were terrible to hear.

"The only reason I don't take you, and do to you everything you did to *her*, and more, is because Josephine wouldn't want it this way," he snarled.

"No, she would not." Nyx stepped into the room. If in this moment Eric was fire, Nyx was ice, cold and merciless as she stared at Ava. "But I'll salt the earth of her shallow grave so nothing grows where her unshriven body lays."

Holy. Fuck.

Jakob felt his eyes get big before he got himself under control. So Nyx was...nuts. He needed to remember to tell his vice admiral to avoid pissing off Hungary's vice admiral at all costs. Then he considered Nikolett and figured they should just avoid the entire territory if possible.

Eric eased his hold, lowered her so her toes touched the

floor. Ava took two shallow, rasping breaths before he once more cut off her air supply.

Jakob nudged Annalise toward the door, but before they could exit, someone else pushed Vadisk—who had been using his big body as a door—out of the way.

Nikolett walked into the safe room, heels clicking, raised the gun she held, and pointed it at Eric.

Holy. Fuck.

Everything was about to get royally fucked up and Jakob had zero idea what the hell he was supposed to do in a situation like this. Protect the fleet admiral? Fuck that, the guy might be bulletproof or something. Maybe his rage could become a physical armor.

Out loud, Jakob said what he always said, cursing. "*Mist.*"

Annalise, tucked against his side, nodded in agreement.

"Release her, Eric."

"Don't threaten me, Nikolett."

"I am not threatening. I'm warning. If you're going to kill her, you do it quick and clean."

"Like she did?" Eric turned his head just enough to stare down the barrel of Nikolett's gun.

"That is why she is a monster. You, we, are not."

Eric bared his teeth in what might have been a smile. "I *am* a monster. I am the *drage*."

"No. You are not." Nikolett shifted the gun, aiming it at Ava's head.

With a snarl, Eric released Ava. She dropped to the ground, barely conscious.

Eric shot Nikolett an unreadable look, then reached down, cupped Ava's jaw with one hand, the back of her head with the other, and twisted. There was an audible pop as her neck broke, and then Eric released her, Ava's body slumping to the floor.

Breaking a neck like that was far harder than it seemed. It

was why Jakob had been trained to first press down, force the spine to compress. Just twisting...that took brute strength.

In the silence that followed, Eric bowed his head, his hand, the hand that had been strangling Ava, curling and uncurling. Nyx glanced at the body, then turned and walked out, Vadisk stepping out of her way at the last minute. Jakob hustled Annalise forward, finally getting her out of the room.

He glanced back over his shoulder just before he made his escape, so he was the only one who saw Eric look up and reach out to Nikolett, his hand blood-spattered and shaking.

She was looking down, putting the safety back on the gun, and didn't see the fleet admiral's moment of need.

Eric hesitated, fingers curling into a fist before he dropped his hand and turned away from Nikolett.

CHAPTER TWENTY-SIX

Annalise blew on her tea to cool it off, but it was still too hot to drink. Then she looked to her side for somewhere to set down the cup. "You need end tables in here," she said to Jakob. It seemed like an inane comment to make, far too normal after all the three of them had been through, but it also felt good to have a conversation that didn't include the words stalker, crazy, or serial killer.

"What style do you want?" he asked.

She rolled her eyes and grinned. Jakob had admitted their first night back in Frankfurt that he'd remodeled this house for her. "Don't you want to pick out anything to your taste?"

Jakob shook his head. "No. This house is for you, Annalise. Always."

She tried to hold on to her smile, not wanting Jakob to see how much his words meant to her, even as they pierced her heart.

They'd returned to Frankfurt the day after Eric showed up in Budapest and killed Ava. She, Jakob, and Walt hadn't even really discussed where they'd go. It had been assumed they'd return here, to this perfect, amazing house. And for three days, they'd shut themselves in, pretending that the world outside them didn't exist, that they hadn't witnessed so many countless horrors it would probably take them a fair amount of therapy to overcome it all.

Every time Annalise closed her eyes, the same two images replayed themselves. Eric snapping Ava's neck. Jakob snapping Axel's. What she couldn't admit, not to Jakob or Walt or even herself, was that she'd felt relief—and in Axel's case, actual happiness—that they'd been killed.

So yeah...she needed therapy.

Upon returning to Frankfurt, it was as if they'd all agreed—though they hadn't discussed it—to shut the past week away, pretending it hadn't happened. Instead, they did what normal couples—or throuples, in their case—did at the beginning of a relationship. They got to know each other.

The three of them spent their days drifting from the bedroom to the kitchen, where Jakob prepared mouthwatering German dishes, from recipes he'd inherited from his Oma. Jakob told them about his lonely childhood and his cold, strict father, about the reasons he was hesitant to speak. His Oma had died when Jakob was only eight and Annalise wondered how his personality might have been different if she had lived longer. According to Jakob, his Oma had never told him to be quiet, not once, and that when she was around, she protected him from his father's ire.

One afternoon, Walt had video chatted with his sister, Sylvia, and his brothers over Zoom. He'd pulled her and Jakob into the screen to introduce them. She had been blown away to see Walt's face on two other men. Of course, it hadn't taken more than a few minutes of listening to the triplets talk before it became quite simple to tell them apart. Oscar's love of the word fuck and Langston's larger-than-life personality were entertaining, but she had to admit she preferred Walt's gentle manner and quiet wit.

Every evening, like this one, the three of them gathered in the living room, sitting before the fire, either reading quietly or talking.

She'd talked in more detail about her hope to rejoin the *Kripo*, admitting that while she'd enjoyed teaching, it had never been her passion.

"It's *not* my house," she forced herself to say. They were living in a fool's paradise and while she'd been the one to originally suggest they focus solely on the present, it was getting harder and harder to ignore that their time together was growing short.

Walt was set to return to Libya in four more days. Just four more.

"Annalise," Jakob started.

"We can't keep ignoring what's coming, Jakob," she said more forcefully than she'd intended.

Walt, who'd been uncharacteristically quiet tonight, nodded. "You're right. We can't. But we also can't change it. One more night, Annalise. Let's pretend for just one more night and then tomorrow morning, we'll sit down and..."

And what?

Walt was right. Nothing they said would change the outcome. The most they could do was share their feelings— their broken hearts—and then, this entire affair would end exactly as they expected. Walt would return to North Africa and eventually join the Trinity Masters. Jakob would remain in Frankfurt at his post as a Ritter, and she would apply for a position with the *Kripo*, or possibly another law enforcement agency. If she got the job, it could mean that she would have to relocate to another city, perhaps Berlin.

"And we'll figure out a way to say goodbye," she finished for Walt, when it was apparent he wasn't going to say it.

Jakob ran his hand over his scalp, frustration rife in his tone. "I hate this. Hate every fucking thing about it."

"Hate fuck, you say? Never tried it, but it sounds hot." Walt, as always, found a way to make them laugh.

"Maybe we should leave the hate fucking to Nikolett and Eric," Annalise said, grinning. It had been a running joke they'd started that Nikolett and Eric were either going to end up killing or fucking one another.

"Sounds like a plan, since I have something else in mind anyway," Walt said, rising and holding out a hand to Annalise. "As your physician, and after this afternoon's quick medical exams, I deem you both well enough for us to branch out into some seriously kinky sex acts."

"Kinky?" Jakob said, standing up quickly. "It's about damn time."

Annalise headed toward the stairs that would lead to Jakob's bedroom, but he grasped her wrist to stop her.

She turned to look at him as he shook his head. "We're starting here," he said. "Want to break in that soft rug in front of the fireplace."

"That sounds more romantic than kinky," Walt pointed out.

"Are you questioning my abilities?" Jakob asked, in that deliciously deep tone of his that told Annalise the game was on.

"Never," she murmured.

"Good. Wait here." Jakob quickly left the room and she heard his footsteps on the stairs.

Walt, who was still holding her, tugged her to him, kissing her softly. Their lips parted and she tasted the sugar from his tea on his tongue. Her lovely American doctor had a serious sweet tooth. As they kissed, he reached up and gently pulled out the hairband she'd used to tie her hair up in a bun this morning. She groaned as he ran his fingers over her scalp before combing the strands out so they hung loose over her shoulders.

"I love your hair," he murmured as his lips left hers, traveling along her cheek to her ear.

Annalise had always thought her hair a rather dull brown, fairly unremarkable as far as hair went.

"Started without me, I see," Jakob said as he reentered the room. Walt kept his arms around her as she turned to face their lover.

Her eyes widened when he held up the tube of lubrication he'd gone to retrieve from the nightstand. Walt placed a kiss on the side of her head.

"So what's the game plan, coach?" Walt asked.

Jakob shook his head, even as he grinned. "So American. Tonight we take our beautiful woman together."

Annalise had loved everything the three of them had done together, even as they'd had to make allowances for her bruises and Jakob's stitches. The past three nights had run more along the lines of taking turns. But this...

This was going to be her favorite night, and they hadn't even started.

Jakob tossed the lubrication to the rug as he approached her. "You like that."

His words weren't a question, but she answered anyway. "So much." Obviously, her poker face was crap.

Jakob reached for her T-shirt, pulling it over her head. None of them had bothered with real clothing since returning to Frankfurt. A big reason this fool's paradise was so perfect was because it involved lounge pants, T-shirts, and no bra. No wonder she never wanted this to end.

Walt was still behind her, so he took advantage of that position, cupping her breasts. It wasn't lost on her that both men really, *really* liked her breasts.

Jakob knocked one of Walt's hands away playfully, making room for his lips on her nipple.

Annalise gripped Jakob's head, moaning when he used his teeth as well as his tongue. With her head thrown back, resting on Walt's shoulder, her eyes closed, she blindly grabbed for Jakob's shirt, determined to get them all naked as quickly as possible.

"So impatient," Jakob murmured, even as he reached back and pulled his shirt off with one hand. Walt released her for just a moment to follow suit.

Jakob and Walt resumed their nipple play, but she still needed more. Reaching lower, she ran her hand over Jakob's erection, now evident beneath his lounge pants. As she stroked him, she pressed her ass back against Walt, wiggling against his hard-on at the same time.

Jakob lifted his head and kissed her deeply and with so much passion, her head spun. Walt's lips were at her neck, then closer to her ear.

"I love you," he whispered.

They weren't new words. In fact, it felt as if the three of them couldn't say them enough. She wondered sometimes if they spoke them so often because they needed to stockpile a lifetime's worth of them in a short time.

Jakob had just reached for the waistband of her pants when there was a loud knock at the door.

Jakob went rigid and alert. He glanced at the clock on the mantel.

Annalise made an exasperated sound. "Who the hell could that be?"

"Every frickin' time." Walt bent over to pick up her T-shirt, pulling it over her head. "I don't know, but, Jakob, you need to get rid of whoever it is quick."

Annalise arched a brow as she glanced at both Jakob and Walt and their very obvious erections. "Maybe I should get the door?" she asked, hating the hesitancy in her tone. She'd been braver back in the hotels in Poland. Coming back to Frankfurt, despite knowing Axel was gone, had dredged up old feelings.

Jakob shook his head. "No. I'll get it. You stay here with Walt."

Old habits died hard, and she knew it would take a long time before Jakob felt comfortable letting her do common things like answering a door or traveling alone. Maybe he never would. The truth was, she wasn't one hundred percent comfortable doing those things on her own yet either.

Walt tossed Jakob his T-shirt just as whoever was outside banged on the door again.

Jakob muttered under his breath, pulling his shirt on as he walked to the front door. He'd picked up a fireplace poker as a weapon before he walked out.

There was a pregnant silence, and then a faint murmur of voices.

Jakob walked back into the living room with a look Annalise didn't understand...until Eric followed him in.

Beside her, Walt groaned and put his head in his hands.

"Fleet Admiral," she said. "We weren't expecting you."

Eric's gaze slid around the room, missing nothing, including the tube of lubrication on the floor. He smirked. "Interrupting, I see."

Jakob quickly walked over to the lube and kicked it under one of the ottomans.

Eric snorted, and then looked at Walt. "Hayden, good. Glad to find you here. Saves me a trip to Libya."

"Eric, go away," Walt groaned.

"Though I wouldn't have minded checking in on the girls," Eric mused.

It took her a minute to figure out he was talking about the girls in Libya he'd rescued from the extremists.

"Is there something we can do for you, Fleet Admiral?" Jakob asked, looking somewhat silly standing at parade rest in his retro Neu! T-shirt, flannel lounge pants, and bare feet.

"Ohh, a whole sentence?" Eric grinned at Jakob, and Annalise hid her own smile. Then the fleet admiral shook his head. "No. You've already done it. I'm sorry it took me so long to get back to you. It was the Albanian mafia at the cafe that day. I had to clean up some of their shit—fucking human traffickers deserve a bloody death—before I could return."

Annalise wasn't sure how to reply. Did the fleet admiral seriously just admit to taking on the mafia?

Eric forged on. "The three of you helped me bring a killer to justice. So I'm here to ask. What do you want? Name it."

Annalise glanced at Jakob and then at Walt. There was only one thing she wanted, but she knew it wasn't Eric's to give.

"Technically, you two had to help me," he went on, pointing at Annalise and Jakob. "But he didn't." Eric jerked his head at Walt.

"It was our honor to serve," Jakob said formally. Annalise nodded her agreement because after all, what else was there to say?

Walt smiled briefly, but there was sadness in his eyes. "It's okay, Eric. What I want—"

"You want them?" Eric interrupted.

Annalise continued to be curious about the closeness between her American doctor and the fleet admiral. Where most people treated Eric with kid gloves or respectful distance, Walt acted almost as if the two of them were old friends, though she knew his association with Eric was as short as his was with them. Of course, Walt was one of those people who simply didn't know a stranger. He was warm, open, and friendly.

"I'm in love with them," Walt admitted. "But I know the rules. Arranged trinity marriages between members." Walt's words were tight.

Annalise felt tears gathering even though the last thing she wanted to do right now was cry.

"If things were different, I'd choose them. I would spend the rest of my life with them, and it would be a good, happy life."

Jakob made a pained noise, and Annalise pressed her fingers to the inner corners of her eyes.

Walt took a breath and went on. "But I, we, can't have that. I'm not a member, and I can't be. I promised Juliette I'd join—"

"A cult," Eric interjected. "You promised to join a cult. And I have one of those."

The drama of the moment evaporated as they all looked at Eric in shock.

Was he saying...

Annalise turned to Walt. For a moment, she thought he was going to argue, but then his frown cleared and brows rose. "You're right. I technically never promised to join the Trinity Masters."

Eric grinned as he stepped closer and slapped Walt on the shoulder. "Nope. You never said those words."

"I just said I'd join a cult." Walt's brief smile faded. "Even so, you and I both know that's what I meant, what I promised. My brothers, the Grand Master...they expect me to come back to join the Trinity Masters."

"Love is hard. Happiness is harder. If you find it, take it. No matter what the cost."

The fleet admiral's words struck her, especially after everything she'd been through in the past few years.

He was right. Absolutely right.

Annalise pressed a hand to her mouth, silently praying. If Walt joined, Eric could—would—place them in a trinity together.

"The Grand Master's going to be pissed off if I don't come back," Walt said slowly. "And my clinic, the funding."

Eric shrugged. "She won't cut your funding. She might be a hard-ass, but the Grand Master isn't cruel. And I seem to be good at pissing women off lately. One more won't matter. To be honest, she's been pissed at me since the day she met me."

"Can't imagine why," Jakob muttered, prompting Eric to laugh loudly.

"Damn, Ritter. Is that a sense of humor?"

"Wait," Annalise said, too afraid to believe everything that was happening. "Are you saying you can join the Masters' Admiralty?" she asked Walt.

Walt hesitated for just a moment, his uncertain gaze locked with Eric's unyielding one. Then a smile slid over his face. "Yeah. I think I can."

Annalise twisted to Eric. "And the three of us..."

Eric waited for a moment. "Ask for what you want, Dr. Fischer."

"I want them. Jakob and Walt. To be my trinity."

Eric nodded and pulled his phone out of his pocket. "Done. I'll call Eburhardt now and tell him what's going on. Then the three of you are flying back to the Isle of Man with me."

CHAPTER TWENTY-SEVEN

·

W alt murmured a quiet "dayum" as they stepped off the private plane that had flown him, Annalise, Jakob, and Eric to the Isle of Man. Nine dangerous-looking people were waiting for them.

"Spartan Guard," Jakob said, pointing. "Their job is to protect the fleet admiral."

"Poor fuckers," Walt muttered.

"The woman in the front is Regina Kagy. Head of the guard."

Eric walked up to the tall dark-haired woman and said, "Honey! I'm home."

From the expression on Regina's face, it was obvious she wasn't amused, but was also professional enough to keep her opinions to herself. She nodded her head slightly. "Welcome home, Fleet Admiral."

"Looks like the whole gang is here," Eric said, his tone somewhere between annoyed and amused. "Admit it, Gina. You missed me."

Regina, who had been doing a good job holding on to her

anger, let the slightest smile slip. It lasted only a second before the frown was firmly back in place and she said, "We almost had you in Dubai."

"I thought that might have been you. You or those asshole exotic animal smugglers."

"We cleaned up that mess for you."

"Good. Did you get to pet a baby tiger?"

"Cub petting is abuse."

"Aww, now you're making me feel guilty."

"You should." Regina arched a brow. "Your crusade is over, I presume?"

Eric grinned. "For now." Then he sobered. "Josephine's killer is dead."

"We would have, could have, helped you," Regina said.

"It was safer for all of you if you were nowhere near me."

The Spartan Guard led them to two SUVs. Eric climbed into the back of the first car, with Regina, while he, Annalise, and Jakob were ushered into the back of the second.

Walt felt a little bit like British royalty or the president of the United States as the guards not driving and occupying the passenger seats climbed onto motorcycles and formed a motorcade to guide them to *Cashtal Ny Tree Cassyn.*

Annalise served as an interesting tour guide as they traversed the island. She pointed out countless tourist attractions, while filling in details about the actual headquarters of the Masters' Admiralty. Keanu Newman, the Spartan Guard driving their vehicle, added his own tidbits as well.

Apparently *Cashtal Ny Tree Cassyn* was a fortified manor house and estate. The main building was where the fleet admiral lived in private quarters on the third floor. The second floor had six bedrooms and a receiving room, while the first floor of the manor had a foyer, library, offices, and kitchen, as well as assorted other small rooms. The majority of the square footage of the first floor was given over to the great hall, which was where any and all large meetings were held.

Walt didn't tell them that he knew the Trinity Masters had a similar place, though theirs was hidden under the Boston Public Library.

Once they arrived, they stepped out of the cars and joined Eric at the front entrance—a heavy wooden door set in a pointy-arched alcove. Walt noted the armed men who appeared atop the walls.

"Come on in," Eric said, entering the place and looking around. When he muttered, "Home sweet home," Walt couldn't help but notice Eric's obvious disdain for the place.

"Gina, my guests and I are going up to my office to take care of some business. Can you see that the guest room—the good one—is ready for them? They'll be staying here tonight."

Gina nodded. "Of course, Fleet Admiral."

Eric gestured toward the stairs and the four of them started to climb, bypassing the second floor entirely as they headed for the third.

Eric opened a door at the top of the stairs and led them into a large office. The room was inviting with comfortable furniture, Oriental rugs, a huge oak desk near a window, and framed photographs on the wall of color shots of nature. Walt was certain Eric had taken the pictures of waterfalls, mountains, and landscapes himself during his travels.

"My office," Eric said, as if that was all the tour they were going to get.

"Nice," Walt said.

"Your sister, Sylvia, was the first person I recruited to the Masters' Admiralty, and hers was the first trinity I married. Traditionally, both ceremonies are done by the admiral of the member's territory, but I'm the boss, so I can change the rules if I want to."

Walt chuckled.

"I want to thank you, Walt, Annalise, Jakob." Eric's voice lost the usual sarcastic tone Walt had become accustomed to. "For helping me find Josephine's killer."

Eric gestured for Walt to join him. "First, you join the Masters' Admiralty. Then the marriage ceremony."

Walt stepped away from Jakob and Annalise.

"Before we do this, you have to know the rules. These are nonnegotiable."

"All right," Walt said, for the first time a little nervous.

There was no teasing in Eric's voice or manner now. "You will obey your territory's laws. You will obey all orders and directives from your admiral and the fleet admiral. Me. You will marry by the age of forty-five—okay, clearly that one is not an issue. Your marriage will be arranged to benefit and preserve our society. When you have kids, you can't tell them the name of, or details about, the Masters' Admiralty. You can tell them you're in a secret club, but no details. Still with me?"

Walt nodded.

"Okay, last one. Your membership is provisional for the first year. If you fail us, you will be assigned a job and a place to live, both of which we control, and you will be watched for the rest of your life."

"That's ominous," Walt murmured.

"I'd say not to worry, but if I get assassinated sometime in the next year it won't be up to me."

"Don't die."

"Not planning on it. You ready?"

Walt looked over at Annalise and Jakob. "I'm more than ready."

"Walter Hayden, you are called before me to join the Masters' Admiralty. Do you stand before me today of your own free will and accord?"

"I do."

"Raise your right hand."

Walt lifted his hand.

"Do you hereby pledge your life to the ideals and principles of the Masters' Admiralty? Will you obey the rules and decrees, maintain the honor and integrity of our society, encourage creative, original thought, and strive to improve the world?"

Walt let those words soak in, the weight, the importance of what he was about to do sinking in for the first time.

He nodded. "I will."

"Repeat after me. *Morumque scientia servabo*."

Walt repeated the words, recalling the Latin he'd learned in medical school. He was vowing to preserve knowledge and morality.

Eric went to the bookshelf and pulled down a large, ancient book. Carrying it to his desk, he flipped through hundreds of pages, before grabbing a pen and what looked like a dagger encased in a scabbard. He turned and jerked his head for Walt to join him.

He handed Walt the pen. "Sign your name here."

Walt scanned the page. The last name entered was one he knew, the handwriting achingly familiar. He touched his sister's signature. "Sylvie." Beside her name there was a faded brown spot.

Smiling, he added his own signature, and then eyed the pages. "Think I could sneak a peek? Who else is in here?"

Eric snorted. "Behave yourself."

Eric grabbed Walt's left hand and poked the sharp tip of the dagger with the embossed triskele into his index finger.

"Ouch."

"Don't be a pussy," Eric said in his normal tone, before once more adopting a more formal attitude. "Place a drop of your blood next to your signature."

Walt squeezed his finger, letting the blood well. He reached out, but Eric gripped his wrist, stopping Walt just before he could drop his blood next to his name. "Membership is for life, and breaking our rules, disobeying our laws, disobeying me, can cost you your life. If you betray us, I will not hesitate to take yours."

Walt had been around Eric enough to know he meant every word he spoke. He also knew there was nothing in this world that would make him betray the vow he was about to take.

He shook off Eric's grip and pressed his bloody finger to the paper without hesitation.

Eric bade him to repeat in Latin once more. "*Cum sanguinis mei, et cor meum recipienti pignori obligo animam meam.*"

Walt spoke the words in Latin, translating them in his own mind. *With my blood, I pledge my heart and my life.*

His chest swelled with pride. He was a part of this now, a member of the Masters' Admiralty.

"Walter Hayden, you have promised your life to the Masters' Admiralty. As Caesar, I welcome you, and bid you to go forth." Eric shook his hand, not in the traditional fashion, but in that of a warrior handshake, the two of them gripping each other's wrists rather than palms.

"Thank you, Fleet Admiral." For the first time, Walt used Eric's title and meant it.

With that ceremony concluded, Jakob and Annalise left their places by the wall and joined him in the center of the office. Annalise kissed him, smiling widely. Jakob reached out as if he intended to shake his hand, but Walt turned that grip against him, pulling him in to grab a kiss from his other lover as well.

Eric cleared his throat, drawing their attention to him.

"We're only halfway done. Are the three of you ready for the rest?"

"So ready," Annalise said. She'd dressed for the occasion, wearing a white sheath dress with a short emerald-green jacket that made her hair seem to glow. She reached into her purse and pulled out a large fascinator with a small net veil. She pinned it on, looking elegant in the way of old Hollywood movie stars, the net over one eye, the edge brushing against her cheek.

Jakob looked extremely handsome in his slacks and dress shirt. Instead of a suit jacket, he wore a shorter military-style leather jacket that didn't interfere with the sword belted to his hip.

Walt was glad he'd still had the suit from Oscar's wedding in his luggage.

"If you're ready." Eric gestured to Jakob, who reached his hand out. Walt and Annalise placed theirs on his.

"I hereby bind you, Jakob Bauer, Annalise Fischer, and Walter Hayden of Germany, in marriage."

Walt chuckled at the idea of suddenly being a German. Despite growing up in South Carolina, he'd spent too many of his adult years as a nomad. It felt good to set down some serious roots. In the short term, he would have to go back to his clinic, but they'd video chat, and in time he'd find someone to take over the clinic and then he'd move to Frankfurt, into the house Jakob had built for Annalise, but which suited the three of them perfectly.

"Your union will serve to better and protect the people of our proud and ancient society. It is your duty to love, protect, and keep your spouses. I will hear your pledge to not only keep and protect one another, but to strive to better our world."

Jakob took the lead, showing Walt what came next as he released their hands and knelt before them. "I pledge on my honor, and as your spouse, to love, protect, and keep you, all of your days."

Annalise knelt next, repeating the same words.

Walt was the last to go to his knees. "I pledge on my honor, and as your spouse, to love, protect, and keep you, all of your days."

"Rise," Eric said. "In the eyes of the law and the Masters' Admiralty, I pronounce you husband and husband and wife."

He was married. He was married and had joined a cult and was now planning to spend the rest of his life living in Germany...

Holy shit.

But also, everything about this felt right.

"Good to have you, Dr. Hayden." The way Eric stressed his last name and the too-pleased, cocky grin he sent his way told Walt he was looking forward to bragging to Juliette about stealing him from the Trinity Masters. Luckily, Walt had no reason to be anywhere near the U.S. Eastern Seaboard, so he wouldn't be in the same country when Eric dropped that bomb.

"Tell Langston that I offered you two hot wives first and you refused," Eric added.

"Duly noted," Walt said.

Eric stared at them, and then shook his head in apparent exasperation. "Kiss already."

The phrase was so close to what Walt had once said to Jakob and Annalise that they all snorted.

"Christ, do you need me to draw you a picture?" Eric said when they didn't immediately start making out. He sighed, then, in a more formal tone, declared, "You may kiss your bride and your groom."

EPILOGUE

"You fucking fucker," Oscar snarled.

Langston grinned. "Congratulations!"

"You fucking promised you'd join the Trinity Masters."

Walt leaned back in the chair, laptop on his knees. A video call wasn't how he'd imagined he would be telling his brothers he'd gotten married, but here they were.

"Well, technically I promised to join a cult." Walt grinned. "I was planning to promise to join the Trinity Masters, but you opened your big mouth and cut me off. You said cult and I agreed, so I didn't break my promise. By your standards, the Masters' Admiralty is a cult too."

"You fucking fuckface!" Oscar snarled.

Langston howled with laughter and Walt smiled gently— which he knew would only piss Oscar off more.

"Fucker! The Grand Master is going to be pissed at me. Somehow this will be my fucking fault."

"Well, it is your fault," Langston said cheerfully. "If you hadn't said cult..."

"Fuck both of you. I hope your husbands fuck your butts without lube."

"Hey now, that's just rude," Walt said.

"Wow, do we need to talk to Luca about anal etiquette?"

"Fucking hate you both so hard..."

"Two and two, probably better that the Trinity Masters and Masters' Admiralty have a tie in the race for the Hayden siblings," Langston said.

"Sad for the Trinity Masters that they got the two dumb ones." Walt made a mock sad face.

"Wow, you gonna do me like that?" Langston demanded.

On screen, Walt could see Oscar thumping his head against the wall behind him.

"On a serious note, we all have to learn German now," Walt said. "I'm not going to play translator when you come visit me."

"I'm never visiting you because I'll be dead, my body tossed into the fucking Boston Harbor like some shit tea," Oscar snapped.

"Hold on, downloading Duolingo." Langston was looking at his phone.

The door to the sitting room where Walt had come to make this call flew open. One of the Spartan Guard stormed into the room. "Come with me, we need to secure you and the other guests."

"What?" Walt said, utterly confused.

"What's going on?" Langston demanded.

"You better not die, you fucker," Oscar snapped, but he was tense, his expression tight and worried.

"There's been an attack. We may be the next target." Keanu, the Spartan Guard, grabbed Walt by the arm, hauling him up.

"Attack." Walt's brain was taking a minute to catch up "Where are Jakob and Annalise?"

"Already secure. The dungeons of the castle are reinforced to prevent a cave-in if the building is bombed."

"Bomb?" Oscar's voice was tense with worry.

"Bomb?" Langston sounded worried, but also interested. "What kind of bomb?"

Keanu glanced at the laptop dangling from Walt's hand, reached over, and snapped it closed on Walt's thumb. Walt tossed the computer aside onto a chair as he was dragged out the door.

Walt caught sight of Eric as he was hustled down the spiral stairs to the basement...no, wait, dungeon. In a castle, it was definitely a dungeon.

"Eric!" Walt called out. "What's going on?"

"Fucking weddings," Eric snarled.

Then Walt was stumbling down spiral stone stairs after Keanu. Jakob and Annalise were there when they reached the bottom, Annalise throwing herself against his chest and hugging him tight.

"Stay here," Keanu ordered.

"What's happening?" Jakob demanded.

"Someone blew up the security minister of Castile's wedding."

"Assassination?" Jakob asked.

"Hopefully," Keanu answered.

"I'm sorry...what?" Annalise asked.

"If it wasn't an assassination attempt, it means the Bellator Dei are back."

NEVER FEAR! Lila and Mari aren't finished yet. Fancy a mafia romance? Check out their latest series, Trinity Masters: The Mafia. It begins with Suspicion's Fire.

· · ·

READ THE ENTIRE TRINITY MASTERS: The Hayden Brothers
Fiery Surrender
Necessary Pursuit
Joyful Engagement (a novella)
Wrath's Storm

AND CHECK out these other series...all part of the Trinity Masters world.

FALL of the Grand Master
Elemental Pleasure
Primal Passion
Scorching Desire
Forbidden Legacy

SECRETS AND SIN SERIES.
Hidden Devotion
Elegant Seduction
Secret Scandal
Delicate Ties
Beloved Sacrifice
Masterful Truth

MASTERS ADMIRALTY
Treachery's Devotion
Loyalty's Betrayal
Pleasure's Fury

Honor's Revenge
Bravery's Sin

THE MAFIA

Suspicion's Fire
Desire's Addiction
Danger's Heir

WARRIOR SCHOLARS

Hollywood Lies

CALLING ALL FACEBOOK FANS! Did you know there's a group for fans of the Trinity Masters series? Come join Mari and Lila for behind-the-scenes stories, contests, exclusive sneak peeks, and hilarious text threads. Join the society right HERE.

TURN to the next page to read chapter one of Suspicion's Fire.

SUSPICION'S FIRE

 hapter One

EMILIANO ORTIZ GLANCED across the courtyard and smiled as he watched his bride conversing with her mother and several other guests, flutes of champagne and small plates of canapes in their hands. She appeared to be telling an entertaining story as the people surrounding her leaned closer, smiling and laughing.

After the ceremony, the wedding party had adjourned to their rooms for a brief respite while guests enjoyed light refreshments, and the staff had set up the courtyard for the cocktail hour and the small ballroom for the seven-course dinner.

Emiliano had remained in his tuxedo, but his new wife had changed out of her wedding dress—a stunning white lace gown that had taken his breath away when he'd first seen her—into an equally eye-catching evening gown, the deep red silk bringing out the dark auburn highlights in her hair.

Among the other women, Gabriella Torres stood out. Not because of her beauty—though she was truly gorgeous—but because of her presence. Gabriella seemed to command the room, her poise, her wit, her intelligence radiating from her, drawing others in, making them want to bask in her glow.

His wedding day had loomed large in his mind ever since joining the Masters' Admiralty, recruited into membership by the previous admiral of Castile, Ricardo Garcia, a decade earlier.

Emiliano had initially been shocked to learn of the centuries' old secret society that operated in the background of much of Europe. The Masters' Admiralty existed in the shadows, influencing not only governments but also advances in science, medicine, and the arts. They recruited the best and the brightest, their membership roster filled with people all dedicated to the idea of making the world a better place.

He'd been honored and astounded when invited to join their ranks, unconcerned about one rather unconventional membership requirement.

He'd agreed to be placed in an arranged marriage.

A marriage between not two but three people.

"She's beautiful."

Emiliano turned and nodded slightly as Vicente Coval—his new husband—stepped next to him.

"She is indeed," Emiliano agreed.

Admiral Santiago De Leon had performed their marriage ceremony only hours ago. A powerful man, Santiago's title of admiral had nothing to do with the Navy and everything to do with ruling a portion of Europe's oldest secret society. De Leon hadn't been the admiral—territory leader—for long, and had only come to power after the previous admiral was killed by a sniper in England.

De Leon was also the person who had arranged Emiliano's marriage, selecting his spouses for him. A month ago, Emiliano went to a dinner party at the admiral's home. De Leon and his two wives, Valery and Carmen, frequently hosted parties, so Emiliano hadn't thought much about the invitation at the time.

Then Santiago had pulled him, Vicente, and Gabriella aside, asking them to join him in his study for a drink. Pouring each of them a glass of brandy, he'd announced that he was placing them in a trinity and that the marriage ceremony should take place in one month's time, which would allow them time to get to know each other and set their affairs in order. He'd then proposed a toast—to their future and their happiness—as if he hadn't just upended all of their well-ordered lives.

The rest of that night had been a blur as Emiliano studied the two people he was expected to spend the rest of his life with. Gabriella, a legacy of the Masters' Admiralty—and therefore raised within the society—had appeared better prepared for the announcement. She had offered both him and Vicente a warm kiss on the cheek, telling them she looked forward to getting to know them.

Emiliano had followed her example, smiling genially, letting excitement take precedence. He'd looked at the upcoming nuptials as an adventure, as a new chapter beginning, and the admiral had certainly placed him in an auspicious trinity.

Vicente had reacted differently. He held a very dangerous and powerful position in the society as the security minister—working immediately under the admiral himself—and had been harder to read, his face revealing nothing of his feelings. It wasn't until Emiliano looked into the other man's eyes that he saw a flash of anger, a split second of emotion that was quickly hidden away once more by an unreadable mask.

Even today during the wedding ceremony, Vicente had been locked down tighter than a drum, the stoic man revealing nothing of his feelings, either through expression or tone. Emiliano wasn't sure what to make of him, his new husband.

It was unusual for Emiliano to struggle to connect with someone at least on some basic level. He prided himself on his ability to not only read people but to find a way to relate to them, to set them at ease. His mother insisted it was that skill that enabled him to find success—as a lawyer and as a politician.

Emiliano lifted his glass of champagne. "To our future happiness," he said, hoping to find some way to draw Vicente out of his shell.

They tapped glasses, Vicente acknowledging the toast with little more than a nod of the head, before turning once more to study their shared bride.

Emiliano regretted not making more of an effort to get to know his future spouses since the dinner party. However, circumstances had not been on their side, as the last four weeks flew by in a flurry of activities.

Gabriella was an heiress and a philanthropist, her parents— two fathers and a mother—billionaire business magnates who had amassed their great wealth in the world of fashion. By sheer force of will and with a shit-ton of money, Gabriella's mother, Genevieve Torres, had managed to organize the wedding and this reception in record time.

By necessity, the wedding party was small—though at over a hundred people, it seemed decent sized to Emiliano. The guests were all successful, brilliant men and women from Spain, Portugal, and France, all fellow members of the Masters' Admiralty, from the territory of Castile—which encompassed

Spain and Portugal—and the territory of France, which included parts of Belgium, as well as France. The territories of the Masters' Admiralty had borders and names that predated the modern geo-political map.

Gabriella's family had offered their Barcelona estate for both the ceremony and reception. The enormous stately mansion—twenty-plus bedrooms strong—had lush, classically Spanish courtyards and also boasted rolling green lawns, countless outbuildings, statuary, fountains, and an impressive view of the ocean.

Emiliano had been knee-deep in work this past month because the Spanish Parliament was still in session, so he hadn't had much to do with the reception planning.

"It's an elegant party," Emiliano said, taking yet another shot at somehow drawing Vicente into conversation. "Quite a guest list. And this house..." He gestured to the mansion, still struggling to take in the sheer luxuriousness of the place.

Unlike Gabriella, Emiliano hadn't grown up wealthy and powerful. He was the son of a single mother, who'd worked two jobs to support their small family of three—Mom, him, and his older brother, Gael. Emiliano had honored her sacrifices for them by dedicating himself to his career path, graduating top of his class in school, working hard to pay his own way through university and then law school. Everything he'd achieved in his life had been through blood, sweat, and tears.

Vicente's gaze seemed to move over the entire area, and it occurred to Emiliano the man wasn't looking at the people or the house, rather the perimeter of the property. "Elegant, yes. Defensible, no."

Defensible? "I hadn't considered that."

Vicente finally looked at him, and Emiliano realized that this time, he wasn't imagining the cold, distant look in his husband's eyes. "A man in your position should pay more attention. You have enemies."

Enemies was a strong word. Obviously, it wasn't unusual for him to come up against a rival or disgruntled constituent, and as such, he was usually very aware of his surroundings. However, he wasn't looking for *enemies* today.

"Of course I'm concerned with security, but this is a wedding, Vicente. A time for celebration, not fear."

Vicente raised a brow. "Nothing bad ever happened at a wedding?"

Emiliano stiffened and resisted the urge to snap at the other man. The Morral affair in 1906 had been an attempted regicide with a bomb in a bouquet. King Alfonso XIII had survived, but now Emiliano was eyeing the flowers suspiciously.

Every conversation with Vicente this past month—and there had been precious few—had felt steeped in landmines. No matter how hard he tried, Emiliano couldn't seem to find any topic that would engage Vicente for more than a few awkward moments before an uneasy silence descended again. He wasn't sure if it was due to Vicente's personality or his position—chief assassin of a secret society probably wasn't a job that made someone chatty.

Emiliano had patience to spare, learning long ago that cooler heads and calmer voices always rang out louder than impassioned voices raised in anger. He tried to swallow down his frustration over his inability to make a connection with this man whom he was expected to share his future, his wife, and...his bed.

Before he could figure out how to proceed, the photographer approached them. "It's time for the fountain pictures."

Emiliano nodded, certain that the low growl that emanated from Vicente hadn't been missed by the photographer, who shot his husband a wary look. They'd already posed for countless photos and according to the "down to the minute" itinerary the wedding planner had shared with them yesterday, they were now going to take pictures on the wide lawn, in front of a stately fountain. In addition to these photographs, there would be three more photo sessions at specific times and places throughout the remainder of the evening.

He and Vicente followed the photographer, and he watched as Gabriella, summoned by the wedding planner, made her way over to them. She gave them a warm smile, which Emiliano returned.

Emiliano offered his arm to help Gabriella walk across the lawn in her delicate-looking heels. The feel of her fingers on his arm had him thinking about their honeymoon, which started tomorrow.

The photographer posed them, placing Gabriella in between himself and Vicente. Emiliano hoped Gabriella couldn't feel his hand trembling as he laid it on her back or the way he jumped when Vicente's fingers brushed his.

They posed, smiled, and then the world exploded.

IT WAS NOT an ideal start to a marriage, and that was before the bomb.

Vicente leaned down to look over the shoulder of one of the people working in the study that had been quickly set up as operational headquarters for the bombing investigation.

"Go," Santiago insisted.

Vicente looked at his admiral. Santiago De Leon was unrumpled, his tuxedo shirt still pristine white. The bowtie that hung loose around his neck seemed more a fashion statement than a sign of exhaustion or stress.

Beside him, Natalia Perez, vice admiral of the territory of Castile, had a silvery emergency blanket wrapped around her shoulders. Her velvet wrap was undoubtedly still draped over the cocktail table she'd been standing beside. That table, along with most of the others, was a tumbled, broken mess, hunks of wood amid the scattering of glass, porcelain, and other debris. The damage at the courtyard cocktail hour had been from the post-blast panic, not the bomb.

"Admiral," Vicente started. "I'm needed here."

"Trust my people," Natalia interjected. "And your own."

He looked at Santiago, then back to Natalia. These people were not his friends, but they were his allies, his compatriots. Together, the three of them were the ruling triad of the territory of Castile.

Vicente wanted to argue. He wanted to be here for the investigation. Technically, it was Natalia's purview—she oversaw the *caballeros*, who served as the territory's law enforcement. Every *caballero* was smart, honorable, and a good person to have at one's back in a fight. His own people, the security officers, walked a darker path. If the *caballeros* were law and justice, the security officers were the monsters in the dark. They did what the *caballeros* could not and would not.

Someone had blown up his wedding reception. He didn't want them captured and questioned. He wanted them shot on sight, with the first shot being to the knee.

"Vicente." This time Santiago sank a bit of authority into the word, an order and a warning in one.

Vicente ground his teeth, but he knew Santiago was right. "Yes, Admiral."

As much as he would prefer to focus on the bomb rather than his marriage, he wasn't needed here. Santiago and Natalia and the *caballeros*, both those who'd been here as guests and those who'd been called in, could handle the investigation. And given that the investigation would include questioning three of his security officers who'd been the active event security, it was arguably better that he wasn't here.

All those sound reasons didn't change the fact that he would rather be here than in the safe house where the *caballeros* had stashed his husband and wife.

His husband and wife.

Vicente nodded to the others and turned on his heel. Javier, one of the *caballeros* who'd been here as a guest, escorted Vicente to a black town car. Unlike Santiago, Javier looked like a man who'd survived a bomb. His tux jacket was gone, there was a rip in the knee of his pants, and his once-white shirt was gray with dust and sprinkled liberally with blood. There was no obvious wound, which meant the blood was someone else's.

It was a short fifteen-minute drive to the safe house, though it would have been shorter if Javier hadn't taken precautionary measures and doubled back several times.

All too soon, the car pulled to a stop. Vicente got out. He tugged on his shirt, which was untucked and dirty, though not as bad as Javier's.

The door to the safe house opened as he approached. Alejandro, another *caballero*, filled the doorway. He glanced from Vicente to Javier and back. Then, with a nod, he stepped back, allowing Vicente in.

"You can go," Vicente told him. There was no foyer, no welcoming entrance, only a long hall that stretched almost to the back of the building.

"I will stay to guard—"

"You are needed there more than you are here."

Alejandro hesitated. "I will send one of the security officers."

"I've already called Xiomara." She was one of his newer security officers, recruited after he lost three people in a bombing in Bucharest.

"I will stay until—"

Vicente cut off Alejandro. "Do you think I am incapable of protecting them, *caballero?*"

Alejandro stiffened. "Of course not, sir."

"Then please, do not insult me. I may be old, but I am not infirm, and the house itself is a fortress." Vicente gestured to the hall, which was a cleverly designed security measure. Anyone who made it through the front door would find themselves in a killing field, thanks to transom windows above the steel doors that lined the hallway. Each room off the hall had a sturdy piece of furniture near the door that could be used to give a gunman inside the height needed to use the window as a modern-day arrow slit.

"Very well, sir." Alejandro nodded his head once, then slipped out.

Vicente bolted the front door, then used the keypad to activate the security system. There was a muffled *thunk* as a second bolt, hidden in the threshold, shot up into the steel door.

"You're not old," a feminine voice said.

Vicente rolled his shoulders and tipped his head to the side to pop his neck before turning.

Gabriella Torres stood at the far end of the long hall. He was surprised to see that she still wore her cocktail dress. It had not fared well. The silk was dirty and torn, her hair was loose around her shoulders. She was beautiful, undeniably so. It was a classic Spanish beauty, with strong cheekbones, full lips, and deep, rich brown eyes. Her disheveled appearance did nothing to lessen her presence. She was the kind of woman who drew attention when she walked into a room, and not just because she was stunning.

He slipped one hand into his pocket. "I am not that young."

Gabriella arched a brow. "True. You are not."

Behind her there came a strangled sound. Emiliano

stepped into the hall, placing a hand on her shoulder. His lips were twitching, but he'd managed to stop from outright laughing.

His new husband's coloring was as dark as Gabriella's, though without the auburn highlights. Emiliano's hair was cut in a conservative, short style that made him look like a lawyer or politician. He was both.

Standing there, they looked like a couple. A dirty, disheveled couple but a couple nonetheless.

Emiliano and Gabriella, they...matched.

"Any news?" Emiliano asked.

"Not yet." Vicente started down the hall. "We've confirmed there were no major injuries."

"My family, are they somewhere safe?" Gabriella asked.

"Yes."

Emiliano nodded tightly, and Vicente wondered if the younger man was sorry he couldn't invite his family to attend. Vicente's family hadn't been among the guests either. Neither he nor Emiliano were legacies. Their families wouldn't have understood the trinity marriage and couldn't know about the Masters' Admiralty.

Someday, perhaps someday soon, Emiliano and Gabriella would marry publicly, and that wedding Emiliano's mother and brother could attend. Vicente knew all about his spouses—Santiago had given him their files the night he announced they were to be married.

The three of them hadn't discussed that yet, that Emiliano and Gabriella would be publicly and legally married. There hadn't been time, but it was the logical course of action.

Vicente walked down the hall, and Emiliano and Gabriella retreated into the room they'd emerged from.

The small living space was elegantly furnished with wide, comfortable chairs, hassocks, and a small fireplace. The fireplace was electric—a chimney would have been a security risk —and the drapes were decorative rather than functional, as there were no windows in the room or anywhere on the ground floor.

Gabriella went to a chair, perching on the edge, dirty, ripped silk splayed out on the floor around her. "Any information, clues as to who planted the bomb?"

Emiliano took a seat in the chair beside her, elbows braced on his knees, hands clasped.

"No, but we will find them, and the would-be assassin will be punished," Vicente said.

"Assassin?" Emiliano looked up. "You think this was an assassination attempt?"

"Bombs kill." Vicente peered down at the other man. "Did you hit your head?"

"I'm not stupid. I mean, do you think the bomb was meant to kill one specific person, or maybe two or three specific people?"

That statement hung heavy in the air.

"If there's no evidence at the scene, we could work backwards." Gabriella tapped her fingers on her knee. "We identify who the bomb was meant to kill and find the villain that way."

Vicente opened his mouth, closed it, then shook his head. Taking a moment to gather himself, he sat in the third chair, stretching out his legs. One knee, the one he'd fallen forward on, was throbbing. "The *caballeros* will handle the investigation."

"They'll need to talk to us, then." Emiliano tapped the heels of his hands together, his brows furrowed in thought.

"Possibly, but for now we should..." Vicente wasn't quite sure how he wanted to end that sentence.

His hesitation gave Gabriella the opportunity to fill in the blank. "Go on our honeymoon? Pretend nothing has happened?" She made a dismissive noise, waving one hand in the air.

"At this time, it's best that we stay in Barcelona and not go to your family's home in Palma de Mallorca." Vicente ignored her tone.

"I figured the honeymoon plans were dead," Emiliano said grimly.

Gabriella looked back and forth between the men. "When are the *caballeros* coming to talk to us? What should we be doing now?"

"Nothing," Vicente assured her.

"Vicente, it is ludicrous for us to not talk about what happened." Emiliano's calm, modulated tone was the perfect accompaniment to his reasonable words.

"There's no need." Vicente was not used to having his authority challenged, and he was fighting down his irritation.

"We almost died tonight," Gabriella added. "Someone tried to kill us."

Vicente had forgotten that most people found that objectionable. "If you need to rest—"

"I do not need to rest. I need you, *husband*," her tone was overly saccharine for that word, "to be honest."

"I haven't lied to you." Lies of omission implied that everyone deserved information, and there were times when that wasn't the case. Times like now.

"Maybe not," Emiliano said. "But you are treating us like we are fools."

Vicente started to get up. "If you two wish to talk about it—"

"You're the security minister. You stayed there while *caballeros* put us in a car and brought us here. You know more about what happened than we do, and you are talking to us," Gabriella snapped.

Vicente hadn't wanted this marriage yet. Originally, he simply hadn't wanted to be married at all—he was devoted to his position and the safety of every member of the territory, but he knew that marriage wasn't something he could avoid, given the requirements of the society.

However, the truth remained that there wasn't time and space in his life for one person, let alone two, and that wasn't fair to his spouses. He'd explained all of this to Santiago, and he'd thought Santiago was in agreement in terms of holding off on placing him in a trinity for another year or even more. At least, he'd believed that until the night of the dinner party.

Perhaps Santiago had an undiagnosed sadistic streak that led him to give Vicente spouses who were strong-willed, intelligent, and fierce. The kind of people who didn't let shadows linger or leave secrets unspoken.

All Vicente had were shadows and secrets.

"I'm sorry you feel this way." Vicente looked from Gabriella to Emiliano, their gazes locked.

My husband.

The words, the idea, took root, suddenly real in a way they hadn't been in the lead up to today.

"That bomb was meant to kill one of us," Emiliano said.

Vicente cursed in the quiet of his head, keeping his expression neutral. "The bomb may have been meant to—"

"Why are you trying so hard to pretend what he said isn't true? To make us stop talking about it?" Gabriella narrowed her eyes. "Perhaps you already know who did it and—"

"Enough!" Vicente surged to his feet. He turned his back to them, running a hand through his hair. It was long enough to brush his cheekbones, and unlike his spouses' hair, his was more gray than brown. He'd started going gray when he was in his early thirties—Emiliano's age—and at forty-four, even his beard would be gray if he let it grow out.

His past lovers had assured him he was sexy, that the color of his hair only enhanced his stern demeanor. He wondered if his spouses agreed, or if they thought he was simply old.

Vicente turned to face them. "Very well." He went to the fireplace, leaning against the mantel. "The schedule for the wedding was not secret—multiple people had it. Anyone who read it knew we would be taking photos by that fountain at that specific time."

Emiliano and Gabriella were both silent, but her expression had softened from accusatory to focused. Emiliano had the same neutral expression he'd had before. It was a lawyer's face, able to dissect any information without showing a reaction.

"There is nothing I can do to apologize," Vicente said in a low voice. "No way to make right what could have happened to you."

"It is not your fault there was a bomb. I, we, are not blaming you for this." Gabriella glanced at Emiliano, who nodded in agreement.

"But you should." Vicente smiled at them, but it felt tight and grim. "The bomb was most likely placed by the Bellator Dei in an effort to kill me. I am the reason you almost died."

The words hung heavy in the air. This was why he hadn't wanted to talk about this. He hadn't wanted to tell them how much danger they were in being married to him. They would have to know, but he'd wanted...wanted to wait. Wait until he knew the danger had passed, the enemy dealt with.

Gabriella and Emiliano looked at each other and then back to Vicente. It was Emiliano who asked, "What are the Bellator Dei?"

SUSPICION'S FIRE is available now.

ABOUT THE AUTHORS

Virginia native Mari Carr is a *New York Times* and *USA TODAY* bestseller of contemporary sexy romance novels. With over two million copies of her books sold, Mari was the winner of the Romance Writers of America's Passionate Plume for her novella, *Erotic Research*.

Join her newsletter so you don't miss new releases and for exclusive subscriber-only content. You can visit Mari's website at https://maricarr.com or email her at mari@maricarr.com.

Lila Dubois is an award winning author of erotic, paranormal and fantasy romance. Her book J is for..., the tenth book in the bestselling checklist series, won the 2019 National Readers' Choice Award. Additionally, she's been nominated for the RT Book Reviews Erotic Novella of the Year for Undone Rebel and the Golden Flogger.

Having spent extensive time in France, Egypt, Turkey, Ireland and England Lila speaks five languages, none of them (including English) fluently. Lila lives in California with her own Irish Farm Boy and loves receiving email from readers.

You can visit Lila's website at www.liladubois.net. She loves to hear from fans! Send an email to author@liladubois.net or join her newsletter.

Made in the USA
Las Vegas, NV
13 March 2026

43609963R00215

Made in the USA
Las Vegas, NV
13 March 2026

43609963R00215